Nothing Like a Dream

Jane Jennings

Copyright © 2014 Jane Jennings

All rights reserved, including the right to reproduce this book, or portions thereof in any form. No part of this text may be reproduced, transmitted, downloaded, decompiled, reverse engineered, or stored, in any form or introduced into any information storage and retrieval system, in any form or by any means, whether electronic or mechanical without the express written permission of the author.

This is a work of fiction. Names and characters are the product of the author's imagination and any resemblance to actual persons, living or dead, is entirely coincidental.

ISBN: 978-1-291-91192-3

PublishNation, London
www.publishnation.co.uk

For Colin

There is nothing like a dream to create the future.
Victor Hugo

1

'Anne! You've got there!'

The double meaning in her friend's words struck Anne Warwick forcibly. She had indeed got there. She was at last living in France.

'How's it all going?' continued Penny eagerly. 'I've been thinking about you all day.'

Anne smiled into the phone. Penny was lovely but, even so, she rather doubted that. No, it was the kind of thing people *said* meaning they cared about you – which in Penny's case was a lot. 'You know what?' Anne gave a little shiver of excitement. 'Not even disposing of more sick bags could dim my ecstasy.'

Penny's infectious giggle echoed in her ear. 'Oh dear, it was a bad crossing, then? It's been pretty blowy here.'

'Blowy? We were standing on our heads. Verity and I were all right, but Dad and Conrad were both very poorly and, although he *seemed* okay, Hayden's face turned green.' Anne paused to recall this with amazement. Again, it was the sort of thing you said but never meant literally. Except in this case, she did.

'Poor man! What about Martha?'

'She was absolutely fine but I don't think babies get seasick. Carpenter wasn't, either.' Carpenter was Anne's wire-haired fox terrier. 'So I'd say the same applies to dogs.'

'What about the house? Does Hayden like the house – after letting you choose it?'

'Um, ask me another.' Things had been so frenetic since their arrival that Anne had not had a minute alone with her husband to ask him what he thought of their new home in Normandy. However, she suspected that he was not enamoured.

Then again, Hayden did not seem enamoured of anything just lately. For the last ten days he had been behaving not so much like a man at the end of his tether, as a man without a tether to be at the end of. Of course, all the last minute arrangements for their move to France had been extremely fraught – the way these things always were. But was that any excuse for him to keep sloping off for hours on end the moment there was anything to be done, and then, when he eventually returned looking boot-faced, to start snapping everyone's heads off?

'Oh, God, Pen.' From nowhere, Anne found herself suddenly assailed by an unpleasantly sharp shaft of panic. 'I do hope it's all going to work out. I mean, in one way I'm over the moon that we're here at last, about to live the dream and all that, but in another, it feels so... so *odd*.'

'How do you mean?'

'I mean, it's for good, it's for keeps, it's *forever*.' Realising she was gabbling, Anne took a deep breath to slow herself down.

'It's not like a holiday,' she explained, 'where you know that, at the end of a fortnight, whether or not you've had a good time, you'll pack up and go home and everything will be back to normal. No, we're going to be *living* here. This *is* normal. So what if... what if it doesn't work out?'

'Oh, Anne, you twit.' Penny sounded amused yet affectionate. 'Of course it's going to work out, once you're settled. Just give yourself time. You know you've always wanted to live in France. You did that year there as an au pair when we left school, and then you were all geared up to move to Paris after university. You were going to go and live with that French guy – remember?'

As if I could forget, thought Anne, shocked that her best friend could remind her of such a thing, whereupon there followed a brief but slightly uncomfortable silence.

'That is... I didn't mean...' Penny's voice faltered and faded.

Anne pressed the mobile closer to her ear. 'Penny! You're breaking up!'

'No, I'm not.' She sounded clear again. 'It just dawned on me that I was being really bloody tactless. The last thing you need, at this stage, is to be reminded about how France went so wrong for you all those years ago. I'm so sorry.'

Feigning nonchalance, Anne told her not to worry about it.

'You're not likely to run into him again, are you?'

'Who – Alain?' God, I hope not, thought Anne in alarm. The possibility had not occurred to her. 'No chance,' she said firmly, trying to muster a conviction she did not feel. 'We're here in

Normandy and, as you just pointed out, he lived in Paris. Anyway, even if I did, I probably wouldn't recognise him. He'll be fat and bald now or, if not, he certainly deserves to be.'

Another, this time slightly forced, giggle came down the line, followed by another short silence. Then, catching sight of the time, Anne sighed. 'I'd better go, Pen. Got to feed the sickly hordes.'

'Okay. We'll speak later in the month, then. When I get back to civilization.'

Penny was off to Australia tomorrow to meet up with her son who was there on a gap year. They were going to do all sorts of intrepid things together like bush walks and diving off the Great Barrier Reef which was great for them, but meant Penny could not guarantee to be in contact for a couple of weeks. 'I'll be seeing you soon, anyway,' she continued. 'At the beginning of September when I come over to fetch Verity.'

As well as being Anne's oldest and closest friend, Penny was godmother to Anne's daughter, Verity. Verity was going to live with her during term time or at least until she had finished her GCSE's.

'You're a saint to do this for me,' Anne said feelingly.

A snort came down the line. 'Don't be daft. We're going to have a great time together.'

Anne knew that here Penny meant exactly what she said; it was borne out by Verity's own enthusiasm when the proposal had first been mooted. 'Oh, that would be sick! Pen is, like, really cool and,' she had added pointedly, '*she* treats me like an adult.'

Yes, well, that was the reaction Anne might have hoped for but, perversely, did not stop her feeling hurt. However, she might have expected as much because from the moment she had announced her pregnancy a year and a half ago, her relationship with her elder daughter had begun seriously to deteriorate. 'I expected shock,' she had wailed to Penny. 'I'm pretty shocked myself – I never intended to have another child. I even expected disgust. You know, that typical teenage 'Yuck, my mother's actually done *that*!' stuff. But it's more than that. Verity seems to hate me.'

'No, she doesn't.' Penny had been as sensible as ever. 'Look, she's thirteen, in hormone overdrive, and you're forty-three and ditto. Everything'll be fine once the baby's here.'

Except it hadn't been. Rather, it had got worse.

Hayden had suggested – tentatively – that he thought Verity might simply be a bit jealous. 'She's had you all to herself all her young life and then suddenly, in the space of less than three years, she's got not just me but a baby competing for your attention. If we make sure she feels just as important as ever, I think she'll eventually stop being so resentful.'

Wise words, doubtless, yet to date there had been no sign of that happening.

We got off on the wrong foot, Anne kept telling herself desperately. Although she didn't feel a bit that way once Martha had arrived, she knew she could have won an Oscar for resentment at the beginning, starting with that evening, that first evening seventeen months ago when she got home from seeing the doctor…

*

'You realise this completely puts the mockers on our plans?'

'What plans?' Hayden Warwick looked at his wife. Her milky pale but always luminous complexion had taken on a dull, almost greyish tinge and her lovely face, normally so open and animated, looked oddly squeezed with exasperation.

She was lying where she had thrown herself when she came in, on the sagging old green velvet sofa in the dining end of the kitchen. It had come with Anne when she had moved in with him six months before, alongside a host of other battered but still beautiful items that had lent his house a character Hayden could never have imagined it possessed. She was wearing a long black full-skirted dress, sashed casually about the waist with a vivid pink scarf, giving her an almost Spanish look belied by her white skin and freckles, and hair of a colour that always made Hayden think, pleasurably, of ripening conkers.

'What do you mean – "what plans?"? We were going to move to France. We said that once Verity and Conrad go off to university, you would take early retirement and we would go and live in France.' Hayden worked for a conference centre in West Sussex run by the Foreign and Commonwealth Office.

'Oh, that.' Hayden had never been wholly convinced by the idea or, perhaps, had not taken it seriously. Which, of course, he should have done, given that if he knew anything at all about his wife, it was that she had always wanted one day to go and live in France. 'Well, we can still do that. Babies are quite portable.'

'No, they're not. And even if they were, they're not cheap. A child is an expensive commodity, as you well know, having, like me, raised one on your own.' Hayden's ex-wife was a woman Anne simply did not understand, not because she had left Hayden, but because she had left their three-year-old son into the bargain. 'With a growing child we simply couldn't manage on your pension alone.'

Hayden knew she was right but said nothing.

'No, a baby means that not only is the French plan kaput but I shall have to carry on working, rather than jacking in my commercial stuff and concentrating on painting. Again something we agreed I could do – *when we moved to France.*'

Anne was a freelance illustrator of book jackets, which was how Hayden had met her. He had commissioned her to design the cover for a book about the history of the conference centre.

'You can still do that bit,' he said cautiously, aware Anne's eyes were becoming suspiciously bright. This made him long to take her in his arms but he sensed she did not want to be touched right at that moment. 'If you were okay being at home with the baby, you could paint then. And we'll manage on my salary.'

Anne sniffed. 'I don't think babies and masterpieces are a compatible equation. The Mona Lisa would never have happened had Leonardo been pegged by four hour feeds. Hayden, will you please stop grinning?'

'Sorry!' Hayden tried and failed to straighten his face. 'I didn't realise I was.' Then he saw Anne was crying and did. However, this meant that at last he could take her in his arms.

'I'm sorry,' he repeated as he crouched down by the sofa. 'But I can't help it. I know it's a shock, and might even be a bit of a dilemma in some ways. But I'm... pleased... delighted... *thrilled.* All the things, in fact, that any expectant father would be – despite my antiquity.'

He was fifty-four, more than ten years older than Anne and no matter how often she assured him that fifty was the new forty and therefore he was really only the same age as her – a logic that completely eluded him - it hadn't taken Hayden long to feel not only delighted but guilty. The baby would grow up with a geriatric father.

Yet, once Martha Jocelyn Warwick had actually arrived, that anxiety suddenly seemed pointless. All that mattered was that Anne was fine and the baby beautiful. It didn't even matter that Anne had indeed given up not just her commercial work but painting too, evincing little inclination to return to either. 'Sorry,' she had murmured with a helpless little shrug. 'But it looks like Martha has sapped any creative instinct I ever possessed.'

'You're just tired – which is entirely understandable. It'll come back.'

'You think so?' Anne had looked sceptical. 'Personally, I'd say we're condemned to single income domesticity in boring old England.'

But then, seven months ago, the offer of a job for Hayden in France had arrived out of the blue. He had been head-hunted in effect, although, as he acknowledged to himself, this made it sound rather more high-powered than it was in reality. In reality, he had been invited to join the small team at a modest, privately funded concern in Caen, running courses and conferences in International Relations. Hayden had resigned from the Foreign and Commonwealth Office, they had sold up, packed up and, until ten days ago, everything looked set fair for success.

But that was then.

Now, those ten days later, on this first evening in their new home in France, Hayden Warwick found himself beset by an anxiety that was anything but pointless and, unlike the anxiety caused by a late child, was one which had no hope of resolving itself happily. And he was facing it alone; he could not tell Anne. In truth, what had happened was so cataclysmic that he still could not quite believe it had.

As he made up her cot and tried to distract himself with the comforting procedure of settling his infant daughter down for the night, Hayden Warwick was suddenly aware of a frighteningly powerful urge to run away and hide.

Except there was nowhere to run to, nowhere to hide. His bed had also been made and the only thing left for him to do was to lie in it.

2

'Is she off?'

Anne turned from the stove as Hayden came down from putting Martha to bed. He was much better at it than she was. She was finishing off cooking supper in between making a list on the back of an old envelope of what needed doing first in the house.

It was a typical old Normandy farmhouse that they had bought, the sort built in stone and timber where once the animals went in one door and people the other and now everyone went in the same. Part of it dating back to before the Revolution, it had originally been the dwelling for a sizeable cider farm. But over the last quarter of a century nearly all the land had been sold off for pasture, leaving one small orchard with a dozen or so apple trees, the straggling boughs of which were now laden with ripening fruit.

In the traditional fashion of the Normandy *longère* or long house, the house ran all in one direction from east to west, with fenestration only on the south side, a centrally placed front entrance door opening straight into the living accommodation. Upstairs, the original fruit loft had been compartmented into four good-sized bedrooms leading off a narrow corridor, and a fifth not so good. But Anne felt that would do as a nursery for Martha, for a year or two at least, or until Verity went off to university. The ground floor found an extremely large open-plan sitting/dining room under a heavily beamed ceiling. This had a rather ugly modern kitchen at one end, and a steep, open tread staircase winding out of the other.

In the standard French provincial style, there was only one, depressingly poky, toilet. But there were two bathrooms, or rather, one shower cubicle and another bathroom with a bath enamelled – unbelievably – in orange and black stripes like a tiger. French provincial style again? As with the shower cubicle and toilet, the bathroom was dank and windowless but Anne planned to do it up. Anne had plans to do everything up. She always did have about houses. Anne Warwick, indeed, thought about houses the way some women think about men; she could never see one without visualising improvements.

She had found the house earlier in the year while Hayden stayed at home to look after Martha. Conrad was at his boarding school and Verity had gone to stay with Penny so, initially, Anne had planned for Hayden and her to go to France together. But, as the time approached, it became clear this was not a very practical plan with such a young baby. Hayden could go, then. Anne had finished feeding but it still made more sense for her to stay with the baby. Until Hayden suddenly confessed himself to be not the slightest use about houses except in terms of them being four walls and a roof over your head. 'I've never heard you say that before,' said Anne.

'Maybe not, but I'm saying it now. I'll stay here with Martha. Besides, I've got piles of stuff to clear up with my job here ending so I'll work from home. I can get a lot done that way.'

Anne had pointed out that if he thought he could get a lot of work done at home with Martha around he had another think coming. But Hayden was adamant: Anne must be the one to go to France and find them somewhere perfect to live.

In the event, the house Anne had found for them was far from perfect. But any misgivings she had brushed aside in favour of the fact that it was cheap – well, not cheap – but, Anne reassured herself, a good deal for what it was, especially as it was being sold by an English couple who had done it up – well, if you could call it that – and were throwing in with the purchase price all the furnishings and fixtures and even the kitchen contents down to pots and pans. Most importantly of all, the place possessed buckets of that elusive, but for Anne vital quality known as *potential*.

Situated half way up a hill on the sunny side of a beautiful river valley on the edge of the Deauville/Trouville region, the house was close enough to the *autoroute* to be an easy commute for Hayden to travel to his new job in Caen, yet still sufficiently remote to be counted as the depths of the country.

'But you've never lived in the country in your life!'

This had been Penny when Anne got back and told her about it.

'Depths or otherwise!'

'Maybe not, but I am now quite ready for the rural idyll.'

'Rural idyll?' Penny had given one of her famously dismissive snorts. 'You'll go rurally off your rocker. What on earth are you going to do with yourself stuck in the country with a baby, for pity's sake? Grow broad beans and carrots?'

Anne had reddened. She had been indulging in happy little dreams of growing broad beans and carrots, not to mention hollyhocks and sweet peas. 'And what's wrong with growing broad beans and carrots,' she said testily. 'Or sweet peas come to that? I may even buy a press and make cider.'

'Cider! You don't even *like* cider! As for the sweet peas lark, the next thing you'll be telling me is you're dreaming about Martha toddling through a wildflower meadow in red spotted wellies from Mini Boden.'

Anne's blush had deepened. Really, Penny could be very annoying sometimes. 'Why are you being so mean?'

'I'm not. I just think you've let your imagination run away with you.'

There had been a twitchy little pause. Then Penny looked contrite. 'Look,' she said. 'The last thing I want to do is upset you and I think the actual house sounds lovely. But you said you were going to find somewhere in a town, if not in Caen itself, then in one of those zingy little French places on the coast with cafés and bars and art galleries and shops and all the things you love – all the things you love here in Brighton.

'You don't want to be stuck at home all day, especially with a small child, in the middle of nowhere, surely?'

'There's a village only ten minutes' walk away.'

'And what's that got? Bugger all, I bet.'

'As a matter of fact you couldn't be more wrong. It's got a nice little boulangerie *and* a bar.'

'Don't tell me, one of those dreary dumps with fat French workmen in blue overalls smoking stinky French fags and swigging cognac at eight o'clock in the morning.'

'Exactly. It's called *atmosphere*.' Anne's eyes took on a faraway look. 'Which is exactly what I want because I am going to paint.'

'Paint!' Penny was even more scandalised. 'You haven't painted for well over a year. All you've said is that Martha has seemed to have sapped any creative instinct you ever possessed, which is quite understandable but do let's be realistic.' Then Penny clocked the faraway look and had given up. There was nothing to be done with Anne when she went all dopey and dreamy.

She had been exactly the same over Alain.

Penny had met Alain Duval, of course – it would have been impossible not to, given he had occupied Anne's life for well over four years. And, at first, she had liked him. He was very good-looking, seemed genuine, and was certainly a talented artist, which was all to the good for Anne who needed someone at that stage of her life to help her develop her own gift.

It was only when she and Anne were both in their third year at university that Penny had started to notice something slightly shifty, slightly *evasive* about the Frenchman. But Anne would have none of it. Anne had been full of the plans she and Alain had made; he had asked her to go and live with him in Paris when she graduated – he wanted them to get married.

'He's actually asked you to marry him?'

'Yes, of course.' Then, seeing Penny's expression, Anne had looked evasive herself. She was someone congenitally incapable of telling a lie. 'Well, perhaps not in so many words,' she had amended reluctantly. 'But it's what we've talked about. It's what he wants, what *I* want. Because I love him.'

Well, that had been the only aspect of the affair that Penny did not doubt. So there was not much she could do except counsel caution, and when did anyone in love ever listen to that? Anne had continued to be starry-eyed and Penny had backed off.

Now, however, she found herself wondering… was Anne making yet another mistake?

No, she told herself sternly. Forget the Alain Duval business. Anne was now married to Hayden Warwick and Hayden was *lovely*. With this comforting thought in mind, Penny resolved not to fret any more. There was no reason now why Anne and France should ever end in tears.

*

Penny's mention of Alain had placed him right back in the forefront of Anne's mind as distinctly as if he had been waiting on the quay for her when she got off the boat. And this was when she hadn't thought of him in years – in the three years since she met Hayden that is.

Now, however, as she chopped an onion and browned mince in the disconcertingly gloomy kitchen of her new home in France, Anne found herself transported a quarter of a century back in time. She was twenty again, a hopeful, naive twenty, and about to enter the real world, the world of hard knocks. Because, of course, Penny had been right. That Alain Duval had truly loved her as Anne had so fondly supposed, had been nothing more than fantasy. Alain had let her down in the foulest way possible.

But this had taught her another salutary lesson. Just because someone does the dirty on you doesn't mean you stop loving them. The reverse was later to prove equally true. If *you* don't truly love someone, then you don't really give a damn when *they* do that dirty. As Anne's first marriage had shown.

Prising open a tin of tomatoes and sloshing the limp red lumps into the pan, Anne suddenly found herself sighing. She found herself wondering if Penny was not once again right and she was again fooling herself, this time about the rural idyll kick. Just as slugs and snails were likely to eat the sweet peas and carrots, wasn't it likely that she would get bored to death stuck in the middle of nowhere? (The house struck her as, weirdly, a good deal more remote than it had seemed when she chose it.) And the painting idea – was that, too, nothing more than fantasy?

She might never recover her desire to paint but even so, she could not blame it on Martha. Her dismay on first discovering her pregnancy now seemed to her bizarre, unholy even. Life without Martha was unthinkable. True, being on your own with a growing child did not leave much space for becoming the next Maggi Hambling, but she could do it if she really wanted. There were nurseries, her father would be here – or would he?

Another little gremlin of doubt pricked in Anne's mind as she remembered that this too was far from certain, even though at first Walter Pepper had been all for the scheme.

*

'What about Walter?' Hayden had asked, that evening back in early January when he had first told her about being offered the job in France. 'We can sort Conrad and Verity, I can take early retirement. Then, with my FCO pension and the new salary, financially we can just about make it work. But what about Walter? Are we going to abandon your widowed father while we swan off to live *la vie en rose*?'

Anne had poured herself a glass of wine at that point, which wasn't a good plan because she was still feeding and it tended to give Martha the burps. But in the excitement of the moment she refused to think of that. Instead, holding up her glass, she had nodded at its pale pink contents. 'Actually, I think with me it would be more la vie en *rosé*.'

This had made Hayden laugh. 'Be serious for a moment,' he had then said. 'With both my parents dead, there's nobody for me to worry about, but you can't desert your father, surely?'

'No, you're quite right, I can't. It's simple – we'll take him with us. If it's okay by you, Dad can come and live with us. He nearly does, anyway,' she had added, thinking of how her father was staying with them at that very moment, as indeed he had been since well before Christmas.

Hayden, however, had continued to look dubious. 'Well, I'm sorry but I don't see that working. *I* don't mind a bit, by the way, but I can't see Walter agreeing. He might spend a lot of time with us but Walter is still deeply attached to his independence. Think of his garden, his bungalow, his chess club, bowls… why would he give all those up? We don't even know if he likes France.'

'I do, and he does.'

And Walter Pepper, it seemed, *did*. When he returned from the pub, Walter Pepper had greeted the idea of moving to Normandy with them with striking enthusiasm, although at the time Hayden did wonder how much of that striking enthusiasm was down to two pints of mild and bitter.

'Do you remember those lovely holidays we had in France when you were a little girl?' he had said to Anne. 'My wife spoke French like a native,' he said to Hayden.

Hayden had later asked Anne if this were true – 'No, of course not.'

Anne had smiled. 'Mum had her old French grammar book from school which wasn't a lot of use because, apart from all that *la plume de ma tante* baloney, all it taught you to say was things like "The Germans are advancing, we must evacuate the village." But to someone like Dad, who left school at fourteen and has never studied a foreign language in his life, she must have seemed bilingual.'

Since then, however, Walter had backtracked. In the last month he had started to mutter about how he did not after all think it a good idea for him to move with them to France. He thought it better that he should stay where he was and just come for holidays – if that was all right?

No, it was not all right! It was not all right at all! It made Anne want to scream. As for Hayden saying 'If he doesn't want to move there, you can't make him, Anne,' well, Anne thought that a feeble attitude. She knew she could. She would bloody well make Walter see sense.

3

'Martha is well and truly off, totally crashed out, in fact.'

'Good.'

'I threatened to sing to her if she didn't go to sleep and that always does the trick.'

Firmly putting the Walter worry and all others to one side for the time being, Anne smiled as her husband came across the room, pausing en route to nod down at the sofa. The dog was lying on it flat on his back, his paws over his eyes as if he could not believe what was happening to him. Anne found herself noticing how tired he looked – Hayden that was, not Carpenter. But then they were both knackered. Still, with the whole of August as holiday, that should sort them out.

Even looking drawn and heavy-eyed, however, could not diminish Hayden's appeal for Anne. When they had first gone out together she had not been particularly struck. Yes, he was a good height and nicely broad-shouldered, with thick, salt and pepper hair, but he had also seemed rather quiet and serious. Once they had been out on a couple of dates, however, Anne had discovered Hayden could be tremendous fun – he made her laugh so much – and his smile when it came was lovely.

Of course, there was a serious side to him, a sort of *deep* side Anne still did not feel she understood too well. But then... Well, it sounded a bit mad but with the baby and everything, they hadn't really had an awful lot of time to concentrate purely on getting to *know* each other. The speed of events in the last three years had left certain things sort of *unsaid*. Anne had never told him about Alain, for instance. From thinking in the early days that she did not know Hayden well enough to trust his reaction, as time went on the moment for such a confession passed – or ceased to matter.

Yes, it had ceased to matter, she now repeated silently to herself. Alain did not *matter*. Here they were in France and all that mattered was that together they had a great future in this wonderful country. She turned to give her saucepan a stir.

'Where are Conrad and Walter?'

Anne glanced over her shoulder at her husband's question, banging a rather crummy wooden spoon on the pan's side. 'They've gone for a walk to check out the estate.'

'It's stopped raining, then?' It had been raining since they left England.

'For now.'

Hayden moved to a car ferry plastic carrier bag on the dining table and, after a sort through screwed-up paper tissues, spare sick bags and empty Coca-Cola tins, withdrew a bottle of whisky and a litre of red burgundy.

'Château bâteau?' He waved the latter at her.

'Fine. We'll get some decent supplies tomorrow.' Handing him a corkscrew and two glasses, Anne added that she hoped he liked the house.

'Like the house?' Hayden forced himself to concentrate; the house was the least of his problems. But he had to say something. He looked about him, noticing for the first time how dark the room was. Despite all the overhead lights being on, with a murky dusk now falling beyond the windows it seemed sunk in a crepuscular gloom more suggestive of a crypt.

Anne was watching him. 'It needs loads of lamps,' she said quickly. 'Which, of course, we'll have once our own stuff is shipped over at the end of the month.'

'I'm sure it's all going to be lovely.' Hayden heard the note of artificiality in his voice and winced. Fortunately, Anne seemed disposed not to notice.

'It will be when I've finished doing it up.'

With a noncommittal grunt, Hayden pulled the cork from the wine, poured a little into one glass, sniffed it, filled both and then sat down at the pine dining table. 'Haven't seen a table like this since the 1980's,' he murmured, blinking at its highly varnished surface.

'I know. And even then they were hideous.'

All the free furnishings in the cottage were hideous, a dire mixture of French cheapo chain store interspersed with British G-Plan – and even that was fake. 'Never mind,' Anne continued bracingly. 'It's good that we've got something to be going on with.'

Our own stuff will look great, although I don't think we've got nearly enough to fill this place so maybe once we get settled we can pick up some nice cheap antiques.'

Thinking antiques were never cheap, Hayden frowned. 'Maybe.'

'I emptied the mail box, by the way, and found this.' She flipped across the table a free local newspaper. 'It's got a section on second-hand cars.'

'Second-hand cars?'

'There's a couple I thought might be worth looking at.' Picking up a packet of spaghetti, Anne ripped it open with her teeth. 'We agreed we'd buy a second car when we got here. Once you start your new job we can't manage with just the one and we sold my old wreck – remember?'

Hayden stared blankly at his wife. Jesus, first doing up the house, then antiques, now new cars, what did she think he was – Rothschild? 'Do we have to talk about this now?' he snapped, so aggressively that Anne started back.

'No, of course not. Not if you don't want to.'

'Sorry!' he cried, and there was a pause while he gulped some wine and Anne sipped hers and looked thoughtfully at him.

'Hayden?' she said, presently. 'What's the matter?'

'What do you mean?'

'What I mean is when are you going to tell me what is wrong with you?'

'There's nothing wrong with me.'

'I see.' Anne chewed her bottom lip. 'So, for the last week, ten days, whatever, I have just been imagining that you have been going round like a bear with a sore head, snapping everybody else's heads off, not to mention looking weirdly or blankly at me whenever I have said anything to you.'

'You're exaggerating. I haven't.'

'No, I'm not and yes, you have. What's upset you?'

'Nothing. I'm fine, just tired.' Hayden bared his teeth in a manufactured grin. 'Honestly, darling, that's all it is.' Then, before she could attack him again, he said quickly, 'Listen, if I were you, I should go upstairs and see Verity.'

'Why? What's the matter with her?'

'Oh, um…' Hayden cleared his throat. 'She's okay but not, alas, at her sunniest. She's saying she wants to go straight back home, straight back home to England that is, because she hates it here. But she did help me to make up the beds,' he added, as Anne's face turned black.

'Really?' Anne put her glass down. 'How sweet of her. Okay, I'll go and see her.'

'Do, but I think you should… ' Hayden floundered. 'Well, you know.'

Anne sighed. She should go easy on the girl was what he had been going to say but hadn't, because generally they tried to make it a rule not to criticise each other's treatment of each other's offspring. 'Okay, point taken.' She wiped her hands on the back of her jeans.

Hayden glanced over to the steaming pan on the stove and twitched his nose. 'What are you cooking?'

'Only some spag bol. Why?'

'There's a funny smell in here, like something burning.'

'I know, but I think it's just dust on the cooker rings because the house has been empty for so long.'

'Possibly, but I don't think it's that. It smells more like burning rubber.'

'Yes, well, never mind that for now.' Anne gave the bolognese saucepan another quick stir. 'This is virtually ready so perhaps you wouldn't mind setting the table, please, and then could you marshal the rest of the troops while I nip upstairs and see Verity? I'll put the pasta on when I come down.'

Hayden heaved himself to his feet. 'Have we got anything to eat *off*?'

'China in that top cupboard.' Anne pointed. 'And cutlery in the drawer beneath.'

'Oh, my giddy aunt, look at this.' Delving into the cupboard indicated, Hayden withdrew a garishly decorated plate. 'Christmas bloody robins!'

All at once feeling got at – she was tired too – Anne lost her good temper. 'Yes, well,' she said coldly, 'I quite forgot to pack the Sevres dinner service.'

'Anne! I wasn't getting at you!'

'Oh, just set the sodding table.'

Fuck, thought Hayden, watching his wife's compact but nicely rounded bottom disappear up the stairs. On top of everything else, it seemed his wife had forgotten to pack her sense of humour.

*

'Dad, you're not eating – are you still feeling rotten?'

'Perhaps he doesn't like spaghetti bolognese.'

'Verity! Don't talk about Grandpa in front of him like that! Can I get you something else, Dad?'

'I don't like it either,' Verity said rebelliously.

'Yes, you do. You have it all the time.'

'Perhaps that's why I've suddenly gone, like, right off it.'

'Verity, will you just for *one minute* stop being so –'

Hayden touched her arm. 'Leave it, Anne, please.'

'I'll have it if she doesn't want it,' mumbled Conrad, sucking up long strands of spaghetti like a hoover.

Anne focused her eyes distractedly on her stepson. Of late, Conrad's capacity for food was nothing short of mind-blowing. Granted, at fifteen he was shooting up – at this rate he would easily top Hayden – but lately he spent so much time with his nose in the fridge she was surprised it hadn't developed frostbite. She shifted her eyes again as across the table her father said something under his breath to his granddaughter, at which point Verity smiled a sneaky little smile, picked up her fork and started desultorily eating again.

'Oh, I do wish you wouldn't do that, Dad!' she cried.

'Do what, m'dear?' Walter Pepper looked up from his plate, aware he was assuming the expression his late dear wife had often teased him about. *Walter Pepper, you might look the picture of innocence, but I know you're up to something.* He had then always smiled at her, which meant they'd simply had a good laugh about it together. Maggie knew he'd never be up to anything *bad*. Yet now he felt so at sea – literally in a way, given the disconcerting way in which room seemed to be moving – he could not summon up the energy to soften his daughter's irritation.

'*Bribe* her,' responded Anne with emphasis. 'You just promised her a tenner if she behaved herself, didn't you?'

'Anne, leave it,' repeated Hayden. 'Please.'

Glaring at her husband, Anne subsided and, except for the clash of stainless steel on robins, for a minute or two there was peace. Then, still with a concerned eye on her father, Anne tried again. 'Listen, Dad, can I make you a cheese sandwich instead?'

Sitting back, Walter gave up the pretence of eating and looked apologetically at his daughter. With her white face and heavy eyes, she looked done for, too. 'I'm sorry, m'dear. It's delicious as always but I'm afraid I'm a little tired. It's been rather a long day. In fact, if you don't mind, I think I'll turn in.'

'Yes, you do that,' agreed Anne. 'And I'll bring you up a nice cup of cocoa.'

'That would be very kind. Good night, all.'

Rising creakily to his feet, Walter Pepper dropped a kiss on the top of his granddaughter's head, squeezed Conrad's shoulder and then lumbered slowly up the stairs. The moment he was out of earshot, Anne turned to her husband. 'Do you think he's all right?'

'Yes, he's fine, just tired. As he said – it's been a long day.'

Unconvinced, Anne chewed her cheeks. 'Perhaps we ought to get a doctor. He doesn't seem himself at all.'

'Can I have that?' asked Conrad, casting a sidelong hungry glance at Verity's plate on which a goodly remainder of spaghetti bolognese was quietly congealing.

'Oh, I'd better go and see him,' said Anne with a sigh, and made to rise from her chair.

'No, *I* will.' A hand on his wife's shoulder, Hayden held her down. 'You take it easy. I'll make the cocoa and sort him out.'

Pushing his chair back with a scrape, Hayden went over to the kitchen and started opening and shutting cupboards in search of the cocoa. 'I think it's on the top somewhere,' Anne said vaguely.

'Right.' Hayden strained his eyes about the littered work surface. 'God, it's dark in here,' he muttered, only a second later to cry, 'Oh, look what I've just found!' His expression brightening, he half turned to Anne.

'Did you realise there is one of those fluorescent strip lights under this unit, darling? Excellent – that's just what we need.'

And leaning forward, Hayden Warwick pressed a switch.

4

The sound of a car drawing into the drive the next morning, followed by a pounding on the front door, found the Warwick family in typical first-day-in-the-new-house chaos made a hundred times worse by a complete absence of electricity.

'Oh, for goodness' sake, leave it alone!' Anne had earlier snapped at Hayden, after his repeated flicking of trip switches and fiddling with fuses had failed to produce anything resembling a spark. She knew it didn't help to get cross, but it didn't help that she was trying to feed the baby cold Heinz chicken dinner for breakfast.

'It's very clear that you have not the remotest idea what you're doing.' She had not the remotest idea what his pressing of the fluorescent strip light switch had done the previous evening, but whatever it was, he shouldn't have done it. 'We'll obviously have to get an electrician.'

Hayden had grunted – obviously.

'For that matter, we'll have to get a gas cooker too, the sort that works off a bottle, and as soon as possible. With Martha we certainly can't risk this happening again.'

Hayden had not repeated his grunt. Besides nearly electrocuting himself, being deprived of his customary morning mug of Earl Grey had rendered him utterly disgruntled. In silence he had sat tea-less at the hideous table in the dark room – the cold light of day didn't seem to have done much to alleviate its gloom – wondering, firstly, how it was wives always contrived to make any disaster your fault and, secondly, what the hell an electrician would charge. In high dudgeon he retreated upstairs to the comfort, if you could call it that, of the dank, and currently torch-lit, toilet. The spaghetti bolognese of the previous evening had settled in his stomach like lead.

As the pounding on the door showed no sign of abating, Anne gave up trying to scoop another spoonful of cold chicken dinner into Martha's unwilling jaws. It hadn't been going down well or, rather, it had – well down Anne's front every time Martha spat it out. Martha looked meaningfully at her. She couldn't manage the words but that look meant, 'What the bloody hell do you call this?'

But there was no option. The baguette from yesterday was too stale for a simple slice of bread and butter and Verity and Conrad, who had set out forty minutes ago with Walter Pepper and Carpenter to walk to the village *boulangerie* for a fresh one, had yet to return.

'Hayden!' she called. 'There's someone at the door!'

No response – he must be in the loo. Muttering curses, Anne got up, scrubbed briefly at the chickeny mess on her front with a paper tissue, and went to answer it.

On the doorstep stood a man in very big footballer's shorts and a very small baseball cap, giving Anne the immediate impression that his head was far too small for his body.

'*Bonjour*,' she said, and then shouted 'Hayden!' again over her shoulder. She felt stale and unkempt and not in the least like dealing with anything or anyone new or novel, or for that matter, French. '*Attendez deux minutes, je vous en prie*,' she said. '*Mon mari arrive toute suite.*'

For a second the man looked completely gone out, which riled Anne – her French wasn't *that* bad for goodness' sake. But the next moment he blew a low whistle. 'My,' he said admiringly. 'Aren't you good at that?'

Removing his baseball cap, which made his head seem even smaller, like a pea balanced on a potato, the man whisked a grubby handkerchief out of a pocket in his shorts and mopped his brow as though it was a boiling hot day – which it most certainly was not. Pocketing the handkerchief, his hand then shot out like a ferret from a trap and seized Anne's. 'Gerry Underwood,' he announced with an ingratiating smile, and replaced his hat.

Resisting the temptation to wipe her own hand on the back of her jeans – his had been astonishingly sweaty – Anne opened the door a little wider. 'Oh – hello. Can we… um, that is, what can we do for you?'

'Other way round, I reckon, Mrs Warwick.'

'I'm sorry?' Anne blinked. How on earth did he know her name?

'It's what *I* can do for *you*.'

Even more bemused, Anne stared at him. 'Perhaps you'd... um... better come in,' she faltered, before realising he already had.

'Hiya, Mr Warwick!'

Spinning round, Anne saw Hayden had appeared at the bottom of the stairs. At the sight of her father Martha crowed and clapped her little hands and looked cheerful for the first time that morning.

'Oh, a *baby*!' cried Underwood, as if beholding a rare and exquisite phenomenon.

'Um... yes.' Anne was beginning to feel completely at sea. 'This is, um, Martha.'

'Lovely, lovely.' Once more whipping off his baseball cap, Gerry Underwood plonked it on the baby's head.

'Oh, no, please!' Unable this time to prevent herself – if his head was as sweaty as his hand – Anne started forward and seized it. 'Sorry!' She collected herself. 'It's just that she might... she might... er, damage it.'

Deprived of her new hat, Martha stopped chortling and commenced upon a series of frantic and penetrating screams. Really, thought Anne, babies had absolutely no sense of discrimination.

'No worries.' Underwood gave a genial chortle. 'It's only a dirty old thing anyway.'

Silently, but with meaning, Hayden removed the cap from Anne's clutches and placed it back on Martha's head. The screams promptly ceased.

'Well, well, well.' With the sideways gait of a giant crab, Underwood had edged further into the room. He seemed possessed of a curious demeanour; theatrically humble one moment and horribly pushy the next. 'I bet you're pleased with this place, aren't you?' he said, looking about him with exaggerated awe.

'I think so.' Anne felt herself thawing slightly.

'We might be even more pleased if we could see it properly,' put in Hayden, earning himself a furious glance from Anne.

She turned to Underwood. 'Unfortunately, we have a slight problem with our electricity.'

Without asking, Underwood bustled over to the nearest light switch and flicked it on and off several times. 'It's not working,' he said.

Who is this man? thought Hayden.

'I expect Kev did something to it.' Underwood treated them to a slow and solemn nod. Then, 'Funny guy our Kev second homers?' he demanded, all in the same breath.

'I'm sorry?' said Hayden.

Underwood flicked the switch again. 'Have you moved over here for good or is this a second home?'

'We've moved here for good,' mumbled Anne, hoping this did not mean Underwood was the sort of neighbour who would move in with you for good.

'Who is Kev?' asked Hayden, but Underwood did not seem to hear him.

'Well, I hope you've got a job. To be honest with you, the showmidge here is something terrible.'

Given Underwood had pronounced *chomage*, the French word for unemployment, like 'sandwich' it took Anne a moment to register what he was talking about. 'My husband is taking up a position at a conference centre in Caen,' she said with dignity. 'Where he will be lecturing in International Relations.'

Hayden twitched.

'Crumbs!' Underwood stared at Hayden. 'So what do we call you, then – Professor?'

Anne frowned. 'As a matter of fact, his correct title is *Doctor War* –'

But Hayden cut her off. 'Hayden will do,' he said with a wintry smile.

'Tell you what, Hayden.' Underwood had turned again to the light switch. 'I can fix this for you in a jiffy. Just a tick.' He sidled back out of the front door.

Hayden and Anne looked at each other but before either of them could speak Underwood had hobbled back in clutching a tool box the size of a small coffin. Dropping it down on the floor with a metallic clang, he beamed at them. 'To be honest with you, I met your kids and their grand-daddy down in the village. They told me you had a problem so I came right on up.'

He made as if to doff his baseball cap, realised it wasn't on his head, and settled for an operatic bow instead. 'Underwood Services at your service,' he muttered to their feet with such abject humility Anne felt like the Queen. 'I fix everything for all us English round here.'

Spitting on the palms of both hands, which was something Anne did not think she had ever seen anyone do in real life, Underwood busied himself with opening the tool box and extracting various evil-looking instruments.

'You are a qualified electrician I take it?' she said suddenly, and then flinched as Hayden kicked her on the ankle.

'No worries. Anything that needs fixing, you come to Uncle Gerry.'

Anne swallowed. 'Oh. Right. Thanks.'

'Right, then.'

Straightening up, Underwood gave a mighty crack of his knuckles. 'I mean, that's what we're all here for, isn't it?' He beamed again at the Warwicks. 'To help each other out in amongst them foreigners.'

*

Twenty minutes later found Anne driving away from the house like a woman possessed. The second Walter and the kids returned, she had left Hayden and Carpenter in charge of her father and Martha – and Underwood – while she hastily changed her t-shirt, grabbed baskets, bags, Conrad and Verity and escaped on the excuse of getting supplies.

This is unbelievable, she thought, as she gunned the Galaxy people carrier through the high-hedged Normandy lanes, all her fond dreams of making friends with the local French mums and of Martha growing up bilingual in smithereens. First day in France and the first person they met had turned out to be Uriah Heep in a baseball cap. Was he the shape – the very peculiar shape – of things to come?

A mile or two later, she was obliged to dispossess herself for fear of getting lost. In the front and rear seats of the Galaxy, Verity and Conrad had embarked upon the total silence perfected by teenagers so she could not expect any help from them. Presently, however, signs for Houlgate, which Anne knew to be a sizeable town, began to appear and she started to relax a little, so much so that she found herself making her usual feeble stabs at conversation. 'Well, it's going to be a lovely day!'

This was far from evident as the sky was still heavily overcast and the countryside looking damp and dismal. Perhaps wisely, therefore, neither teenager responded. Nevertheless, Anne persisted. Really, there was no limit to a mother's grim determination. 'So what do you think of your new home in France, then?' she asked, with a sideways glance at Verity.

There followed a long pause during which Verity turned her head away to look out of the side window and Anne studied her out of the corners of her eyes.

As usual, Verity was clad in the nastiest clothes she could muster. Today wearing a drab polyester A-line skirt with the hem coming down, a washed-out cardigan and slutty-looking slingbacks, Verity might have been a devotee of the original Kate Moss grunge look, even though that had ceased to be fashionable before she was born. Miniskirts, Per Una tops, Gap jeans and little dresses, all bought hopefully by Anne, all gathered dust in Verity's wardrobe. In as much rubbish as her pocket money would allow her to acquire from charity shops, Verity was dedicated to the pursuit of ugliness. And other mothers complained about their daughters so dolled-up they resembled teenage hookers.

I wish, Anne sighed, I only wish.

'It's good,' volunteered Conrad, in answer to her question and earning himself a backward glance of withering contempt from his stepsister.

Conrad was always politer to her than Verity but, really, Anne did not know why she bothered. Suddenly she remembered something. 'Did you give Grandpa a croissant when you ate yours down in the village?'

More silence.

'He didn't want one.' Conrad again. 'We offered him one but he said they stick to his false teeth.'

Damn, thought Anne. I hope Hayden sorts out some breakfast for him.

'I guess Grandpa doesn't like it here,' remarked Verity.

Anne opened her mouth to lay into her daughter for this unhelpful contribution and just as quickly closed it again. She was not going to argue. *Not*. Instead, she decided to concentrate on her own thoughts although, it had to be said, these were far from encouraging. Any elation she had expressed on the phone to Penny had evaporated, not least because she had visualised the ensuing evening being quite a triumphal occasion, with everyone recovered from the awful journey and in transports of rapture over their lovely new home.

But perhaps that was precisely the problem – their new home was anything but lovely.

Anne felt baffled; she could not recall the house being quite so run down when she bought it. Even if she accepted that imagination frequently blinded her to reality, she could not recall it being quite so grotty.

Setting aside the electricity problem, a night of her father's little snorts and snores sounding almost as if they were in her right ear had made it clear that the partition walls between the five bedrooms were no more than plasterboard, and extremely thin plasterboard at that. Anne seriously suspected they were merely lengths of wallpaper stretched between battens.

Which brought her to another realisation; the decor was gruesome, massively gruesome, not just in parts, but everything, everywhere. Even discounting the tiger bath, which in its way was so monumental Anne wondered if she really ought to preserve it as an ironic *homage* to bad taste the way some people went in for kitsch collections of things like plastic herons or snow globes – but everything, *everywhere*.

On the ground floor, for instance, the exposed stone walls had been painted – well, fair enough – but painted pink. *Pink*. Who on earth painted exposed stone walls pink? Upstairs, every wall in every bedroom had been papered, each in different colours yet each in the same pattern, a kind of surrealist scribble like a Jackson Pollock, but nowhere near as well-executed and that was even if you liked him – which Anne did not. The ceilings were clad in polystyrene tiles.

Shit, she thought, in sudden alarm, I hope they aren't the dangerous type. Inflicting Jackson Pollocks on Martha, Verity and Conrad was one thing, asbestosis quite another. Downstairs, the floor also was covered in synthetic tiles, in that unfortunate shade only ever known as tangerine, their bobbly texture even feeling, rather creepily, like tangerine peel. Well, at least they wouldn't kill anyone.

But they must be the first to go, Anne resolved, as she cruised the car cautiously down the steep hill into Houlgate town. I'd rather we walked on the bare boards. Then she remembered there wouldn't be boards, bare or otherwise. French houses of that age and type had concrete on the ground floor – if you were lucky. But then, as they reached the bottom of the hill, her spirits rose for the first time that morning. 'Oh, look!' she cried. 'There's a market!'

'Fuff,' muttered Verity under her breath, or at least that's what Anne thought she muttered. If it was anything else, she simply did not want to know.

She found a space in a car park on the seafront, whereupon the sky suddenly cleared and the sun burst into splendour, making the sea sparkle and everything bright and normal, save for a bizarre and enormous diplodocus constructed out of privet and rearing out of the centre of one of those fantastically gaudy flower beds beloved of the French.

Simultaneously seizing backpacks, Verity and Conrad leapt out. 'We're going to the beach,' announced Verity.

Why does she never *ask*? sighed Anne. Looking round for a ticket machine, she observed *le parking* was *gratuit*.

'If that's okay?' put in Conrad the courteous.

Anne relented. 'All right.' She would rather do the market on her own, anyway. 'Just for an hour or so. When I'm finished I'll wait for you in that café over there.'

Following the direction of her eyes, Verity and Conrad turned to the rows of white plastic tables and chairs set out in front of a bar opposite the diplodocus. A waiter was placing a blackboard outside chalked with "*Moules et frites €21.*"

Anne double took in dismay. Jesus – twenty-one euros for a simple bowl of mussels with chips? But she refused to be discouraged. 'Wow, yummy,' she purred. Then, aware of sounding silly, elaborately consulted her watch to cover this. 'Come back at twelve,' she said.

'Oh, Mer-um...' began Verity.

'Twelve o'clock.'

'We can get a bus home.'

'You most certainly will not.' Anne turned to the car to collect her bags and baskets. 'We don't even know if the buses run out there yet, let alone at what times. Twelve o'clock, Verity, please, and don't glower at me like that and don't be late.' She locked the car, adding, 'And *don't* talk to strangers.'

The kids trooped off and Anne set off back up the hill, feeling better by the second. She adored French markets.

*

'Don't talk to strangers – Jesus! Does she so treat me like a child.'

'She doesn't mean it.' Conrad peeled off his t-shirt and fleece in one go, chucking them down on the sand. 'I mean, only like all grown-ups do,' he amended confusedly, with a nervous glance at his stepsister. Always, whenever he said anything in Anne's favour, Verity told him he was a turdy little minger. However, with one hand shading her eyes, he saw she was peering back at the town. 'What are you looking for?' he asked curiously.

'A *tabac*.'

'Why?'

'Because I want to buy some cigarettes, prat.'

Conrad pulled off his jeans and surveyed his legs with distaste. Pallid, straight, hairless and skinny, they might have been lollipop sticks. He examined his arms and torso. Just as bad. Complete absence of pecs and not even the hint of a six-pack. Growing six inches in the last eighteen months seemed to have stretched every hope of a muscle he'd ever had – and that wasn't much. '*You're* the prat, not me,' he said crossly. 'Anyone who does smoking is a prat.'

'Gitânes are different. Gitânes are, like, cool.'

'Cool!' Conrad made a vulgar noise. 'They're still cigs. Look at Dad. He's spent his life trying to give up. Cool just isn't in it. I bet you anything he doesn't last this time. Giving up does your head in.'

Verity looked superior. 'Yes, well, I'm not thinking of *giving up*.'

Stuffing his clothes untidily into his backpack, Conrad yanked out a pair of goggles and a snorkel from the side pocket. 'In fact, Mum once said it was him giving up fags that made them get divorced.'

'Don't be a turdy little minger. Nobody gets divorced over *cigarettes*.'

Conrad looked glum. '*They* did. According to Mum, he was just too bloody impossible to live with any more.'

5

'How do you do? Agnes Fenn.'

'Oh! Hello. Hayden Warwick. Come in.'

Bloody hell, thought Hayden, trying not to let the chagrin show on his face, as for the second time that morning he prepared to welcome yet another obviously and unimpeachably English person into his new home. Economically, France was not exactly healthy, but did that mean there had been a mass exodus of the native population? Were there no French left in France? 'Do come in,' he repeated, as this latest of his countrymen hesitated on the doorstep.

A countrywoman, in fact, of any age between sixty and seventy, she was tall and spare-boned, the brown, sinewy arms of the dedicated gardener protruding from a sleeveless denim dress faded to the same colour as her blue and rather penetrating eyes, both of which were now fixed in unabashed scrutiny of his face.

'No, I won't come in, thank you,' she said, as she bent down to stroke Carpenter. The dog was cavorting with his usual shameless abandon all over her sandalled feet. 'I know what you're thinking.'

Hayden felt himself redden. 'I'm not thinking anything,' he blustered, a trifle too heartily to be convincing.

'Yes, you are.' She straightened up, the look in the blue eyes so candid that Hayden's blush deepened. He swallowed.

'I'm sorry if you think that. It's just that – oh, hell.' Giving up pretence, he decided to opt for honesty. 'It's just that we seem to be rather popular this morning.'

'So I saw.' She inclined her head in the direction of the lane. 'I saw Gerry Underwood's van out there earlier. Can I ask you – do you know Gerry?'

'Do I know Gerry?'

'Yes, that is – from home.'

'From home?'

'Yes. From England.'

'From England?'

'I'm just trying to ascertain,' she said with elaborate patience, 'whether Gerry Underwood is a personal friend of yours.'

'A personal friend?' For God's *sake* – Hayden gave a sudden start. Why on earth was he repeating everything the woman said? He got a grip on himself. 'No, he is not a personal friend. In fact, until this morning I'd never set eyes on the man.'

'I thought as much.' Agnes Fenn gave a satisfied nod. 'And now I must ask you another question. Has he by any chance just done some work for you?'

'Done some work –?' Oh, don't start that again!

Hayden shook himself like a dog trying to get water out of its ears. 'He has, indeed,' he confirmed with a bright smile. 'Indeed, he has just fixed our electricity.'

Then he realised that, in truth, although the electricity was working again, he was not absolutely certain Gerry Underwood had fixed anything. Eschewing his coffin toolbox for twenty minutes of wittering on about fuses and terminals and junction boxes, all Underwood had actually *done* was to wrench the fluorescent light tube away from its bearings and fling it outside, obliging Hayden to rescue it from Carpenter – or the other way round. Telling Hayden he wanted "Sixty euros, guv'nor, in cash and no questions asked" in return for this less than scientific operation, Gerry Underwood had then departed whistling.

'Too late, then.' Agnes Fenn half turned to go. 'A pity, because I only came to warn you.'

Hayden stared at her, feeling a twinge of alarm. 'To *warn* me?' This time repetition seemed appropriate. 'Warn me about what?'

'To warn you that, whatever you do, do not let Gerry Underwood do any work on your house.'

'I see.' Hayden rubbed his jaw and thought a minute. 'That bad, is it?'

'That bad. The man's a complete charlatan.'

'How do you – sorry – how do you know?'

'I know in the same way that I know he would have offered to do anything for you, anything for, as he puts it, "Sixty euros, guv'nor, in cash and no questions asked."'

There was a pause while they looked at each other. Then, stepping back, Hayden opened the door wider. 'Come in,' he said, and this time he meant it. 'Please. Come in and have a drink.'

*

Anne bought cheeses and fruit, pâté and huge tomatoes warm from the sun, saucisson and salad. After a certain amount of deliberation and a quick squint at the dog-eared Elizabeth David in her shoulder bag, she also bought a clutch of *andouilles*, the smoked chitterling sausages famous in Normandy. They looked rather repulsive bulging away in their shiny skins like over-fed slugs, but Hayden would love them. Hayden loved unusual cooking.

At this point it occurred to her that she might not have anything to cook the *andouilles* on, so she augmented her purchases with a demi-kilo of *rillettes*, the soft squidgy paste of pork and lard also famous in Normandy, and also looking pretty unappetising, Anne had to admit – but only to herself.

As an afterthought she added from the *traiteur* a bottle of Calvados, the famous apple brandy of Normandy. She could pop into the supermarket to pick up a case of wine on the way home. Next door to the *traiteur*, however, she paused on the pavement outside one of those expensive little art galleries that spring up like daisies in French seaside towns. It was showing an exhibition of drawings by Raoul Dufy. Anne cupped her hand against the window to peer in. Then, with a quick glance at her watch to confirm she had a bit of time left before meeting the kids, she decided to have a proper look.

Half an hour and two bunches of dried lavender later she lugged her purchases back down the now hot hill, packed them into the car boot and settled herself with a glass of Provençal rosé at the seafront café.

It was a quarter to twelve, a time when normally at home she would not dream of settling herself with a glass of Provençal rosé, a glass of anything. Then again, at home she would not dream of going into a bar by herself and ordering one. People would think you a wino. But this was France. In France life was different.

She leant back with a beatific sigh, closing her eyes and turning her face to the sun. As the rosé crept down to her empty stomach and dizzily back up to her head – she must not have another when she was driving – Anne felt her habitual optimism returning. Hayden would be fine; the house would be fine – *fine*. She had always, she reminded herself, always been able to perform miracles with a tin of paint. She would paint over the orange-peel tiles; she would paint over the Jackson Pollocks. Lifting her glass to her lips without opening her eyes, Anne drifted off into a happy reverie of paint.

It was several seconds before she realised someone was saying her name.

*

'Wouldn't your father-in-law like a drink?' inquired Agnes Fenn, as Hayden poured them both another whisky.

He had apologised for only having Scotch on offer; he and Anne had finished off the bottle of boat plonk in the unlit misery of yesterday evening. To which Agnes Fenn had replied, with what he was beginning to recognise was her disarming candour, that she never drank anything else and only in great quantities at that.

Outside, in an old deck chair under the apple trees, Walter Pepper was asleep which, Hayden thought hazily, was just as well, since the amount of whisky Agnes Fenn seemed able to put away would have knocked him flat. 'He's a little tired,' he explained tactfully.

Agnes Fenn nodded as if she completely understood.

Earlier going upstairs to put Martha down for her morning rest, Hayden had been concerned to find his father-in-law sitting morosely on a hard little chair in the darkest corner of his bedroom. Clad in the cavalry twills he always wore, his wool tie neatly knotted and tweed jacket buttoned, Walter Pepper had seemed so pathetically abandoned that all he needed was a label round his neck to make him look like a displaced person.

Trying to coax him downstairs, Hayden explained how he had found an old plastic sun lounger from somewhere and placed it in a sunny spot in the garden for him. But this did not go down at all well.

'Plastic, my boy,' Walter had promptly and loudly asseverated, 'plays merry hell with your piles.'

'All right, then.'

Not wanting to go into the details of Walter Pepper's bottom, Hayden had said, all right, then, he would put a cushion on it. But Walter would not budge. It was only when, after another prolonged search, Hayden managed to dredge up the battered canvas deck chair from somewhere else that Walter had consented grudgingly to descend and sit in that.

But, grumpy though Anne's father might be, Hayden realised the old man was unnaturally strained and exhausted. The journey over had more than taken it out of him and last night's debacle with the electricity hadn't helped. Once under the apple trees, Walter had fallen into a heavy doze and was there sleeping still.

'Grim, that crossing can be,' remarked Agnes, fishing a crumpled packet of Gauloises out of a pocket in her dress and offering one to Hayden. With minimal hesitation he accepted it, at the same time making a mental note to clean his teeth before Anne got back.

'Tell me,' he said, puffing furiously as the nicotine kicked in. 'Are there a lot of English people living in this area?'

'Is that what Gerry said?'

'He...inferred it.'

'He would, but no.' Spreading her hands, she lifted her shoulders in what seemed to be a curiously Gallic shrug. 'There aren't that many, not in this particular *commune* at any rate.'

'What about in Normandy as a whole?'

'Oh, there's plenty around the place, although,' she conceded, 'a lot have run home like scared rabbits in the last few years. Only the stalwarts stay. But you'll see for yourself soon enough.' She drank some whisky and looked amused.

'What does that mean?'

'It means they're very easy to identify.'

'Really?'

'Really. All the men wear Marks and Spencer slacks and linen shirts creased beyond redemption, because their wives can never be bothered to press them properly.'

Hayden looked down at his shirt. 'And what do the wives wear?'

'It's not so much what the wives *wear*, as the way they rush about markets foaming at the mouth over precisely the same stuff you can buy in Waitrose in Salisbury.'

Hayden thought of Anne foaming at the mouth at the prospect of French markets.

'And on winter Sundays when it's raining, they all go to junk shops in the Pays d'Auge and get cheated out of a fortune for garden tables welded together out of bits of rusty old iron. Then they always get the grass on their land cut instead of grazing a donkey or sheep on it, their houses always have all the lights blazing, and in August they scream with drunken mirth over their stinky barbecues.'

Clearly, Agnes Fenn was warming to a favourite theme.

'And, of course, they always live in houses like this one, exactly like this one.'

'Whoa!' Hayden held up a hand as if stopping a bolting horse. 'What's the matter with this house?' Granted, he could not claim to have fallen in love with his new home – he was beginning to wonder what had possessed Anne to buy the place – but that did not mean he would allow it to be insulted.

'Nothing at all.' Agnes Fenn sipped her whisky. 'Beyond the fact that a Frenchman would never dream of living in it.'

Hayden lowered his chin at her. 'But a Frenchman must have lived in it once. In fact, a Frenchman must have built it.'

'I meant a Frenchman of your *class*,' Agnes said smoothly. 'It was built by a peasant.'

Hayden wasn't sure he liked the sound of that. But she saw his expression.

'That isn't a pejorative term to the French, you know,' she said, looking even more amused. 'Besides, you bought it from English people, didn't you? The English people, who,' she made a scissor of her fingers in the air, '*did it up.*'

Hayden hesitated. 'We did. In fact, I've just realised that must be who Kev is, or was,' he amended.

'Oh, Kevin was all right,' Agnes said unexpectedly. 'Nice fellow, really. He used to drop in on me from time to time. To get away from his wife, I think. She was a pain in the neck.'

'Is that so?'

'Then again, if you spend your life teetering about in skin-tight white trousers and stiletto heels I rather doubt that the Normandy *bocage* is going to be quite your Shangri-la.'

Gaping at her for a moment, Hayden roared with sudden laughter. This was partly down to the whisky but also, somehow, God knows how, he was beginning to feel better than he had felt for days. He finished his drink. 'How long have *you* lived here?'

'Oh, Lord knows. Forty years? Fifty?' She gave another typically Gallic shrug which was at last explained when she said, 'I married a Frenchman.'

'Did you, now?'

'But he died.'

Hayden sobered. 'I'm sorry to hear that.'

Agnes flicked him a naughty grin. 'You wouldn't be, if you'd met him.'

A plaintive little wail drifted down from upstairs.

'That's the baby.' With difficulty, Hayden got to his feet and stood there swaying slightly. 'Would you excuse me for a minute, while I go and get her up?'

'Have you got a baby, then? I mean, your own baby?'

'I sincerely hope so.'

Agnes Fenn pulled a face. 'Tut tut, how disgraceful. At your age.'

'I beg your pardon!' Then Hayden saw the twinkle in her eye and managed a weak smile.

'Only teasing,' she said. 'But I do admire the way you people these days plan your families so late. I had my children all up and running before I was thirty.'

'Martha wasn't exactly planned.'

'Ah.' Agnes Fenn looked knowing. 'Then you're on your second marriage. Have you got – what is it they call it now – a trophy wife?'

Hayden guffawed. The phrase sounded bizarre in her pre-war BBC accent. 'Couldn't afford one,' he said, and suppressed a hiccup. There was another muted squawk from upstairs. 'Back in a mo. Help yourself to another drink.'

But Agnes also rose to her feet. 'No, thank you, I must get on. However, before I go, let me give you the number of my *plombier/electricien* – they tend to be combined here. Are you on the telephone?'

'No land-line yet but I've got a mobile.'

'Oh, dear.' Agnes Fenn's mouth turned down in mock disapproval. 'Do tell me you're not one of those idiots who prances around with it permanently glued to his ear. Last time I went to confession I had to compete with the beeping. One of these days the priest will start giving out Hail Marys over his I-phone.'

Hayden laughed. 'I'm not, no. We're rather strict about mobiles in this family – pretty much the only thing we *are* strict about, actually. The kids are rationed, to stop them spending their every waking hour texting their friends. But we've all got one for essentials.'

'Good. Then give my chap a ring.' Ferreting in the pocket of her dress, she found a pencil stub and an old plant tag. 'I assume you speak French. He is a Frenchman.'

'You assume correctly. I spent a year studying politics at the Sorbonne as part of my doctorate.'

'Yes, I thought you seemed intelligent.' Scribbling down a number, Agnes handed him the plant tag. 'There you are. This man is excellent and you're going to need him.'

'What makes you say that?'

For the first time since she had arrived, Agnes Fenn looked ill at ease, almost, it seemed, embarrassed. 'Because,' she touched his arm as if in sympathy, 'it was Gerry Underwood who installed your electricity.'

*

'You stink of those fags, you know.'

'Don't be so fucking personal.'

Conrad felt himself blush to his hairline. It always made him blush when a girl used that word, even when the girl concerned was his stepsister. He had quite a bit of trouble using it himself.

He paused at the top of the beach to scrub perfunctorily at his bare legs and feet. They were coated in wads of what seemed to be superglue sand. He shook his backpack; a lot of sand poured out. He shook his trainers; a lot more sand poured out of them but as much stayed behind. Giving up, he levered them on and hobbled gingerly after Verity, hoping for the best. 'I didn't mean that,' he said, striding out as forcefully as he could, which was tricky given his feet felt as if they were encased in wet grit. 'I meant that your mother will smell it on you.'

'So?'

'Well, she'll go,' he paused before enunciating bravely, 'fucking berserk.'

Verity threw him a sidelong but acute glance. 'So?' she repeated, in what Conrad recognised as her defiant voice. 'What's new? She goes fucking berserk about anything I do.'

Conrad looked away in discomfort because it was true. His stepmother did always seem to be in a strop with Verity over something, which was weird because Anne was always really nice to him. While this made him feel good, it also made him feel a bit bad about Verity. He quite liked Verity, despite the fact that she was always calling him a turdy little minger. She could be really amusing when she felt like it, and her knowledge of film was *sick*. 'Tell you what,' he said, as if on an inspiration. 'We'll say there was a French family right next to us on the beach and they were smoking their heads off. Everyone knows French fags really stink, don't they?'

Verity did not reply. She had halted at the top of the steps from the beach. 'Well, look at that,' she said indignantly. 'And she has the nerve to tell *me* not to talk to strangers.'

Conrad followed the direction of her eyes. At a table on the edge of the bar across the car park, his stepmother was talking animatedly to a girl he had never seen before. She was slim and blonde, wearing the skinniest of skinny white jeans and a fabulously groovy black and white top, her yellow mane of hair held back from her suntanned face by a pair of silver wraparounds perched on her head.

Conrad knew immediately that she was French because, no matter how hard they tried, no English girl could ever achieve that effortless pseudo-celebrity pizazz. French girls, it seemed, could. But this is what made them so sophisticated and also made Conrad wish with all his might that he had put his clothes back on. As he stared, Anne turned her head, spotted them and flapped her hands as if dispelling smoke.

Verity ambled over at her best saunter, Conrad following a good deal more reluctantly, holding his backpack firmly in front of his body like a shield.

Anne jumped up as they arrived at her table, pink-cheeked, and seeming in state of great excitement. Conrad glanced covertly at the French girl. Close to, he could now see she was much older than he had first thought, *very* much older, in fact. Quite, in fact, a wrinkly – if a glam one. Her skin had that woody look that brown old women always got. Anne seemed very taken with her, though.

'Darlings!' she squawked, making them both flinch, and swept an arm in the direction of the Frenchwoman as if she were Ant or Dec presenting the winner of *Britain's Got Talent*.

'You'll never guess who this is!'

6

'But who *is* she?' demanded Hayden, as Anne returned from putting Martha down for her afternoon nap. He gulped to suppress a burp; the *andouilles* had been a mighty experience.

'I told you.'

She bent over him to clear his plate, then bent closer and sniffed his hair. 'Have you been smoking?' she said suspiciously.

'Of course not!' Hayden spread his hands and lifted his shoulders in what was, for him, an uncharacteristically Gallic gesture. They must be infectious. 'It was that neighbour I told you about – Agnes Fenn. She was heavily into Gauloises and everyone knows how French cigarettes stink.'

Anne looked unconvinced but Hayden treated her to a guileless smile. 'But tell me again about who *your* woman is. With Martha screaming I couldn't take in what you said.' It was battling with the *andouilles* that had sapped his concentration, which was in any case far from great at the moment. 'Who is she?'

Anne sighed. 'She's a Frenchwoman I bumped into in Houlgate, who invited Verity and Conrad back to her house for lunch and a swim in her pool, and also to meet her daughter, which I thought was very nice of her and would also be nice for Verity and Conrad.'

Hayden's guileless smile switched off like a light bulb. 'Are you saying you let Conrad and Verity go off with an unknown Frenchwoman?'

Anne looked exasperated. 'Hayden, what on earth is the matter with you just lately? Of course I didn't let Verity and Conrad go off with an unknown Frenchwoman! She isn't! Unknown, I mean! Her name's Stephanie Dérain and I *told* you. I told you I used to know her years ago and, by extraordinary coincidence, I met up with her again this morning in Houlgate.'

'You knew her? How did you know her?'

Anne tossed her head a little. 'I was once an au pair to her daughter,' she said indifferently.

Hayden sat back with his mouth open.

'Oh, for goodness' sake,' exclaimed Anne. 'Why are you looking at me as if I've just confessed to being a drugs mule?'

Hayden closed his mouth with a snap. 'I'm sorry. You just rather took me aback.'

'Why? I told you I lived with a French family for a year after school.'

'You did, but I assumed it was some sort of exchange thing. I didn't know you were actually an au pair.'

'Yes, well.' Anne resumed clearing the table, flinging a crust of baguette to Carpenter who swallowed it whole and then gave a strangled cough. 'I expect there's a lot you don't know about me.' That was true enough, she realised, but she wished she hadn't said it because it sounded sinister.

'Anyway,' she said, briskly stacking plates, 'you'll be able to see for yourself because she's invited us as well, for tea this afternoon and then dinner this evening.'

'Tea? Dinner?' After the *andouilles* Hayden felt like never eating again. 'But what about Martha?' he cried, aware of an edge of hysteria creeping into his voice. 'And Walter?'

'What about them? They're invited too, of course.'

'Ohmigod.'

'What do you mean – ohmigod?' Anne sat down suddenly and looked at her husband. 'Are you all right?' she asked in a more concerned tone. 'Did Underwood the Unctuous upset you or something?'

'What? No.'

'He fixed it, didn't he? The electricity, I mean. The electricity *is* okay, isn't it?'

Hayden shifted his bottom about as though his chair was uncomfortable, which it was – very – but that was not why he was shifting about. 'Yes.'

'What's the matter, then?'

'Nothing.' He gave himself a little shake. 'Listen, I know we agreed not to have a full survey done, but I've been meaning to ask you – what did the estate agent, the *immobilière* woman, tell you about this house?'

Anne stood up again and scrunched together a pile of paper napkins. 'Not a lot as far I can remember. Or could understand,' she added. She paused and furrowed her brow. 'Whatever she told me about anything wasn't very easy to understand. Why do you want to know?'

Hayden frowned. 'Surely it would have been wise of you to have engaged an interpreter, then? If you couldn't understand her, if your French wasn't up to understanding the wretched woman?'

Anne considered him a moment, an expression of he did not know quite what on her face. 'I could not understand the wretched woman,' she said, presently and patiently but unmistakeably sarcastically, 'not on account of my pathetic French, but because the wretched woman kept insisting on speaking *English* to me. Her English was about fifty times worse than my French and, as you have just obliquely pointed out, that's saying something.'

'I'm sorry.' Hayden looked chastened.

'Furthermore, from the moment I mentioned to her that I was a painter, all she could do was witter on about her artist brother who, as she so unfortunately put it, was *exposing* himself in Paris.'

Walter Pepper came downstairs.

'But why do you want to know?' Anne asked again.

Hayden debated whether to tell her what Agnes Fenn had said about the electricity and Gerry Underwood and then changed his mind, partly because the *andouilles* had regrouped for a second assault.

'Anne, m'dear.' Walter patted his daughter's shoulder with an affectionate but reproachful hand. 'I hope you don't mind me saying but,' he paused to emit a restrained but heartfelt belch, 'I think you should watch your step with them French bangers.'

*

Verity could not believe what was happening to her. She had never met anyone in her life like Stephanie Dérain and as for where Stephanie Dérain lived, it was like something out of a feature in *Hello!* magazine. She'd gathered that Mum had centuries ago been a sort of nanny to Stephanie's daughter, which was even more unbelievable. For the life of her, Verity couldn't imagine her mother in this set-up.

But the daughter wasn't there, anyway, so maybe it was all some weird dream.

Stephanie was dead nice to her, though, and gave her a glass of wine with lunch before showing her round the amazing house – it was, like, a mansion, like, *epic* – leaving Conrad cavorting palely in the swimming pool like a bleached grasshopper. He was even whiter than she was. Which brought Verity right back to another problem – this mythical daughter of Stephanie's. Going round the house, it had suddenly occurred to her that Stephanie's daughter was probably ten times as chic as Stephanie, and Stephanie Dérain was the chicest of chic.

She began to wish that she had washed her hair that morning, even if the water had been stone cold. She began to wish with all her might that she was wearing anything but the disgusting old polyester skirt and cardy that she had put on only to spite her mother. Mostly, whatever she wore was to spite her mother but all of a sudden this seemed like a totally dumb idea. Perhaps when she came on later Mum would bring her something cool to wear; she longed to change into some cool gear.

Then Verity realised she hadn't got any cool gear to change into, or not that she had packed. This made her start to feel desperate, so desperate that, after a bit, she began to long for something that *really* did her head in.

She began to long for her mother to arrive.

*

'So they still live in the same place,' said Hayden, as they careened round the Cabourg ring road and out onto the coast road leading north.

'That's right. That is, they don't exactly *live* here, or not all the year round at any rate. They live in Paris. This is just a house where the family congregate in August.'

Hayden changed down for the start of a hill. 'A holiday home, then?'

'A holiday home,' Anne confirmed dutifully, but still managing to sound peculiarly doubtful.

'Did you keep in touch with them after you left?'

'Not really.' Anne now sounded vague. 'A few years of Christmas cards and so on. Then it tailed off, the way these things do. I think the last thing I sent them was a wedding photograph when I got married to Mark. That's how Stephanie recognised me today.' She gave a rueful little laugh. 'God knows how, though. I've changed a bit since those days – or at least I hope I have.'

Hayden placed his left hand on her knee. 'Were you as sexy then as you are now?'

'Oh, red hot,' murmured Anne in her best *femme fatale* tones. Which is so untrue, she thought silently. Even though I thought I did with Alain and later, Mark, I didn't really know what sex was about until I met Hayden. With a brief squeeze of her knee, he had returned his hand to the wheel.

'What was the daughter you looked after like? A bolshy French adolescent?'

'Oh, no, she was a *baby*.' Anne reflected a second. 'About the same age then, in fact, as Martha is now.'

There was a pause as Hayden braked on the winding road and fell in behind a chugging tractor. 'Look for me, will you?' As he clicked on the indicator, Anne craned her neck to the side window.

'How odd,' he said a few minutes later, as they reached a straight bit and zoomed past the tractor. 'Or rather, how poignant.'

'What is?'

'That you looked after a Frenchwoman's baby daughter, what was it – when you were eighteen? And now you're back in France twenty-seven years later about to see her again with your own baby daughter.' He gave a proud little chuckle. 'You'll be able to show her off.'

The Galaxy swerved slightly as something suddenly struck Hayden a light but stinging blow on his left ear.

'Martha! That's naughty! You mustn't throw things at Daddy when he's driving!' Releasing her seat belt, Anne dived round Hayden's ankles to retrieve a pink furry rabbit with a blue plastic nose.

Twisting round in her seat, she thrust it back into the baby's arms. Martha promptly flung the rabbit on the floor with a high squeaky scream whereupon Carpenter equally promptly pounced on it.

'Dad?' begged Anne, wresting the rabbit from the dog's teeth and turning round to her father. 'Could you keep an eye on the baby for me, please? I can't quite remember where this place is so I'm watching the road for signs.'

'I've forgotten m' stick,' complained Walter, irrelevantly and for about the fourth time.

'Yes, well, you won't need your walking stick where we're going,' said Anne. 'We won't be walking anywhere,' she added firmly, but a bit pointlessly, thought Hayden, since Anne knew as well as he did that her father never used his walking stick to help him walk. Walter Pepper was perfectly sound in mind and limb. Walter Pepper used his walking stick to point at things.

Anne twisted back to face the front. 'This is it,' she said suddenly. 'I remember now. It's just round this next bend.'

Hayden slowed the Galaxy to a crawl.

'There!' she cried, pointing.

Turning the wheel to the right, Hayden pulled off the road onto a narrow drive angled at thirty degrees away from the main route and winding down into a densely wooded valley. A sign with *Voie Strictement Privée* flashed past and then another, slightly crooked on its post, *Manoir des Tilleuls*. Lime Tree Manor, thought Hayden in some surprise, I wasn't quite expecting a manor house. Nobody spoke as he negotiated bends and chicanes, emerging into a wider, straight avenue lined, unsurprisingly, with lime trees. The house lay at the end of it.

Hayden brought the car to an abrupt halt and looked. No, it was not a house. Even the term *manoir* was a misnomer.

'Some holiday home,' he murmured. He was looking at a château.

*

'*Ou est la salle de bain?*' Verity inquired of the maid, wishing she'd paid a little more attention in French lessons at school, although perhaps it wouldn't have helped much given the woman looked completely out to lunch. '*Stephanie m'a dit que... que je peux laver mes cheveux,*' she enlarged haltingly, rubbing her hands demonstratively through her hair for good measure.

Light dawned on the leathery old face and letting off a stream of what sounded bafflingly like Spanish – whatever it was, it certainly wasn't French – the maid hustled her off to an enormously exotic bathroom with a bath the size of a swimming pool.

'*Merci bien.*'

Twiddling the tails of two gold-plated dolphins, the maid handed her an equally exotic bottle full of pale gold liquid and said something that sounded like champagne. It couldn't be that. Or could it? It was the sort of bathroom where people drank champagne. Verity looked at the label on the bottle. *Shampooing* stood out in crabbed black letters. 'Ah, *merci, merci,*' she cried in relief.

The maid rubbed her own hair in the same washing gesture and then touched Verity's head.

'*Oui, oui, merci, merci,*' repeated Verity, and then wondered why she was saying everything twice. 'Sham-pwang,' she said once and extremely firmly so that they all knew where they stood.

The maid gave a single satisfied nod and left.

Lowering herself inch by inch into the scalding water, Verity settled back in the huge bath and reached for her moby to do what she had been dying to do all afternoon but couldn't because of Stephanie being around.

'Hiya – Suze? You'll never guess where me and Condy are...'

*

'You might have told me,' said Hayden, the second Stephanie Dérain had disappeared to organise tea.

'Told you what?'

'Told me about this – *this.*' Hayden heard himself speaking in a clandestine hiss, even though there was nobody else remotely in earshot, nor had been for some time.

Verity had rushed inside to change into the dress Anne had brought for her the moment they arrived, Martha had fallen asleep in her buggy, Carpenter was doing his best to fornicate with the tartiest of the Dérain poodles, and Walter had borne Conrad off to admire the exterior of the château. They could just see them from where they were by the swimming pool, Walter with a plastic spike he had commandeered by his nonchalant dismembering of a parasol, and pointing out transoms and turrets with a lordly air.

Nothing fazed Walter Pepper.

Tucking up the skirts of her red cotton sundress, Anne sat down on a sun lounger, kicked off her sandals and put her feet up. Come to that, thought Hayden, watching his wife wiggle her bare toes, not a lot fazed Anne either.

'Sorry,' she said, not sounding it. 'I was going to tell you over lunch. But, given you didn't listen to a thing I *did* tell you over lunch, there probably wouldn't have been much point.' She turned to look critically at him. 'In fact, Hayden, you're acting so strangely just lately that, at the risk of sounding melodramatic, I'm beginning to wonder what it is you're not telling *me*.'

Their eyes locked for a second, until Hayden looked uncomfortably away. He knew very well what his wife was getting at, and he could not deny it. But, in between skirmishes with *andouilles*, his lunch had been a worry fest about what Agnes Fenn had said about Gerry Underwood and his installing of their electricity. It looked very much like the entire system would need replacing and soon, too, before the house and everyone in it went up in smoke.

And this, he had now decided, he simply could not tell Anne, because the first thing she would demand was that they got it sorted, pronto. Which was impossible. If nothing else, the one thing he now had to do was keep a massively close eye on whatever funds they had left in their bank account – which were nothing like a lot.

'Hayden?'

'What? Sorry. Miles away.'

'Please tell me what's the matter.'

'Nothing's the matter. I'm sorry, darling. I know I've been a bit funny just lately but I'm fine, really. Come on.' He waved a hand to distract her. 'Spill the French beans. Where does all this come from?'

Reluctantly shifting her eyes, Anne said, 'The Dérains' wealth, you mean?'

He nodded and, looking about him, forced himself to concentrate on his environs – and very imposing environs they were. Although not quite on the scale of Chenonceau, Manoir des Tilleuls could only be described as *grand* in the French sense of big as well as the word's more prosaic English meaning. With its clean symmetrical lines and majestic gabled roof, its double row of well-proportioned windows, some shuttered, some propped open, the Manoir qualified as one of the best examples of French provincial architecture of the lesser aristocracy, not to mention its exquisite surroundings.

At the front of the property lay the avenue of lime trees culminating in a gracious sweep of gravel drive, to the rear a wide, flag-stoned terrace giving onto shaved lawns and a sparkling swimming pool. Elegant and unpretentious, it was the type of house now usually converted into a hotel, the upkeep of such places being beyond anything like a normal family. So who on earth was this family?

'It's funny you should ask that,' said Anne, as if in answer to his unspoken question. 'Because I don't really know. I never did know really, even back then, back when I lived with them, or rather, was employed by them. They're not old French aristos, however. I can tell you that for sure.' Leaning forward, she picked a bit of flaky skin off her big toe. 'I suspect – and this is perhaps why they were always cagey about it – that virtually all the millions come from Maxine's husbands.'

'And who is Maxine?'

'Oh, sorry! Maxine is Stephanie's mother-in-law. She's the *grand-mère* of the Dérain family, and a very grand *grand-mère* I can tell you, in the sense that she calls the shots. Anyway, as far as I could make out back when I was the au pair, Maxine's first husband made a packet after the war – although doing what I have no idea – and then died quite young, leaving her an absolute fortune.'

Hayden was intrigued. 'You said hus*bands*, plural.'

Anne gave a nod. 'Yes, well, that's right. She's had quite a few in her time. When I first met her she was in the process of divorcing husband number three, her second having apparently also fallen off his perch. Whatever – two and three had also been rolling in it. After that, I seem to recall Stephanie writing to tell me that she had married for a fourth time.'

'Blimey, you make her sound like Zsa Zsa Gabor!'

Anne turned to him with a quizzical smile. 'Is she that ancient Hungarian woman who's never done anything but marry super rich men?'

'That's the one, although, to be fair, I think she started out as quite a talented actress.'

'My mother was always intrigued in her shenanigans.'

'So was mine –'

'Champagne!'

Both Warwicks jumped.

'Oh, Stephanie.' Anne recovered herself first. 'You shouldn't do this.'

'No hour for tea!' Stephanie Dérain cried gaily. 'We are in a cause of celebration!' She placed down on a table before them a silver salver loaded with glasses, a dish of green olives and an ice bucket with a bottle of Bollinger which she then picked up. Leaping to his feet, Hayden took it from her and began untwisting the wire.

'It's very kind of you,' he said.

'It is no more than I can do.'

'It's very kind,' he repeated, struggling with the cork. The Frenchwoman hovered over him, elegant, poised, her scent so spicy it made him want to sneeze, until Verity suddenly hoved to, coppery hair clean and flopping and looking unrecognisably svelte in a fitted linen mini dress the colour of fading lavender.

'Why, Verity, you look gorgeous!' Hayden exclaimed, in tones of what he immediately realised were distinctly unflattering amazement.

'*I* bought it for her.' Anne sounded tart. '*And* packed it and I haven't seen it on her till this moment.'

Stephanie Dérain came to everyone's rescue. She bent to finger the hem of the dress. 'The Laura Ashley, is it not?' she purred. 'So simple, so *gamine*.' She straightened up with a theatrical sigh. 'I could wish only I were so beautiful and so *yong* as to wear the Laura Ashley.'

Everyone laughed nervously and Verity blushed bright pink and looked more gorgeous than ever.

The next minute, however, some kind of commotion seemed to break out at the French windows of the château. Everyone turned to look except Stephanie, who seemed bent on steadfastly ignoring whatever it was, imploring Hayden to pour the champagne. Hayden made to do as he was bid but with difficulty, finding himself once more distracted as this time a young woman not so much entered as charged into their midst.

Without a word to anyone, she flung herself down in the lounging chair next to Anne's, tilting it back at the same time as throwing off a man's Fedora hat to reveal a frizzy mop of purple hair bleached white at the roots and eyes so dark a blue as to be almost black. She was wearing miniscule denim shorts, honeycombed with artistic tears and rips, so low slung that they would have revealed her pubic hair if she'd had any to reveal, which, observed Anne, did not seem to be the case. Completing the picture were crimson platform boots and an ancient white boob tube covered in so much graffiti it qualified as a boob underground. Her naked shoulders were thick with tattoos.

Everyone looked thunderstruck – except for Stephanie.

'Pour the champagne, 'Ayden,' she said again.

'Who are you?' asked Verity at last, with the kind of bald curiosity only the very young can get away with.

The girl smiled but said nothing.

Stephanie Dérain moved to place her hands on the tattooed shoulders. 'This,' she said simply, 'is my daughter. Do you remember?' She looked calmly and directly at Anne.

'Yes,' Anne said faintly. 'I remember. She's Juno.'

7

'And the very next time,' growled Hayden two days later, 'that someone calls me 'Ayden, I shall ...I shall... '

'Yes, darling?'

'I shall make a noise like the Suez canal!'

'Yes, darling.' Anne turned back to her painting.

Yes, Anne was at last painting again but, decided Hayden in despair, it was the type of painting diametrically opposed to anything he would now, of all times, encourage her to return to, given the brush in her hand was a standard four-inch and the paint the cheapest and sloshiest white emulsion.

'We can't afford to replace those floor tiles, you know,' he said desperately.

While what she was doing was a definite improvement on the sitting-room walls' previous appearance – anything would have been a definite improvement – Hayden felt only alarm that she had not put any newspaper down and great sweeps of white emulsion were also sweeping all over the floor.

Anne gave an airy wave of her four-inch. 'Oh, I shall paint them as well. Stephanie took me to this marvellous interior decor place in Cabourg and I bought a great pot of a superb potion you simply whisk over tiles. In no time at all we will be looking at Italian terracotta.'

Hayden gave up. Stephanie had pronounced the house *charmante*, a judgement – bearing in mind Château Dérain – that was bound to be more patronising than sincere. Not, however, that the Dérains seemed, on the face of it, anything but charming themselves. Nevertheless, one could have too much of a good thing and in the last day or so Hayden's house seemed to have turned into a sort of *entente cordiale* staging post. His ears rang with Anglo-French shrieks.

There were, he estimated, four Dérains, that is, four currently on the scene, in that at that first dinner at the Manoir there had been a good many more. But, after declaring the weather to be *vraiment plus mauvais que l'Angleterre*, various sisters and *beaux-frères* had taken themselves off to Antibes and what was doubtless another Dérain holiday home.

Funnily enough, the moment they departed the rain stopped for good and a blistering heat wave descended, but they did not return which Hayden decided was fortuitous. Anne, of course, was in her seventh heaven. Not only was she at last living in France, but she had struck up a terrific friendship with Stephanie Dérain. The two women seemed to have discovered they had more in common than Hayden would have dreamt possible, given the disparity in their circumstances.

Even so, Hayden sensed Anne also felt a quartet of Dérains was quite enough to be going on with, not to mention the addition of a handsome, if rather haughty, youth introduced simply as Jean-Pierre. He seemed to be Juno's boyfriend besides being, as Juno had assured Hayden, an artistic genius on the brink of fame. Hayden had yet to see any evidence of this – either the genius or the fame – although Anne had said she thought he looked vaguely familiar. So perhaps he was – almost famous, that is.

'I hear you're a painter,' Hayden had said, in an attempt at genial conversation with the prodigy. 'You must talk to Anne. She's an artist, too. I'm sure she'd be fascinated to see your work.'

The young Frenchman had hesitated. Then 'I do not show my work,' he said bluntly, which seemed rather an odd thing for a genius on the brink of fame to say but there you were; artistic genii were nothing if not contrary.

Besides him and Juno, there was Gilles, Juno's father and Stephanie's husband, albeit only in the traditionally Gallic sense in that he wasn't around as much as the others because he was always shooting off to Honfleur where, he had informed Hayden *homme* to *homme*, he kept a yacht and a mistress. 'She costs me a packet,' he had moaned, but whether he meant the yacht or the mistress when he said this was not entirely clear.

Last, but by absolutely no means least, there was Gilles's mother, Maxine – the grand grandmother Anne had told him about. No matter she had indeed got through three more husbands after her first had died, Maxine still counted herself as an original Dérain, so to speak, and certainly seemed to call the shots as far as the family millions were concerned.

In fact, it seemed that Hayden had hit the nail on the head with the Zsa Zsa Gabor comparison in more ways than one. Although in her late eighties, Maxine Dérain could have passed for seventy and a hugely glamorous seventy at that, even if it was the type of glamour that personally left Hayden cold. He found all that rigorously-dieted chocolate flesh utterly unappealing. Give him Anne's pale and voluptuous comfort any day.

However, Maxine, Hayden could not deny, was a woman to be reckoned with. She had also taken an inexplicable but tremendous fancy to Walter Pepper, seizing every opportunity to secrete herself away with him for whispery little *tête-à-têtes* in intimate corners or, more ambitiously, country drives in her Porsche.

It was Maxine now who came into the house from the orchard where she had spent the last half hour nose-to-nose with Walter under an apple tree.

''Ayden,' she said throatily.

Anne lowered her paintbrush and looked expectantly at her husband.

'Maxine.' Hayden managed a weak smile.

'Wal-tèrre and I depart but I return him,' she consulted her Patek Philippe, 'towards five clocks.'

For some reason she always deferred to Hayden as if he were his father-in-law's keeper. That settled, she left to the accompaniment of engine roar huskier than her voice and much grinding of gears. Besides husbands, Maxine Dérain had also got through four Porsches.

'Where are those two off to now?' Abandoning her sloshing, Anne had turned to wipe her painty hands on a disposable nappy apropos to sorting out Martha, who was sitting on her play mat hurling plastic bricks into the log basket. Hayden put on the kettle.

'According to Wal-tèrre, somewhere I've never heard of called Le Grand Hôtel in Cabourg. She's treating him to lunch.'

'Wow.' Straightening up, Anne looked impressed. 'I've always wanted to go there. It's famous. In fact, it's where Proust used to stay when he was writing *Remembrance of Things Past*.'

'Really? Well, that's curiously appropriate given what Maxine told me earlier.'

'What was that, then?'

Hayden grinned. '"Ayden,' she said, 'Wal-tèrre and I are going to reminisce."'

'Reminisce?' Opening the fridge to take the milk out, Anne smiled. 'About Proust? Hardly. I very much doubt my father knows anything about Proust.'

'I wouldn't count on that.' It never ceased to amaze Hayden the things Walter Pepper did know about. 'But that's not the idea. They are not going to reminisce about Proust, they are reminiscing about Juno.'

'Juno?'

'Quite.' Acknowledging Anne's expression, Hayden took some mugs down from a cupboard. 'It confused me too for a moment. But Maxine did not mean her granddaughter. She was referring to an earlier model – Juno as in the beach, the D-Day Landings beach.

'As far as I can gather,' he went on, picking up the coffee jar, 'Maxine was a founder member of the Resistance in the Second World War. So she is going to relate her *'Allo 'Allo!* exploits and Walter is going to do a Spielberg on her, and describe how he battled up Juno Beach in 1944.'

Anne halted in the process of pouring the milk into a jug. 'But my father was nowhere near Juno Beach in 1944!' she cried.

Also halting, in his case in the process of spooning coffee, Hayden looked nonplussed. 'Where was he near?'

'Wolverhampton.'

Hayden blinked. Before he could respond, however, they were interrupted by another guttural roar from outside, albeit a less expensive-sounding one, and another clashing of gears, albeit a more proficient-sounding one.

Anne cocked an ear. 'There's Juno now. But listen, Hayden, I think you've got your arithmetic up the creek. In 1944 my father was still a boy.'

'Of course he was. How stupid of me. But what could he have meant, then?'

'No idea. He was probably exaggerating for dramatic effect. You know how Dad loves a good tale.' She glanced out of the window.

Hayden smiled to himself. 'I do indeed'

'But never mind that for now.' Anne turned to face him square on. 'We need to talk about something far more serious, and quickly, before Juno comes in.'

Hayden's smile faded. The past couple of days had seen him making a supreme effort to dissemble. And he had largely succeeded, at least in the sense that Anne had relaxed a little and stopped quizzing him. Of course, this head-in-the-sand approach could not continue ad infinitum, but the very last thing Hayden wanted at this moment was a return to confrontation with his wife. Instinctively turning away therefore, he said lightly, 'That sounds ominous. What's up?'

'Hayden, I don't think that young woman is a good influence on Verity and Conrad.'

Taken aback, he turned back. 'What young woman?'

'Juno, of course – who else?' Anne looked exasperated. 'Look, there's something up the creek with the girl. By that I mean she's odd... strange. I don't know but I'm beginning to think Juno is taking drugs or something.'

'Oh, surely not?' Hayden now felt not so much taken aback as shocked. 'I know she's a bit on the quiet side, a bit reserved, but I think she's just shy. She seems very sweet to me. Conrad and Verity adore her and it's incredibly kind of her to keep offering to take them to the beach. What on earth makes you think she might be taking drugs?'

'Her eyes, principally. Hayden, Juno's eyes are all pupil. I don't remember her having such black eyes as a baby. Yet now she looks, well... almost *demonic*.'

He shrugged. 'Her father's very dark.'

'But her hair, her clothes...'

'Her clothes?' Hayden frowned. 'I can't see anything wrong with her clothes. In fact, as far as sartorial influence goes, she seems to have had a rather positive effect on Verity.'

Anne knew what he meant. Since meeting Juno, Verity's appearance had transformed overnight from gruesome grunge to galloping glamour. All well and good except it pissed Anne off and for three very good reasons. One, the conversion owed nothing to her efforts. Two, she had received not so much as a whisper of thanks when Verity blithely trotted out all the nice clothes Anne had bought for her – and packed – but which she had never previously deigned to consider. And three, worst of all, Verity was showing early but definitive signs of shopaholism. 'I don't know about positive,' she said sourly. 'All Verity does now is pester me to go shopping in Cabourg for new gear.'

'Surely that's better than looking as though she's slept under Hungerford Bridge?'

'Is it? Have you seen the prices in those Cabourg boutiques?'

Hayden hadn't – and thought he preferred not to.

'I tell you,' Anne said with feeling, 'I'm not shelling out a fortune for Verity to emulate Juno. Especially when, expensive as they doubtless are, most of Juno's clothes are ghastly.'

'Oh, come *on*.' Hayden gave a little hoot of derision. 'They're fashionable, that's all. Fashion always looks ghastly to us oldies. Besides, didn't you wear ghastly clothes when you were a kid?'

'Juno is not a kid! She's twenty-seven and I certainly never had tattoos.'

Juno chose this moment to enter clad in what appeared to be a dustbin liner but minus the tattoos – they must have been the stick-on variety. Hard on her heels followed Verity, Conrad and Carpenter, Verity brandishing a dog-eared photograph and wearing an expression of sneaky triumph. 'Hayden?' she giggled. 'Do look at what Juno's given me.'

Hayden glanced at the snap Verity was holding and then glanced closer. In the grounds of a château he now saw was the Dérain pile, and clutching a plump fair-haired baby that might or might not have been an infant Juno, he deciphered what was patently, if incredibly, a teenage edition of Anne.

'Love the big hair, Mum.'

Anne snatched the photograph.

'And those padded shoulders – wow!' crowed Verity. 'Were you thinking of taking up American football?'

Hayden laughed.

'It's not funny, Hayden!' Anne flung the photo into the kitchen bin.

'Oh,' pouted Verity. 'And I was going to frame it.'

'Juno?' Anne turned to the girl. 'If you are taking the children to the beach,' she emphasised the word "children," 'then you had best get going.'

With kids and dog departed, Hayden carried their coffee to the table where they drank it without looking at each other, Anne sensing her husband was not pleased with her. Minutes passed in silence, save for the occasional crash and gurgle from Martha who was now hurling plastic bricks at the walls, painted and unpainted alike.

'Well, your hair looked a darn sight better than mine did at the age of eighteen.'

'How do you mean?' Anne looked up.

'I had a mullet.'

'You didn't!' Anne laughed suddenly and shamefacedly. Jumping up, she dived into the kitchen bin and retrieved the photograph. Rinsing some tea leaves off, she wiped it clean with the dishcloth and placed it on the draining board to dry. 'I'll give it back to her,' she said.

'Good plan.'

They smiled at each other in relief because they had seemed again on the verge of a row and rows were beginning to frighten them, because all at once rows seemed remarkably easy to come by.

Hayden knew this was his fault. Try as he might to conceal it, he knew Anne was picking up on his tension. Sooner or later something had to give, especially given the problems piling up. Monsieur Martin, Agnes Fenn's plumber/electrician, had called yesterday when Anne was out with Stephanie, only to confirm what he had suspected: their electricity was in need of a radical overhaul.

Panic-stricken, Hayden had embarked upon a voluble plea for the system to be patched up, only to grind to a wordless halt when he realised that, fluent as he was in the language, he hadn't a bloody clue what the French was for 'to patch things up'. Monsieur Martin had caught the gist, nonetheless, albeit he looked so intensely offended Hayden was then obliged to embark upon a voluble apology – he had evidently insulted the man's professionalism.

Although far from appeased, at length Monsieur Martin consented grudgingly to check over the junction box which he duly did, accompanied by a goodly rendering of 'Poof!' on his part and fizzing on the fuses. He then departed, waving away all offers of payment, however, which, while relieving, had left Hayden feeling very small indeed.

'I'm sorry.' Anne had crossed the room to stand behind him, winding her arms about his chest and nuzzling his neck.

'What for?'

'I've turned into such a grumpy old woman since having Martha,' she whispered, and planted rather a loud kiss in his right ear.

'No, it's me that's the grumpy old man.' He stroked her freckled arms, turning her hands palm upwards. 'Tell you what.' He planted a kiss on each palm. 'Let's pop Martha down for her rest and go and be grumpy together.'

'Actually,' Anne immediately detached herself, 'I was going to suggest you went to the beach as well.'

Great, thought Hayden, on top of everything else, he'd just got the good old brush-off. 'Why?' he said aloud.

'It would do you good and, anyway,' Anne glanced at her white emulsion now fast drying into what struck Hayden as alarmingly purple streaks, 'I want to get on with this.'

'Don't you want me to help you?' He nodded at the walls. 'That looks to me,' he said tactfully, 'like quite a lot of work.' But Anne gave a sanguine yawn.

'Oh, it only needs a second skim. No, you go to the beach. You can check on the kids and I can get along fine on my own.'

Hayden flexed his stiff shoulders and decided on a policy of least resistance. Besides, it had suddenly occurred to him that getting away from the house on his own would at least allow him some time to think things through clearly and calmly – something he had to do at some point.

It was impossible to think in any way at all with the kids and his father-in-law around 24/7, not to mention the French invasion. If he went into the garden, Conrad, Walter or even Verity generally trailed after him. If he tried going for a walk, Anne did the same. But here was his opportunity to get a grip. 'Okay,' he said, affecting a shrug of resignation – God, he was crap at this acting lark. 'If you're sure. What about lunch?'

'Can you buy yourself a sandwich? And also –' From nowhere Anne whipped out a shopping list. 'Perhaps at the same time you wouldn't mind picking up one or two things from the supermarket, plus a kilo of *andouilles* from the *charcuterie*. You know I've invited the Dérains to supper this evening? Well, I want to do that thing I did the other day for lunch.'

Hayden hesitated.

'What?'

'I was just thinking.' He gave another shrug, this time theatrically casual. 'Why don't you do something English?'

Anne sat down and looked at him suspiciously. 'Didn't you like my *andouilles*?'

'Darling, they were delicious!' Hayden heard yet another unmistakeable ring of insincerity in his voice, too late tried to curb it, and too late realised she had already heard it. He gulped. 'I was just wondering that, as you are cooking for French people, if it might not be more fun to cook something quintessentially English. Something like... like roast lamb, for instance!' he exclaimed, as if roast lamb were a sudden miraculous inspiration. 'The French love roast lamb.'

Anne looked far from appeased, but gave a martyred sigh.

'Oh, all *right*.' She got heavily to her feet. 'Get a leg of lamb instead, then, a *gigot d'agneau*.'

Hayden stood up.

'And take Martha with you,' she added, picking up her paint brush.

Revenge, thought Hayden, as he gathered together the astonishing amount of paraphernalia required to transport the twenty-first century baby ten yards let alone ten miles. Hell hath no fury, he reflected glumly, like a woman with her *andouilles* scorned.

8

Maxine was urging him to have something called An-yo. Or rather, that's what it sounded like she was urging him to have. Then again, Maxine dropped so many aitches it might have been Han-yo, which sounded suspiciously like that Chinese grub. Whatever it was, he was not going to risk it and he couldn't understand this blessed menu for love nor money.

'I'd like a nice steak,' Walter Pepper said firmly. 'A nice, rare steak.'

'Ah!' Maxine looked excited. 'An Englishman of the full blood.'

Walter felt his chest swell. It was donkey's years since a woman had said something like that to him. The waiter came over and Maxine ordered their food in rapid French, only to break off to remind Walter he hadn't chosen a starter. She pressed him to try the house special. What was it? Oysters. Walter considered this. Except for prawn cocktail, the only shellfish he had ever eaten were whelks, on Brighton Pier, and with vinegar.

'Wal-tèrre?'

Her eyes bright as a button, Maxine was asking him if he knew what oysters were famous for. Well, yes, he did but, slightly shocked that a lady should refer to such a thing, told himself she meant pearls. 'Of course,' he replied uneasily, thinking it was high time the conversation moved on.

The next moment, however, Maxine cast him such a roguish look from under her eyelashes that Walter decided he didn't care if she had meant what he had thought she meant because a woman hadn't looked at him like that in donkey's years, either.

'Right, then.' With a fortifying swig of champagne, he got down to business. 'Now, what was it you were telling me about what you did in the war?'

*

Conrad rebuilt the sandcastle for the fourth time. Martha was a terrible person to build sandcastles for because the moment they were completed – and she always waited until then – all she wanted to do was whack them to smithereens. Conrad felt like giving up but knew if he did all she would do was crawl off and whack someone else's sandcastle to smithereens, and then there'd be hell to pay. Actually, he had a terrifically soft spot for his baby half-sister but always tried to conceal it ferociously in front of Verity in case she called him a turdy little minger.

Patiently, he filled the plastic bucket with sand and showed Martha how to pat it down. Wrenching the spade off him, Martha swung it round her head like an Olympic hammer thrower and let go. The spade sailed through the air landing in another child's moat. Conrad rushed to retrieve it with as many *pardon*s as seemed necessary – which was a lot.

Back at the ruined castle, he sat down again on the sand and wedged Martha into a sort of loose vice between his knees. She could almost stand up on her own now and, anyway, she was always more controllable when she was being cuddled. Then he remembered Verity and glanced anxiously back to where she was lying propped on her elbows a little way up the beach above them.

He needn't have bothered. Verity was paying no attention to him and Martha. She was too intent on Jean-Pierre reclining next to her, gazing at him in an open-mouthed admiration that in anyone else she would say was pathetic. It was, too – not cool, at any rate. Not that Conrad blamed her. He also found it difficult to keep his eyes off Jean-Pierre. Oh, not in *that* way, for heaven's sake. Or maybe it was. Maybe it was a bit suspect the way he kept finding his eyes drawn to all that muscle. Jean-Pierre had abs like slabs.

'Bugger off!' screamed Verity suddenly, making Martha jump. Carpenter had arrived back from his tenth swim and was shaking himself all over her. Jean-Pierre cracked up with laughter.

Offended, Carpenter loped over to them whereupon Martha bent over to smack her hand on the sand to make the dog sit down. Her nappy stuck up in the air. Carpenter sniffed it in an experimental sort of way and then looked meaningfully at Conrad. Conrad leaned forward and caught the whiff. Oh, bloody hell. He might have known this would happen if his father left them alone for five minutes. 'Verity?' he called, twisting round. 'She needs changing.'

Verity ignored him not so much studiously as devotedly. Jean-Pierre, however, sprang upright in one fluid movement.

'Come!' Bounding down the beach, he stretched out a hand to haul Conrad to his feet, lifting the baby gently into his other arm. 'There is a room at the topping of the stairs, a room for the changing of the *bébé*. Come. I help you.'

Gratefully, Conrad went with him, Verity looking suddenly a little disconsolate.

*

With a growing sense of panic, Anne loaded her brush so full that when she lifted it, emulsion trickled down her arm into her sleeve. Scooping off the gobs with the other hand, she slapped them manually onto the walls with the desperation of someone trying to block a crack in a dam.

She stepped back. Not good, not good at all. A second skim of white had only made matters worse. From bearing streaks of deep purple, the walls were now a uniform sweaty mauve. Candy-floss pink was clearly not giving up without a fight.

Anne girded her decorating loins. It was her own fault; she had not allowed the first coat to dry properly. She must not rush so. Throwing the paintbrush dripping into the sink – she never could be bothered to wash decorating brushes – she turned to the tin of floor treatment.

The instructions were in French and in German, in Dutch, Arabic, Chinese, Serbo-Croat, Latvian and Outer Mongolian, but none, it seemed, in English. Never mind, she could perfectly well translate the French ones. Two hours, they seemed to say, to touch dry, three to completely – depending on the conditions. Well, the conditions could not be more boiling and, Anne checked her watch, it was ages before anyone would return.

Prising off the lid with the bread knife, she gave the treacly brown liquid a brief examination, selected a new brush and headed for the farthest corner of the sitting room. She should really hoover first but, after a quick mop of white spirit at the paint smears, the floor was reasonably clean. In any case, the tangerine peel tiles were so bobbly any blips wouldn't notice.

Ninety minutes later, breathing heavily, she straightened up from her hands and knees and thought how exhausting life must be for Martha. But it looked fantastic, fantastic! It really had transformed the floor into something akin to terracotta. With a flood of pleasure, Anne stepped outside and sank down on a hairy old rug on the unmown grass to pour herself a glass of cold rosé from the bottle she had placed ready before she did the last bit – she wasn't stupid.

Actually, she was.

She should have put a bottle of water out as well because she was, she now realised, absolutely parched with thirst. Knocking back a glass of wine to assuage this, Anne realised something else. She was dying for a pee. At a loss, she knocked back another glass of wine to assuage this, too, and inevitably only made matters worse.

Lying flat on her back, she concentrated on lifting her mind above the banal, the way some women claimed they got through labour. This succeeded only in making her feel unpleasantly as if she were *in* labour and her waters about to break. She turned on her side and closed her eyes.

There followed an inestimable period of time during which she did not feel anything at all.

'Anne? Anne! Are you all right?'

Anne rolled over, detaching a strand of rug stuck to her face with emulsion. Blearily, she focussed on her husband and dog looming over her.

'Don't go inside!' she squeaked, sitting up and suddenly remembering.

'Shit!' Hayden clutched his head as he also suddenly remembered something. 'I've forgotten the bloody lamb.'

9

'You mustn't choose anything expensive,' hissed Anne, the moment she and Verity got inside the *dames* or rather the *hommes* and *dames* in accordance with standard French loo practice. Verity got a comb out and started teasing it through her now always gleaming locks. 'Say you just want an omelette.'

Verity stared at her mother's reflection in the mirror. 'But I don't just want an omelette,' she said, her voice rising. 'I'm *hungry*.'

Anne gave her a fierce nudge. 'Shush. Just do as you're told for once.'

'But you're always going on at me not to diet.'

'Yes, well, this is one occasion when I want you to pretend you're a chronic anorexic.'

'Mum?' Verity turned from the mirror to face her mother, looking strangely adult. 'You're being very silly. The Dérains have kindly invited us out to dinner in a restaurant presumably in the expectation that we will *eat* that dinner in a restaurant.'

'That's not the point and you know it.'

'No, but I don't see why I should starve simply because Hayden forgets the meat and you choose to stick everyone to the floor.'

'Oh, shut up.'

Verity turned back to the mirror. 'Besides,' she continued indifferently, 'the Dérains are such breadheads it will do them good to part with a bit of dosh.'

'Breadheads? And what on earth does that peculiar idiom mean?'

Verity looked away. 'Oh, you know,' she said vaguely. 'They're, like, obsessed with money. Juno told me.'

'Typical!' Anne gave a snort. 'That girl has everything, *had* everything when she was a child, and now she pours scorn on it. Even as a baby her dresses were specially designed and made for her in Liberty prints.'

Verity faced her mother again. 'Exactly,' she said calmly. 'Everything material, everything meaningless. Nothing important, nothing real, just money, money, money.'

'But – ' Anne began, and then drew to an abrupt halt as a memory from twenty-seven years ago reared in her mind.

There had been certain aspects of Stephanie's behaviour towards the infant Juno that had shocked her, that is, not shocked her at the time, at the time when she was only eighteen, but had shocked her much later when she had her own daughter and recalled them. With a start she realised Verity was watching her.

'What's up, Mum? You look, like – blown away.'

'Nothing.' Anne shook herself. 'Are you saying you don't like the Dérains?'

Verity did not reply immediately, putting her comb away in a fluorescent orange nylon bag shaped like a flowerpot that Anne did not recognise.

'And where did you get that?' she demanded.

'Juno gave it to me.'

This was getting to be something of a refrain. As far as Anne could ascertain, Juno had to date given Verity a yellow suede miniskirt, a chain belt apparently constructed from gold doubloons and a string vest which, with the exception of its label, looked exactly the same as the ones Walter Pepper had always worn.

'Listen to me, Verity.' Anne looked severe. 'You must not keep accepting these hand-outs from Juno.'

'They're not *hand-outs* – that sounds horrible. They're presents. Juno just likes giving people things. And, anyway, why not?' Verity leant forward again to the mirror to examine her nose for peeling. 'She's got so much gear she doesn't, like, know what to do with it. Besides, you asked me whether I like the Dérains – well, I do. That is, I really, really like Juno,' she said, sounding pleased. 'And I really, really like,' she reddened a little and averted her eyes, 'Jean-Pierre.'

'He's not a Dérain and, besides,' added Anne, seeing the blush, 'he's going steady with Juno.'

'Oh, Mum.' Verity now sounded disgusted. 'We're not into all that oiky boyfriend/girlfriend stuff these days. These days people, like, stay loose.'

'All right, but Jean-Pierre is much too old for you to stay loose with.'

'He's twenty-five, Mum! Ten years is, like, peanuts between a man and a woman provided it's, like, that way round.'

'Oh, do stop saying *'like'* like that and what do you mean?'

'I mean it's, like, gross if a woman of forty-five goes lusting after a hunk.'

'I beg your pardon!' cried Anne, affronted, but before she could do anything about it had to hustle Verity out of the toilet as a fat man barged past them and headed for the urinal.

'Anyway,' Verity said coolly, as they made their way back to the dining room, 'Hayden is ten years older than you.'

Something struck Anne. 'That reminds me. Did Hayden fall asleep on the beach or something?'

'No.' Verity halted in her footsteps and looked at her. 'Why do you ask?'

'Because of him forgetting to go to the butcher's.'

Verity lifted her shoulders. 'Well, I don't know about that. All I know is he wasn't even at the beach for very long. He just stayed for about five minutes and then dumped Martha on me and Condy.'

'What do you mean?'

Verity walked on. 'He went off somewhere with Juno.'

*

Back at the table, Walter Pepper was saying, 'I think I'd like a pork chop,' Maxine was persuading everyone to start with *moules marinières* and Juno seemed to have disappeared.

Conrad tugged at Anne's shirt sleeve as she squeezed past.

'I don't have to have those mussel things, do I?' he whispered fearfully as she bent over him.

'You have what you want,' she murmured, giving him a quick hug. 'Maxine?' she called, sitting down very deliberately next to Jean-Pierre and casting Verity an avenging glance. Verity looked loftily away. 'Would you mind terribly if Conrad and I gave the mussels a miss? We're not awfully good with shellfish.'

Conrad threw her a grateful smile.

'*Moi non plus.*' Closing his menu, Jean-Pierre stretched across her to pour her some wine. 'The mussels, they do not like me.'

I wouldn't have said that, thought Anne, watching his rippling brown forearm. He was certainly very attractive, quite fair-skinned for a Frenchman but nicely tanned with sun-bleached streaks in his long mousy hair, full pouty lips and a bum-fluff/little boy beard like a young Brad Pitt...

But that was it! His striking resemblance to a young Brad Pitt was obviously why she kept thinking she had seen him somewhere before. And you can bet he cultivates it as well, thought Anne in amusement. Still, he was only a kid and seemed quite sweet, especially as he was now guiding Conrad through the menu. 'Try the *selle d'agneau pré salé*,' he was saying kindly.

'What's that?'

'Lamb, grazed on the salt marshes of Mont St Michel.'

'Lamb!' exclaimed Conrad without thinking. 'We were going to have lamb at ho –' Catching his father's eye, he broke off and blushed furiously.

'Quite,' said Anne, looking grim.

At the opposite end of the table, Hayden looked miserable.

'Yes, I'll have that,' Conrad said hastily, adding, 'Thanks, Jean-Pierre.'

'Yes – thank you,' echoed Anne in a low aside.

Everyone settled on fish soup or *pâté de foie gras* to start, except for Maxine and Walter, who had surrendered to her blandishments and was tackling mussels with caution. Oh, dear, fretted Anne, I do hope they don't disagree with him. As far as she knew, except for prawn cocktail, the only shellfish her father had ever eaten were whelks, on Brighton Pier, and with vinegar.

She turned to Gilles on her other side.

'This is such a treat,' she said, with a slightly forced smile because she had always found Gilles a trifle hard-going. 'We haven't been out to a restaurant for ages. It's so difficult with a young baby.' Martha had been left at the Manoir in the tender if gloomy care of Maxine's Spanish maid, Dolores, who, if nothing else, certainly lived up to her name.

Gilles waved a dismissive hand as if considerations such as babies were beyond him. 'Perhaps you are in need of a beautiful au pair?'

'Um, perhaps,' mumbled Anne, and then didn't know what to say next. It was the sort of leaden compliment that put a dampener on repartee.

'Ignore him,' cooed a silky voice in her other ear. 'He is – how do you say – the boring old fart? Speak with me instead.'

Suppressing a schoolgirlish desire to giggle, Anne turned back to Jean-Pierre. 'He's paying for that wine you're knocking back,' she said primly.

Jean-Pierre lowered his glass and looked unmoved. 'I think, in fact, Maxine will pay. But – *tant pis*.' He waved away the remark. 'The gift of money,' he continued with gravity, 'means something only when you have little of it to give. They all have too much.'

Anne considered him. 'I think you've been talking to my daughter.'

'*Bien sûr*.' He spread his suntanned hands. 'She is a pretty girl.'

'Very pretty – and very young.'

Jean-Pierre shot her one of those hot French looks. Goodness, thought Anne, feeling her colour rise, he could dry my tile skim in a second with that. 'I am never the cradle-snatcher,' he said laconically. 'I prefer the woman who, like fine wine,' he pinged his empty glass with one long brown finger, 'has arrived at her *maturitée*.'

'Yes, well, I expect you'll grow out of it.'

He studied her. 'Why do you give me the putting down?'

Anne shrugged. 'Sorry, but I don't like being fawned over.'

'So you think I was meaning you?' he retorted, with a look of such cynical contempt Anne cringed.

'No, of course I didn't.' She turned away in embarrassment. But the next moment he touched her arm.

'Please, I apologise.' He flashed a penitent smile. 'You are a very beautiful woman.'

Oh, *God*, thought Anne, feeling oddly like Verity. Why could they not have a, like, *normal* conversation? But before she could say as much Maxine had jumped to her feet and clapped her hands in the air.

'Friends!' she trilled.

'Romans, countrymen,' muttered a voice from somewhere.

Anne turned furiously on Jean-Pierre but he frogged his lips at her. Maxine in any case swept on regardless.

'I 'ave a leetle announcement to make! I would wait until your stomachs are full but my 'eart, 'e is so full I am not able.' Seizing Walter Pepper's wrist, she dragged him to his feet, whereupon Walter beamed happily if bemusedly round.

'Yes!' cried Maxine in ringing tones, pumping Walter's arm up and down like a bell rope. 'It is true.' She turned and planted a smacking kiss on each of his cheeks. 'Wal-tèrre and I are engaged to be married!'

'Jesus Christ,' said Anne.

*

'Anne, calm down. For heaven's sake, calm down.'

'Stop bloody telling me to calm down!'

'Okay, okay!' Hayden backed off, his palms raised as if in surrender. God, Anne was almost frightening him. He'd never seen her like this.

'But frankly,' he said, from a safe distance, 'I can't understand what you're getting yourself into such a state about.' Finding the bottle of Calvados in the kitchen he poured two generous measures and knocked his back in one. 'It probably isn't serious but even if it is, don't you think you're being a bit mean? You could think it rather nice.'

'Nice?' Anne slumped into a chair. '*Nice*? It's a bloody catastrophe.'

Wedging the Calvados bottle in his armpit, Hayden trod carefully across the room to sit opposite her, lifting his feet in a way that made him feel like Olga Korbet on her Olympic medal routine. The floor was still tacky which meant even Carpenter was picking daintily about like a reed bunting. Gingerly patting her arm, he handed his wife a glass.

'Here,' he said, and poured himself another. 'Just think of it this way. Your father has found romance.' He decided to try that last word again because on three glasses of Pernod and at least a bottle of

Gevrey Chambertin, not to mention the top-up of Calvados, it had sounded more like romansh.

'Romanch.' Still not quite right. And what on earth did he think he was doing? He never got drunk, never. Thank God Anne had been sensible and able to drive them all home although, he observed, as she also downed her Calvados in one gulp, it looked very much as though she was now going to make up for lost time. He poured her another.

'Yes,' put in Conrad, nervously eyeing his father. 'Good for Grandpepper.' Conrad had always called Anne's father Grandpepper.

Anne turned to him. 'Go to bed, Conrad.'

Conrad left without another word, Carpenter slinking after him.

'I agree with Condy,' said Verity. 'I think it's wicked.'

Anne rounded on her. 'And you can keep out of it too! None of this would have happened if you hadn't kept hobnobbing with that awful Juno.'

Verity burst into tears and fled upstairs.

Anne jackknifed upright and began to pace about, her sandals making grating tears on the sticky floor like sellotape being wrenched off bubble-wrap.

'That was very unnecessary, you know.' Hayden found himself feeling abruptly sober. 'However upset you are, that's no excuse for taking it out on the kids. You're being childish, Anne.'

She ripped past him.

'And do you think you could stop striding about like that? The noise is driving me bananas.'

Anne flung herself back into her chair with a final resounding rent. 'Oh, you don't understand,' she said contemptuously, and downed her second Calvados in another single gulp.

Hayden refilled her glass. 'Why is it,' he mused, 'that people always say you don't understand when they really mean you don't agree?'

'Oh, don't start playing intellectual semantics with me, buster. You don't understand because he's not your father.'

'It's precisely because he's not my father that I do understand. I see Walter as a nice old gentleman, and here he is finding himself a nice *rich* old lady. And, just in case you've forgotten, *you* were the one determined he should come and live here in France. Well, now he will be, and in the lap of luxury. As Conrad so rightly put it – good for Grandpepper.'

Anne said nothing. She emptied her third Calvados down her throat.

'Are you jealous?' Hayden asked suddenly.

Anne went still. 'Jealous? No, of course I'm not jealous. Why the hell should I be jealous?'

'Because he'll have a château and pots of money and all you'll have is a broken-down old cider farm with tacky tiles.'

There followed a not long but deeply unpleasant silence.

'Well, well, well,' Anne said at last. 'Who's being childish now? And nasty. Is that what you really think of me? How you really see me – as some moron who wants nothing more out of life but a fucking French château without tacky tiles?'

'No, of course I don't and I'm sorry.' Hayden drained his glass. 'Truly sorry. I should not have said that and I didn't mean it. You're right that I don't understand quite why you're so upset, but I'm too tired and too pissed to go into that now and if we shout any more we'll wake Martha – which is the very last thing either of us want. We'll have to talk about it in the morning. I'm going to bed.'

And leaping to his feet, he headed for the stairs.

That is, Hayden headed literally for the stairs. There was an almighty crash as both Hayden's feet stuck irretrievably to the floor.

'Dad!' came a wail from above. 'Are you okay?'

10

Walter Pepper woke in the spare bedroom at the château. That is, he woke in what seemed to be a spare château. There was an adjoining lounge as big as his bungalow and a bathroom you could have held a ball in, not to mention a canopy over the bed that must have started life as Napoleon's campaign tent.

Notwithstanding the luxury, however, Walter had slept anything but well, drifting into a fretful doze only around dawn. It might have been down to the hard mattress – that felt like it dated from Waterloo – or more likely on account of the pyjamas Maxine had pressed on him.

Not that the pyjamas were not nice of Maxine and, with their pocket monogrammed in gold, he supposed nice pyjamas. But they were made out of some slippery stuff which had made him feel so simultaneously sweaty and cold that for quite a lot of the night Walter had wished with all his might that he were in his own bed in his own bungalow and his own pyjamas.

Wincing, he levered himself upright. He had a headache, and a stiff neck to boot, probably on account of the pillow being lumpier than one of those damned bangers Anne had cooked. Stretching his neck upwards like a goose, he looked round for his tea. Anne always brought him a cup of tea in the morning when he was staying with her, just leaving it quietly by the bed. Now, however, a loud knock on the door made him jump.

Walter heaved himself out of bed with a frown; he didn't like loud noises in the morning. Realising he hadn't got a dressing gown, he hitched up the painful pyjamas, clutched the jacket round his chest and opened the door a crack.

The strange Spanish maid was standing there with a tray.

Walter frowned anew. He didn't like encountering strange Spanish maids in the morning either, especially without his dressing gown on. But before he could close the door, she barged in and slapped the tray down on a side table.

'Thank you,' he said coldly.

Giving him a hostile stare, she muttered something incomprehensible and barged out again, slamming the door for good measure and making him feel like one those poor devils stuck in an old folk's home.

Shifting his eyes from the door, he examined the tray.

It held a conical pot, a cup the size of a gusunder, and a couple of those greasy French roll things, the crumbs of which always stuck to his plate. There was no toast and she had forgotten the milk.

With a sigh, Walter decided tea without milk was better than no tea and poured a cup. Immediately he reared back, swayed forwards again and sniffed the pot. It was coffee and black coffee at that. Coffee! Coffee played merry hell with your bowels in the morning, as he was always telling Anne.

Walter sat down on his hard bed with a crunch, suddenly feeling he would do anything for a nice cup of tea. He would do anything to be at home with his daughter as well, with his daughter making his nice cup of tea, his toast and maybe frying up a spot of bacon.

Then he remembered his daughter's expression of the previous evening…

*

By eleven o'clock it had become clear Hayden was not suffering from terminal brain damage, Hayden was suffering from a terminal hangover. Even so, Anne kept peering into his pupils – he had an absolute shiner of a black eye from catching it on Martha's buggy on his way down – asking him if he knew what day it was and whether he could remember what he'd eaten for breakfast. Until, eventually, Hayden lost his temper and shouted at her that he didn't even know what bloody *year* it was and, as she bloody well knew, he never ate bloody breakfast so would she therefore bloody well leave him alone.

'You shouldn't drink so much,' observed Verity, looking up from pressing French transfers onto her backpack.

Hayden shot his stepdaughter a baleful glance.

All at once, Anne abandoned fussing over her husband's appearance and rushed upstairs to fuss over her own. She was in an uncharacteristic ferment of anxiety about what she should wear today.

As fond of nice clothes as the next woman, Anne's years of raising Verity on her own with the money coming in anything but regularly – her first husband was a complete shit when it came to supporting his daughter – had been a boot camp in the art of Being Sensible. Being Sensible meant a collection of Indian cotton skirts which never dated (well, they did but she tried to pretend they didn't), t-shirts and jeans and the odd ethnic dress bought on e-bay which recently (age really did creep up on you) had begun to make her look like Mother Courage.

Except for an incurable addiction to decent soap, she bought her make-up in Tesco and for scent relied on birthday presents. Hayden had given her some beautiful Turkish jewellery and a lovely deep violet pashmina last Christmas which was the only remotely classy thing she possessed. But you couldn't wear a deep violet pashmina in twenty-seven degrees of heat in a restaurant in France in August, and that was the problem. The problem was that she was meeting Stephanie Dérain for lunch and she hadn't a clue what to wear.

As soon as she had deemed it an acceptable hour that morning, Anne had got on the phone to Stephanie Dérain and not so much asked as demanded they get together. Stephanie took the demand in her stride, just another lady who lunched she was doubtless thinking, or maybe she missed the campaign note in Anne's voice. Whatever, the Frenchwoman had proposed Houlgate as a suitable venue. She would come and collect Anne and they could go to a little place on the seafront that was quite acceptable.

Unsure as to whether quite acceptable meant Macdonald's or three-star Michelin, Anne decided to opt for overkill. She was planning to be on the attack and therefore needed as much reinforcement as possible. With this in mind, she sat down in front of her dressing table and scrutinized her reflection in the mirror.

Everything looked the same. Eyes the colour of pondweed, chin length, straight hair that had once been a glossy copper like Verity's but was now more the dull rust of an old garden fork, and passable features in a face that was unfashionably round. Her teeth looked okay, but that was only because of spending money she could ill afford on private dental care to keep them looking nice. But, in truth, everything looked exactly the same.

Sighing, she slapped on some tinted moisturizer and then powdered it down to a scone-like consistency. Her own excess of Calvados the previous evening had left her cheeks wan and drooping, her freckles standing out like specks of iron mould on a pillow case. Not a bad simile given her face looked as though someone had slept on it.

Drama sits ill on the old, she thought despondently, remembering the dreadful scene of yesterday evening. It was the worst row – the only serious row – she and Hayden had ever had and, although he had apologised again this morning, by far the nastiest thing he had ever said to her. Actually, Hayden had never said anything nasty to her before which was why it had been such a shock.

Anne examined her conscience. Was she being unreasonable? Was she being mean about her father? What was the problem with Walter having a little romance? What was the problem with Walter getting married again – if that is what he genuinely wanted to do? She should be pleased for him, surely? Everybody else seemed to be – well, nearly everyone. It had been obvious that Gilles was far from ecstatic about the engagement. Yet, even he had toasted the "'appy couple" with his customary concrete gallantry. As for Hayden, on his own admission, he failed to understand why she was so upset.

But that was the point. Hayden did not understand.

With an effort, because it was another time in her life she did not like to remember and yet would never forget, Anne cast her mind back seventeen years to the bitterly cold February day when her mother had died. Coronary thrombosis – there was no warning. One minute Maggie Pepper was alive, the next she was dead.

Walter had gone completely to pieces. Oh, not in the now fashionable emotionally incontinent way. He did not even cry, or at least not in front of Anne. He simply went quiet, so desperately quiet that as time went on Anne feared he was going to follow her mother. But, of course, he did not. With that inexorable plasticity of the human spirit, Walter had eventually returned to something like normality.

Yet… a shift had taken place.

'It's as if you have depended on your parents all your life,' Anne had said when she tried to explain it to Penny – her first husband being not remotely interested. 'And then the positions are suddenly reversed. It's as if *you* become the parent.'

Penny had understood, only gently cautioning Anne that, while what she was feeling was completely normal, she must try to keep some distance. Walter was not a child and she was not his mother. Anne saw the wisdom in this, yet it did not stop her continuing to feel intensely protective of her father.

Oh, how she wished she could talk to Penny now! But Penny was incommunicado. Bush walks and diving off the Great Barrier Reef – they had agreed not to phone each other until Penny got back to civilisation. Then again, Penny would probably only have given her the same advice: back off, Anne, let Walter Pepper live his own life.

Anne could not. She could not now sweep those seventeen years of fearful love on one side, simply because a rich old Frenchwoman had decided to annex her father as her fifth husband.

Her *fifth* husband!

That was the other point Hayden did not understand.

Maybe Hayden was labouring under the fond delusion that Maxine was simply spectacularly unfortunate in losing all these husbands to death or divorce, but Anne knew there was a bit more to it than that. It wasn't that she expected Maxine to be a poverty-stricken little widow hobbling about on a Zimmer frame, but there had to be something suspect in the way Maxine had ended up not just so many times married but so phenomenally rich. Anne did not trust her motives. There was no way she was going to let the woman do a praying mantis act on Walter.

She caught sight of the time. Stephanie would be here any minute.

Quickly settling on an extremely full Indian cotton skirt in bright turquoise, Anne grabbed a scoop-necked plain black t-shirt and then the lovely Turkish necklace and earrings. Not bad, she decided, assessing her appearance through half-closed eyes. Not bad at all. Her outfit could even, at a pinch, pass as boho chic.

Downstairs, Hayden had gone that seasick green colour again, making Anne wonder for the first time how much he had really had to drink yesterday evening and why. It was completely unlike him to get pissed. Fiddling with the elasticated waist of her vast skirt, Anne suddenly wondered whether it made her look very fat. She caught Verity eyeing her critically.

'You wouldn't look too bad at all, Mum,' she remarked with her mouth full of transfers, 'If you junked the old hippie look and got yourself something new and trendy.'

Well, that's rich, thought Anne, coming from the erstwhile face of Miss Oxfam.

She turned her attention to Martha, sitting gurgling on her play mat and admiring the collapsed coffee table with all the awestruck satisfaction of a demolition engineer. Hayden's headlong dive across it the previous evening had rendered the coffee table not so much G as V-Plan.

'I can leave her with you, can't I?' Anne asked him, as she bent to kiss the baby. 'If you decide to take her to the beach, do make sure you keep her well protected in the sun, won't you?'

Hayden nodded a weary affirmative. He was sipping a mug of black coffee and trying not to retch. Anne hovered, debated whether to kiss him goodbye as well, heard the sound of car outside, decided against, and made for the door.

'You can come to the beach with Martha later, Dad,' Conrad informed his father kindly. 'When you've got over your hangover. Juno is picking me and Verity up at half past.'

Anne stopped dead in her tracks, turned back and opened her mouth. Verity caught her eye, saw her expression and then frowned in an inquiring sort of way. Anne closed her mouth and gave up. She was not sure Hayden had heard Conrad in any event, given Hayden now had his head in his hands.

The single good thing about the day so far, she reflected, as she settled herself into the expensive confines of Stephanie's Lancia, was that at least the bloody floor had dried.

*

Walter thought about Anne as he washed and shaved – a funny thing for him *to* think about since as rule he never exactly thought about

Anne. Anne was just there, always there; he did not need to think about her.

Now, however, as he scraped away with a disposable razor and great puffs of an aerosol disgorging that blooming squidgy stuff like synthetic cream – it was decent of them to put it out but personally, he had always been one for a good old-fashioned cut-throat and soap – he found himself thinking about her a great deal. He found himself wondering for the first time if he might not have upset her.

Anne was a good girl, of course, a very good girl. Mind you, she was a headstrong one, too, good and headstrong; always wanting her own way and getting it. Maggie had been fond of saying it was because she was an only child. *Walter, we spoil that girl.* But, true as this might have been, it was one of the very few things Walter had not liked his wife saying. It made it sound as if they had never had more than one child.

It made it sound as if Jack had never been born.

Swilling his face in the basin, Walter patted it dry with an oversoft towel and noticed his eyes were watering. Funny how they should do that the moment he was remembering Jack. No, it couldn't be that, not forty-nine years on. Nobody wept about a baby who died forty-nine years ago. It was the blooming shaving foam. It had a stink like a – well, like something unmentionable.

Back in the bedroom, he was about to put on his drawers when he saw something on the bed. Someone must have been in while he was next door because they had left laid out for him a clean shirt. Like the pyjamas, it was shiny-looking and a bit flashy.

Walter stood in his socks and vest, pondering on which was the worst evil, feeling like a spiv or wearing a stained shirt; his own had got rather familiar with those damned mussels yesterday evening. The flashy clean one, he decided, opting for the line of least resistance. He might upset Maxine if he spurned her shirt and somehow he suspected upsetting Maxine might have worse repercussions than upsetting Anne.

Maxine... *Maxine.*

For the life of him, Walter could not remember proposing to Maxine.

He could remember proposing to his wife; remember it like it was yesterday. Oh, he had even got down on the old one knee. But for the life of him he could not remember proposing marriage to Maxine.

He wondered whether he'd had one over the eight but no, Walter knew he had never been the sort of gent to get squiffy with a lady. Then, was it Maxine? Maxine was such a chatterbox, which he liked, but it meant sometimes he found it a touch tricky to keep abreast of the conversation.

Had Maxine somehow got hold of the wrong end of the stick? If she had it wouldn't be the first time. There was, for instance, that mix-up over Juno when they were first getting to know each other. One minute he was asking Maxine about her granddaughter – he had been rather struck by Anne being Juno's au pair when the girl was a baby – and the next it seemed he had stormed the D-Day Landing Beach! Very confusing, in fact, pretty blooming funny given he had barely been out of short trousers in 1944.

But he hadn't put Maxine right because it seemed... well, it seemed... well, he hadn't and that was that. Now, however, Walter began to wish he had.

What had he said this time that Maxine could possibly have misconstrued?

They had simply been talking, talking about everything under the sun. When had he *said* what it seemed he must have said? Then he remembered, all of a sudden Walter remembered. It was when they were drinking coffee after lunch and he'd remarked – when he could get a word in edgeways – that he had always wanted to travel.

'But Wal-tèrre,' she had replied in that grating voice that he found so surprisingly attractive, 'You must already have seen so much of ze world.'

Well, actually, he hadn't. A bit of a time in Germany, you know, on his National Service, and then the couple of holidays here in France when Anne was a little girl. Oh, when he was a young man he had wanted to see the world, he'd wanted to go to places like Italy, Spain, even America. But, you know, times were different then.

'We go to these places on our honeymoon, Wal-tèrre,' Maxine had then declared. 'We go anywhere you are wishing to go.' And that was it.

No, it wasn't it! He must have said something before that, something to lead her on although for the life of him he could not recall what…

He decided to wear the shirt.

Actually, once he had it on, he felt better. It looked natty, rather swish, he decided, admiring himself in the looking-glass above the dressing table. Tidying his hair with a silver-backed brush, he stood back and contemplated his appearance. 'A man's gotta do what a man's gotta do,' he drawled sternly to his reflection in his best John Wayne impersonation.

It sounded as impressive as always but for some reason did not fortify him the way his John Wayne impersonations usually did. With a conscious effort to dispel a slight but persistent feeling of unease, he transferred his thoughts back to Maxine. Maxine was a wonderful woman, he told himself as he pottered from the room, a really wonderful woman.

11

'Anne, *chérie*.' Stephanie looked sympathetic but baffled. 'I am sorry but I do not understand.' The Frenchwoman lifted her hands in a graceful gesture of helplessness. 'I do not know what it is you are asking me to do. Tell me, 'ow is it you say? Tell me in the plain English what it is you want me to *do*.'

Plain English. Right, then, that was all right, then. Except the trouble was Anne was not entirely sure she knew what she was expecting Stephanie Dérain to do either.

In search of inspiration Anne looked away, her eyes wandering abstractedly over the blue sky beyond the restaurant terrace, the blue sea below the blue sky, the blue awning flapping overhead and the blue cloth on their table before coming to rest on Stephanie's blue plate. Far from being three-star Michelin, the restaurant Stephanie had chosen was one of those seaside affairs where the decor gets stuck in such a blue funk you're relieved not to be served blue food.

Inspiration did not arrive. Oh, dear, this was not going to be easy. In fact, nothing about this lunch with Stephanie Dérain was turning out to be easy, not the least Stephanie's plate and her rigid determination to permit as little as possible to be placed upon it.

Take the starters. They had ordered a Caesar salad apiece or rather, Anne had. In view of Stephanie requesting hers to be served without dressing, egg, croutons or parmesan, she had ended up with more of a seizure salad. From this they had both moved on to the dish of the day – *sole Normande*. Examining her fish as if she were about to circumcise it, Stephanie had assiduously scraped aside every drop of its sauce. Toying with about a quarter of what was left, she then ate two French beans and one and a half *frites* (Anne counted), and drank a glass of Badôit.

'I admire your self-discipline,' Anne had remarked, as, for her part, she swallowed at least twenty chips and half the bread basket – she always did eat a lot when she was hungover – not to mention a carafe of rosé. But she was not being entirely truthful. Far from admiring her, all Anne could think was how restaurants must absolutely detest customers like Stephanie Dérain. Indeed, Anne found herself suddenly not all that keen either. 'Stephanie?' she had asked abruptly. 'Don't you ever give yourself a break?'

'A break?'

'A break, a holiday – from dieting.' Anne picked up a chip with her fingers and ate it to demonstrate. 'You know, from the *régime*.'

'Ah, *non*.' Stephanie took this to be a joke – doubtless one those strange English ones – and gave a tinkling little laugh. 'I take no break.'

And Stephanie *was* being truthful. By this stage in their friendship, Anne knew enough about the Frenchwoman to realise that, for her, appearance was a full-time, on-time, absolutely no-time-out occupation. But then, apart from a creepy old fart of a husband and weird daughter, there was nothing else *to* occupy her. She had never had a job. At home in Paris she employed a full entourage of domestic staff to iron Gilles's designer underpants and cook the designer meals she never ate, as well as paying for a personal trainer to maintain her designer size six figure. All in all, Stephanie's life struck Anne as excruciatingly boring and not a little painful.

Then Anne asked herself if she were not simply envious, because the results were undeniable. There was not an eyebrow unplucked, not a toe nor fingernail unpolished. Stephanie's clothes were beautifully fitting and always fitting to the occasion which meant, in deference to what she must have after all anticipated as a sober encounter, she was today decked out in a restrained, pale grey linen trouser suit with a demure white silk camisole underneath. There was not a speck on her black ballet pumps, not a scuff on her quilted Dior bag. Anne wondered what happened if she ever got it wrong. You got the impression with Stephanie Dérain that if she had a bad hair day she'd slit her throat.

However, Anne knew she was probably the one out of step. Penny was always nagging her to go to the gym; she had been once since Martha and found it very smelly. Some of her other friends had gone in for Botox, which Anne herself had considered but ultimately declined. Her face was already quite fat enough, thank you very much. No, Anne had to admit she was a low maintenance female –

and happy to be so. Women like Stephanie simultaneously awed and aggravated her. There seemed something so self-absorbed in all that dedicated vanity.

Yet, there was also something Anne could not prevent herself liking about Stephanie Dérain, especially when Stephanie now leaned forward, placed a cool but affectionate hand on Anne's wrist and said kindly, 'Speak to me. You look *désolée*. I worry myself for you.'

Leaning back to let the waiter remove her empty plate, Anne waved away the pudding menu and decided the time to speak had come indeed, and to speak plain English. 'Stephanie,' she began, placing her elbows purposefully on the table and grinding to a halt anyway.

'*Continue.*'

'This is difficult.' Anne chewed her lip. 'I don't want to seem insulting to your family but you must see in what an unsatisfactory situation we find ourselves.'

Stephanie flashed an enigmatic smile. 'Ah,' she cooed, '*ma belle-mère et ses amours.*'

'Yes, well,' Anne felt suddenly irritated all over again. 'You may find it entertaining that your mother-in-law has seduced my father but I don't.'

Stephanie withdrew a little, concealing affront if she felt it. 'But what can I do?' she asked serenely.

'For a start you can talk to her, *talk* to Maxine. You can tell her to find her *amour* with someone other than my father.'

Stephanie now looked both amused and incredulous. She did not reply.

'Well?' prompted Anne.

'Anne.' The Frenchwoman's expression became sorrowful. 'You are surely not believing Maxine would ever 'ear a word that could pass my lips?'

Anne frowned. Put like that, it did sound pretty unlikely. 'All right,' she conceded. 'You can tell Gilles to talk to her, then. He is her son.'

Stephanie's beautifully painted lips twisted into an abrupt *moue* of distaste. 'Gilles – pah!' she spat with such venom that Anne blinked. 'Gilles is useless at this moment.'

'I'm sorry?'

''E is having problems with 'is mistress.' The Frenchwoman lifted her shoulders in a faint but scornful shrug. 'I tell 'im she is the fat peasant but 'e does not listen. Gilles listens to nothing at this moment.'

Anne sat back with a gasp. From thinking during the last twelve hours that nothing could ever shock her again, Stephanie Dérain had just managed to shock her to her very core.

*

Today, Martha was not interested in smashing up sandcastles, Martha was interested in water. Fetching another pail full for her, Conrad wondered what she might be interested in tomorrow. It made him think it must be a soothing sort of life, being interested in something new every day and every day someone obligingly providing you with the wherewithal to be interested in it. Anyway, today Martha was really into water, scooping up great fistfuls and splashing them over her feet and forearms with all the reverent dedication of a Muslim performing ritual washing. Okay, if it kept her happy.

Conrad lay back and looked up at the sky. It had gone overcast and sullen, turning the sea a silent glassy grey. It was still very hot, though. Even Carpenter had given up cavorting and was collapsed panting on the sand, his tongue twice its normal length as he attempted to expel heat from his boiling little body.

Conrad rolled over onto his side, resting his head on his hand. Nearby, a German couple were having a blazing row. That is, he couldn't understand what they were saying to each other but it certainly wasn't the German equivalent of you are the sunshine of my life.

Holidays were funny things, he reflected. People spent all year saving and planning and looking forward to them, and then when they arrived, hardly ever seemed to enjoy them. Yet they would never admit defeat. There seemed to be a sort of strict and universal code of honour: this is my holiday and I will have a good time if it bloody well kills me. Take Dad and Anne, for instance. It was obvious to anyone that neither of them were having a good time. They never argued at home, yet, here in France, they seemed to have embarked upon a kind of heated cold war. They'd be better off going home.

Then Conrad remembered.

This *was* home now, at least for them. Anne and Dad weren't really on holiday and, at the end of the summer, only he and Verity would be going back to England. It felt weird; he couldn't get his head round it. Maybe that was Anne and Dad's problem, too, and that's why they were being so picky with each other. Whatever, it was beginning to look as if moving to France had not been a particularly smart idea.

He looked down the length of his body as Martha gave him a testing thump on the ankle. 'Ouch,' he said obligingly and she giggled, holding out the empty bucket to him for about the tenth time.

'Conconconconconcon!'

She started to sing at the top of her voice. It was really awesome the way she'd got his name but it made Conrad nervous. Pathetic as his French was, he knew enough to know that what she was singing sounded exactly like a certain French word, and a highly unrepeatable one at that.

'Now shush, Martha, there's a good girl' he tried. 'No more now.' She was in a horrible mess of sandy nappy and sandy hands. Her face looked as if it had been pebble-dashed. Filling her lungs with air, Martha held out her bucket more imperiously.

'CONCONCON – '

'Oh, stop it, Martha.' Verity had turned over towards them, adding 'You're being boring,' which was rich of her considering all Verity had been doing was boring Jean-Pierre with how much she hated boring Normandy. She said stop it quite nastily too which meant Martha's face crumpled.

Oh, *bugger* Verity, cursed Conrad as he raced down the beach with the empty bucket. He really could not stand it when Martha cried.

*

'Don't you care?'

Stephanie had continued to look cool and tranquil, even faintly superior. 'In France, we do not think of these things the way you English ladies do.' She had considered a moment, her head on one side. '*Non*, I think it the more honest arrangement. No deceit.'

'No *deceit*!' Anne's eyes popped. 'For God's sake, Stephanie, how the hell can your husband cheating on you be anything but –' Then she twigged. 'Oh, I get it,' she said dubiously. 'Or at least I think I do. You're saying it's better to know what he's up to rather than for him to go behind your back.'

'*Exactement*. I am Gilles's wife, I and I only. No mistress will ever take my place, but in a situation that is always going to be the same, it is better for the wife to know and for her to accept.'

'*I* wouldn't accept. If I found out Hayden was keeping a mistress, it wouldn't just be the legs of his trousers I'd cut off, I can assure you.' Anne expected the Frenchwoman to blush at that but Stephanie did not blush. Her regular open pore closing treatments did not allow for blushing.

'You are yong. You are certain in life. You will learn.'

'I'm not *yong*, Stephanie, and by the way, it's pronounced "yung". I'm forty-five and far from certain about anything in life, especially not the claim you seem to be making that all men are inevitable adulterers.'

Stephanie cast her a knowing look. 'And are they not?'

Anne gulped at her wine. Insisting upon ordering another carafe of rosé for her, things had got so cosy Stephanie had even unbent from her *régime* and commandeered a *tarte aux pommes*. 'This is my sin,' she had confessed, tucking in with all the fearful relish of a Jesuit priest discovering sex.

'But tell me,' she now said, as she delicately scraped her plate. ''Ow does 'Ayden see the engagement?'

They were back to Walter Pepper. 'Oh, Hayden can't see anything wrong in it,' sighed Anne. 'Then again, Hayden can't see anything very clearly at the moment on account of having a black eye.'

Stephanie looked at Anne with her most admiring glance to date and poured her more wine.

'Oh, I didn't mean that!' squeaked Anne. 'We had... he had, that is, a little... er, accident.'

Stephanie looked doubly impressed. 'Always, always you English ladies are so *diplomatique* about your control over your men.'

It was Anne's turn to blush. 'It wasn't quite what I meant, Stephanie, but never mind that for a moment.' She paused. 'I'm more interested in what Maxine could possibly see in my father. He's not rich, you know,' she said, quietly but with meaning. But Stephanie waved a dismissive hand.

'Oh, it is not the riches. Maxine 'as so much, she does not know what with it to do. *Non.*' Finishing her pudding with a replete sigh, Stephanie lit a Disque Bleu with the flare of a gold Dunhill lighter, offering one to Anne as an afterthought.

Shit, thought Anne, as she accepted it. She would have crucified Hayden for breaking their pact on smoking but these were extreme circumstances. She just had to have a cigarette.

'What, then? What can she see in him? I mean, for goodness' sake,' she rushed on, inhaling as if her life depended on it, 'I've nothing against late romance but don't you think my father a trifle on the antique side for a holiday fling? And that's all it is going to be,' she added. 'Because I cannot think what else Maxine would want him for.'

'Anne.' Stephanie looked reproachful. 'Your father is a very charming man.'

'Oh, don't talk crap.'

'*Comment?*'

'Sorry.' Anne collected herself. The cigarette had made her feel headier than the wine. 'I just cannot see,' she said, choosing her words with care, 'why someone like Maxine would find someone like my father, charming as he is, attractive.'

Stephanie considered, summoned the waiter and ordered another helping of *tarte aux pommes*. 'Okay, I see maybe the point you make.' She stubbed out her Disque Bleu. 'I think, then, maybe it is this: Maxine is excited by 'im being an 'ero of *la guerre*.'

Yes! Even though she personally detested the gesture, Anne had to restrain herself from punching a victorious fist in the air. This was it, this she could deal with, this she could *fix*. 'Stephanie?' She took a deep breath. 'My father is not a war hero.'

'No?' The Frenchwoman frowned, thought about what Anne had just said, and then frowned again. 'So why does 'e tell Maxine – '

'I know,' Anne cut in with an apologetic smile. 'But things have got... well, have got a little mixed up.' That was the most tactful way of putting it short of making Walter Pepper out to be Walter Mitty. 'I'm sorry to destroy Maxine's illusions but the fact is that in the Second World War my father was never anywhere near the Battle of Normandy, never near France at all. He was on the home front – home in England.'

'Aha! A boy from the back room!' Stephanie fell on the tart the waiter had placed before her. 'This Maxine would like also.'

'No!' Anne nearly screamed. 'Not a back room boy either! In 1944 my father was barely out of school. He was about to start his apprenticeship to train as an engineer.'

Stephanie raised her laden spoon to her lips and waited, her eyes fixed wonderingly on Anne.

'Listen,' began Anne, suddenly aware that she had got herself into a bit of a minefield. 'What my father did in the Second World War is absolutely nothing to be ashamed of. Indeed, it's quite the reverse because if he had been a few years older, he would undoubtedly have been one the brilliant men helping to design the Spitfires that won the Battle of Britain.'

There was a pause while Anne finished her carafe of rosé.

'Of course, they are the unsung heroes,' she said dreamily. 'Indeed, without men like my father, we would be enslaved. We would not enjoy the liberty, the freedom, the freedom to live, to eat, the freedom you have to eat that pudding before you, that pudding you are eating today.'

Stephanie lowered her laden spoon and looked guilt-stricken. Oh, bloody hell, thought Anne. Why do I always go over the top? It was the damned wine. 'Sorry,' she said. 'Eat your pudding.'

Stephanie tentatively picked up her spoon. 'Anne.' She sounded awed. 'Sometimes you are frightening in your passion.'

Anne signalled the waiter for some coffee. 'All I want to say,' she said, and hoped it was all, 'is that I don't want Maxine thinking that while she risked life and limb in the Resistance that, in his turn, Walter Pepper stormed the Normandy beaches because he most certainly did not.'

There was another pause, this time a long one.

'What's the matter?' Anne asked at last. Stephanie had the most peculiar expression on her face.

'Maxine told 'im she risked life and limb?'

'So I understand – why?'

'That she was in *La Résistance*?'

'Yes. Why?'

'I think,' Stephanie began, speaking slowly and deliberately, 'I think that maybe Maxine – what do you say – maybe Maxine 'as at last met 'er matching?'

'Met her match, you mean, but what are you saying? Are you telling me that she didn't risk life and limb?'

Stephanie hesitated, a strange little smile playing about her lips. 'Anne, *mon amie*.' She took Anne's hand. 'All I know for sure is that in the war Maxine was not a member of *La Résistance*. Oh, I 'ave no doubt she joined in the uprising in the streets of Paris in August 1944 as so many yong girls were doing at this time. They were children, you know? But I assure you that she was never in *La Résistance*.'

Anne stared at her friend. 'Then why would she tell my father that? What could she possibly hope to gain?'

'Nothing.' Stephanie gave a mirthless little laugh. '*Elle est une fantaisiste*,' she said shortly.

Anne frowned, translated and then frowned again. 'A fantasist? You're saying Maxine is a fantasist?'

'That's right.' The Frenchwoman nodded. 'Maxine likes making up stories.'

12

Waking alone in bed the next morning, Anne opened her eyes to the discouraging realisation that her dream life in France was in smithereens before it had even properly begun. Not only had her father hitched his star to a fruitcake, there was now another more serious problem plaguing her.

And that was the business of Hayden and Juno.

Hayden and Juno, Juno and Hayden – they sounded like a pair of bloody planets. The pairing sounded ridiculous in another way, too. Because, even with her over-active imagination, Anne could not conjure up an image of her husband being turned on by a bin bag. Yet the undeniable fact remained that Hayden kept going AWOL *and* he always seemed to absent himself at the same time as Juno.

Take yesterday, for instance.

Just as she and Stephanie were finishing their coffee, it had started to pelt down with rain, obliging Anne to call a summary halt to mind-blowing revelations and persuade Stephanie to rush her off to the usual spot on Cabourg beach to make sure the kids were all right.

Well, the kids were all right, all right. She had found the three of them huddled together in the shelter of a sun pavilion on the promenade, Carpenter looking martyred and Martha swathed like an insect pupa in a green designer windcheater belonging to Jean-Pierre. For all his surliness, Jean-Pierre had evidently acted quickly and responsibly as far as the baby was concerned.

Hayden had not, though. Hayden had not acted anything like responsibly and quickly for the simple reason that Hayden was not there – any more than Juno was.

To be sure, Hayden had arrived back at a sprint, saying he had just popped into town for some paint from the *quincaillerie*. But, when later Anne had casually raised this with Conrad, Conrad said vaguely that he thought his father had been gone a couple of hours. To be sure, Hayden had bought some paint, but it took less than ten minutes to walk from the beach to the shops in Cabourg. Anne knew because she had walked it herself.

Of course, the scenario was unlikely and even if it wasn't, she could simply confront him, simply ask him outright 'I say, dear husband of mine, are you by any chance having an affair with young Juno?' On Stephanie's precept, this would be the mature, the dignified way to behave. But every time she girded herself up to do exactly that Anne lost her nerve at the last minute. She was terrified he might actually admit it and then where would she be? Who knows? He might even be seduced by some Gallic principle and expect her to put up with it. Well, she bloody well wouldn't.

Turning over onto her back and staring up at the polystyrene ceiling, Anne debated whether to get up or whether to simply stay here in hiding with only Carpenter for company; the dog was lying at the bottom of the bed, gnawing on what seemed to be a windfall cider apple. But just as she was deciding she really could not face anyone, the door opened and Hayden marched in.

'One baby breakfasted, bathed and booted,' he said cheerily. 'With two teenagers bribed to look after her for an hour or so.'

And without further ado he yanked off all his clothes and leapt into bed beside her. Taken completely by surprise, Anne found herself submitting as her husband pulled her into his arms, even giving a grunt of contentment as Hayden got down to business, feeling him all warm and ready and starting herself to feel terrifically randy in anticipation. It suddenly seemed exactly what she needed.

But no sooner had she entered into the spirit of the thing than Anne began to visualize in graphic detail the image that had earlier eluded her, the image of Hayden making love to Juno. Never mind the bin bag, she found herself reflecting on Juno's long legs, Juno's rosebud mouth, Juno's youth.

''Ayden,'Ayden,' she heard murmured in a Gallic purr inside her head. 'You drive me wild with desire, 'Ayden.' Which was not was quite right really because Juno never called Hayden ''Ayden.' Juno, indeed, never called Hayden anything but a courteous Monsieur Warwick in the same way that she also always called Anne 'Madame.' A nicety, however, that Anne had lately come to suspect was merely a dastardly ploy designed to emphasise her age.

Hayden was now working up a head of steam which was a pity because Anne felt herself going right off the boil. 'No,' she mumbled at the last possible moment.

'No?'

'No.'

'Okay.'

With the merest hint of a sigh, he kissed the base of her throat, gave her left breast a valedictory squeeze and rolled off her. She turned over the other way from him, her head spinning with the contradictory sensation of having scored a point at the same time as having kicked herself squarely in the teeth.

This is idiocy, she decided, I'm going mad, and prepared to turn back to him. But, before she could move, she heard him get out of bed, pull on his clothes and go to the bathroom, whereupon there followed a very long and unnaturally deep silence.

When he comes back, I'll make it up to him, resolved Anne. I love him so we will *make* love.

The silence continued.

I want him, she told herself. I really, really want him.

More silence. More minutes ticked by.

What the hell was he *doing* in there? Indulging in a session of Juno-fantasizing auto-eroticism? Suddenly livid, Anne was about to leap out of bed and go and accost him mid-wank when she caught sight of Carpenter.

'Hayden!' she screamed. 'The dog's foaming at the mouth!'

Hayden rushed in, his face covered in shaving lather. After a quick examination, he extracted what was left of a bar of soap from Carpenter's scented jaws.

'Oh, the rotten meanie,' said Anne indignantly. 'That was my best Roget et Gallet.'

*

'So, what are you two going to do today?' Hayden asked the kids, as they all gathered round the dining table with mugs of coffee. Verity looked at her stepfather as if he were simple.

'We're going to the beach, of course.'

'And there was me thinking you might be taking up extreme tiddlywinks.'

'What?'

'Nothing,' said Hayden.

'Is Juno... ahem... is Juno picking you up?' The name had seemed to stick in Anne's throat like a cough drop.

Verity shook her head. 'Not this morning. She said she's got, like, something she's got to do this morning.'

Anne pounced. 'What?'

Verity looked taken aback. 'I've no idea. She didn't, like, say.' She looked curiously at her mother. 'Why do you want to know?'

Lowering her eyes, Anne gave a deflective sort of grunt in reply. She wished this feeling would stop, this feeling that she needed to pin down Juno as if she were marking her in netball. In silence, she stood up to clear the breakfast dishes.

'When's Grandpa coming home?' Verity asked suddenly.

Her hand arrested on the butter dish, Anne looked at her daughter in surprise. 'I only wish I knew, darling. Why? What made you ask that?'

Verity pondered. 'Dunno. It's just, like, I've never realised it before, but you don't really notice Grandpa when he's around but when he's not, you, like, really miss him, don't you?'

Anne felt her throat close. 'You do indeed,' she croaked.

'Are you going to take us to the beach, Dad?' Conrad looked up from teasing Carpenter with an old flip-flop and making Martha gurgle with pleasure.

'Actually,' Hayden turned to Anne, 'why don't you go down with them?'

'Go down with them?' Anne heard her voice sounding as if it was coming from somewhere else, as if she were a ventriloquist's dummy.

Hayden stood up and stretched. 'Yeah, I thought I'd stay here and give the roller and that new paint I got from the *quincaillerie* a whirl.' He glanced at the mauve walls. 'The man in the shop said it was better than Dulux Once – guaranteed to cover a multitude of skims.'

Anne did not laugh. Juno at large and Hayden home alone. Wonderful.

'Tell you what,' suggested Hayden, as she took the mugs over to the sink and started crashing plates about to relieve her feelings. 'Let's all have a day out tomorrow. Go somewhere different.'

Verity looked suspiciously at her stepfather and asked him what he had, like, in mind. What he had, like, in *mind*, Hayden informed Verity with elaborate sarcasm, was taking her poor old mum out somewhere she would enjoy.

Jesus, thought Anne. He makes me sound like *his* old mum.

'She's trying to have a bit of a holiday as well, you know,' Hayden was saying sententiously. 'But what do you think, darling?' he asked to Anne's back. 'We could go to Giverny. It's not too far for a day trip and I know how much you've always wanted to see Manet's house.'

'Oh, for God's sake, how dim can you get!' Anne whipped round so fast she nearly fell over. 'Giverny is *Mon*et not *Man*et!' Clutching the back of a chair to steady herself, she registered her family's faces.

'Ouch.' With a wink at Hayden, Verity wagged her hand as if it had been slapped. Martha started to whimper and even Carpenter dropped the flip-flop in shock.

'Sorry.' Anne gulped and swallowed. 'Extremely sorry, everyone.' She bent over the baby to soothe her, burying her burning face in Martha's fat little neck.

'Well?' said Hayden, a moment or two later when she had straightened up. His expression looked unnaturally bland. 'Are you going to take them to the beach?'

'Yeah, come on, Mum.' Leaping up, Verity enveloped her mother in a bear hug.

'Are you feeling all right?'

'I'm dying to show you this really funky top I've seen in a boutique in Cabourg.'

'That sounds more like it.'

Detaching herself, Anne shakily picked up the bread board and went over to the open doorway. Before she could knock the crumbs off it, however, Gerry Underwood appeared from nowhere, yelled,

'Right, then, Mister Warwick!' and in his without-so-much-as-a-by-your-leave fashion, barged past Anne into the room.

'*Do* come in,' she said ironically.

Fuck, thought Hayden, getting quickly to his feet.

'And what, pray, can we do for you this morning?' Anne asked sweetly. She was determined to be accommodating, determined not to be snobbish. Then, something in his manner made her look more closely at Underwood. Yes, the shiny shorts were still there, and the weeny baseball cap, but therein ended the tale.

Gone was the ingratiating manner, gone the slimy smiles. This was Uriah Heap turned mad axe man, an impression that was immediately reinforced when he took a threatening step towards Hayden and shouted in his face, 'WHADDYA MEAN! Whaddya mean by getting another electrician? We gotta a contract!'

'Hang on a sec,' interjected Anne. 'What's going on?'

'Conrad?' Hayden spoke quietly but gravely to his son. 'Take Martha and Verity upstairs, please, and stay there until I tell you to come down.'

'What?' Verity looked comically amazed. 'What is this? An action replay of *Titanic* or something? Women and children first?'

Dragging Martha out of her high chair and noting with passing disgust that she looked as beguiled as ever by Underwood, Anne piloted the baby into her elder daughter's arms. 'Go on, darling,' she said, with a conspiratorial wink. 'Do as Hayden asks, please. Go upstairs for a minute.'

Verity stared at her mother for a second and then capitulated. 'Oh, all *right*, but I don't need *him*,' she jerked a contemptuous shoulder at her stepbrother, 'to take me.'

That left Carpenter, Anne realised too late, as the kids clattered up the stairs. But the way things were going they might need him.

'Now.' Turning to Underwood, Hayden looked him straight in the eye. 'Can we discuss this sensibly?'

*

'I'm going to call the police,' said Anne for the third time.

'No, you are not,' Hayden said for the second time.

'For Christ's sake, you've just been seriously assaulted! What are you, a martyr or something? That man has just punched you in the eye!'

'It only evens things up.' Hayden gingerly reapplied the cold compress Anne had made from ice cubes wrapped in a tea towel. 'I needed a black eye on the other side to look regular. It was decent of him to choose the right one.'

'Hayden, this isn't funny, we're dealing with a lunatic.'

'Tell me about it.'

'But what was all that about a contract?'

Hayden held the tea towel over both his eyes. 'How the hell should I know? As you correctly observed, the man's a lunatic.'

'But a contract...'

Lowering his improvised mask, Hayden looked oddly at her. 'Maybe he meant a contract to murder me.'

'What! Oh, Hayden, please don't joke about things like that!'

'Or maybe he's just after my money.' Hayden met his wife's look with a cold stare. 'Or should I say – my *Mon*et?'

There was a pause as they locked eyes.

'Look, I'm sorry about that.' Anne felt terrible. 'I said I was sorry and I am. I've just been a bit cross with you because you're not on my side about Walter but I didn't mean to put you down like that. Truly.'

'Forget it.' Hayden flung the tea towel into a wet heap on the table.

'No, I really *am* sorry. How can I –'

'I said forget it.'

Silence fell except for a muted slurping as Carpenter crept between them and started licking up the pool of compress water dripping onto the floor. Unable to sustain Hayden's grim expression, Anne looked down at the dog.

'And you were a great help,' she informed him. All Carpenter had done when Underwood ran amok was shoot under the table. 'Where was Lassie to the rescue?' she demanded, hoping to make Hayden laugh but failing dismally. She sighed. 'I do wish somebody had socked the horrible creep back, though.'

'Does 'somebody' mean me?'

'What? No! No, of course it doesn't.'

Without warning, Hayden sprang to his feet and seizing the wet tea towel, balled it up in his hands as if about to throw it at something – or someone – but then stopped and drew in a deep breath. 'Well, I'm sorry I couldn't oblige but fisticuffs are not my line. In fact, I'm not sure quite what is my line these days.'

There was a pause while Anne stared at him. Her husband's eyes had gone strangely opaque. 'Hayden, what do you mean? What's going on? You haven't been yourself for days. What's wrong?'

'Nothing.'

Sounding unutterably weary, he turned away from her. 'Go to the beach. Go to the damn beach with the kids and let me get on with the decorating. Maybe we'll talk later but for now all I want to do is watch bloody paint dry.'

13

Which, all in all, Anne told herself drearily, as she loaded teenagers, dog, snorkels, towels, flippers, baby and boules into the Galaxy, was not the optimum way to approach a fun little day at the beach. Even more galling was the knowledge that Hayden was a million times more hacked off by her putting him down than anything that jerk Underwood had done. And it was all down to her working herself up into a ridiculous lather over stupid suspicions about Juno. Well, it had to stop.

She resolved there and then never to think about Juno again, or at least not Juno in connection with Hayden.

At Cabourg seafront she made three trips to the promenade to unload everything and everyone, and then wondered whatever had happened to the days when you went to the beach with a bucket and spade. However, just as she was about to descend the stairs for the final time 'Anne!' squealed a voice behind her.

'Is this not enchanting? I was *pining* to see you!'

Anne shifted Martha to her other hip as she and Stephanie Dérain embarked upon all the double kissing malarkey. She was trying hard to feel enchanted and pining to see Stephanie, but yesterday lunchtime's confession session had left her feeling distinctly awkward in the Frenchwoman's company.

'This morning I am solitaire.' Stephanie looked soulful. 'Gilles abandon me, Maxine, Juno…'

Yes, where *was* Juno, Anne started to say and stopped herself just in time.

'But now I 'ave my friend.' Tucking her arm cosily into Anne's, Stephanie propelled her in the direction of the Grand Hôtel lido. 'We beetch together, yes?' she said happily.

Momentarily nonplussed, Anne suddenly laughed and felt more cheerful. She could not possibly have explained the joke to Stephanie but perhaps a good beach/bitch with another woman was just what she needed.

It took less than ten minutes, however, for Anne to realise that Stephanie Dérain was The Number One Woman You Should Never Go To The Beach With.

While the kids flung down their towels and raced off to the sea with Carpenter, Stephanie appeared to regard the placing of her exquisite bottom on something as lowly as sand as tantamount to revolution. Instead, she insisted on going through the immense palaver of renting from the hotel not only a couple of immaculate sun loungers, but also a striped pavilion bathing tent that could have graced Brighton Beach in 1899.

Hot and bowed with exhaustion from holding Martha – this baby had better start walking soon or she would end up like Quasimodo – Anne had gone off the whole enterprise long before they were eventually at ease. Worse still, Stephanie then disappeared into the hotel with a vast Prada holdall, only to emerge an age later decked out in a stunning pareo printed in silvery swirls of blue like the inside of a mussel shell, topped by a see-through voile shirt knotted over a matching bikini.

Anne considered her own ancient bikini and decided that, come what may, she would keep her clothes on. The combination of grand hotel and Stephanie Dérain was enough to give anyone an inferiority complex.

When Stephanie, however, immediately summoned a minion and ordered iced coffee for herself and a glass of rosé for Anne, Anne began to feel there were some positive aspects to the life of luxury. Then she thought about the automatic way Stephanie had ordered wine for her without even asking and began to feel insulted instead. Damn woman must think her a dipso.

'So,' breathed Stephanie, at last at gleaming repose on her lounger. She had just spent twenty minutes assiduously plastering every centimetre of her body in Clinique's entire range of sun care.

Human oil slick hits Cabourg, mused Anne, envisaging headlines as she slapped Boots Factor 30 on Martha and stuck her under the bathing tent awning. **Seabirds dead. Ecological disaster threatened.**

'So,' repeated the Frenchwoman. 'How proceeds your crisis?'

'My crisis?' Anne abruptly stopped musing, mortified to think anyone might know about that morning's shenanigans. 'What crisis?'

'Your father, Anne.' Stephanie looked puzzled – as well she might. 'I ask about the... *situation*. I am using the wrong word maybe? I ask about Maxine and your father.'

'Oh! I... I don't know.'

With a start, Anne realised she had completely forgotten about Walter in the last couple of hours; they had been far too traumatic. Looking away, she concealed her confusion by tending to the baby. Rocking back and forth on her rug, Martha was contemplating the oiling and boiling of bodies around her with all the beady glee of a *tricoteuse*. 'Some flunky arrived from the Manoir yesterday evening to collect all his belongings,' she said, trying not to remember how much this had hurt her. 'But apart from that, I've had neither sight nor sound of either of them.'

'*Moi non plus*.' With a dejected little sigh, Stephanie sat up to sort through her holdall. Withdrawing four pairs of sunglasses – that bag could rival the Tardis in its hidden capacity – she settled for some tortoiseshell Ray-Bans and put them on. 'I 'ave not seen them for days.'

Days? A fresh wave of panic assailed Anne. 'What do you mean, *days*? Are you saying Walter and Maxine have left the Manoir – have left home? Oh, my God, Stephanie,' she rushed on before the Frenchwoman could answer, 'they haven't *eloped*, have they?'

'Ah *non*! *Non, non, non*.' Removing the Ray-Bans, Stephanie replaced them with a Versace pair studded with diamonds. Then she giggled. 'Anne, people of this age do not elope, I think.'

Anne thought she wouldn't put anything past Maxine. 'So where are they, then?'

'Oh, they are still at *Le Manoir* but –' Stephanie broke off, pushed her sunglasses up onto her head and raised her eyes to heaven. 'Maxine with 'er M'sieur Peppaire! 'E is – what do you say – the new toy boy? She bring 'im 'ere, she bring 'im there. Today the *polo de Deauville*, tomorrow the *casino*.'

'Goodness.' Anne found herself trying to keep a straight face. Cross as she was with her father, the idea of him as a toy boy was hysterical. 'She'll wear him out.'

'Per'aps.' Stephanie lay back down. 'But I think 'e die 'appy.'

Before Anne could respond to this somewhat macabre observation Verity and Conrad arrived back, skidding to a halt in a shower of sand, Carpenter at their heels.

'Come and swim, Mum,' panted Verity, looking dishevelled and happy.

It was because Jean-Pierre wasn't around. When he was in the vicinity, Verity never fooled about with Conrad. All her energy was concentrated on disposing her body into attitudes of slavish elegance. Yet, notwithstanding her irritation with this, Anne felt a sudden rush of love for her daughter. It was foul being fifteen. One moment you were a child, the next a woman, and you didn't even stay like that. You kept flicking back and forth between the two until you didn't know where you were.

'Oh, I don't know, darling,' she said, feeling her eyes moisten.

'Mum, come *on*.' Verity did a cartwheel and then three handstands.

Anne squinted down at the sea. It looked very inviting and she was baking hot sitting here, togged up in jeans and an old shirt of Hayden's. She undid an experimental button at the same moment Stephanie unfolded herself from her sun lounger.

'I swim also!' the Frenchwoman cried, and whipped off her pareo to reveal knobbly knees and a stomach with more tucks than a Cornish pasty. Nevertheless, she was undeniably streamlined.

Ann did up the button. 'No,' she said firmly. 'I think I'd better stay here. The water's too cold for Martha.'

Verity and Conrad raced off, Carpenter bounding between them in great four-footed leaps and Stephanie following at a discrete distance, tripping along in the sort of seductive little shimmy that really only worked if you were twenty. Oh, dear, thought Anne, with a despondent swig of wine, I'm turning into a right bitch.

She looked at her watch and wondered what Hayden was doing now – Juno probably. No, she must stop this. But if only she could rush home and make up the quarrel, prostrate herself before him – literally if necessary. A massive longing flooded her. He would take me to bed, she thought yearningly, and this time I would *not* be such a prat, this time... But why not? Why could she not do precisely what she was imagining?

Anne stared into space as she made her plan.

'Stephanie?' she began casually, when the Frenchwoman came back from her swim, bronzed limbs artistically sprinkled with sea water, not a hair out of place – there was no justice in this world. 'Could I ask you a big if not to say tremendous favour?'

'But of course, *cherie*.' Stephanie was assiduously patting herself dry.

'It's just there's an art exhibition currently on in Houlgate. Dufy sketches, actually. And I should so *love* to see it. I'm absolutely *crazy* about Dufy.' Anne steadied herself. Don't overdo it, rebuked an inner warning voice, but Stephanie smiled with immediate understanding.

'You wish to go and see this exposition?'

'Do you mind? That is, would you mind terribly looking after Martha for me while I nip over there and take a look?'

Stephanie beamed. 'It is my pleasure,' she declared, and seizing her pareo, plumped herself down on the baby's rug to play peek-a-boo with it. Martha screamed with joy.

Anne blinked and dithered; she had not anticipated such alacrity. 'I'll only be a couple of hours. All Martha's things are in her bag.'

'Be as long as you desire. *Je m'amuse*.' The Frenchwoman flashed a smile so seraphic Anne nearly flinched. 'I give too the children their lunch, and then this will give you every time in the world to see your artist exposing 'imself.'

Oh, blimey, thought Anne, not another one.

*

'I owe you an apology.'

'What on earth for? Gerry Underwood assaulting me is not your fault.'

'It is, you know.'

'How do you make that out?' Agnes Fenn had arrived about half an hour after Anne and the children had departed and, on seeing his face, had promptly suggested Hayden pour them both whiskies. For shock, she had said, and she was right.

'Listen,' she now began, taking a huge gulp of hers. 'Had he been drinking?'

'Well, now.' With his head on one side, Hayden affected to consider. 'I have to say I didn't get close enough to the man to be able to tell whether he had the Colgate ring of confidence. That is, not while he was punching my lights out.'

'Oh, dear.' Finishing her drink, Agnes sniffed and looked uncharacteristically abject. 'It *is* my fault. I should have warned you. He came and had an absolute *fit* on my doorstep yesterday evening – because he'd seen François Martin's van here. So when I saw Gerry's own van shooting up the lane this morning, I knew where he was coming and probably what he was going to do…' Dragging a gardening glove from her pocket, she gulped and blew her nose on it.

'Oh, no, please don't cry!' Taking her other hand, Hayden chafed it gently.

'Oh, dear,' she said again, and gave another disgusted little sniff. 'I'm making a fool of myself, aren't I? And all over him, a man who is such an absolute *bounder*.'

In any other circumstances, the lovely archaic word would have made Hayden smile. As it was he simply waited as Agnes Fenn politely detached her hand, sat erect and breathed deeply in and out for a second or two. 'Better now?' he asked, when he thought it was.

'Fine. And I apologise.'

'Don't. Ever again. Here.' He took her glass. 'Let me get you another one of those.'

But Agnes shook her head, rose rather wearily to her feet and said thank you but she must get on. She had fourteen ladies of the commune arriving that afternoon to learn how to divide regale lilies. 'Besides, you've got your decorating to do.' With a glance at the walls, she nodded at the roller and tray standing ready, turned to the door and then hesitated.

'Forgive me for saying this,' she said, 'but, you see, in my heart of hearts, I actually feel quite sorry for Gerry Underwood. He's a bit of a sad case.'

'Is he?' Hayden stood up. 'Why is that?'

'Because, in the first place, he is one of those unfortunate Englishmen who came to live in France without properly thinking things through – and there are plenty of them,' Agnes added, with a reflective little shake of her head. 'They poured in back in the early 1990s when the price of property in the UK was getting silly and yet here you could still buy a house for tuppence ha'penny. So I can well understand why they came, but they still seemed to me to have been irresponsible. Indeed, I'd go so far as to say reckless.'

Reckless. Hayden winced at the word. Just how reckless would Agnes Fenn think him, if she knew how irresponsible he had been?

'Oh, don't look so pained!' she cried in alarm. 'I don't mean you!' She patted his arm. 'I mean the people who could not be bothered to learn a word of the language nor gave a fig about this country's culture. The tradesmen who thought they could swan over here and start grabbing the work from all the perfectly adequate plumbers, electricians and builders we already have. Men like Gerry Underwood – I'm afraid they've antagonized a lot of French people.

'And then, as if it wasn't enough that the man had come here in the first place, it all went very badly wrong for Gerry last year when his wife suddenly left him and high-tailed it back home, leaving him with a wreck of a house he can't sell and a mountain of debt. Which meant that recently, as so often happens in these cases, he's taken refuge in the bottle.'

'I see.' Hayden tried and failed to look sympathetic.

Agnes registered his expression. 'I know – why should you care? But she took the children with her, of course, and even if he does not amount to much in other ways, Gerry is a genuinely good and devoted father. Hence I felt... I *feel* sorry for him, even if he has largely himself to blame for being so foolhardy.'

Foolhardy. There it was again. Like 'reckless' the word made Hayden cringe.

'Still, I – ' Agnes started to say something else, broke off and suddenly peered into his face. 'What on earth's the matter?' she asked in concern. 'What have I said? You look terrible.'

Hayden managed a twisted grin. 'Nobody looks their best with two black eyes,' he said feebly.

'No, it's more than that, more than Gerry Underwood's idiocy.'

'Is it?' The candid eyes held nothing but tenderness; it made him want to weep.

'You know it is.' She touched his arm again. 'Please tell me. What's happened? Has something awful happened?'

Hayden stared at her, battling with conflicting emotions. Then the fight went out of him. 'Yes,' he said hopelessly, and turning away, slumped down into a chair. 'Something awful has.'

*

'Where's Mum gone?'

Stephanie looked up from building sandcastles for Martha and told her.

Verity frowned. How weird. Mum had popped into the Dufy exhibition the day they arrived and while she frequently went twice or even three times to art exhibitions, it was only ever when she thought they were good. With the Dufy, she had said it was disappointing, pretty crappy she had actually said, adding something about how annoyed she got when these galleries showed, like, three pin man drawings a painter had done when he was two for his nanny, and then expected you to drool over them.

'Come!'

Stephanie had stood up and was shrugging on her shirt and knotting her pareo. Slinging her huge Prada bag over her shoulder, she stooped to pick up Martha. She looked funny holding Martha, Verity decided, sort of inappropriate, like the Queen holding a cat. But 'Put on your clothings,' she was saying excitedly to them.

'I want to take you all into the town and buy each of you a *cadeau*.'

Verity exchanged looks with Conrad. Mum wouldn't like that. In fact, she doubted whether Hayden would be too thrilled, either. 'Thank you,' she said. 'But I don't think...' She hesitated and bit her lip, not quite knowing how to refuse politely.

But in any case Stephanie was paying no attention, jogging Martha up and down like a milkshake and calling her an angel in French. Martha looked entirely won over but then, Martha was not known for her discrimination.

'Please.' Stephanie suddenly looked wheedling. 'I make it fine with your *maman*.'

Verity couldn't help feeling impressed; Stephanie was certainly quick on the uptake.

'Well,' she said reluctantly. 'It just so happens there's this top I saw...'

*

People are surprising, Anne decided, as she hared along the Normandy lanes; just lately she seemed to spend her life haring along Normandy lanes. Stephanie Dérain had never struck her as the maternal type. Casting her mind back, she summoned up the young Stephanie, the Stephanie who had been her employer twenty-seven years ago.

Stephanie had always been kind, she recalled, always friendly and courteous, in every way a pleasant person to work for. But not, Anne also recalled, what one might by any stretch of the imagination call a devoted mother. Indeed, within two seconds of Anne's arrival, Stephanie had handed over the infant Juno rather in the way you might rid yourself of a cumbersome parcel at the post office: signed, sealed, delivered, that's yours.

Juno was clearly intended to be – and ended up being – Anne's for the duration.

Oh, maybe she was being unfair. After all, she realised with a guilty little start, of late she had not exactly lavished maternal attention on her *own* infant daughter. If the young Stephanie Dérain had been adept at dumping her child on someone else, then the same could be said of the old Anne Warwick.

'This must all stop,' Anne muttered to herself, as she swung the Galaxy into the winding lane leading up to their house. She was going to pull herself together, get motherhood properly back on line and – *and* – stop all this idiotic nonsense about Hayden and Juno.

I am a mature and rational woman, she reminded herself. I will therefore act like one. Once she and Hayden had settled their differences – in the way she was hoping for – they would all start doing things as a family. Juno was not important. Juno was merely a figure of fantasy. She reached the house in a fever of anticipation and nearly drove into the gate post.

There on the grassy drive, gleaming and innocent in the bright sunshine, sat Juno's red Mercedes.

14

He did not weep, which was fortuitous, because not only would that have compounded his shame and humiliation but an hour after Agnes had left Anne rolled up. She would certainly have immediately noticed what an abject state he was in and wanted to know why and he would have had to tell her – which, of course, was precisely what Agnes Fenn had advised.

'You must tell her. The first thing you must do is tell your wife what has happened.'

'I can't,' he had said. 'I've let her down so badly.'

'Oh, for pity's sake!' Agnes had been brisk, almost rough. 'Stop being a hero! Heroes are like martyrs, highly admirable but also impossible to live with. Be sensible,' she had continued in a gentler but still firm tone. 'You've lost your job. That can happen to any man – to any woman.'

'Not lost it,' Hayden had replied morosely. 'I never had it in the first place.'

'All right, the organisation you were going to work for here in France has suddenly gone bust – gone into administration, whatever one calls it these days. Well, it doesn't surprise me given the stupid mess this country is in at the moment. But that's not the point. The point is that for you it is extremely bad luck and obviously lands you in a bit of a fix. However, it is *not* your fault.'

'I'm sorry but I think it is,' Hayden had countered, aware of sounding obstinate but that was how he felt. 'I should never have resigned my job in England, not with two teenage children and a baby, not to mention a wife, to support. It was secure and we wouldn't be in this mess now if I hadn't. Frankly, I cannot now understand what on earth I thought I was doing, other than being – what was the word you used – *reckless*?'

There had been a little pause between them at that point, Agnes eyeing him thoughtfully until Hayden suddenly burst out, 'Haven't you ever done something you bitterly regret?' and she had flashed back, 'I'm an old woman – how long have you got?' and the tension between them had eased.

'Listen to me,' Agnes said, after they had both lit and were smoking one of her Gauloises. 'I'm not going to lecture you any more, except to point out that, as with guilt, regret is one of the most unprofitable emotions in the human psyche. Let's instead look at practicalities.' She hesitated. 'I don't suppose you would let me lend you some money?'

'No, I certainly would not!' Hayden was horrified. He swallowed and added awkwardly, 'Sorry – no. I'm very grateful but it wouldn't be the answer, would it?'

'No, perhaps not.' Agnes had given a reluctant nod of agreement. 'Then leave it with me. I might be able to help you in other ways. You're fluent in French, aren't you? Well, I might be able to get you some translation work. I used to do a fair bit myself until a year or so ago, so I have contacts in that field. Come and see me in a day or two – I'm only just down the lane, the house in the walled garden – and in the meantime I'll make some telephone calls. I'm sure you'll get something. For now, whatever happens, please remember that you can always come to me if you need urgent help.'

The kindness had brought a lump to Hayden's throat. 'I don't know how to thank you.'

'Good, because I don't want thanks. Just do one thing for me.'

'What?'

'Tell your wife.' Agnes had cast him a coolly ironic look. 'Nothing upsets our 'pretty little heads' more than being treated like an imbecile. So, listen to an old woman, an old woman who knows, and *tell your wife.*'

After she had gone, Hayden realised she was right. He'd been an idiot to think he could keep this all to himself. At the first opportunity he would come clean, in fact, the very next time he saw Anne. Except when Anne turned up it hadn't quite worked out like that.

*

'What the hell was she doing here?'

Juno had gone, which was something of a relief because Anne felt her eyeballs literally aching, so out on stalks had they been from staring at Juno. And not because she had stumbled on Juno in anything like a passionate clinch with Hayden. Anne doubted any sort of clinch could have shocked her more than what she had seen. No, it was the way Juno had looked. Juno had looked completely unrecognisable.

Gone was the frizzy purple hair, Juno's head had been covered in a sleek crop fairer than Martha's, delicate tendrils curling about a face as seductively elfin as Keira Knightly's. Gone were the demonic eyes and in their place, two round orbs of the clearest blue. As for her clothes, she had been wearing a short but exquisitely demure little dress, its silky fabric clinging so lusciously to every inch of her lissom curves that for a split second Anne had wanted to kill her.

The vision of beauty had been sprawled casually on the sofa, head angled away from Anne and the little dress rucked up – which had made Anne wonder if she had any pants on. She bet she hadn't. She had even tilted her head slightly to check at which point she suddenly realised Hayden had stepped back from painting the wall and was watching her in concern. 'Have you done something to your neck, darling?' he said.

But before she could reply, Juno had chosen the moment to spring up with the grace of a gazelle and take her leave. At which point all Anne's fears had flooded back to swamp her.

'Why was Juno here?' Hayden now echoed her question. Once again, he had that oddly evasive look about him. 'Oh, nothing vital. I'll tell you in a minute. Have you left Martha with the kids?'

'No, she's with Stephanie.'

'Oh! Right. What did you come back for, then?'

'What?' Anne tried to remember what she had come back for but her mind refused to see past the lingering vision of Juno.

'Did you forget something?'

'Hayden, would you answer my question, please? What was Juno doing here?' But instead of doing as she bid, he swiftly crossed the room with his arms outstretched.

'I can't tell you how sorry I am for being such a bastard earlier. I love you, Anne,' he said, and then seized her whereupon Anne immediately caught the acrid, burnt toffee whiff on his shirt. Gauloises. Fucking Gauloises. Juno smoked Gauloises.

Before she knew what she was doing, she had pushed him roughly away.

And now they were staring at each other in slightly shocked silence, Anne thinking he looked horribly guilty and Hayden in his turn thinking that, all-seeing as she might be in her ageless wisdom, Agnes Fenn did not envisage this.

'Hayden?'

'What?'

'Tell me what Juno was doing here.'

What the hell did that matter? Aware the shutters that had trapped him for days were once more clanging down, Hayden moved to the table and picked up two cards that were lying there. 'She came to leave these for Verity and Conrad.'

'What are they?'

'See for yourself.' He flipped them at her. 'Personal invitations to the opening of some fantastic new night club in Cabourg.'

'Oh, no way.' Anne backed away, hands raised as if to defend herself and her expression so hostile Hayden could scarcely recognise her.

'Hey, come on, what's your problem? They'll love it. There's no harm in the odd night club and Juno said she would take them. I thought it very sweet of her. She really is such a lovely girl.'

That did it. 'I said no.'

In fact, Anne resolved grimly, over my dead body.

*

'No.'

It was the following day.

'Oh, Mer-um.'

'I said no.'

'But I could wear my new top.'

Anne looked critically at her daughter. 'You know, you really shouldn't have let Stephanie buy you that.'

'I did try and stop her.' Verity opened her eyes very wide. 'I did, honestly. Besides, she bought you a present as well.'

Didn't she just, thought Anne in disgust.

Stephanie's present to her was an expensive but rather common-looking peach t-shirt embossed with gold pansies on the bosom. It was not Anne's sort of thing at all but that was not what got up her nose. What got up Anne's nose was the large XL on the size label.

'Hayden's said to Condy he can go.'

Anne rounded furiously on her daughter. 'Did Conrad really tell you that?' She and Hayden still did not agree but they had pledged to maintain a united front. Although Anne did wonder how much the united front was down to a kind of desperation on both their parts not to rock the marital boat when it was so very clearly on the point of sinking.

'No.' Verity looked sulky. 'I made it up. But I know Hayden's on our side.'

'Tough luck.'

'But I've got to get into clubbing some time and you know what Juno said. She said she'll take us and bring us back and stay with us the whole time we're there.'

'What is it with that girl?' demanded Anne. 'Is she aiming to become a quick-change artist or something?' This morning Juno had been sporting a floaty cream creation and hair in white tresses down to her ankles.

'She just likes recreating herself. Like Madonna. Did you see her dress? Fab, wasn't it? It's from Ghost.'

'She looked like one with that hair.'

'Extensions.' Verity squinted at a strand of her own. 'I must get some.'

'You most certainly will not. They damage your own hair.' But Anne could not resist asking, 'How does she do the eye colour switch?'

'Tinted contact lenses. She's, like, into them. She's got some yellow ones that, like, make her look like a panther.'

'With or without panth?'

'What was that, Mum?'

'Nothing.' Anne collected herself.

'Anyway, I think Juno is a, like, crazy lady.'

'Oh, for mercy's sake stop saying *like* like that!'

'Will you let me go to the night club opening if I promise never to say it again?'

'No.'

Verity made a last ditch attempt. 'But you let me go to parties and discos at home.'

'Discos and parties are not the same as night clubs and, besides, here we find ourselves strangers in a strange land. Who knows what hazards might await us?'

'Blimey, Mum, you sound like something out of *Star Trek*.'

Anne blushed. 'Yes, well, you're not going and that's that.'

*

'Oh, Hayden, I love you!' Verity flung her arms round her stepfather's neck and smothered him in kisses.

Hayden had the decency to look abashed.

'I must call Juno and give her the good news.' Seizing her mother's mobile phone, Verity rushed out into the garden. Conrad followed her, also looking slightly sheepish. Anne had the impression that, for some reason he was keeping to himself, Conrad was not keen on the night club escapade.

She looked sternly at her husband. 'I'm holding you entirely responsible for this, you know. If she gets bombed on Ecstasy or comes back a trainee coke-sniffer, it'll be down to you.'

'Oh, Anne, give the girl a break. She's a sensible kid.' Hayden leaned across the table and took her hand. 'Besides, just think. We can have an evening to ourselves for once. We could... talk.'

'Talk?'

Talk was the last thing Anne felt like doing with Hayden, given he would doubtless want to talk of things she did not want to talk about. Detaching her hand, she said indifferently, 'No, I don't think so, thanks. I'm going to ask the Dérains to supper.'

Hayden's face fell. On top of everything else, it struck him that the fraternizing was getting a little out of hand. 'You should have warned me that moving to France was going to make us founder members of the Normandy social set.'

'Very funny,' Anne said coldly. 'It's evidently escaped your notice that we still haven't returned their hospitality for either the dinner at the Manoir or the one at the restaurant. Not forgetting the lunch I had with Stephanie,' she said, adding pointedly, 'She insisted on paying for that, you know.'

Hayden sighed. 'Okay. Have it your own way but what about Maxine and Walter?'

'What about them?'

'Shouldn't you invite them as well?'

Anne considered. Actually, she hadn't thought of that but it could be a good plan. True, a joint invitation smacked of tacit approval of the engagement but at least it would get her father here and then perhaps she could fashion a straightjacket for him – or even Maxine if she went off on one.

'All right, I'll ask them. Although,' she said, bethinking herself, 'I'm not sure they will accept. They are up to their necks in social engagements because, according to Stephanie, Maxine has launched my father on *le beau monde*.'

'Poor Walter,' mused Hayden despondently. 'Perhaps he can give me a few tips.'

*

He hadn't had a time like this since he was a lad. In fact, he hadn't had a time like this then, because then it was the post-war years and nobody had any money and there was still rationing and although everyone said a girl would do anything for a pair of nylons, he'd never found one who would. By the time the '50's had got going and Harold Macmillan was telling everyone they'd never had it so good, he was married and those were his salad days over. Now, however, it seemed they had returned.

Every day brought something different.

'Bonjour, Wal-tèrre!' Maxine would cry the moment he got downstairs for breakfast. He'd stopped all that basin of coffee/greasy bun lark. Now he just had a nice pot of tea in his room, followed by another nice pot with toast when he got up.

'Today we make the special eventing,' Maxine would say and then usually give him a present. He had four walking sticks now, two with gold tops, except he had stopped this as well after a while because it was making him feel like one of those 'jiggle-lows' as darling Maggie used to call them.

But then they'd be off.

Marvellous restaurants and oysters (except he'd cut down on those ever since one tried to crawl back up), the racing (except Maxine kept wanting to back a horse called Pepper Potty which didn't strike him as a bit funny), and the polo (except he couldn't say he cared for the way she kept licking her lips over those young beggars in tight breeches). She had even taken him up in a light aeroplane belonging to a friend of hers which was marvellous, except he couldn't help noticing the landing gear looked a mite dodgy to him.

But he was having a marvellous time. Maxine seemed to know people wherever they went or, if not, she soon did. She introduced him to all kinds of marvellous characters, one or two perhaps a bit what you might call shady but most were marvellous. One of them even called him Sir Walter which, although odd, made him feel marvellous. But then someone else asked if they could see his V.C. which was taking things a bit too far. Never mind. He was having a marvellous time.

The only problem was he felt bad about Anne and – well, he was missing her. He was missing his granddaughters as well and that boy of Hayden's. He was missing him a lot which was odd because Conrad wasn't even properly related to him. Oddest of all, he found himself missing Carpenter and that really floored him.

You would never have thought Carpenter someone you could miss.

*

'This is just the opportunity I've been waiting for.'

It was the day of the night club opening and Verity was so spaced out with excitement she hadn't even noticed Carpenter was chewing her precious flowerpot bag. Conrad wasn't going to tell her, though. He was too pissed off with her.

'You don't even know he's going to be there.'

'I do. I asked Juno and she said he was definitely.'

'Oh, bloody hell,' muttered Conrad.

'It's hopeless here at the beach. But,' Verity's eyes gleamed, 'in a club I just know I can get him.'

Conrad dug a shell out of the sand and chucked it away. Carpenter must be into that bag; he normally pounced on chucked shells. 'Well, frankly,' he dusted off his hands, 'if all you're going to do is drool over Jean-Pierre, I'm not coming.'

Verity's eyes narrowed. 'You've got to come,' she said haughtily. 'It would be rude to Juno not to.'

'What you mean is that your mother wouldn't let you go on your own with Juno.'

Verity treated him to her best withering glare. 'God, you are a child, Conrad.'

'I'm the same age as you. In fact, I'm two months older.'

'Act it, then.'

Conrad sprang to his feet. 'You're the one who needs to act their age. Do you honestly think someone like Jean-Pierre could be interested in you?'

'Oh, fuck off.'

'With pleasure.' Conrad grabbed his snorkel. Then he paused deliberately and looked down at her. 'I can tell you who is interested in something, though.'

'Who? What?'

'Carpenter. In your bag.'

And with that he fled before screams rent the air.

*

Back at the house Anne was in a fever of preparations. Nothing stimulated her more than preparing for a dinner party. Well, not quite nothing but she knew what she meant. Actually, it wasn't going to be a dinner party as such, not a formal one that is. Anne had no intention of attempting to emulate the haute cuisine of Château Dérain even if she could persuade Hayden to dress up as Dolores.

No, it would be relaxed, *in*formal, she would create an atmosphere exquisitely *dégagé* ; a shimmering oil lamp here, a plate of cheeses there, lemons and grapes piled *à la* Cezanne, a dish of shiny olives. And the food would be stupendous, nothing pretentious, of course, but perfectly executed with a nonchalant wonder that would make Gilles kiss his fingertips and proclaim her *magnifique*.

This was quite important, not because she gave a shit about impressing Gilles Dérain, but because Anne was determined to excel in something in front of Stephanie other than an XL t-shirt. She was quite positive Stephanie Dérain could not slice a French bean even if she looked like one. Anne, however, knew herself to be a good cook so this was her opportunity to shine. Moreover, she was determined Stephanie would eat even if Anne had to pin her feet to the floor and force food down her throat like a Strasbourg goose; quite an appropriate analogy in a way because, amongst other things, she was going to be cooking goose.

She had settled on cassoulet as being simple but stylish fare. She had never cooked cassoulet in her life but Elizabeth David had come into her own and it all looked quite straightforward. Just a question of soaking great quantities of haricot beans overnight, flinging them, some of the dreaded *andouilles*, salt pork, onions, garlic and a few legs of preserved goose into a huge pot, and then sitting back to await the heady aroma of peasant France.

By five o'clock everything was ready, the cassoulet heaving away in the oven. Hayden had given up hinting about roast lamb and mint sauce and was hinting about being hungry instead. The food chez Warwick had been somewhat scrappy in the last twenty-four hours, the way it always was when Anne was building herself up to a feast. Never mind, Hayden was suddenly being surprisingly sweet and obliging. It made Anne wonder – hope – that everything might be going to be all right between them after all.

Besides somehow extracting an acceptance to her invitation from Walter and Maxine, Hayden had looked after Martha and, in between ferrying the kids to the beach, finished off painting the walls. True, these were now so blindingly white you perhaps felt the need for a pair of sunglasses from Stephanie's private collection, but they looked good. And this was quite important because, as well as dazzling the Dérains with her culinary skills, Anne was going to dazzle them with her interior decor.

There were her new throws from the supermarket waiting to be thrown over the G-Plan sofa and a pretty red checked tablecloth standing by to disguise the crummy dining table. She still only had the Christmas dinner plates but cassoulet would blot out the reddest of the robins.

Besides hanging bunches of lavender from the beams, Hayden had filled the log basket full of early apples, an idea Anne had hit upon to inject the room with a homely, rustic touch. Unfortunately, however, the only rustic, homely touch the log basket of apples seemed to have injected was great swarms of wasps. But, after doggedly killing any wasps who failed to make good their escape, Hayden had sportingly praised her spirit of enterprise and, better still – much better still – there had been neither sound nor sight of Juno.

'Shall I get some flowers when I collect the kids?' he offered, as Anne sat down to rest for a moment. He always went out and got flowers when they were entertaining friends at home.

'No need, thanks. There are masses of those big white daisies in the garden. I'm going out to pick a bunch of them in a sec.'

She stood up again and moved back to the kitchen to put the finishing touches to her salad dressing. Sticking it in the fridge, she wiped her hands on her skirt. She must have a bath and wash her hair. Then there was something casual but suitably *soignée* to find to wear in order to measure up to Stephanie, who was doubtless at this very second pouring herself into Armani.

Martha had had her tea but there was still the kids' supper to do when they got back from the beach. Then the Dérains were coming quite early so that they could all have a drink together before Juno bore Verity and Conrad off to the night club opening. She hadn't a lot of time, Anne realised with a quick glance at her watch, so without further ado grabbed the kitchen scissors and rushed out into the garden.

In the orchard the apple trees were bowed, sagging with ripening fruit, and on the far side of the valley, the sun was balanced on a ridge of early evening mist like a great golden orb. Hayden had roughly scythed down the worst of the long grass, its new-mown sweetness filling the air. From the distant village came the faint but soulful peal of church bells and somewhere in the dusky meadows a donkey brayed. Entranced, Anne caught her breath. All at once she knew, as she had not known since she had arrived in France, why she had fallen in love with this place.

It was beautiful, she thought wonderingly, beautiful. With its darkening trees and lengthening shadows, the landscape before her might have been a Corot painting. She could paint it herself this moment. In fact, tomorrow, she resolved, she would do exactly that.

Brimming with inspiration, she cut a huge armful of the daisies, straightened her skirt, tossed her hair back into a romantic sweep and glided smoothly back towards the house. Hayden would be entranced as well, captivated by this vision of a rural goddess bringing flowers. Then she heard his voice. He clicked off his mobile phone the second she entered the room.

Anne put down her daisies.

'Who were you talking to?' she asked, her rural goddess act evaporating into thin air.

'Nobody. Wrong number.'

'No, it wasn't, Hayden. I heard you talking to someone.'

'Martha,' he said, with what sounded remarkably like desperation. 'I was talking to Martha.'

Simultaneously, they both turned to look at their daughter. Martha was asleep in her buggy with her mouth open, as indeed Martha had been asleep in her buggy with her mouth open for the last half hour, having as usual nodded off straight after her tea.

'Hayden, you were talking to someone on the phone. I heard you.'

'Must go and pick up the kids.' He seized the car keys and with a horribly jocular – and painful – chuck of her chin, headed for the door. 'Won't be long!'

Anne sank down in a chair at the table and looked at her red checked cloth. She looked at her new throws, her blinding white walls, her basket of apples, her lavender hanging from the beams. She looked at her bunch of daisies and burst into tears.

It was true. She had been right all along. Hayden was having an affair.

15

Walter and Maxine did not turn up which Anne felt really was the last straw. Now even her father was casting her aside for the delights of his *grande passion*. For the first and only time in her life, she felt a bitter surge of hatred for France. If they had never come here, none of this would have happened.

Walter had not even bothered to send a proper apology, just a mangled message from somewhere that might or might not have been Paris, but wasn't clear because it reached Stephanie via Dolores who could scarcely be regarded as the Alexander Graham Bell of communication. As Stephanie related this, Anne caught Hayden looking pityingly at her. 'Never mind, darling. I'm sure there's a perfectly reasonable explanation.'

Flashing a bright and unseeing smile in the general direction of everyone, Anne sprang to the kitchen to fix some drinks. Hayden followed her.

'What's the matter?' he asked in a low voice, placing a hand on her shoulder. He'd had the nerve to keep asking her what the matter was ever since he got back from fetching the kids.

Anne shrugged him off with a toss of her dirty hair. Sitting sobbing in the kitchen meant she had left it too late to have a bath before the kids got back whereupon, when she went up to have one, it became immediately plain that Verity had pinched every bloody drop of hot water.

Hayden swore softly under his breath.

'Stephanie?' Anne called, ignoring him. 'I'm afraid we're out of Badôit.'

Gilles said he would have whisky whereupon Hayden told him sorry, but they were out of Scotch, too.

'What about that bottle from the ferry?' hissed Anne.

'Finished,' Hayden said shortly, and turned away to prevent further argument.

Both Dérains accepting chilled Sancerre with the reluctant air of aristos being dragged to the guillotine, everyone sat down and tried to think of something to say.

Martha saved them the bother by suddenly bursting into a positive frenzy of screaming, possibly on account of Stephanie having also burst into such a sprightly routine of baby billing and cooing it was enough to give anyone the heebie-jeebies. Carpenter added to the commotion by equally suddenly charging about snapping his teeth at a new invasion of wasps – with an aside clash of his jaws at Stephanie Dérain every time he passed her way. Clad in a Breton sailor top striped in black and yellow, the Frenchwoman could, Anne had to concede, have easily been mistaken for an anorexic bee.

Nonetheless, she felt obliged to step in and roared at the dog.

'Carpenter,' mused Gilles Dérain, once a semblance of order had been restored. 'Carpenter. This I find truly an amusing name for a dog.' He hooded his eyes in disdain as if it wasn't amusing at all but beyond all reason. 'Why are you calling him Carpenter?'

'Because,' Verity piped up before Anne could stop her, 'when he was a puppy he did odd jobs about the house.'

Hayden guffawed.

'Odd jobs… odd jobs?' The Frenchman frowned. 'What are these odd jobs?'

Anne closed her eyes in despair. Not that it did not serve Gilles right, the superior prick, but somehow she had a feeling of doom about this evening.

*

It started the second they got inside the club, the way Conrad had known it would. Bloody irritating because the club was actually quite empty when they walked in, it still being very early, and if Verity had decided to be sensible they could have all sat around chatting for a bit while he got his bearings.

Conrad was not wild about clubbing. Well, okay, he'd never been clubbing but that was exactly the point, exactly why he felt he needed to distance himself and chill. He'd been hoping Jean-Pierre wouldn't turn up until much later, half hoping Jean-Pierre wouldn't turn up at all, but, of course, he did. In he strolled about two minutes after they arrived, looking the coolest of cool (as usual), and coming straight over to them with the sexiest of all his sexy grins (as usual). Conrad wondered if he really ought to warn him to tone down the heartthrob act but then again, if he did, he could not for the life of him see how.

When they arrived, Juno had immediately ordered a round of drinks for them, agreeing, after a slight hesitation, to a shot of vodka in an orange juice for Verity. Now, as Verity knocked this back and Jean-Pierre asked her if she would like another, Conrad tried to catch his or Juno's eye. The last thing Verity needed in her manic state was booze. But before he could manage to catch anyone's eye, Jean-Pierre had ordered the second round of drinks in French too rapid for Conrad to understand a word.

They sat in the bar while Juno and Verity disappeared to the loo, doubtless in Verity's case to apply yet another layer of make-up despite already having so much black around her eyes she looked as if she had gone six rounds with Amir Khan. After a pause, during which Conrad surveyed the interior of the night club so studiously he might have been taking it for A-level, Jean-Pierre leaned forward and touched his arm.

'Hey, chill,' he said pleasantly.

'I'm fine,' Conrad said stiffly, not turning.

Jean-Pierre clicked his teeth. 'There was no vodka in it,' he said very loudly.

Conrad spun round. 'I'm sorry?'

'This time I asked them to serve your sister's drink without the vodka. It was only the orange juice but I think she will not know the difference.'

Conrad blushed, feeling awkward. 'Thanks, that was decent of you.'

'And fear not, my friend,' continued Jean-Pierre, sounding like Antonio Banderas in *The Mask of Zoro*. 'I know – what is it you say? I know the score.'

'I'm sorry?' repeated Conrad, trying to decide if Jean-Pierre was saying what he very much hoped he was saying.

Jean-Pierre gave a shrug. 'I know *Veritée* makes the lustings after me.'

Conrad could not now decide whether this made Jean-Pierre sound sensible or like a conceited bastard, but as Jean-Pierre quickly added there would be no trouble he decided to concentrate very hard on the first option.

Then Verity arrived back, her eyes smouldering under a shedload of mascara and an expression on her face that to Conrad was only too familiar. That was the problem, he thought in despair, any glimmer of reassurance fading rapidly away. Jean-Pierre, Juno – neither of them – had absolutely any idea just how determined Verity could be when she set her mind on something.

*

Walter Pepper was not enjoying himself. He could not help feeling Paris was not quite up his street, principally on account of the street where Maxine lived being so narrow, dark and spooky it reminded him of that old film, *Murders in the Rue Morgue*. He had found himself glancing over his shoulder and then up at the looming buildings and wondering if he would ever see Wolverhampton again.

Once inside Maxine's flat, he had hoped he'd feel better. But, despite Maxine chivvying away at some landlady woman, ordering her to drag the dust sheets off the furniture, turn on the lamps and open all the curtains, the place had still been gloomy, still what you might call eerie.

And it was quieter than the grave.

While Maxine went to powder her nose, Walter took off his jacket, poked about a bit, found a portable telly on a table in the corner of the ornate and chilly lounge – it reminded him of Wolverhampton town hall – and switched it on, not just for a bit of cheerful noise but because one of the things he had really missed in France was a spot of telly.

Not a day had passed when he hadn't wondered what was happening in *Coronation Street*. Of course, there wouldn't be *Coronation Street* on French telly but, surprisingly, the first thing that came up was that Michael Crawford in an old episode of *Some*

Mothers Do 'Ave 'Em. Brightening, Walter saw it was in English as well, with those subtitle things that always flashed so quickly across the bottom of the screen you wondered how anyone ever managed to read them, even when they were in your own language.

Pulling up a chair – hard but it would do – he settled down with enjoyment. They'd had a busy day in Paris seeing the sights and this was just what he fancied. Seeing the sights of Paris with Maxine was what you might call a once-in-a-lifetime experience.

Once in a lifetime because if it happened more than that, Walter had a feeling you would not live to tell the tale.

It wasn't that Maxine was one of those people who showed you every last little thing on sightseeing, insisting you admire this point and that point, putting you through a sort of third degree if you dared to forget what it was you were supposed to be admiring. As a tourist guide, attention to detail was not Maxine's line. Oh, no. As a tourist guide Maxine's line was Maxine. The Paris Maxine showed you was Maxine's Paris.

Take the Place de l'Opera, for instance. This was where Maxine fell in love for the first time, Sacré-Coeur the second. In the Jardins du Luxembourg Philippe told Maxine he adored her, at Notre Dame, Antoine. By the time they had walked the length and breadth of the Boulevard St Michel and Walter had heard about Jacques, Gustave, Georges, René, Louis, Alexandre and Herbèrt, it looked as though half the population of France had told Maxine they adored her in Paris.

Then there was Maxine and Paris in the war.

One minute Maxine was plotting to blow up the Gestapo, the next escaping a firing squad. In a cellar on the Left Bank, Maxine had single-handedly constructed a radio receiver, in a church tower, a transmitter. As for the liberation of Paris, it was down to one person – Maxine. By the end of the day Walter had got the message. He was living the gospel of Paris according to Maxine and bloomin' exhausting it was too, even if he did not believe a word of it.

So, a quiet evening in with a spot of telly had been just what he needed. Maybe Maxine could persuade that landlady woman to knock them up a shepherd's pie. There might even be a bottle of light ale in the place.

Well, Maxine had not seemed to see things that way at all. The moment she got back from powdering her nose, he saw that she had, so to speak, powdered everything else, even to changing into a cocktail dress which, while it was very elegant, was a mite on the young side for her. They were going out to dinner, she announced. They were going to dine at the Ritz.

Walter decided to dig his heels in. He was tired, he didn't want any more rich food, he wasn't getting in another of those French taxis with cabbies who drove like lunatics and he wanted a quiet night in. If she couldn't manage the shepherd's pie, then there must be a take-away nearby and that would do. Anne sometimes got take-aways for supper when he stayed with her and Hayden. The Chinese didn't do much for him but the Indian ones weren't bad at all.

Well, you'd have thought he'd suggested something indecent. Screaming at him that she'd never been so insulted in her life, Maxine ranted away for a good five minutes. Walter gave up listening after a bit and concentrated on Michele Dotrice instead. Now there was a nice little woman, a nice little wife, doing all that was expected of her even when lumbered with that bloomin' twit of a husband.

Maxine eventually ran out of breath, or rather, as she was breathing heavily, she must have run out of things to shout at him. If he had wanted to stay at home with a tedious little supper, she concluded nastily, he could have gone to his daughter's.

Walter turned his eyes slowly and coldly to her. What the devil was she talking about? And then he remembered. With a sudden painful thud of his heart he remembered. Today was Thursday. It was seven o'clock on Thursday evening, the Thursday evening Anne had invited him and Maxine to supper.

And here they were in Paris.

He had panicked a bit at that, found he was pacing about the room, and then seeing a telephone sitting on a side table seized it. But it had been as dead as a doornail and he'd left that portable thing Anne had forced on him back in Normandy. He loathed the damn thing, anyway. But he had to ring Anne…

'I must telephone Anne,' he said urgently to Maxine, picking up his jacket and patting the pockets to find his little address book. 'Is there a public call box near here?'

And that had been when Maxine started to laugh. Snatching up her evening bag, she whisked out what looked like a gold ingot studded with emeralds, punched out a number and, before he could ask her who she was ringing, gabbled something into it in French and clicked it off.

'There you are,' she snapped. 'Your *bourgeois* little excuses made.'

And it had been at that point, Walter reflected later, the point when she started telling him he was bourgeois, that he had begun to get quite cross with Maxine.

*

'Do you have *une petite amie?*' Gilles asked Hayden in an undertone.

In the kitchen end of the room Stephanie was rocking and crooning over Martha while Anne heated a saucepan for the baby's bedtime milk.

Hayden contemplated Gilles with veiled distaste. With his flashy leather jacket, his tight jeans, his assiduously nurtured suntan and his suggestive nudges and leers, Gilles Dérain seemed bent on putting himself across as a caricature of the randy old Frenchman. Mumbling something inarticulate in reply, Hayden turned in relief to Anne who had crossed the room and, with an aggressive thrust of her arms, was shoving the corkscrew and a bottle of red wine in his face as if serving him with a writ. 'Gilles very kindly brought it,' she said to a space somewhere above his head.

Hayden flicked a smile up at her but Anne just turned on her heel and stomped off back to the kitchen. Smothering a sigh, he withdrew the cork with such a vicious wrench he might have been garrotting someone, which indeed he felt like doing – preferably Gilles Dérain. The prat was now making a great show of sniffing the wine cork like an expert in viticulture but more reminiscent of the way Carpenter sniffed Martha's nappies.

In due course, Martha was put to bed and dinner served. Hayden found himself casting frequent and not very surreptitious glances at his watch, counting each interminable minute as it passed.

*

'Verity, stop it!' he shouted in her ear.

'WHAT?' she screamed back in his face. At least, that's what Conrad guessed from the shape of her mouth that she was screaming. With the music now at fifty squillion decibels you couldn't hear a bloody word anyone was saying, which probably meant she had not heard him either.

Conrad was beginning to feel desperate. He could see Juno and Jean-Pierre were looking concerned as well. Shit, he thought, as Verity swayed forward to take yet another gigantic swig of her drink. Some ran down her throat but most over her new top, which under any other circumstances would have made Conrad laugh – except this was getting way beyond a joke. Anne would go ballistic. 'Do something,' he mouthed frantically at Jean-Pierre.

'DO SOMETHING!'

*

Well, if this was peasant food, no wonder they were always revolting. The *andouilles* were so impenetrable they could have auditioned for a job as sleeping policemen and as for the legs of preserved goose, they must have been preserved in a morgue. Of course, it could have been down to Anne discovering – a little too late in the day – that the thermostat on her new gas oven was a touch unreliable. In fact, it seemed it operated at only two temperatures: burning and cremation.

Neither of the Dérains made any attempt to eat more than a mouthful and, in truth, Anne could not blame them. Hayden alone struggled manfully through his helping while for her part, as she pushed despondently at disintegrating beans, Anne felt her supper party disintegrating round her ears. She found herself drinking too much, which was not so unusual at supper parties, but with a morose concentration – which was.

It was not only the disastrous food, they none of them seemed to know what to say to each other. Although normally great value in company, Hayden was either too pissed off to bother or he needed every ounce of his concentration to conquer the cassoulet. As for Stephanie, in the presence of her husband she was behaving with an artifice quite alien to her cosy luncheon self, talking, if she talked at all, in funny little disconnected phrases delivered in a warbly gush that made her sound like Edna Everage.

Then – Gilles. Anne decided that the very next time Gilles groped her thigh she'd knock his fucking capped teeth out. Pudding, a classic *tarte aux pommes* Anne had bought from the patisserie, was served in silence.

That is, until both Dérains refused it.

'But Stephanie! This is your favourite! I only bought it because I know how much you –' Anne's words died on her lips as she caught sight of an expression of not so much alarm as active fear on the Frenchwoman's face. Sculpted eyebrows rushing together, Gilles had slowly and threateningly turned to look at his wife.

Oh, I get it, thought Anne in disgust; the bully behind the bulimia.

'No, sorry, wait,' she interjected before Gilles could speak. 'I was getting Stephanie mixed up with someone else.' Throwing the tart in the bin, out came the cheese which again, except for Hayden, nobody touched.

'Strange.' Gilles was lighting a gold tipped Sobranie, 'This English custom of serving cheese after *le dessert.*'

'Nearly as strange,' remarked Hayden, rage making him reckless, 'as our custom of not smoking until coffee is served.'

'*Comment?*'

'Nothing.'

Anne shot Hayden a warning glance. 'Now, tell me.' She turned confidentially to Gilles in an effort to distract him. 'I am so curious to know,' she continued, all at once aware of a worrying need to enunciate with care. 'Have they really gone to Paris?'

''Oo?' Gilles wasn't too hot on aitches, either.

'My father and Macsheen.' Shit, that was no good.

The briefest glimmer of a smile passed over Hayden's face.

'Yes, I believe so.' Stephanie flicked a wary glance at her husband. 'It is possible they visit for the *tourisme*.'

Gilles threw his wife a look of utter contempt. 'Nobody visits Paris in August.'

Seeing Stephanie's miserable flush, Anne felt a tidal wave of tipsy sympathy for her. Being married to Gilles was clearly not a bowl of cherries. 'Except for the tourists,' she said sweetly.

Stephanie threw her a grateful smile and then cast her eyes round the room to indicate appreciation. 'You know, Anne, I so adore this little 'ouse, It 'as a quality so without sophistication, a quality so *primitif*.'

Anne's tidal wave of sympathy flattened to a ripple. Patronising cow.

'And your dog,' Stephanie continued sublimely. 'Your *M'sieur Charpentier*. Does 'e like 'is French food? Per'aps 'e would like a bone of the goose?' She lowered her eyes inquiringly to the floor.

As if expecting to see straw there, Anne thought savagely. After all, where else would we primitive English fling our bones? Before she could decide whether to say this, however, everybody jumped out of their skin as Carpenter suddenly burst into an unearthly yowling and started charging about again – this time on three legs.

'*Mon dieu*!' shrieked Stephanie. '*Il a une attaque! Le chien a une attaque!*'

She and her husband made a bolt for the door.

'He is not having an attack,' snapped Hayden, also leaping to his feet but in his case to find the bottle of vinegar in the kitchen and pour out a bowl which immediately made the room stink like a chip shop, possibly an improvement on the previous burnt baked bean smell of the cassoulet.

Capturing Carpenter, he unceremoniously plunged the dog's injured paw into the vinegar. 'He's been stung by a wasp,' he explained coldly.

Presently, Carpenter calmed down to lick his paw and silence reigned once more. Anne decided the time had come for action. 'Coffee,' she announced, in tones more threatening than inviting, and sprang to her feet to make it.

Taking the lid off the kettle, she turned on the tap. Nothing happened save for an anticipatory gurgle sounding uncannily like Martha when she was about to spit out her dinner. Except, unlike Martha, nothing did out spit. Desperately if covertly, Anne spun both taps – nothing. Not a dribble, not a drop. Great. That was all they needed. She glanced over her shoulder.

Hayden had started up a desultory conversation about French politics so, as she saw Gilles lean forward as if to take issue with something, Anne swiftly grabbed the bottle of Evian reserved for the baby. No matter how enlightened the French might be, she was never going to trust their mains water for Martha.

'Coffee coming up!' she cried with nauseating jollity, slamming the lid back on the kettle, switching it on and then reaching up to get the cups down.

'Anne, my darlink.'

Gilles had sidled up behind her, sneaking a claw-like hand round her waist.

'You can tell me the location of the room for little boys?'

Wriggling away, Anne thought she wouldn't be surprised if that was exactly what he did mean – he was just the type to be into little boys. However, if the taps were anything to go by, the loo would be done for. 'Oh, we go in the garden,' she said tersely.

Gilles Dérain lifted his cosmetically lifted eyelids. She could see him thinking, yet another primitive English habit. Nuts to him. She turned to pour boiling Evian into the coffee pot and then stopped, her hand arrested on the kettle handle. The roar of a vehicle drawing up outside meant the kids must be back. She glanced at the kitchen clock. How odd. It was still very early.

The door slammed open and in burst Conrad and Juno, followed immediately by a staggering Jean-Pierre; staggering because in his arms he was carrying Verity. Her head lolling unconscious on his shoulder, her face chalk white, she looked horribly dead.

Anne felt as if she had been literally turned to stone.

Hayden was the first to react. 'My God, what's happened?'

'It's okay,' panted Jean-Pierre. 'No panic. She's okay.'

Unable to move a muscle, Anne watched as with Hayden's help Jean-Pierre lowered Verity onto the sofa. Hayden knelt down by his stepdaughter, briefly examined her and then looked up at Anne. 'I think we are going to need that coffee, darling,' he said ruefully.

There followed a minute but unfathomable pause before everything became too much.

'Damn you!' screeched Anne, and with a sudden huge leap, flew at Juno. Jean-Pierre stepped quickly between them and grabbed her.

'You bloody, bloody bitch, Juno!' Anne collapsed howling against Jean-Pierre's chest. 'What is wrong with you? You did this deliberately, didn't you! For God's sake, what is fucking wrong with you?'

16

'I shall have to apologise to Juno.'

'Why?' As his wife came down the stairs, Hayden looked up from feeding the baby her breakfast. 'I mean, maybe you shouldn't have flown at her quite like that, darling, but frankly, if it was her fault that Verity got so drunk then Juno is the one who should apologise.'

Sitting down opposite him, Anne picked at the toast crumbs on the tablecloth. She actually felt disgusted with herself for flying at Juno. Whatever the provocation, she loathed the thought that she was turning into some kind of bunny boiler.

'It wasn't her fault,' she said, biting her lip. 'Verity's confessed. She kept sneaking off on the pretext of going to the loo but in reality to buy vodka shots with her own money – her holiday money – to put in the orange juices Juno and Jean-Pierre had bought her.'

'Jesus!' Hayden looked appalled. 'That club could be prosecuted for that, you know.'

'I do know.'

'And why on earth would Verity do a thing like that, anyway?'

Anne glanced at Martha. The baby was frowning impassively down at them from her high chair like a Wimbledon umpire on a disputed line call. 'A thing like what?'

'Set out to deliberately get drunk.'

'I don't think she did set out *deliberately* to get drunk –' Anne began. Verity in the grip of a monstrous hangover might not have been at her most articulate, but she had said enough for Anne to glean that her daughter had been trying to get off with Jean-Pierre and he had given her the brush-off or, at least, behaved like an adult. Which made a welcome change given it was about time someone round here did.

Yet Anne felt curiously reluctant to explain all this to Hayden. Angry as she was with her daughter, she also knew Verity was genuinely and desperately ashamed of her behaviour. Anne found she could not bring herself to further humiliate the girl by telling Hayden what a fool she had been.

The next moment, however, she felt ashamed of herself. Why could she not tell Hayden? He was her husband, for goodness' sake. He was Verity's stepfather as well, and a far better parent to the girl than her own father had ever been. But just as she was trying to think how to explain everything, Conrad came leaping down the stairs.

'Are we going to the beach, Dad?'

'Would the world stop turning if you did not go to the beach? Yeah, all right. In a minute. Go and get your stuff together.'

Conrad thumped back up the stairs, making Anne wince. Never mind Verity's, her own head felt like a bucket this morning. She watched as Hayden unpeeled a banana, gave it to Martha and licked his fingers. Martha promptly squashed the banana flat on her high chair tray. Anne sighed.

'When she's finished that I'd better get her into the bath.'

'Ahem,' coughed Hayden pointedly.

Anne looked at him. 'Oh, God, yes, I forgot. No bath for baby.'

Until they got hold of a plumber, her family had yet again joined the ranks of the great unwashed. Hayden had only managed to keep the loo going by using up thirteen bottles of Evian and Carpenter's water bowl. Anne's hair now felt as if it was crawling off her head and the kitchen was an assault course of dirty pans and dishes from last night.

'What are we going to do?' she asked Hayden, wiping Martha's mouth with a paper napkin whereupon the baby immediately squashed banana up her nose.

'What about?'

'The water, of course. We can't ask that headcase Underwood.'

'God forbid.' Pouring himself a second cup of tea, Hayden said as soon as he had drunk this he would ring the electrician/plumber.

'What electrician/plumber?'

'Oh! Um... just someone Agnes Fenn recommended.'

Anne frowned. 'You never mentioned that before. Why on earth didn't you say?'

On the table Anne's mobile phone suddenly shrilled into action, making them both start. Relieved at the stay of execution, Hayden seized it before Anne could. He listened a moment before handing it to her.

'Stephanie Dérain. For you.'

Conrad came down just as she was ringing off, warily clocked his father's expression, and collecting Carpenter, disappeared into the garden. 'Give me a shout when you're ready to go, Dad.'

'Well?' Hayden watched his son slouch out before turning to Anne. 'What did Stephanie want? To thank you for the delightful evening?'

Anne made a face. 'She did, actually. That woman never ceases to amaze me. She's even asked me to have lunch with her today.'

Hayden stroked his unshaven chin. 'Are you going?'

'I said I would but, on second thoughts, I don't think I will. Apart from the fact that I feel a complete wreck, I think I should be here for when my daughter is slightly less comatose so that I can have a serious talk with her.'

'Oh, no, wait a minute.' Hayden ran weary hands all over his face. 'Please don't start that stuff.'

'What stuff?'

'Recrimination. Look, Verity got drunk, made a damn fool of herself – end of story. Don't rub her nose in it.'

'She's fifteen, Hayden!'

'Exactly.' He stood up. 'Old enough to know better and no doubt in future she will without the need of a torture session from you or me – or anyone else.

'Go and have your lunch with Stephanie. Go and have a girly session with her and you'll feel better afterwards. Take Conrad to the beach on your way where he'll be okay on his own for a couple of hours, and I'll stay here with Verity and Martha and wait for the bloody plumber. Settled. All right?'

With that Hayden marched to the front door, was about to step outside but then turned round and hesitated.

Anne frowned at him. 'What?'

'There is one other thing. I'm not convinced the Dérains are people I am personally panting to keep in with.'

Anne dropped her eyes. Carpenter had come in from the garden and placed a soggy muzzle on her knee. He had a pigeon's feather stuck behind one ear like Hiawatha. Removing it, Anne smoothed it between her fingers. 'I take it,' she said quietly, 'that you've forgotten my father is intending to marry one of them.'

'No, I haven't.'

Anne looked up.

'Oh, I've nothing against Maxine – even if she does strike me as a bit dotty, or Stephanie for that matter. I feel sorry for Stephanie, actually.' He reflected a second. 'But don't ever invite that creep here again.'

Anne frowned again. 'What creep? Gilles, do you mean? Why? Don't you like him?'

'*Like* him?' Hayden looked disgusted. 'I can't stand the man.'

'But... but...' Anne found herself stuttering. True, she was nothing like enamoured of Gilles Dérain but it was unlike Hayden to express such a strong antipathy.

'But why?' Seeing his wife lost for words, Hayden supplied them. 'I'll tell you why. Many, many reasons but two will suffice. In the first place, he's a bully.'

She could not deny that.

'And if that doesn't suffice, he gropes other men's wives under the dining table.'

Anne flushed bright red. She hadn't realised Hayden had noticed.

'I would have said something if I hadn't been waiting for you any moment to stab the pillock in the thigh with your fork.'

Anne stared at her husband a second and then started to giggle weakly. 'Oh, Lord, I nearly did as well,' she croaked.

But Hayden did not laugh. 'Not that it would have made the slightest difference to him. Gilles Dérain is one of us males so entirely dedicated to lechery he would probably applaud if I told him I was screwing his daughter.'

All desire to giggle promptly left Anne. She could not believe her ears.

'Go and get yourself ready.' Hayden turned back to the door. 'I'm going to find Conrad. Somehow I don't think he feels too wonderful about yesterday evening's antics.'

*

There are few things more demoralising to a woman than dirty hair. One of them, however, is the suspicion that the love of her life is cheating. Not knowing which to tackle first, her lank locks or Hayden's peculiar comment about screwing Gilles Derain's daughter, Anne scraped a damp flannel over her face and armpits and gave up. She simply could not face lunching with Stephanie Dérain in this state.

Downstairs, Hayden was back sitting at the kitchen table, absently flicking through the pages of Verity's *Hello!* He looked up as she came in. 'Seeing as this thing seems to consist entirely of photographs of celebrity babies,' he remarked with a glance at the cover, 'I don't know why they don't call it *Bellow!*' He closed the magazine. 'Agnes Fenn's plumber is coming, by the way.'

Anne hovered over him. 'Good, but you go to the beach with Conrad. I've decided to cancel my lunch with Stephanie so I'll wait in for him.'

There was a long pause until Hayden said with finality, 'No.'

'What do you mean – no?'

'I mean I have to stay here.'

Anne looked closer at her husband whereupon he immediately shifted his eyes. That did it. It was time she got to the bottom of this once and for all. 'Hayden,' she began, 'I think we need after all to have a little talk – oh, bugger!'

Her phone had rung again. Pouncing on it, Anne rammed the receive button and snapped, 'I can't make it.'

'What can't you make?' said a male voice.

It was Jean-Pierre. 'Oh! I thought you were Stephanie.'

'Do I sound like Stephanie?'

'Er, no.' Holding the phone away from her ear for a second, Anne frowned at it. 'What do you want, anyway?' she said.

Jean-Pierre explained that he was ringing to see how she was.

'Don't you mean to see how Verity is?'

'No. I mean you.'

'Oh. Thank you.' Jean-Pierre sounded different on the phone – older and more mature. In fact, he had quite a striking voice on the phone. 'And I'm sorry. I didn't mean to be rude.'

Conrad came in as she was ringing off. 'That was Jean-Pierre,' she said to him. 'He's going to the beach with the kids of some friends. You can join them if you want to.'

'Okay. Are we going now?'

'In a minute. Your father's taking you.'

'No, you are.' And picking up the last bottle of Evian from the sink and *Hello!* from the table, Hayden went upstairs without another word.

Conrad and Anne looked at each other as they heard the loo door clang shut.

*

Jean-Pierre must have been watching out for them, because the second she and Conrad arrived at the top of the steps near their usual spot on the beach he came loping up the sand. Barefoot and clad in plain black swimming shorts, Anne could not help noticing how attractive he looked, and how attractively he moved, in a nicely supple way but a way utterly bereft of all that stupid fitness fanatic, look-at-me stuff.

Reaching them, Jean-Pierre turned to indicate where he was camped. A girl was crouched down on the sand about twenty metres away, fixing a sail to a windsurfer, and near to her was a boy sitting cross-legged on a towel, reading. To Anne they seemed at this distance to be about the same age as Conrad and Verity.

'That is Danielle and Hugo,' Jean-Pierre was explaining to Conrad. 'They are expecting you. Do you want to go say 'Hi'?'

'Okay.'

As the boy ambled off with Carpenter, Anne shifted her gaze back to Jean-Pierre, then shifted it away again. Now she was faced with him she kept thinking about having hysterics all over his chest last night, which meant she could not quite look him in the eye. The trouble was it was a bit difficult to know what else to look him in when presented with all that naked taut flesh. My word, she thought with a little shiver, they didn't make 'em like that in my day.

'Who are they?' she asked, nodding at the two kids below them.

'The son and the daughter of some friends of Juno.'

Juno, Anne thought drearily, always Juno.

'Are you okay?' He tilted his head to peer into her face. 'You did not reply to my question when I asked you on the telephone.'

'I'm fine,' she said brightly.

'If you do not mind me saying this, you do not look so fine.'

'Thanks!'

'No, no.' He frowned. 'That I do not mean, as I think you know.'

'Yes, well...' Anne forced herself to meet his eyes. 'Listen, I want to apologise for the scene yesterday evening.'

He shrugged. '*C'est pas grave*. It was a bad situation, you had a shock. Forget it.'

'Thank you – that's nice of you. And thank you for bringing my daughter home.' Anne looked away again.

'So. You are coming down?'

Anne looked back at him. He was holding out his hand as if to guide her down the steps. 'Oh, I'm not stopping.'

His face seemed to fall a little. 'No?'

There was a tiny pause.

'But you will come back later?'

She nodded. 'Around four thirty to pick up Conrad and Carpenter. Why?'

He considered her a moment. 'Return at three. I meet you at the Café de la Digue. You know this place? Good. So, maybe we have a glass of wine together or who knows?' He winked one suggestive eye at her. 'Maybe I just give you the nice surprise.'

Anne blinked. Was that a pass? If so, she'd never come across one quite like it. 'Oh, Jean-Pierre, I'm flattered, really, but I don't think I can –'

Jean-Pierre leaned forward suddenly and kissed her lightly on the cheek. Anne immediately hoped he could not smell her dirty hair.

'Three,' he repeated and embraced her other cheek.

'All right,' she said faintly. 'Three o'clock.'

*

Today Monsieur Martin was wearing his plumbing hat – literally, in that he had swapped his previous traditional blue French workman's cap for a green rubber sou'wester. It made Hayden wonder what happened if he ever got mixed up and wore the sou'wester for electricity. Maybe that was why it was rubber.

But notwithstanding his change in role, Monsieur Martin was his usual quasi aggressive/genial self, that peculiar mixture of admiration and disparagement. So that now, as he entered the battleground of a kitchen, he wrinkled his nose in distaste whilst simultaneously observing the remains of the cassoulet with a grunt of approval.

'*Les andouilles,* eh?' he barked with a smile.

'*Oui,*' confirmed Hayden, and resolved to say no more on the subject, having already made a private vow that the very next time an *andouille* attempted to cross his threshold, he'd throttle it.

Monsieur Martin set to work, turning taps on and off, stopcocks off and on, and clumping upstairs and down with plungers, spanners and suction pumps. Presently, low but penetrating explosions began to rumble round the cottage, a baritone accompaniment to the soprano sound effects issuing from Hayden's digestive system; that preserved goose had certainly been shot on a windy day. Wondering how on earth Verity could sleep through the barrage, he decided to take Martha out into the garden and chew some Rennies while he waited.

In due course Monsieur Martin appeared with an armful of pipes, threw them down with a clatter and told Hayden he had incredible locks of air. Now, however, all had been evacuated. You don't say, thought Hayden, swallowing Rennies and wincing at the phrase. He asked if the problem would happen again, three minutes into Monsieur Martin's reply realising that he had never in his life asked such a stupid question.

Not so much a stream as a raging torrent of French was pouring over him, peppered with obscure terminology and abbreviations. Raising a hand as if stopping a taxi, Hayden called a halt in the proceedings and said he had got the general picture. He had got anything but. However, as Monsieur Martin had seized and was somewhat disconcertingly brandishing a pipe to emphasise one of his more impenetrable points, this seemed a wise course of action.

Not daring to ask for a quotation for re-plumbing, and Monsieur Martin evidently appreciating this was not the time to offer one, they settled for a quick check of the wiring. In the kitchen, having flicked various switches, the now electrical version of Monsieur Martin – albeit he was still wearing the sou'wester – pondered a while before sticking a long band of thick black insulating tape over the row of sockets above the work surface, leaving just one in use.

He handed the electric kettle to Hayden and wagged an admonitory finger. '*Non*,' he said. '*Dangereux*.'

Hayden put the kettle in a cupboard. First his fluorescent light strip, now his electric kettle. He had a sudden and vivid mental vision of his house being dismantled piece by piece. 'But everything is all right for now?' he asked in French.

Monsieur Martin shrugged. '*Le jour s'approche*,' he replied, which sounded rather Delphic.

Then suddenly he gave a broad smile and added in severely broken English, 'Next time you 'ave a poof! 'e is ze beeg one.'

Terrific, thought Hayden. I can't wait.

17

Like Jean-Pierre had been, Stephanie was waiting for her – at the same restaurant in Houlgate. 'Gilles 'as left 'is mistress,' she announced the second Anne arrived.

'Oh!' Having just spent the entire journey concocting abject apologies for her behaviour towards Stephanie's daughter, Anne found the wind slightly taken out of her sails. Sitting down opposite the Frenchwoman, she cast round for appropriate expressions of delight.

'Well, that's… that's wonderful news, Stephanie. I'm so pleased for you.'

Stephanie looked at her as if she had grown a second head.

'What's the matter?' Anne asked cautiously. 'Isn't it wonderful news?'

'Of course not,' Stephanie said impatiently. 'It is the fucking catastrophe.'

Oh dear, how to say this. Language was such a responsibility. One little slip and she had turned Stephanie Dérain into Mohamed Al Fayed. 'Erm, Stephanie?'

'*Oui*?'

'I don't know quite how to put this but you mustn't, that is, I don't advise you to use that word – not in public, at least.'

Stephanie frowned. 'What word? Fucking?'

'Yes.' Anne glanced uneasily around. The restaurant was almost full.

'Why not? You use 'im yourself when you are in the big passion.'

'Yes, I know I did but I shouldn't have done. It's really very impolite, very rude. In fact, it's extremely insulting.'

Stephanie gave a satisfied nod. '*Bon*. Because I tell Gilles 'e is the fucking idiot.'

A waiter came over with the menu. After a quick perusal, Anne decided on *crevettes grillée* followed by steak and chips; very heavy on the cholesterol, but what the hell. If unhealthy food did not give her a heart attack, her dream life in France soon would.

Stephanie summoned the waiter and asked the ingredients of about ten starters before eventually settling on melon, which didn't have any ingredients. This she would follow with a very small *salade paysanne, sans vinaigrette*. Oh, well, Anne reflected cynically, I'm sure she'll make it up with prohibited puddings.

'But tell me,' she began, once Stephanie's Badôit and her glass of rosé had arrived; it was beginning to feel like a ritual. 'Why is Gilles the fucking id –' she controlled herself. 'I mean, why is Gilles an idiot? I thought you said his mistress was a fat peasant.'

'*Tu as raison.* She is.'

Stephanie lifted her shoulders inside her striped blazer. Today she was arrayed in such an immaculate reproduction of Thames wear, circa 1920, Anne almost expected her to strike up the Eton Boating Song.

'But this is not the point.'

'What is the point?'

Stephanie smoothed the flannel knees of her Oxford bags. 'I did not want 'im to finish with 'er. She is cheap and besides,' she hesitated, looking slyly up at Anne from under her lashes, 'she supplies 'im.'

For the second time that morning, Anne could not quite believe her ears. This was getting out of hand. She began to wish with all her heart that she had never even heard of the Dérains, let alone bumped into them again.

First the loopy grandmother had done a Mata Hari on her father, then the daughter had probably seduced her husband, and now here was the wife blithely confessing her husband was a junkie. Frankly, you needed a fast forward button to keep up with them.

'Anne, *chèrie*? Are you well? I think you go a little pale.'

And you're beyond the pale, thought Anne. 'Yes, well, you've given me a shock.'

She paused a moment. She must get to the bottom of this and then scarper. She adopted a severe expression. 'With precisely what does Gilles's mistress supply him, Stephanie?'

'Sex,' the Frenchwoman said simply. 'What did you think I am meaning?'

*

Verity surfaced at lunchtime looking completely normal. The recuperative powers of youth, reflected Hayden gloomily. If I drank myself into a stretcher case I'd be prostrate for a week, and that would be in the unlikely event of me surviving it.

'Where is everyone?' she asked on a yawn.

'Your Mum's out to lunch with Stephanie and Conrad's beaching.'

Verity stretched and twitched her nose.

'I was just about to make some scrambled eggs for Martha's and my lunch,' explained Hayden. 'Do you want some too?'

'Yeah, okay,' said Verity, as if this were a concession.

'Well, set the table, then.'

Verity looked immediately as though food was the last thing on her mind.

'Come on, I've done everything this morning.' Hayden heard the whine in his voice and too late tried to curb it. But he was done in.

He had washed up all the dishes from last night, dried and put them away, then had to get some out again because Martha fancied a snack, cleared away and washed up after that, mopped the floor because everybody was sticking to it again – this time with dirt – tried not to notice what seemed on a brief examination to be large flakes of tile paint attached to the mop – and on a closer one stayed being them – bathed Martha and dressed her, popped her down for a rest while he took a shower, dried himself, dressed himself, got Martha up and changed her, stuck various articles of clothing strewn about the bedrooms to soak in a bowl the way Anne did every morning in the absence of a washing machine, rinsed and wrung out the soaked articles of clothing, noticed with some dismay that they were all a sort of grimy pink colour, hung them out on the line nevertheless and hoped for the best, changed Martha and sat down for two minutes only to realise it was nearly lunchtime.

He was beginning to understand what Anne meant when she complained there was nothing more exhausting than being at home with a baby.

They sat down to eat in silence, Verity not being famed for her dedication to polite conversation. 'So,' Hayden asked presently, 'what are you going to do with yourself this afternoon?'

'Why?' she said suspiciously.

'Because I was thinking of making a start on painting the bedrooms and I just wondered whether if you had nothing better to do, you might like to give me a hand.'

Verity's face now took on the perfected blank expression of a teenager who knows precisely what you are suggesting but has not the slightest intention of admitting it. Before Hayden could pursue the point, however, the familiar sound of a car sweeping into the drive induced in his stepdaughter the greatest show of enthusiasm she had displayed since rising from her sickbed.

'That's Juno!' she cried, leaping to the window and then charging upstairs. Thundering down a second later with her backpack, she rushed to the door.

'Aren't you going to invite her in for a minute?'

Verity stared at her stepfather as if he had proposed something outlandish. 'What for?'

'Because maybe I'd like to see her.'

Verity frowned. 'What for?' she said again.

Hayden gave up. 'Oh, never mind. Go on, then. But make sure,' he added, bethinking future ructions, 'that you tell her that you are very sorry for your behaviour yesterday evening.'

This time his stepdaughter looked not so much blank as totally dumbfounded. The second gift of youth, thought Hayden with envy – a memory as conveniently short as your recovery time. But without another word Verity was gone.

As the drone of the car engine faded into the distance, Hayden looked at his daughter. 'And how are you with a paint roller?' he said.

Martha smiled at him, rubbed her fists together and chortled.

'Yes,' he sighed, 'I thought you might say that.'

*

Things were looking up. Although Conrad would not have dreamed in a million years of admitting it, he had actually been getting pretty pissed off with the beach. This, of course, was partly down to Verity acting so dumb over Jean-Pierre. The only times she had been anything like fun at the beach was when Jean-Pierre hadn't been around, and there hadn't been many of them.

It had often occurred to him that, if Verity was anything to go by, girls were a weird bunch of tricks. He just could not suss them out. They wanted guys to like them and yet the second one appeared they went all stupid and posing. In Verity's case the change was so dramatic it was like she was two people.

The other 'partly' was what he had often heard Dad say about holidays; that lolling about on a beach was tedious. It was, actually. The snorkelling here was no good; you needed rocks for that to work. Except for the sun making his zits vanish – like, a big consideration – Conrad felt on the whole he'd rather be at home. Except this was home now! School, then. No, that was going a bit far. All in all, however, it had been getting so boring that Conrad had wondered how he was going to stick out the rest of the month. But that had been before.

Before he met Danielle.

Danielle was unlike any girl he had ever met. Okay, he hadn't met too many but that was the problem with going to an all boys' boarding school. You saw a few at a disco or a party when all they did was behave like Verity. Danielle was different. Danielle did not behave anything like Verity. Danielle, in fact, did not behave anything like a girl. But she was one, though, and a bloody pretty one at that.

Conrad guessed she was around the same age as him but he did not get to confirm this because that was not the type of thing that interested Danielle.

Danielle did not go in for poxy little chat up lines like how old was he and what year was he in at school. The only question Danielle asked him was to establish whether he knew enough French to be able to understand her. He didn't, quite, but she apparently could not speak a word of English so after a bit he felt he might. At which point all she wanted him to do was help her try out her windsurfer. In a way, this was a bit pathetic because there wasn't a breath of wind, but Danielle wasn't going to let a little thing like no wind put her off.

Leaving her brother, Hugo, to discuss some book he was reading with Jean-Pierre – Hugo was older, around seventeen, and quite an okay guy but a bit geeky – they dragged it down to the shore and for the next couple of hours Conrad found himself having the greatest fun of the holiday so far.

Eventually, however, he said they had to give it a rest. He had shouted himself hoarse and laughed himself into a stitch not to mention being starving hungry. Back with Jean-Pierre, Hugo and Carpenter, Conrad got out the saucisson baguette Anne had bought him on the way to the beach and offered some to Dani – it was Dani by now.

She tore it expertly in half. She was really strong for a girl, which was probably why she was such a fantastic swimmer, and immediately handed him in return a huge slice of wicked pizza. Then they all sat around on the sand eating and drinking – Jean-Pierre gave him a bottle of Stella – and all talking in French. Danielle made a fuss if anyone said anything in English.

But that turned out to be really great, too, because nobody corrected him if he made a mistake. It struck Conrad that this was what holidays should be about; feeling chilled, feeling cool, feeling you never wanted the time to end. Until Verity appeared and he stopped feeling any of those things.

Thinking he should make an effort, he introduced her to Dani and Hugo in French.

'Are you showing off or something?' she said.

Sometimes, he thought, now feeling murderous, sometimes he just could not *suss* Verity. Juno was with her, however, and said something pleasant in reply to him, also in French.

But the next minute Jean-Pierre had jumped up and put his arm round Juno's shoulders, saying something to her that was too low for anyone else to hear. And it was at this moment that Conrad saw in some surprise that Juno, in fact, looked awful; really stressed-out and white and her mouth wobbling as if she was about to burst into tears.

Juno, thought Conrad, as Jean-Pierre gently guided her away down the beach from them, Juno. Now there's another girl I can't suss.

18

All around them now the terrace was full of people slurping oysters and spearing snails. Some tables even had miniature boats moored on little stands, loaded to the gunnels with every crustacean known to fish-kind. It was quite a scene, exactly the sort Anne would at any other time have found enchanting. On a table near them, a handsome Frenchman was assiduously picking winkles out of their shells with a dwarf harpoon and feeding them to his sleek girlfriend as though she were a performing seal.

But, looking down at her prawns, Anne tried valiantly to summon up some appetite and failed. Far from being in the mood for misery eating, she was beginning to feel almost queasy, mainly on account of the conversation. 'Are you seriously saying,' she said, keeping her voice low, 'that you like Gilles having a mistress because it means you don't have to sleep with him?'

Stephanie nodded an affirmative. 'I am,' she said gaily.

Anne seized a prawn, pulled off a head and legs, washed down the torso with a swig of wine and then felt like Hannibal Lecter. 'But Stephanie, if you can't stand the thought of sleeping with your husband, why do you stay married to him?'

Stephanie pondered, a spoonful of melon suspended before her lips.

'After all,' continued Anne, 'it can't be for Juno's sake. She's grown up. And by the way, I was going to say earlier, but I do apologise for flying at her like that yesterday evening. Please tell her from me that I am extremely sorry.'

Stephanie puffed out her lips. 'No, it is not important.' She swallowed the melon with a contemptuous gulp. 'I 'ave no doubt she was to blame for the condition of Verity.'

'I now know she wasn't, actually.' Anne looked curiously at her friend. 'In fact, if you don't mind me saying so, Stephanie, you're very down on Juno, aren't you?'

'Per'aps.' Averting her face, Stephanie stared across the square at the sea. 'But if I am, then it is the fault of Gilles.'

'How do you make that out?'

The Frenchwoman turned back to look at Anne, her eyes so suspiciously bright that for a second Anne feared she was about to weep. But no, Stephanie got a grip on herself. Rivulets of tears trickling down the Diorskin were not her line.

'Because I do not *know* my daughter,' she said with fervent meaning. 'I cannot love 'er. Gilles kept my baby from me all through 'er youth. Gilles was able to control everything I did. 'E controlled my relationship with my daughter. It was Gilles who insisted upon the au pairs, the nannies, the summer camps.'

'Oh, come on!'

Try as she might, Anne could not recall a single occasion when she had been the Dérains' au pair, of Stephanie trying to wrest the infant Juno from her arms. On the contrary, Stephanie had been quite content to beetle off on her social round leaving Anne lumbered with a baby screaming herself stupid. Moreover, she hadn't much sympathy for women who made their husbands out to be monsters while continuing to air their credit cards.

'What 'situation'?' Anne picked up on Stephanie's own phraseology. 'I'm sorry, but I fail to see what situation could have kept you from your own child.'

Stephanie looked cast down. 'Ah, now you are angry with me.'

'No, I'm not.' Anne suppressed her exasperation. Women like this drove you to screaming pitch. One minute you felt sorry for them, the next you wanted to shake their bones dry. 'I'm just pointing out that you could surely have stopped all that if you'd really wanted to.'

'Maybe.'

'Besides,' Anne continued encouragingly, 'Juno is grown-up now. And a decent young woman.' This was wild – she was sticking up for Juno. 'You could try just liking her.'

''Ow can I like her when Juno does things of which I do not, I *will* not approve? She is unspeakable. If you knew, you would understand. Indeed, if you knew what she was doing, doing per'aps at this very moment...' Stephanie's voice faded away, her head bowing so dejectedly that for a moment Anne thought she had after all decided to sacrifice the Diorskin.

'Stephanie? *Stephanie*? Whatever is the matter?'

'*Non*! I cannot speak of it to anyone, above all not to you.'

There was a little silence, until Stephanie's head suddenly jerked up. 'Tell me,' she said, affecting one of her disconcertingly seraphic smiles. ''Ow did you meet 'Ayden?'

'Hayden? How did I meet Hayden?' Anne blinked. 'Why on earth do you want to know that? I mean, what's how I met Hayden got to do with what we have been talking about?'

'Oh, I do not know.' Stephanie looked dejected again. 'But please tell me.'

At a loss, Anne scratched her ear. 'Okay, right, um, well, I suppose it was through my work. I met Hayden when he was my, um, sort of... *employer*.'

The Frenchwoman now affected an expression of operatic wistfulness. 'And you fall in *lorve*?'

Anne smiled. 'Reader, I married him.'

'*Comment*?'

'Sorry, private joke.' Anne felt a pang. Were the days of private jokes over? Oh, how in love they had been. Was that all gone forever? She shook herself. 'We fell in love? Well, yes, of course we fell in love, Stephanie. That's why we got married, why anyone gets married, isn't it?'

'I knew it!' Stephanie gave a little clap of her hands. 'And so,' she added, 'you will now understand.'

The waiter arrived to clear their first course.

'What will I understand?' asked Anne, distracted by the waiter examining her scarcely touched plate with undisguised disapproval.

'Why I stay with Gilles.' Offering her a Disque Bleu, Stephanie lit Anne's and then her own. 'I never marry Gilles for lorve,' she said mournfully, and exhaled a long plume of smoke.

'What did you marry him for, then?' Anne drained her glass of wine.

''Ave another.' Stephanie made to beckon the waiter.

'No, I can't, I'm driving. Tell me instead what you married Gilles for.'

'Money, of course.'

'Of course.' Ask a silly question...thought Anne.

Stephanie's eyes went dreamy. 'I was poor, you see, so beautiful but so poor.'

'Really.' Except in novels you'd be ashamed to be caught reading, Anne did not think she had ever come across a woman who said that.

Their main courses arriving, Stephanie ground out her cigarette and picked up a fork. 'Gilles wanted a beautiful wife. I wanted money.' She stirred her salad as if it were a cup of coffee. 'It was a bargain. On both sides.'

Watching her, Anne nibbled a chip. 'I'm sorry,' she said at last. 'But if that is really true, then I think it's revolting.'

Stephanie looked unmoved.

'And as for the bed angle,' Anne nibbled another chip. 'I can't imagine being as rich as Croesus compensating for having to sleep with someone you find repulsive. Unless,' she conceded, 'you just don't like sex and therefore it's neither here nor there.'

The Frenchwoman burst into peals of laughter. 'Oh, Anne, *que tu es drôle*! Of course I like sex! It's just sex with Gilles that makes me sick!'

'Hush!' Anne glanced round in alarm. 'Don't talk so loudly.' On an adjacent table, an elderly English couple were trying not to listen.

'Gilles 'as 'is little friends,' Stephanie resumed more quietly but still firmly. 'And I 'ave mine.'

Anne frowned. 'Are you saying you have lovers?'

'In the singular.' Stephanie looked modest. 'I 'ave a lover.'

'Who?'

Irritating the hell out of Anne, the Frenchwoman wagged a playful finger. 'Ah, now you ask too many questions. I will say only that I nearly always choose someone *yong*. They can give me what I want.' She ate half a slice of tomato. 'And, of course, I can give them what they want, too.'

'What's that?'

'Money.' Stephanie twitched her nose in an unemotional sniff. 'The money that is the reason why I stay with Gilles.'

*

'Hello! I was going to come and see you later on.'

Turning round from deadheading a huge rose climbing over her front door, Agnes Fenn whipped off her gardening glove and extended a hand to Hayden in a reassuringly English way. 'Although I'm afraid I haven't anything useful to tell you as yet. Everyone I try to contact seems to be on holiday. August in France, you know? But I was going to come and see you, anyway. How are things? How are *you*?'

'Fine, fine. I hope I'm not disturbing you.' He found himself drawing deep breaths of the fragrant air.

'Kiftsgate.' She nodded at the rose. 'An absolute so-and-so to get going but once one has, the scent makes it all worthwhile.'

'It's lovely.' Hayden looked about him at the verdant lawn and the flowerbeds crammed with an old-fashioned riot of hollyhocks, larkspur and red hot pokers. 'But so is your entire garden.'

'Not as lovely as this little poppet.'

Agnes was smiling down at Martha who was sitting in her buggy clutching her bare toes and occasionally putting one in her mouth. 'Come in, or rather come and sit down.' Throwing her gloves and pruning knife into a battered trug on the doorstep, Agnes indicated a wicker table and chairs set out across the lawn in the shade of a massive chestnut tree. 'And I'll make us some tea.'

'Oh, no, please don't go to any trouble. I only came to thank you for putting me onto François Martin. We had to call him out again this morning.'

'Oh dear, did you really?'

'This time in his plumbing hat.' Hayden forced a smile. 'We'd turned into the Kalahari Desert. As far as I can make out,' he explained, 'it's now the water system that should be condemned. It transpires that my U-bends are all upside down or back to front. In fact, it seems I have non-U bends.'

Agnes laughed but looked concerned. 'Come and sit down,' she said cajolingly. 'And tell me all about it.'

Hayden hesitated.

Far from getting on with some decorating, he had started feeling so horribly depressed at home on his own with the baby that it had actually frightened him. Even telling himself – with inescapable irony – that at least he was learning something about the problems of the majority of the female sex had failed to raise his spirits. He'd had to get out of the house; he'd had to *talk* to someone. And Agnes Fenn had been the only person he could think of. Yet, now he was here, he felt foolish, embarrassed by his weakness.

'No. You're very kind but as I said, I really only came to –'

'No, you didn't.' Agnes was watching him with an extraordinarily tender look in her cool blue eyes. 'Come on, come and have some tea with me.' Then she smiled.

'Or perhaps you'd prefer whisky?'

*

As the day ground on Verity felt more and more awful, a really awful sort of awful too in that she did not know how to stop feeling it. Everyone had cleared off and left her: Conrad messing about with the windsurfer and the bossy little French girl, and Jean-Pierre and that boring Hugo playing volley ball. Even Carpenter had abandoned her for a Dutch family further down the beach.

The Dutch family were screaming in ecstasy over his antics. But people always did scream in ecstasy over Carpenter when he did his shadow boxing act. It was only because they were eating ice-creams. Carpenter's performances were never free. At some point he would do his canine version of passing the hat round and steal an unguarded cornet, and then there would be screams of anything but ecstasy.

Until then, she was on her own.

To be fair, everyone had asked her to join in with whatever they were doing, except for Juno. She'd no idea where Juno had cleared off to but it was pretty mean of her to dump her like this. But if she felt left out Verity knew that it was her own fault; she knew she was being rude and surly. The problem was she couldn't stop being rude and surly because she didn't want to do any of the things everyone else was doing. All she wanted to do was to have a private chat with Jean-Pierre to try and find out exactly what she had done yesterday evening. She'd asked Juno on the way here but Juno wouldn't tell her. Juno, in fact, had been, like, quiet, in a funny mood; almost, like, unfriendly.

It was quite worrying in a way, this business of not being able to remember things and nobody willing to remind her. It made Verity all the more convinced that whatever she had done, it had been pretty atrocious. Yet, concentrating very hard, the sole memory she could dredge from yesterday evening was dancing with Jean-Pierre. There was no harm in that was there?

Suddenly she froze, or rather she burned. Every centimetre of her skin caught fire as a mental vision of her dancing with Jean-Pierre came sharply into focus. She had not been dancing with Jean-Pierre – she had been practically trying to have it off with him. Or rather, she had been trying to rape him because he had been trying to stop her. Her mind went blank again. What had she done then? Had she actually gone the whole hog and taken her clothes off in the middle of the dance floor?

Two French girls strolled by, glanced at her and then said something to each other and giggled. Verity turned on her stomach and buried her head in her arms. She wished she could bury her whole body, sink, disappear, do anything to get away from this horrible feeling that she had made a complete and total prat of herself. Everybody was watching her. Everybody was laughing at her. The thought made her want to cry and so she did, the tears trickling saltily down her cheeks and falling in black little plops on the sand beneath her eyes.

After a bit, Carpenter returned – ice-cream-less – the Dutch family must have been on the ball – and flopped down heavily across her back. His claws scratched her skin and he was hot and wet and gritty but she didn't care; the weight of him was consoling. It made her almost stop crying.

After all, she told herself, whatever she had done, Carpenter wouldn't mind.

*

'No, no alcohol for me, thank you,' said Hayden. 'Since yesterday I'm on the wagon for a bit.'

'And me,' said Agnes, clearing a space on the garden table for him to put down the tea tray. 'In my case by order of my doctor.'

'Oh?' Hayden watched as she poured the pale liquid into two bone china cups translucent with age and delicacy. 'You're not poorly, are you?'

'No more than usual.' She pulled what was for her a slightly exasperated face. 'The good doctor merely told me I must stop drinking whisky but he always tells me that.' The exasperation relaxed into one of her mischievous grins. 'So I asked him what he thought about me taking up gin instead.'

There was a pause as Hayden chuckled and Agnes stooped to lift Martha up from the grass and perch her on her lap. 'That's the only tedious thing about being old,' she said, giving the baby a tarnished silver teaspoon to play with.

'What is?'

'The way it is always assumed one is desperate to prolong one's life.'

'But surely,' Hayden looked quizzically at her, 'most people are?'

'Are they?'

Absently slipping off her battered sandals, the old woman pushed her toes into the velvety thick grass. Martha craned her head to look down at them, and then back up wonderingly at Agnes as if amazed to discover that someone else had feet, too.

'I thought they were but I could be wrong. You see, I was thinking about my father-in-law. He seems determined to squeeze every last ounce of mileage out of his life.'

'Is that so?'

'He even thinks he's in love.'

Agnes smiled, lowering her eyes to contemplate her naked feet. Misshapen and lumpy with knotted veins, they were as gnarled as the exposed roots of the chestnut tree. 'E.M. Forster was rather good on love and old age,' she remarked sadly. '*Passage to India,* you know.'

'Forgive my ignorance but I haven't read Forster since I was at school.'

A sort of shadow seemed to pass over her face. 'No, well, it doesn't matter. I only mentioned it because some days I feel I have a lot in common with Mrs Moore.'

Hayden felt a twinge of anxiety. He hesitated a second, then said, 'Are you sure you're all right?'

She looked up. 'Yes, of course I am. Why do you ask?'

'You seem a bit... low.'

'Low?' She also hesitated and then shook her head. 'No, I'm not low. I wouldn't mind seeing my son a little more frequently but I understand that he's very busy, as is my daughter. But no, I'm not low. How about you?' She changed the subject very deliberately. 'Can you bear to tell me how things are going or are you cringing with embarrassment at having let your guard down?'

This was so close to the truth Hayden blushed slightly. 'I was a bit at first,' he admitted wryly. 'But that didn't mean I wasn't extremely grateful to you. Just telling someone – telling *you* – helped enormously.'

'And your wife?'

'Ah, now that didn't pan out quite as one might have anticipated.' It wasn't quite what he wanted to say. He wanted to say help me, help me again. Tell me why my wife suddenly seems to detest me. He wanted to lie down on the sweet, soft grass and have Agnes solve all his problems. Instead, he smiled. 'But I expect I'm handling it all the wrong way.'

Agnes did not return his smile. Rather, she looked pensive. 'You know,' she said, affecting a quoting voice, *'one does not discover new lands without consenting to lose sight of the shore for a very long time.'*

Hayden stared at her. 'How very apt – who said that?'

'André Gide.'

Hayden gave a slow nod. 'The French novelist.'

'More of a philosopher, really. I was reading him after the last time we talked. That particular epigram is often attributed to Christopher Columbus but it's actually from Gide. Would you like to read him too?' At this point Agnes did smile, but only with a kind of wry shame. 'Or are you becoming weary of my homilies?'

'Never,' Hayden said firmly. 'And I should like to read him very much.'

*

Today Stephanie's eating crime consisted of a chocolate soufflé and two helpings of crème brulée. Anne couldn't understand why she didn't simply start at the end of a menu and work backwards. Then again, she had eaten virtually nothing herself. If she hadn't had much appetite to start with, Stephanie's true confessions had done for what remained. Light years away from being moralistic, Anne could not help feeling a little disgusted at the clinical arrangement of the Dérain marriage. Oh, well, it was their funeral. Remembering the time, she glanced at her watch.

'I'm sorry, Stephanie.' She signalled for the bill. 'But I'm afraid I'm going to have to go. I've got to be somewhere at three.'

'You meet a little friend?' Stephanie said archly.

Anne blushed. 'No, of course not.' She took the bill from the waiter. Aside from the puddings, it seemed a hell of a sum for what had basically been one prawn, half a melon and two chips.

'I know. I make only the joke. I know you are devoted to your 'Ayden.'

'Yes, well.' With a slightly sickly smile, Anne paid and closed her purse. 'I've really got to go, I'm afraid. I've got a ... a dental appointment.'

God will strike me dead with a thunderbolt for such lies, she thought, as she shot back to Cabourg. But what a very peculiar thing for Stephanie to say, even as a joke! One minute she was wittering on about how Anne had found true *lorve* and the next practically inciting her to adultery.

Then, as she reached the outskirts of the town, it struck Anne that Stephanie had said something else peculiar, something about Juno. *If you knew what she was doing, perhaps at this very moment... I cannot speak of it to anyone, above all to you.* But what could Juno be doing that Stephanie could not tell her? Anne had a sudden vile thought. Oh, no, Stephanie could not have meant that, surely?

Or could she?

*

By three o'clock Verity felt so jittery she could not keep still. The tide was right out, the sea a distant band as unreachable as her peace of mind.

Conrad and Danielle were playing boules with Hugo. At least, they were trying to play boules, but with Carpenter carrying off the *cochon* all the time it was tricky. Jean-Pierre had left, saying he had to meet someone at the Café de la Digue.

With a fresh wave of paranoia, Verity sprang up, yanking on her jeans, t-shirt and trainers. Conrad looked over at her.

'Where are you going?'

'For a walk,' she said shortly.

'Anne's coming to pick us up at half past four, you know.'

'Yeah, yeah,' she muttered, thinking bloody little goody-goody as she marched off. It was always the same with Conrad. Conrad never did anything awful. Conrad never made a fool of himself. Conrad was always so well behaved it made you sick.

Bounding up the steps, Verity sprinted along the promenade. She knew roughly where the Café de la Digue was and if she just, like, hung about around there she might just, like, *spot* Jean-Pierre and then pretend to bump into him and then maybe they could talk and then maybe she could get her head sorted.

Yeah. It was a good plan.

*

Anne steamed into Cabourg – a date with Jean-Pierre was a far more attractive prospect than mulling over Stephanie's strange utterings – by some miracle found somewhere to park straightaway, and then galloped up towards the promenade. The Café de la Digue was on the seafront, a bit further along from where they usually sat on the beach, somewhere she knew only in passing.

And here it was. Anne came to halt, running a hand quickly over her head to check her hair and reflecting that the only good thing about dirty hair was at least it didn't fly all over the place. She scanned the tables; they were nearly all full of people either still eating lunch or drinking coffee or just generally relaxing. At one of furthest, a man stood up.

He came over to her.
'Alain,' she said weakly.
'Hello, Anne,' said Alain Duval.

19

At half past nine the next morning, a plastic Grecian urn arrived on the Warwick's doorstep. Beneath it were the legs of a delivery boy and above what seemed to be the entire stock of a florist's shop.

'Good grief!' exclaimed Hayden, edging it sideways through the door. 'Perhaps he's got the wrong house.' He flipped a small envelope attached to the top right hand corner of the cellophane. 'No, they're for you, darling,' he said in surprise, unpinning the envelope and passing it to Anne.

Taking it, Anne had a split second's panic that the flowers were from Alain. No, of course they wouldn't be. She and Alain had drunk a glass of wine together, nothing more. Well, okay, there had been a kiss but only a kiss that had happened because it had taken her completely off guard, but nothing more.

And there wasn't going to be anything more, either.

Hayden was admiring the bouquet. 'Who on earth could have sent you such lovely flowers?'

Anne snorted.

The flowers were hideous: giant salmon-pink gladioli clashing horribly with maroon dahlias and pus-yellow carnations but, like so many of his gender, Hayden was colour-blind. This, however, was not what had made her snort. What had made Anne snort was Hayden's evident assumption that nobody would send her flowers. That pissed her off so much that for a second split second she hoped with all her might that they *were* from Alain – that would show him.

Slitting open the envelope, she withdrew a thick, ivory-coloured card. It was the French equivalent of an At Home invitation from Maxine Dérain, the print so heavily engraved it could have passed for braille. In a biro scrawl across the bottom, her father had written, '*My dear Anne, Please come to this if you can. Just a few friends for a picnic round the pool. I am very sorry about missing your dinner. Hope you like the flowers. With my love, Dad xxx.*'

Anne felt almost unbearably touched; her father could be so sweet sometimes. Swallowing rapidly, she looked up to see Verity watching her in what seemed to be an unwontedly beady fashion.

'Well?' she jeered. 'Who are they from? Your boyfriend?'

'That's right,' Anne said merrily. 'The eighteenth of my nineteen lovers.' She turned to Hayden. 'The flowers are from my father to apologise for not turning up to dinner the other evening and the invitation is from Maxine. She is having a few friends round to a picnic by the pool at the Manoir today and would like us all to join them.'

'Fantastic!' exclaimed Conrad.

Anne turned to him. 'Why fantastic?'

'Because Dani is going there today.'

'Danny?' Anne frowned. 'Who's Danny?'

'A ladette,' sniffed Verity.

'In my day,' sighed Hayden, 'we called them tomboys.'

'Oh, you mean Danielle! Is she nice?' Anne said teasingly to her stepson.

'Very.' Tearing up his second croissant, Conrad reached for the jam.

Verity muttered something under her breath.

Conrad's head jerked up. 'She is not a stupid little tart!' he shouted. 'And as if you could talk after the pathetic way you tried to get off with Jean-Pierre at the nightclub.'

'Oh, you fucking little tell-tale!' screamed Verity, leaping to her feet.

'Verity, Verity,' Hayden said mildly. 'Is that really necessary?'

She rounded on him. 'Don't you bloody criticise me – you're not my father! If you want to tell someone how to behave,' she spat, pointing at her mother, 'try *her*.' Turning on her heel, she stomped upstairs and slammed her bedroom door.

The dust settling, Conrad took his croissant and said if they didn't mind he would finish his breakfast in the garden.

Martha began to grizzle.

'It would be so nice,' remarked Hayden, as Anne picked up the baby, 'so award-winningly welcome if one's beloved stepdaughter could occasionally think of a more *original* insult to fling at one.'

'She didn't mean it.' Anne clutched Martha to her in self-defence.

'There's nothing *to* mean. I know I'm not her father.'

'Do you want me to have a word with her?'

'Certainly not.' Hayden lifted his shoulders in an irritable little shrug. 'I am curious, however, as to what she meant by the other stuff.'

'What other stuff?'

'The bit about me telling *you* to behave.'

'Oh, that.' Gently detaching Martha's jammy little fists from her hair, Anne affected nonchalance. 'I'm not a hundred per cent sure. But, hazarding a guess, I would say she's got some bee in her bonnet about me and Jean-Pierre.'

'You and Jean-Pierre? Why on earth should Verity have a bee in her bonnet about you and Jean-Pierre?'

Anne looked her husband directly in the eye. 'Because he invited me to go for a drink yesterday afternoon in Cabourg.' There, that wasn't a lie, was it? 'And it would appear she has somehow found out about that.'

Hayden yawned. 'That's all right, then.'

'What is?'

'That it's just teenage hormones in overdrive as usual. But do you think,' he said on a stretch, 'that there is any remote chance of us having a nice quiet family day for once? You know, doing something soothing and tranquil such as bungee jumping from Concorde or feeding man-eating sharks by hand?'

'Oh, but we must go to the Manoir. It's the ideal opportunity for me to talk to my father and sort things out.'

'Quite.' Hayden gave another cavernous yawn. 'That's precisely what I meant.'

*

After washing up the breakfast things, Anne arranged the flowers – she couldn't leave them in that gruesome urn thing. As her hands mechanically divided up the bouquet into about six less frightening bunches diluted with white daisies from the garden, she mulled over what Hayden had said.

He was right in the sense of Verity overreacting if she had found out about her harmless little date with Jean-Pierre – what Anne had *thought* was going to be her harmless little date with Jean-Pierre. But then children always did overreact about things like that. No matter their own extremes, they were more censorious than a public morals committee when it came to their parents' behaviour.

It was odd, though, how and if Verity *had* found out. Maybe Jean-Pierre had simply told her because, obviously, she could not have seen them together because they hadn't been. Anne had been very surprised to see her daughter at the beach when she got back there to pick up Conrad, given she had thought Verity was at home with Hayden. Then again, she hadn't really been at all surprised because her life was getting more like a game of Cluedo with each passing hour. People were never where you expected them to be. The minute you left them safely in one place, they turned up in another, usually with a metaphorical length of lead piping.

Her hands suddenly arrested in the process of squashing stalks of gladioli into a pared down Evian bottle. Oh, God, maybe Verity had seen her with Alain. And if she had, that would look a bit odd, her mother having a drink with a total stranger – oh, shit, maybe Verity had actually seen Alain *kissing* her.

Abandoning flower arranging, Anne made to rush upstairs and have a word with Verity, to tell her to keep quiet about what she had seen – if she had seen it. Then she halted, feeling dizzy with subterfuge. She couldn't tell Verity not to say anything about seeing her with Alain because she had not told Hayden anything about seeing Alain because Verity would think that completely dishonest. Oh, God and double God – what a stupid, stupid mess.

She had fully intended to tell Hayden about Alain yesterday evening but, aside from the fact that with the kids around all the time it was very difficult to have anything like a private chat, Hayden had spent the whole of yesterday evening with his nose in some book by André Gide.

While Anne had cooked supper, fed the baby and got her down for the night, cleared away, washed up, dried up, tidied up and then played a couple of games of Bezique with Conrad, Hayden had sat glued to the sofa with his book. He even took it up to bed with him.

'Where did you get that from?' she asked, as she climbed in beside him. Hayden had not looked up, only muttered that Agnes Fenn had lent it to him.

'And when am I going to meet this Agnes Fenn?' Anne had then asked pleasantly enough, expecting Hayden to say any time. Instead, although he did turn over to face her at this point, it had been with a peculiarly mulish expression on his face.

'Why do you want to meet her?'

Anne had felt baffled. It was such an odd response and he *looked* so odd. She half expected him to say childishly, 'Agnes is my friend, not yours.' But neither of them said anything more at all and – he turned back to his book.

So she had not told him about Alain, and now felt even less like doing so, principally because of his reaction when she had told him about the date with Jean-Pierre.

She had actually had the temerity to assume Hayden might be jealous but no, he had yawned. He had bloody well *yawned*. That must mean he either, a) had such blind faith in her loyalty he could not imagine her straying, or b) thought it impossible that Jean-Pierre could ever be attracted to a wilted old bag like her, or c) did not give a monkey's what she did. Of these options c) was definitely the worst or perhaps b). Then again, a) did not exactly fill her with rapture.

Sighing with exasperation, Anne trawled the kitchen cupboards for another makeshift vase. Seizing the electric kettle – if, as Hayden had mysteriously ruled, they must not use it to boil water it may as well be used for something – Anne crammed it full of the last dahlias, wiped her hands on her jeans and looked distractedly out of the window.

Conrad was showing Martha how to throw windfall apples for Carpenter and Hayden was chopping up the defunct coffee table with an old axe he'd found from somewhere, breaking off occasionally to laugh at Carpenter's antics. Anne felt herself soften; her husband looked lovely. Manual labour in the open air seemed to suit him. It brought out the son of the soil in him, but with an extra dimension. The swain with a brain, she thought dreamily, and gave a long sigh.

She had briefly contemplated leaping on Hayden in bed last night – hopefully squashing André Gide in the process. But she hadn't really been in the mood and there was something horribly demoralising about sex when you weren't in the mood for it. Anyway, she knew very well that she had not been in a fever of passion but rather a fever of desperation to do anything to expunge Alain from her mind.

Damn the wretched man, she cursed, why the hell did he have turn up out of the blue? Hadn't he already done her enough damage? And damn Jean-Pierre, the Machiavellian little jerk. Well, she now knew precisely where he had got *that* particular quality from. The moment she had sat down yesterday and looked properly at Alain, she had understood why Jean-Pierre had always seemed to her to be so peculiarly familiar. The young Frenchman's fair colouring had misled her because it was nothing like courtesy of a young Brad Pitt.

'Ah, yes, Jean-Pierre,' Alain had said, looking smug. 'My son looks wonderfully like me, doesn't he?' Smoothing back his black hair, he had grinned. 'Flirtatious young devil as well. I bet he's made a pass at you.'

'I wouldn't have noticed,' had been Anne's crushing response, privately squirming in the knowledge that a pass was exactly what she had thought Jean-Pierre had been making. But Alain merely roared with laughter.

'Wow, are you still adorably pompous when you want to be?' And, before she could respond, he had leaned impudently across the table and kissed her full on her half-open mouth.

Why on earth had she not walked off at that point? She should never have sat down, never have agreed to have a drink with him in the first place. She only did so because it had seemed the mature and dignified way to behave. But when the arrogant bastard had then had the audacity to kiss her, why did she not just *go*? Because he had got to her, that's why, he still got to her. Whether it was because she and Hayden hadn't been getting on at all well of late, or whether all these years she had merely been kidding herself that she was over him, the fact was that Alain Duval still had the power to get under her skin.

And he knew it.

Giving herself a little shake, Anne fought to demystify the man. He only disturbed her because she suffered from pique. Now in his late fifties, he wasn't even that attractive any longer – no, that was no good. He was. Far from becoming fat and bald, his thick black hair was still remarkably thick and black and his physique remarkably trim, if a tad heavy about the neck and waist. Okay, she could take comfort in the fact that he hadn't made the grade as a painter.

Except 'Oh, I quit *painting* years ago,' he had yesterday informed her, with the condescension of one who finds such an occupation infantile. His English had improved out of all recognition, his accent now sounding oddly American.

'I deal in art now,' he went on, adding as if reading her thoughts, 'working mainly out of New York. Your buddy Gilles helps me out this end.'

'He's not my buddy,' Anne had started to say, when suddenly she realised how infantile *this* sounded. In any event, Alain wasn't listening. He was instead asking her where she would like to go for dinner that evening, at which point she *had* stalked off, a little too late, however, to gain much mileage out of the gesture.

Oh, enough. This wasn't getting her anywhere.

Turning from the window, Anne trudged upstairs. Outside Verity's door, she hesitated and lifted her hand to knock. Then she lowered it again. Britney Spears' *I Wanna Go* was reverberating through the wall – Verity was evidently having a wallow. Best leave her to it, Anne resolved feebly.

Besides, she must wash her disgusting hair and find something to wear. God knows what when Hayden's washing efforts had unfortunately involved a red scrunchie of Verity's, thereby turning not only most of her pants and bras dirty pink but also her best white shirt. All her dresses and skirts were grubby and her jeans downright filthy. Life without a washing machine might be ecologically sound but it had its limitations.

Dispiritedly, Anne settled on a pair of khaki shorts she had bought in a sale and hardly ever wore because Penny said they made her look like a 1960's scoutmaster. All she had left to go on top was a white sleeveless t-shirt, clean but so badly shrunken it flattened her tits into fried eggs. It also meant the wrinkly bits of her upper arms would be on show and the entire outfit was not at all smart, but it was going to be an extremely hot day again and so would do for a casual little poolside picnic.

She filled the tiger bath and got in.

Rubbing shampoo into her hair, Anne expelled Alain from her mind and concentrated on what she was going to say to her father. The flowers were a cunning trick to get in her good books but she must not be blown off course by them. Here, at last, was an opportunity for her to tackle him properly and to try – no, to *make* him see sense. He'd had his cakes and ale. The day of reckoning had arrived.

She would have him home by this evening.

20

By the time they left for the Dérains' diplomatic relations had more or less been restored. The atmosphere was not exactly overflowing with peace and goodwill but Verity had apologised to Hayden, and also to Conrad. In the latter's case, however, because she had wanted to annex his fake Gucci leather belt. Re dress as opposed to redress, Anne reflected cynically. With Verity it was always a trade-off.

At the Manoir awaited another scene.

'Oh, no, please,' whimpered Hayden, as they tripped out of the French windows leading onto the terrace.

Anne might have guessed. Maxine's casual little picnic for a few friends round the pool was a full-blown sit down reception for at least seventy.

An enormous yellow and white striped marquee had been erected on the lawn, its looped-up sides revealing ranks of white-clothed tables bristling with glass and silverware. Squadrons of rented staff with trays of champagne and canapés were zooming all over the place in that legless glide perfected by French waiters. Maxine had even hired a small band with a synthesizer and Celine Dion lookalike. All the male guests seemed to be in suits and ties and the women tarted up to the nines.

Anne stood with her scruffy children and tie-less husband by the door, the baby in her arms and feeling like some downtrodden refugee family brought along to one of those gruesome fund-raising events to bring a tear to the eye. Even Carpenter was looking a wreck because nobody had brushed him since leaving England.

Spotting them, Maxine flapped over wearing a hideous paisley shirtdress that wasn't her sort of thing at all. Perhaps in deference to Walter Pepper she was trying to turn herself into an archetype of the English country gentlewoman. Lady of the Manoir, thought Anne, feeling hysterical. It must be Maxine's latest fantasy.

'The War-wicks!' she squawked, making them sound like embattled candles, and then embraced them all very fondly with the exception of Carpenter. Martha she seized from Anne to embrace twice more before passing her like a tea tray to Dolores, who was hovering nearby looking mutinous in a blue serge uniform apparently modelled on a 1900 British nanny.

Hayden tried to protest as Dolores disappeared with the stunned baby.

'Leave it,' Anne said to him under her breath. 'I'll go and get her back in a minute. Just for God's sake don't anyone let Carpenter off the lead.'

Walter Pepper appeared as Maxine turned to shriek at new arrivals.

'Dad!' Anne was so pleased to see her father that for a moment she forgot she was supposed to be cross with him. They kissed and hugged and then Walter hugged Verity and Conrad and made a great fuss of Carpenter. Finally, he shook hands very warmly with Hayden.

'Glad you were able to make it,' he said, directing them towards the throng of people milling around the terrace. He looked apologetic. 'Sorry about this, though. Not quite what I was expecting. But Gilles and Stephanie are here,' he added, 'and Juno's around somewhere. I don't think you'll know anyone else but will you be all right for a while? Maxine's expecting me to be on parade to greet people.'

'Wait a minute, Dad.' Anne placed a detaining hand on her father's arm. 'I want to have a little talk with –'

'We'll be fine, thanks, Walter.' Taking a firm grip of Anne's elbow, Hayden whisked her off.

'What the hell are you doing?' Anne tried to pull away from him.

'Now is not the time,' he muttered through clenched teeth.

'Then when *is* the time?' she hissed fiercely back. 'I didn't come here to play Happy fucking Families.'

'André!'

Hayden had stopped dead in his tracks, looking thunder-struck as a tall, rangy man glanced round at them from the edge of the crowd. As he turned properly, Anne saw he was one of the very few not in a tie. Instead, he was wearing an ancient safari suit which, coupled with his smile of innocent wonder, made him look like David Attenborough stumbling across mountain gorillas mating.

'Whatever are you doing here, André?' cried Hayden.

The man gave a booming laugh. 'I could say the same to you.'

Conrad was jigging from one foot to the other. 'Dad?' He touched his father's arm. 'This is Danielle.'

Hayden looked at the pretty, boyish teenager. 'Danielle is *your* daughter?' he said to David Attenborough. 'I had no idea. Anne, darling?' He drew her forward. 'This is such a surprise. Let me introduce you. This is André – André Laurent. André lectures in International Affairs at the Sorbonne and used to come to quite a few of my conferences in Brighton.'

Everyone shook hands, André Laurent introducing his wife, Brigitte, and his son, Hugo. The kids then mooched off with Carpenter while Hayden drew André apart to talk shop, leaving the women together.

Brigitte Laurent helped herself to two glasses of champagne from a passing waiter and, handing one to Anne, winced at the Celine Dion clone giving her all to *My Heart Will Go On*. 'Ohmigod,' she said, raising her eyes to heaven.

Anne smiled, feeling suddenly more cheerful.

'Do you know what all this in aid of?' Brigitte waved a hand at the marquee.

Like her husband, Brigitte Laurent's English was completely idiomatic with no more than a trace of an accent. Like her husband, she was tall and lanky and, judging by her hippie kaftan, equally impervious to the dictates of fashion. 'Is Maxine getting married today or something?' she said.

'Heavens, I hope not.' Anne looked alarmed. 'But it is slightly unexpected. According to my father, this was going to be a casual little poolside picnic.'

Brigitte looked curiously at her. 'Is it your father who is going to marry Maxine?'

Not if I can help it, Anne said to herself. 'Possibly. But do you know Maxine well, then?' On first impressions she wouldn't have thought the Laurents at all Maxine's type.

Brigitte shook her head. 'Hardly at all, really. No, it's Juno that André and I know. She invited us today.'

'Oh, yes.' Anne recalled what Jean-Pierre had said about Danielle and Hugo being the children of Juno's friends. 'How do you know Juno?'

'I taught her English at school in Paris and she used to babysit for us when the children were little.' Brigitte smiled. 'She's a lovely young woman. We're all terribly fond of her.'

Another Juno supporter, thought Anne, with an inward groan. Perhaps she ought to start a fan club. Still, Brigitte Laurent did seem rather nice. 'You must be a fantastic teacher,' she said sincerely. 'Juno speaks English brilliantly.'

Brigitte grinned again. Although her face with its strong features was rather masculine, she had a surprisingly attractive smile which made her almost but not quite the *jolie laide* type.

'Thank you. That's nice of you. But I think you'd change your mind if you could hear my own daughter. When it comes to speaking English Danielle seems to be a complete Anglophobe. Either that, or it's simply because *I* want her to speak it – which I suppose is far more likely.'

'Sounds just like Verity.' Anne gave a sympathetic nod. 'I've got to the point where I deliberately don't suggest she does something because I know she'll only straightaway do precisely the opposite.'

'Bloody pubescent daughters,' grumbled Brigitte. 'Who'd have 'em?'

Anne laughed and then they both started giggling, united in the trials of motherhood.

'Why can't they stay babies forever?'

'Which reminds me – ' Anne explained about Martha. 'The doughty Dolores whisked her off.'

'Oh, you are lucky to have a baby.' The Frenchwoman looked wistful. 'Not so long ago André fancied a third child, but I must have left it too late because I found I simply could not get pregnant.'

'No, I know I was really very fortunate.' Anne told her about Martha being a bit of a surprise. 'The best of surprises, though. Because she's gorgeous.'

'Are you bringing her down?'

Anne flicked a glance at the marquee and its glittering tables and pulled a face. 'Don't think so somehow, but I must go and see if she's all right. I'll just get her bag from Hayden.'

'I'll join the men, then.' Brigitte followed behind as Anne wormed her way back through the throng. 'Shall we save you a place at lunch?'

'Yes, please,' said Anne over her shoulder, as she reached the edge of the crowd and saw Hayden and André standing on the lawn where they had drifted apart from the main crush.

Hayden had his back to her, André Laurent holding forth to him about something. 'Of course, I completely understand your problem,' the Frenchman was saying in his fruity but penetrating voice. 'At this stage, I probably wouldn't tell my wife either, but –' His bushy eyebrows suddenly shooting ludicrously skywards, the Frenchman broke off mid-sentence as he caught sight of Anne over Hayden's shoulder.

'LADIES!' he yelled at the top of his voice. At which point Hayden wheeled round so sharply he nearly fell over her.

'ANNE!' he shouted, and, as Brigitte Laurent appeared at Anne's elbow, both men gave a sort of uneasy chortle.

Brigitte considered them. 'And what are you two looking so guilty about?' she demanded teasingly, with an aside wink at Anne. 'Just look at them, Anne. What can they be up to?'

*

Walter Pepper was getting desperate. No sooner did he escape a guest's clutches than Maxine dragged him off to introduce him to someone else. So far he had been pinned down by a la-di-dah miss done up like a dog's dinner, a couple of blimps in blazers with badges on the pocket and now he was trapped by this raddled old crone batting eyelashes like a road sweeper.

They had all turned out to be English as well, which was very shaming.

Maxine had promised that to make up for being so insulting to him in Paris, she would throw a nice little impromptu family do at home *especially* for him, inviting one or two British friends whom she just knew would be his kind of people.

Well, even setting aside the fact that this shindig was not a bit his idea of a little family do, Walter felt insulted all over again if she thought he would have anything in common with these characters. Where on earth had she dug them up from? They were ten times more dubious than the most dubious of some of the dubious types he had already met with Maxine. Was it her idea of a joke or something? Was she, Lord forbid, making *fun* of him?

Craning his neck round the eyelashes, Walter raked the crowd for Anne and Hayden. Anne had looked extremely put out when they arrived and, frankly, he didn't blame her. He had been on the point of ringing at the last minute and telling her not to come after all. But he couldn't think how to say this without sounding rude or nasty – or both. And he had already behaved quite badly enough where his daughter was concerned. In any event, it was quite clear from the determined glint in her eye that she was thinking it high time they had a little chat.

Walter heaved a sigh. The last thing he fancied was a little chat with Anne, or at least a little chat about the subject he knew she wanted a little chat about. Why couldn't she just leave him to paddle his own canoe? Why could she not accept that whether he sank or swam it was his business and his alone?

But it was the same old story. Everybody always thought they knew what was best for you. The first third of your life was spent with your parents thinking they knew what was best for you and the last third with your children thinking the same. Except for the bit in between, when, admittedly, you thought you knew what was best for everyone else, nobody ever allowed you to make your own mistakes in peace.

Maybe this thing with Maxine would turn out to be not such a good idea in the long run but Walter felt it was up to *him* to decide that, if and when the time came. He would make that plain to Anne when he spoke to her, if he ever spoke to her. For now, it was hopeless. He couldn't see anyone in this crush and, anyway, Eyelashes was asking him something.

'What was that?'

'I gather,' she said, treating him to a gummy smile, 'that you are about to become Mr Maxine Dérain Number Five. Or is it Six? I never can keep count.'

Walter stared at her, sorely tempted to point out that she had lipstick on her tooth. 'No,' he said coldly. 'You've got the wrong man.'

*

Her espadrilles making no sound on the tiled floor, Anne padded quickly across the hall and up the wide staircase, pausing a second on the landing. Inside the Manoir all was cool and quiet, save for a distant clattering from the kitchens and the rhubarb hum of partying outside.

She assumed Dolores would have taken Martha to the same little sitting room on the first floor where she had babysat her on the night they all went to the restaurant. It might be better to leave her there if she was all right, at any rate until after lunch, Martha and tables loaded with glassware not being a marriage made in heaven. But first she needed a moment to collect herself.

Nipping into a bathroom further along the powder-blue panelled corridor, she crossed to a linen box and sank down on its cork seat in despair. Was she going mad? She must have misheard André Laurent. Yet the Frenchman's words, or the gist of them, echoed at full volume in her head; something about Hayden having a problem. What problem? Then – what was it he said? *At this stage, I probably wouldn't tell my wife, either.* What wouldn't he tell his wife? Did he mean...? Well, there was only one explanation, wasn't there? Hayden had confessed all to David Attenborough.

Hayden was having an affair.

Anne felt on a sudden physically ill. She *must* have misheard. Yet, if they had been talking about something perfectly innocent, then why had André shut up the way he did? And why had he and Hayden looked so uncomfortable? It wasn't just her. Brigitte had noticed that as well.

All at once, Anne felt like rushing back down to the terrace and demanding a showdown with her husband. This had gone quite far enough, she decided, working herself up into such a lather that, before she knew what she was doing, she had jumped up and marched across the bathroom to fling open the door.

Silently, she closed it again. She *was* going mad, completely off her trolley if she thought she could have some sort of confrontation with Hayden here. Maxine might call the *flics*. No, André had meant something entirely different...

Utterly unconvinced, Anne moved back to the mirror above the basin and listlessly examined her reflection. It wasn't an edifying prospect. Travelling in the Galaxy with all the windows open had whipped her newly washed hair into a thatch of matted ropes like a rusting Rastafarian. Dreadful locks, thought Anne, seizing a comb from her bag and viciously yanking out the tangles.

Why was it that the tousled look, so enchanting at twenty, at forty-five merely turned you into Medusa? She stuck her tongue out. It looked grey and mouldy, which was not surprising because there was a revolting taste in her mouth. She probably had halitosis; she was rotting from the inside out.

Opening the medicine cabinet, she found a bottle of mouthwash and gargled about three caps' full. They left her mouth dry and stinging but that was preferable to gassing people out. Finally, she hitched up her Baden-Powell shorts and tucked in the t-shirt. It hadn't looked too bad in the gloom of the tiger bathroom but now Anne could see it really was indecently tight, each nipple standing out like a glacé cherry on a cupcake. Perhaps she should find Stephanie and ask her to lend her a shirt.

Except Stephanie would doubtless take one look at the cupcakes and offer her one of Dolores' outsize overalls. Oh dear, what was the matter with her these days? It was most unlike her to be so paranoid. Next thing she knew she'd be having hot flushes, which reminded her to flush the loo even though she hadn't used it.

She went in search of Martha.

Well, at least Martha was enjoying herself. Dolores had settled her down in front of a DVD of *Lady and the Tramp*. Martha adored *Lady and the Tramp*. So, it seemed, did Dolores who, having jettisoned her nanny regalia for one of the aforementioned overalls, was engaged upon a credible imitation of Peggy Lee. Leaving the baby's bag, Anne kissed her daughter, thanked Dolores and slipped back out.

Back in the corridor, however, she dithered.

Ever since coming back to Manoir des Tilleuls, she had been possessed by an overwhelming desire to see her old room. Nobody had offered to show her and she had resisted asking because it made her sound like an aged retainer. Perhaps she could just take a quick peek now. Revisiting a scene of her youth might be just what she needed to restore her self-confidence, to rid her mind of mad fancies, to reconcile her with herself.

Leaning over the stairwell, she checked the hall was still empty, galloped swiftly to the far end of the blue passage, and then quietly opened a little door concealed in the panelling. It gave onto a turret with a tiny flight of twisting stone steps. Panting a little with anticipation, she tiptoed up them.

Her room had been in a sort of attic right at the top. Sort of attic because, while it had a skylight window and sloping ceiling and had probably originally been servants' quarters, in Anne's time it had been refurbished in the worst taste of the late 1980's, meaning flock wallpaper, a ruched Austrian blind and fitted shag-pile carpet.

Of course, she'd only spent a couple of months there in the summer of the year she worked for Stephanie. Nonetheless, the room had pissed her off because, although it was warm and comfortable, Anne had felt if she had to be banished to an attic she'd rather bare boards and an iron bedstead so that at least she could imagine herself a struggling painter starving in a garret.

The fantasy did not lend itself to flock wallpaper and fitted shag-pile.

Reaching the last step, she pushed open a door shaped like a bishop's mitre and gasped. It looked lovely. It had been refurbished. Or rather it had been un-refurbished. It had been turned into an artist's studio.

Stepping inside, she padded over what were now stripped floorboards to the centre of the room, blinking at the sunlight flooding the stark white walls and exposed roof beams. A classic *bateau lit*, unmade, stretched along the opposite wall, and under the skylight stood a long, scrubbed pine work bench holding a mishmash of old French mustard jars crammed with brushes, a sketch block and trays of oil paint, palettes and a bottle of turpentine. An easel bearing a blank canvas occupied the far corner, with more blank canvases stacked behind it.

Moving to the work bench, Anne picked up the sketch block and flicked through it – nothing. The palettes were pristine, the brushes new. None of the oil paints had been used and the turps was still sealed. All the paraphernalia of the artist but no sign any of it had ever been used. Puzzled, Anne turned away, immediately spying another, smaller, sketch block partly concealed in the jumble of sheets on the unmade bed.

She stepped forward to pick it up.

This one had been used; it was nearly full of intricate pencil studies. Intrigued, Anne flipped over the pages. The drawings recalled Leonardo's designs for fantastical machines – slightly mad, yet exquisitely executed and possessed of a singular force.

Suddenly she froze. She saw the empty wine bottle, the smeared glass and the crumpled cigarette packet on the floor beside the bed. She saw draped over the back of a wooden chair a white t-shirt and what looked like a pair of men's underpants. She saw the ashtray on the bedside table spilling butts everywhere. What on earth did she think she was doing? The bed had obviously been slept in; this was obviously someone's room – someone's *bed*room – and that someone's personal possessions. And here was she prying into them.

Dropping the sketch block back on the bed so quickly it might have burnt her, Anne made to turn and run when, before she could move a muscle, a voice behind her made her jump out of her skin.

Scarlet with embarrassment, she wheeled round.

Alain was lounging in the doorway, sporting a white suit and a quizzical smile.

'Looking for something?' he said.

21

There were times, Verity decided exhaustedly, when you could really go off Carpenter. If he wasn't giving great graveyard coughs because he had throttled himself pulling – Carpenter never had been any good on the lead, even an extending one – he was winding himself like a yo-yo round people's legs or lifting *his* leg on every tree and shrub. Carpenter eked out his pee too so that each received individual attention. Hugo kept offering to hold him to give her wrists a break, which was nice of him.

Hugo was far less boring than she had thought yesterday. She had discovered he spoke English brilliantly, like an English person, in fact. Unfortunately, however, he still hadn't anything in the looks department, being neck-achingly tall and skinny – his parents were like streaks. And his clothes were mega gross. Today he was wearing a gruesome Hawaiian shirt thing and a pair of nerdish brown corduroys that made his legs look so like tree trunks – if very thin ones – that Verity dare not let Carpenter near them.

Hugo was, however, amazingly easy to chill with. Conrad and the ladette had gone for a swim in the pool, but Hugo had opted to stay with her and Carpenter, asking her a lot of questions about herself and really listening to the answers. She could see he fancied her, he wasn't just being polite. It was funny the way that stood out a mile in someone when you didn't fancy them. Whereas when you did, you could never tell. It was a pity she didn't.

But still, it made her feel better after all that rubbish with Jean-Pierre, not to mention this latest business of her mother snogging some total stranger in the middle of Cabourg. That was pretty iffy whichever way you looked at it. Yet, could Mum really be having an affair? Mum despised infidelity. The reason she and Dad had split was because Dad was forever cheating – or so Anne had told her years later. Verity had been able to see Anne's point of view, although it had turned her off both of them for quite a while.

Carpenter had at last calmed down a bit and was panting like a headcase instead. Hugo went off and fetched him some water, bringing it back in a champagne ice bucket which struck Verity as rather a cool thing to do, especially as Hugo also brought back some glasses and the remains of a bottle of champagne for them. 'I wish we had some strawberries,' he said, pouring the wine.

'Why?'

'Because champagne tastes beautiful with strawberries. Haven't you seen *Pretty Woman*? I'm crazy about film and that's one of my favourite old movies.'

He gave her a kind of cute grin. 'You look like Julia Roberts,' he said shyly.

Verity looked at him to see if he meant it. He did. She could tell he did. Julia Roberts. Well. She looked away because the compliment had made her feel a bit hot and then back at him again.

You know, Hugo wasn't really *that* bad looking...

*

'What the hell are you doing here?'

'I could ask you precisely the same question.'

Backing away, Anne tossed her head. 'It's none of your damn business.'

'No?' Alain looked amused. 'Well, you see, I was looking for my son. This is Jean-Pierre's bedroom. You are in my son's bedroom.'

Shit, thought Anne, that's all I need. 'I'm sorry, I didn't know that,' she said stiffly. 'Anyway, I'm going now. So let me by, please.' She made a gesture for him to step aside but he did not move, continuing to stand bang in front of the door, blocking her exit with his big white-clad body. Coolly and casually, he glanced over at the untouched work bench.

'Not much of a painter, is he?' he said, throwing her an audacious little wink.

Anne treated him to a stony stare. 'Let me by, Alain.'

'But Anne, my love, you have not answered my question. Or shall I answer it for you? Shall I say it seems to me that you are here in this room on a little trip down what you English call the 'memory lane' – no?'

Anne felt her heart begin to thump unpleasantly hard. 'I'm not your *love*,' she said, as calmly as possible, 'and I have not the slightest idea what you're talking about.'

'Of course you do. This was *your* bedroom.'

'Was it?'

'You know it was. As do I. That summer I came down from Paris for the weekend and you sneaked me up here one night – remember?' Alain gave a little laugh of pleasure at the recollection. 'Yes, I think you will agree it was a night to remember.'

'You flatter yourself. Now please get out of my way.'

Still he did not move. Instead, he affected a soulful expression. 'You know, I am so glad we meet again like this. I had no chance yesterday but I wanted to apologise to you.'

'Apologise to me?' Anne eyed him suspiciously. 'Apologise to me for what?'

'For the way I treated you those many years ago. It was very bad, but you know what?' Waving a hand, Alain resumed his self-satisfied smirk. 'I could not help myself. You were so beautiful it was not my fault. You made me forget myself.'

For a long moment Anne considered him. How, she asked herself, had she ever managed to get herself mixed up with a man like this? Was she indeed a fool, or was it not her fault? She had thought him the best thing that had ever happened to her. How could she have known he would turn out to be the worst?

'I think the only thing you forgot, Alain,' she said, presently but pointedly, 'was your *wife*.'

'I am divorced now,' he replied, as if that made it better.

'So? You weren't divorced then. Your wife then was someone you found it convenient to –' Anne twiddled her fingers in the air '– *forget*. And, as far as I was concerned, someone you continued to forget for the best part of four years.'

'But Anne, my love –'

Anne lost her temper. 'Oh, for goodness' sake, shut up!' she shrieked. 'My love, my arse! It wasn't only your wife you forgot! When I turned up at your studio in Paris all those years ago, believing I was going to give you a lovely surprise, believing everything you had promised about us living together, about me moving to Paris, about *us* marrying, what was it I found? Not just you and your wife together, all lovey-dovey, but another tiny detail you so conveniently *forgot*.' Anne paused, almost panting with fury.

'She was pregnant. Your wife was bloody pregnant!'

In the dead silence that followed, she was gratified to notice Alain had at last begun to look discomfited – if not nearly enough.

'It was an accident,' he muttered.

'An *accident*?' Anne started to laugh only abruptly to stop as something incredible occurred to her. 'My God, I've just realised who that child was – is. The child your wife was carrying then is Jean-Pierre, isn't it? Well, from the little I know of Jean-Pierre, I somehow doubt that he'd appreciate being called an accident.'

There was a short pause as they glared at each other.

Then Alain gave a shrug. 'You knew what you were doing,' he said.

*

Verity was just about to say something nice to Hugo in return for his lovely Julia Roberts compliment when Hayden came over.

Where was her mother, he asked. Verity said she had no idea, thinking it was funny the way Hayden sometimes did that, acting like she was her mother's jailer or something. But Condy had once told her that Mum did it to him about Hayden, so doubtless it was just another one of those weird things step parents did. Anyway, Hayden then ordered her to go and find her mother because everyone was about to sit down and eat.

She was in the house with Martha, he added, at which point Verity was just about to ask why he didn't go and get her himself, then, when the synthesizer shut off with a strangled bleep. As an awed hush fell everywhere, Verity saw her grandfather straightening up from bending down behind it.

Grandpa, it seemed, had literally pulled the plug on the band. After a second or two, however, people started to drift over to the marquee.

'Will you sit next to me?' said Hugo.

*

Trapped in the attic, Anne felt a huge surge of contempt for Alain, and a smaller one for herself. 'Oh, I know,' she said bitterly. 'I know I was only too willing to play Trilby to your stupid Svengali, except –'

'Exactly.' He cut across her. 'So you cannot put the blame on me.'

'Except when we started I was eighteen and you were thirty-two.'

'It makes no difference.' Alain looked sulky. 'You were an adult. You were free to choose. We were two people free to fall in love.'

'Oh, for God's sake, how can anybody be *free* when they're married?'

He looked hard at her. 'The point is that I never meant to hurt you.'

'*Hurt* me? You wasted four fucking years of my life!'

Realising she was on the point of tears, Anne knew she had to get out. 'You're nothing but a vain and ridiculous old man,' she said icily. 'And I'm a fool to give you the time of day. Now get out of my way.'

She made to barge past him but he grabbed her.

'Please, Anne, I'm so sorry! I loved you! I think I still love you!'

'Oh, grow up!' Fighting to get away from him, Anne caught sight of something over his shoulder and was suddenly still. Verity and Carpenter were standing in the doorway.

It was difficult to say which of them looked the most shocked.

*

'Let go of me! LET ME GO!'

'No, stop!' Alain struggled to restrain her. 'Don't leave me like this! I love you!'

But Anne wrenched herself away from him, leaping down the turret staircase faster than a free runner.

At the bottom the blue-panelled passage was empty. Racing to the end, Anne almost hurled herself over the gallery as she frantically scanned the hall below. The red hair was just bobbing through the French windows. 'Verity, wait!' she screeched, but it was no good.

Daughter and dog disappeared.

By the time she had galloped down the staircase four steps at a time, skidded across the hall and out into the garden there was no sign of either of them – or anyone else for that matter. The terrace was deserted save for a bow-tied waiter collecting glasses.

Anne looked over to the marquee. It was throbbing with noise and occupants, the light breeze ruffling the pennant flying from its top and making it look like an ocean liner about to sail away across the lawn. Wincing, she hobbled over, her calves killing her. You certainly needed to be fit for this life of drama.

Inside, the roar of conversation hit her like a slap in the face. It was packed in there, waiters contorting themselves like giant eels between tables crammed with such a sea of gabbling faces that for a moment Anne could not make out anyone. A fresh wave of panic assailed her. She was terrified Verity might do something silly.

Then she spotted her, sitting with Conrad and some other kids at a table in the far corner. She looked absolutely fine. In fact, judging by the way she was giggling, Verity was having a high old time. Carpenter was sitting on a chair between her and Hugo Laurent, also having a high old time because they had tucked a napkin into his collar and were feeding him breadsticks. Verity glanced up at that moment and frowned briefly at her mother but with no more than the sort of mild irritation usually reserved for finding that annoying last teaspoon once you've started up the dishwasher.

Anne looked away, feeling relieved but at the same time oddly deflated. Hayden's arm was waving at her from another table. Wearily, she squeezed through the gaps to the place they had saved for her between André Laurent and a huge man.

'I am Hans,' the man informed her, leaping to his feet and not quite clicking his heels but somehow giving the impression he very much wanted to – he was German. His eyes lighted on the fried eggs. Not surprising when, as a result of her exertions, they were wobbling about all over the place. 'And I am coming in Hamburg,' he said excitedly.

'Is Martha all right, darling?' Hayden asked, as she fumbled into her chair.

'Fine,' she croaked.

'This is Cindy.' His tone deceptively expressionless, Hayden introduced the young woman between him and Hans. 'And her husband Malc.'

From across the table, a man in a baby blue seersucker suit raised a hand but otherwise did not pause in telling Brigitte Laurent how many millions he made out of microchips.

On Hayden's other side, Anne saw Juno, back to her usual outlandish attire, this time consisting of a fringed suede squaw dress and Red Indian plaits. Given Cindy was sporting a white leather waistcoat and ponyskin cowboy hat, Hayden looked like a bandit captured by the Lone Ranger and Tonto.

'Hiya, Annie!' cried Cindy. She was apparently American with an artificially pumped-up bosom and teeth whiter than a miniature picket fence. 'Your man Hi-den has been tellin' us all about you,' she went on, whereupon Anne heard Estuary English breaking through California.

'Have I?' said Hayden in surprise.

Cindy didn't appear to hear him. 'All about your cute liddle Marsha –'

'Martha,' Anne corrected quietly.

'And how your wonderful old poppa is marryin' Maxy.'

Hayden contemplated the tented ceiling for a moment before turning very deliberately to talk to Juno. Cindy had just opened her mouth for the next assault when, fortunately, a waiter chose the moment to slide in front of her a gold-rimmed white plate laden with a shiny tranche of *pâté de fois gras*.

'Wot's this?' she demanded in horror, poking the truffle in its centre and completely forgetting her accent.

Malc looked up. 'Don't eat this stuff, babes,' he ordered. 'It'll send your salt levels way over.'

'Okay.' Cindy obediently pushed her plate away. 'There's a bleedin' stone in it, anyway.'

A comical rictus of disbelief curving his mouth, André Laurent seemed on the point of saying something and then changed his mind as, leaning forward to spear up the rejected pâté, Hans swallowed it in a single magnificent gulp.

'*Das is gut.*' The German beamed happily at Anne.

'Very,' she agreed. Hans was really rather sweet.

'I hear from Hayden that you've moved over here,' André said on her other side.

Anne turned warily to him. He sounded friendly enough but, if he was in cahoots with Hayden, it might just be an act. 'That's right,' she said cautiously. 'Hayden's got a fantastic new job in Caen. Has he told you about it?'

'Um, not really.' Averting his eyes, André concentrated on pouring her some wine. 'Actually, he was talking mostly about you.'

'Me?'

'Yep. He told me that you're an illustrator, quite a brilliant one, I hear, but that you are also an extremely talented painter.'

'Oh, I don't know about that.'

'Gosh, Anne!' Grabbing a respite from microchips, Brigitte looked admiringly across the table. 'Are you really a painter? How very exciting. I'd love to see your work. André and I buy quite a lot of contemporary –'

Malc cut straight across her. 'Don't waste your money on modern crap,' he said contemptuously. 'Go for the real stuff. Paid two million bucks for a Monet in New York last month but, believe me, it's a no brainer when it comes to turning a fast trick.'

'I don't like that Monnit,' droned Cindy. 'He can't colour in proper.'

There was a slightly stunned pause before everyone began talking at once.

'*Pour l'amour de Dieu*!' muttered André Laurent to Anne under the babel. 'Where does one find a woman like that?'

'On the Phoney Express?'

Looking for a second baffled, André gave a sudden loud guffaw of amusement. 'You and Hayden must come to dinner,' he said warmly.

'Thank you, we'd love to.' It must be okay, thought Anne. This man is lovely and I'm just imagining things. But the next moment she wasn't so sure.

'Actually, I'm glad we've got this chance to talk. I want to tell you about something I think might interest you.' Oblivious of Anne's sudden change of expression, the Frenchman picked up a fork to tuck into his pâté.

'What... what do you mean?'

'Hey, don't look so alarmed!'

André flicked her a puzzled little smile. 'It's good, or at least, I think it could be good for you. You see, I've got these English friends who have bought a vineyard in Provence. The place was pretty run down when they bought it but they've got it going again with a view to specialising in producing rosé – rosé wine specifically for the British market.'

'Oh, what a fantastic idea!' Anne felt herself perking up. 'I love rosé.'

'Do you?' André wrinkled his nose. 'Not a fan, myself. Anyway, there is, of course, a lot of rosé already on the British market, but my friends believe it still has unexploited potential, that it could catch on in Britain a little the way Prosecco has become so fashionable. However, they are desperate for someone to design a label for them, someone to create a *look* for their promotional material, and to date all they've ended up with are proposals for pretty little pictures of pink grapes.'

'Yuck.'

'Quite. So, would you be interested, then?'

'Possibly, although it's not an area I normally go for.'

'But surely,' André said pleasantly, 'there's nothing to lose in trying something different, is there?'

'No, not really.'

In fact, Anne was surprised to find that for the first time in over a year her head had immediately begun to buzz with all the old inspiration. She had never lacked ideas. Her attention drifted...

What was that joke she had cracked to Hayden that evening all those months ago when the possibility of them moving to France first came up? La vie en *rosé*, punning on the famous song by Edith Piaf. Could she work up something along those lines? *La vie en rose.* It was such a beautiful emotion. Suddenly she choked on her pâté. How full of joy life had seemed then and how different reality was now.

'Anne? Are you okay?'

'Fine. Sorry. It went down the wrong way.' Drinking some water, she cleared her throat. 'And I am interested.' She smiled at the Frenchman. '*Very.*'

'Great! Well, how about I give my friends a call and pass on to them your number and you can take it from there? It's not just the wine they're launching; they're also setting up wine-tasting holidays.'

André launched into a detailed explanation of his friends' business but, however hard she tried to concentrate, Anne found herself distracted once again. Alain had chosen the moment to stroll into the marquee.

There he was, prancing around in his stupid white suit, stopping at tables, laughing down at some, embracing proffered cheeks at others – he might have been Gérard sodding Depardieu for all the lick-lipping adulation he was receiving. He obviously knew a lot of people but then he was just the type to be in with Maxine and her gang. The next minute Anne's heart missed a beat as she watched him at last slide into a place someone had saved for him.

Stephanie's friends, Stephanie's little friends. Right. So now she knew. Anne didn't need another confession session over blasted apple tart to work out what was going on.

Alain's place was being saved by none other than Stephanie Dérain.

'Hey, are you still with me?'

'I'm so sorry!' Anne suddenly realised André was peering curiously into her face. 'I was... er... I was ... um...goodness, there's such a din in here! What were you saying?'

'I was telling you how I know these people with the vineyard. We were all students together years ago at the LSE. You see, we – '

What was it Stephanie had said? Anne cast her mind back. *I nearly always choose someone young* – sorry – *yong. They can give me what I want.* Well, there was no way Alain could be classed as young. Nevertheless, he would certainly be able to give Stephanie what she wanted. In fact, judging by the way Stephanie was now whispering in his ear, her fingers trailing proprietorially through the thick Byronic curls in the nape of his neck, he'd already given it.

Anne felt her whole body on fire with rage and humiliation. Up to this point, she had been assuming Jean-Pierre had put Alain onto her, although she had never quite fathomed how Jean-Pierre could have made the connection between her and his father. Clearly, she now saw, it hadn't been Jean-Pierre at all, it had been Stephanie. *Stephanie.*

Stephanie and Alain had been amusing themselves – at Anne's expense. Anne experienced an abrupt crucifying mental vision of them lying in bed together laughing at her, laughing themselves sick. Far from being Anne's friend, Stephanie had compromised her in the foulest way possible. She had –

'Anne? Are you really okay?'

Oh, God. André Laurent was peering at her again, this time in concern.

'Your hands are shaking.' He nodded down at them.

'It's the drink,' Anne said desperately, and then squawked 'Sorry!' as the Frenchman looked alarmed.

She forced a laugh. 'Sorry,' she repeated. 'Silly joke. I'm absolutely fine.'

André inclined his head across the marquee. 'Who's that man you were watching, the charmer pawing Madame Stephanie? Do you know him?'

'No.' Anne flicked a last look at her one-time lover. 'I don't know him at all.'

22

'Are you feeling better now?'

'Much.' Verity tried to smile. 'I just suddenly felt really sick for some reason.'

'It was very hot under that canopy,' Hugo said kindly. 'I expect that was it.'

'I expect so,' she agreed noncommittally.

It wasn't why at all. She had felt sick in the middle of lunch not because of the heat, but because in her feverish attempts to act normal, she had been forcing down such great lumps of un-chewed food that a wodge of potato had stuck in her throat and nearly choked her. And that was when she had already been feeling completely choked.

She cast a sidelong timid look at Hugo. He looked calmly back. This wasn't fair. Hugo was too nice to be lied to. Verity drew a deep breath. 'Actually, it wasn't that at all.'

'No.'

'I was upset about something.'

'I know.'

'But I can't tell you what.'

'That's okay.'

She smiled at him in relief. 'But I'm fine now. We can go back if you want.'

Hugo shook his head. 'I don't unless you do.' He glanced down at Carpenter wagging his stumpy tail hopefully between them. 'But he does.'

'No, he wants a walk.'

The French boy hesitated for a fraction of a second before passing her the dog's lead and then taking Verity's other hand very firmly in his own. 'Let's blow, then.'

*

'Thank God!' said Hayden, as he and Anne escaped with the Laurents to the terrace. 'Another minute of that and I would have been sick in her Stetson.'

'Oh, Hi-den,' squeaked André, imitating Cindy's tinny little voice. He was a bit tight. 'You need Ten Gallon Hat Re-adjustment Therapy.'

'Quite – how many therapists did she say she had? I lost count.'

'Nine,' Brigitte informed him, 'not including the two for Malc.'

'I don't know who was worse.' Hayden shook his head in disbelief. 'Microchip-on-his-shoulder or Cindy Doll.'

'Barbie, you mean,' Brigitte corrected him with mock severity. 'Definitely Barbie, given the anatomically impossible figure.'

'An American guy I knew at university,' mused André, 'wrote his entire PhD thesis on Ken's suppressed violence towards Barbie. Could this be the case here?'

'Uh huh.' Brigitte now corrected her husband. 'Cindy said Malc was her *rock*.'

'Oh, how original,' drawled André. 'Did you write it down so we won't forget it?'

'Help!' Hayden looked nervously round as guests started spilling out of the marquee and moving to help themselves to coffee from a trestle table set up by the side of the swimming pool. 'They'll be out in a minute. Can't we go somewhere they won't find us?'

'You mean you want to play Hi-den seek?' André was obviously in his element.

The next minute Hans came over to them, looking deeply puzzled. Brigitte asked him what was the matter.

'I think Fraulein Cindy is very furious with me,' he said.

'Now why should that be?'

'I do not know.' Hans looked as if he might be about to cry. 'I ask only how often she is mounted.'

André started practically to cry with laughter.

'It is because of her cowboy hat,' Hans explained quite seriously. 'But this is a bad thing I am saying to a lady?'

André wiped his eyes. 'Hans, my friend?' He clapped the German on his mighty shoulder. 'That was no lady.'

Hans looked more puzzled than ever. 'No lady?' He looked down at his chest and then suspiciously back at André. 'You are saying she is a man?'

'I shouldn't worry about it.' Brigitte patted the German's arm. 'Let me get you some coffee instead.'

'I've got a better idea.' Hayden eyed the waiters whizzing round with vast trays of *petit fours*. 'Why don't we sneak off and you all come back to our place for coffee? You too, Hans.'

'We can't go now,' said Anne.

'Oh, come on, darling.' Hayden gave her shoulders a jollying hug. 'I know you wanted to have a chat with your father but it's hopeless in this set-up.'

'I didn't mean that, I meant Verity has gone off somewhere. According to Conrad, she felt poorly during lunch and went outside with Carpenter. And Hugo apparently went with her,' she added to Brigitte. 'I don't know where they went but we'll have to wait for them to come back.'

'Oh, bloody hell.' Hayden looked thoroughly fed up.

'Never mind,' said André. 'Another time, maybe.'

Hans agreed and explained he was sorry but he was obliged to leave now also, because his Mutter was arriving from Hamburg this afternoon.

'Give me your phone number, Anne,' Brigitte said to her when Hans had gone, having bade a fond farewell to them all. She got a pencil and diary out of her bag. 'It would be lovely to meet up.'

Anne told her. 'Yes, look, I'm sorry about the coffee.'

'Don't worry about it.' Brigitte tucked the diary away. 'We've got a missing son, anyway. We'll fix up to get together soon.'

'It's just bloody annoying,' chuntered Hayden. 'I've had quite enough of this place for one afternoon.'

'It sounds to me,' observed André, 'as if your mutter has arrived already.'

Hayden gave an unwilling grin. 'Actually, my mutter arrived about –' His eyes suddenly fixed on something beyond their group. 'There she is!' he exclaimed.

Turning round, Anne saw Verity and Hugo about to edge their way past the trestle coffee table in front of the swimming pool,

Verity hanging on to a straining Carpenter and Hugo hanging on to a blushing Verity.

'Verity!' yelled Hayden.

'Don't tell her off!' squeaked Anne – too late.

'Where the hell have you been?' her husband bellowed.

As if in slow motion, Anne watched her daughter come to a complete halt, her face turn chalk white and her thumb very slowly but entirely deliberately depress the black button on the extending lead.

Anne closed her eyes as Carpenter shot forward.

*

'Well, that's all I needed,' snarled Hayden, getting back into the Galaxy and yanking the door shut. In his haste to remove his family from the scene of the crime, he had backed into a Maserati. 'Now I've got to shell out for a designer bumper as well as for the cleaning of a sodding swimming pool.'

In the back of the car, Verity began to cry. 'Maxine won't expect you to pay for the pool,' she sobbed.

'If you think for one moment that I'm going to be beholden to someone who has such appalling friends then you've got another think coming.'

Slamming the Galaxy into first gear, Hayden picked a chocolate fondant out of his ear. Besides knocking the coffee table and its considerable contents into the swimming pool, Carpenter's extended lead frolics had sent a tray of *petit fours* airborne. 'Anyone would think these damn things were *petit millions*,' he snapped as he hurled it out of the window. 'They're all over the bloody place.'

'What did that Maserati man say to you, Dad?' asked Conrad.

'It pains me to repeat it.'

'Was he very angry?'

'Put it this way,' growled Hayden as they shot off down the drive. 'In the last five minutes I've learnt a whole new vocabulary of French obscenities.'

*

'What do you want?'

Verity had opened the door a crack. She had her hair scraped back under a black stretch bandeau and dabs of spot blaster all over her face.

'I've brought you some breakfast.'

'I don't want any breakfast.'

'Come on,' Anne said cajolingly. 'You haven't had anything to eat since yesterday lunchtime.'

'I'm not hungry.'

'Well, just come downstairs, then.'

'No.'

Anne felt a twitch of exasperation. 'Verity, you can't stay locked away up here forever.' Verity's expression clearly told her she could. The moment they got home yesterday Verity had taken to her bedroom, refusing even to come down for supper. Unable to see how she could risk any sort of confrontation that might expose the Alain incident with Hayden around, Anne had been obliged to leave her to it.

Early this morning, however, with the clean clothes situation reaching crisis point, Hayden had taken six dustbin bags of mainly pants along with Martha and Conrad in search of a launderette, so the coast was clear. 'Will you let me in, then?' she asked patiently.

Verity remained sullen and unbudgeable. 'Why should I?'

'Because I think it's high time we had a little talk.'

'What you really mean,' Verity said stonily, 'is that you want to tell me a load of lies.' But she turned away, leaving the door open.

Anne pushed in before her daughter could change her mind and, kicking the door shut behind her, looked for somewhere to put the breakfast tray. The bedside table was a forest of apple cores, empty Coca-Cola tins and CDs, and the chest of drawers bristling with make-up, every spot cure under the sun and squeezed-out tubes of Piz Buin. Shoving the tray down on the floor, she removed a tangle of bras and bikini tops from a chair and sat down. 'Okay. Let's start by you telling me when I have ever lied to you.'

Verity flumped herself down on the bed. 'You're screwing that funny old man.'

'I'm not.'

'That's the first time.'

'Verity –' Anne searched for the right words. 'Things aren't always what they seem, you know.'

'I know that, I'm not a child. But don't tell me that when I found you wrapped round that guy yesterday lunchtime – in a *bedroom*, not to mention snogging him in a bar in Cabourg – that it wasn't obvious what you were doing with him.'

'For heaven's sake!' Guilt made Anne irritable. 'I was not *snogging* him in Cabourg any more than I was wrapped round him yesterday afternoon. How did you know where I was, anyway?'

'I heard your voice. And I saw you with him in Cabourg.'

There was pause while Anne racked her brains for what to say next.

'There you are, you see?' Verity looked triumphant. 'You look guilty.'

'Well, I don't know why. I hardly know the man –'

'Yes, you do. You know you do. Who is he?'

'If you must know, he's Jean-Pierre's father.' There was another pause. Anne decided to come clean.

'Look, okay, I used to know him years ago, when I was an au pair to Juno. We had a relationship, actually. But not a very happy one. And then I... bumped into him in Cabourg. As for yesterday lunchtime... well, he turned up when I was sneaking a peek at my old room.'

'It strikes me that you did a lot more than just bump into him.'

'Yes, well, he jumped on me. He's a shit.'

There was further silence while Verity picked at her drying spot blaster. 'Then that's entirely different,' she conceded with a disapproving little sniff. With that headband on she looked like poor old Mo Mowlam defending the Good Friday Peace Agreement. 'Have you told Hayden about it?'

Anne hesitated. 'Um... no.'

'Well, why not, if you've got nothing to hide?'

Why not indeed? 'Because it's not important,' Anne said aloud. 'He's a creep and I prefer to forget the whole silly business.'

'So you're not having an affair?'

'Is that what's really bothering you?'

'Not exactly,' said Verity, in her occasional adult fashion. 'What you choose to do is entirely up to you.'

'What, then?'

Verity let out a long sigh. 'It's just the way you, like, seem to have, like, double standards.'

'How do you mean?' For once the 'like' encouraged rather than aggravated. Its reinsertion meant Verity was beginning to feel better.

'Okay.' Verity spoke rapidly. 'I mean that one minute you're divorcing Dad because he's cheating on you and the next you're, like, doing exactly the same thing yourself.'

Anne considered her daughter. It was true what she had said a moment ago – Verity wasn't a child any more. 'Well, of course, if I were having an affair,' she said carefully, 'then what you say would be entirely justified. But I'm not,' she added firmly. 'I promise you, I am not.'

There was yet another pause.

'Don't you believe me?'

Instead of answering the question, Verity looked oddly at her mother. 'Hayden wouldn't do that to you, you know.'

Anne stared at her daughter. 'You say that very convincingly. What makes you so sure?'

'Oh, I don't know.' Dropping her eyes, Verity lifted her shoulders in a vague shrug. 'I just know. I just, like, know that about Hayden.'

'ANNE!'

Hayden's voice shouting up the stairs made them both start.

'Are you up there?'

Anne called an affirmative. There followed the sound of pounding feet, a knock on the door and then it flew open.

'Guess what?' Hayden looked pleased with himself. 'The Laurents have just rung me and invited us all over to their place for the rest of the day. Or rather, darling,' he explained, 'you can have lunch with Brigitte. André and I are going to play a round of golf.'

'Golf?' Anne blinked.

'The washing's all done and dried,' Hayden went on. 'And the Laurents' house is right on the seafront at Cabourg so no problem about the beach. But if you like the idea,' he turned to Verity, 'there's a Jean-Luc Godard film showing at the ciné-club in Caen this afternoon, which I'm told Hugo would very much like to see if you would like to see it with him. You can go over on the train.'

'Sick!' Tearing off her bandeau, Verity leapt for the door. 'Must wash my hair!' Then she stopped short and hung her head. 'Sorry about the swimming pool,' she mumbled to her stepfather.

'Forget it.'

Verity looked up in surprise – Hayden was smiling.

'I phoned Maxine a while ago,' he said, 'to apologise and ask what the cost of cleaning would be. She was still in her *boudoir* but she very kindly refused, on account of the pool being due to be emptied and cleaned this week in any event. So there's no great harm done.'

'Oh, *good*.' Verity stood on one leg and looked relieved.

'Well, jump to it, then,' Hayden chided. 'Get your glad rags on because I want to leave in half an hour."

'Oh, shit – I mean, oh, gosh.' Verity shot out.

'Hayden?'

'Mmm?' He turned to Anne. 'You know, I feel quite grateful to Carpenter.'

'Why?'

'Because, according to Maxine in her *boudoir*, the only person annoyed about the pool is that pillock Gilles because he's missing his morning swim.' Hayden's shoulders shook with laughter.

'Hayden?'

'Yep?'

'Did I hear you say you were going to play golf?'

23

The very next time Gilles was rude about Carpenter, Walter decided he'd say something very rude to him. Whatever Carpenter had done had been an accident. The swimming pool was perfectly all right, anyway, now the handyman had sucked the sugar lumps off the bottom with his hoover thingamajig. The water might perhaps be a trifle on the instant coffee side, but in view of Gilles's weedy body already being tanned to that colour, Walter couldn't see it making a lot of difference if he was busting to swim his stupid lengths.

Debating whether to point this out, Walter decided against, reflecting that Gilles was only making the most of the opportunity yet again to provoke him, to provoke him the way Gilles had been trying to provoke him ever since Walter had returned from Paris with Maxine.

Gilles, of course, had never been what one might term friendly, but before the Paris trip Walter hadn't noticed him much. Gilles had hardly ever been around, occupying himself, Walter had gathered, with some old dinghy he kept at the seaside. But whether she had sunk – pity if she had that she hadn't gone down with him on board – lately Gilles always seemed to be hanging about, especially at breakfast, going out of his way to be goading.

Be it snide little digs at Englishmen in general or at Walter in particular, he never missed a chance to play the smart alec which meant, unfortunately, that Carpenter's folly had simply been grist to his mill. Now, for the third time, he was whining about the expense of cleaning the pool and not because it was anything like down to him. As far as Walter could make out, Gilles was a complete limpet on his mother – Maxine paid for everything. But because it was another way to wind up Walter.

Walter listened to him in silence. Not that he had not fully intended all along to bear the entire cost of cleaning the pool himself but he wasn't going to tell Gilles that. It was between him and Maxine, whom he began to hope very much would come down before he gave Gilles the satisfaction of making him lose his temper.

Fortunately, Maxine chose that very moment to sweep onto the terrace with a great swirl of a long diaphanous housecoat thing that made Walter think of Isadora Duncan. Actually, it really was rather hussy-ish but he was so relieved to see her, even though he was cheesed off with her too on account of that awful party yesterday, that he stroked her hand and kissed her back as she embraced him on both cheeks.

Gilles promptly directed a flood of violent French at his mother. Again bloomin' ill-mannered when he knew perfectly well that Walter would not be able to understand a word of it.

Walter decided to ignore him, concentrating instead on pouring Maxine her bowl of black coffee, stirring in three sugars the way he knew she liked it. 'Does he always behave like this in the mornings?' he said quietly to her, jerking his head at Gilles.

Maxine did not reply, but her face seemed to turn rather pale and the hand that wavered towards her coffee trembled. That did it.

'How dare you speak to your mother like that?' Walter heard himself saying suddenly and very loudly.

There followed a ringing pause during which Maxine's eyes widened in admiration and Gilles's narrowed in fury. 'It is nothing to do with you what I say to my *maman*,' he said haughtily.

'It's everything to do with me when you're upsetting her. *Disgraceful* way to behave to a lady.' Walter felt the bit between his teeth. 'I tell you, if I were younger and you my son, I'd not think twice about giving you a damned good hiding.'

'This is *incroyable*, unbelievable,' sputtered the Frenchman. ''Oo do you think you are? First you make the seduction of my mother for 'er riches and now your crazy dog ruins my exercise programme. You look at the water.'

Leaping to his feet, Gilles stalked over to the edge of the pool. 'You come and you look,' he demanded, gesticulating away in his silly G-string trunks. 'The dog is mad, a *lunatique*. 'The dog 'as destroyed the pool. It is all dirty. Your crazy dog 'as denied me my morning lengths.'

'Denied you your morning lengths?' Rising slowly to his feet, Walter strolled over to the Frenchman, pausing in front of him for a fraction of a second before giving the puny chest a hefty shove. 'Well, how about measuring one, then.'

It was the most childish thing he had ever done – and the most gratifying. 'There.' Ripping his wallet from the inside pocket of his jacket, he seized a wad of notes and flung them into the heaving brown water. 'This'll pay for your bloomin' pool.

'Just don't ever let me hear you insulting my grand-dog again.'

*

'But you've always said you hate golf.'

'I used to play a lot when I was married to Julia.'

'No, you didn't, you didn't play at all. You told me that you only joined the golf club because it was somewhere you could go to get away from Julia. You told me you used to sit in the clubhouse and read John Le Carré.'

Hayden remarked that he wished Anne were not always possessed of such a devastatingly accurate memory.

'Yes, well, why do you want to play now? Are you trying to get away from me?'

'No, of course I'm not,' expostulated Hayden, looking harassed. 'For Pete's sake, Anne, I thought you said you liked Brigitte Laurent.'

'I did. I do.'

'Then what's the problem?'

Anne looked down at the table, pleating the red check cloth in her fingers. 'I just thought we might have a nice family day for once. That's all.'

'Ahem,' coughed Hayden quietly but pointedly.

Anne looked up. 'What?'

'I seem to recall that when I suggested something yesterday about a nice family day, I ended up being hauled off to a party that would have given Harold Pinter a nervous breakdown.'

'I didn't know it was going to be like that,' Anne said miserably.

'No, I know you didn't. But it doesn't negate the fact that it was largely on your account that I spent most of yesterday stuck with the human equivalent of the Californian Fault.' Getting to his feet, Hayden went across to the bottom of the stairs to shout Verity again.

'So just for once,' he said, coming back, '*I* am deciding what we're going to do. That means Brigitte for you and André for me. I am – for the moment at least – on holiday. And like a million other husbands and fathers on holiday and trying to enjoy themselves,' he treated Anne to his smoothest and most charming smile 'today I am going to play a little golf.'

*

Oh, bugger, there was Hayden calling her for the third time.

Yanking off her fifth choice of top, Verity stood in her bra and jeans and a quandary. This was hopeless. All her tops and t-shirts made her look as if she was about twelve and while she had no idea if the film Hugo wanted to see was 18 classification or even if France went in for that sort of thing, it was faint-making to contemplate being turned away at the door. She would never live down the humiliation.

Perhaps she shouldn't wear jeans, anyway. They weren't very smart for somewhere sounding as sophisticated as a ciné-club and besides, they were so tight she was sure they made her bum look huge.

Wriggling them down her hips, she trod the legs off while simultaneously riffling through the wardrobe to save time. Not that there was much to riffle through. All her old charity shop grunge gear looked gross, inexplicably gross – what had she thought she looked like in it? No, better not think about that at all. But what had she left? The suede mini Juno had given her was great but a bit on the hot side. Then there were some boring shirts, a blue and white check shift that her mother had bought her and in which she looked about ten, and then the new top she had worn to the nightclub. Verity was nearly sick at the thought. She certainly wasn't wearing *that*.

Finally, there was the Laura Ashley linen dress. No, she didn't want to wear that either, partly because Laura Ashley was so bloody naff these days, and she wasn't wild on the wishy-washy colour, and partly because – again – Mum had bought it for her. They might be back on speaking terms but there was a limit as to how far you should climb down with your mother. Hugo had said she looked like Julia Roberts.

What would Julia Roberts wear to a ciné-club?

'VERITY! We're leaving in FIVE minutes! WITH or WITHOUT you!'

Oh, fuck! There was nothing else for it; she would have to wear the Laura Ashley.

Actually, she thought, taking a last quick look in the mirror, it looked not at all bad now she had a tan. She would opt for total simplicity to set it off. No jewellery and just a slick of lip sheen. Ramming her feet into a pair of grey cotton pumps, Verity grabbed her backpack and hared downstairs.

'Well,' said Hayden, looking her up and down. 'After all that time the very least I expected was Lady Gaga.'

*

'*Jamais dans ma vie*,' moaned Maxine.

Since the dripping Gilles had removed himself with as much dignity as he could muster – which wasn't a lot – Maxine had moaned *jamais dans ma vie* about six times. Walter had enough French or, more accurately, sense to gather she was saying such a thing had never happened in her life. 'Well, I'm sorry, m'dear,' he said, eventually and briskly. 'But there's a limit to what a man can stand and, as far as I'm concerned, your son just exceeded it.'

Maxine murmured something else in French which Walter did not gather.

He stood looking down at her for a moment.

'You know, Maxine, m'dear,' he said, speaking in as calm and gentle a way as he could manage. 'I think this might be the time for us to call it a day. I didn't want it to end like this but maybe it's for the best. We've had a jolly time, you and I, and you're a wonderful woman, Maxine, a really wonderful woman. But I think what has just happened must prove to you that it's not –'

Maxine suddenly flew out of her chair, clashing her jaw against his in such a fervent embrace she knocked his plate sideways.

'Steady on, old girl,' Walter remonstrated mildly, resettling his teeth at the same time as clutching her to save his balance.

'Wal-tèrre!' she shrieked in his ear, nearly deafening him. 'You do not understand! Never in my life has a gentleman defended me against Gilles. Always my son is the bully to me. Always he puts me in the fright. But you –' she burst into a storm of weeping all over his best necktie. 'You are my 'ero!'

'There, there, m'dear. You have a good bellow.' Hands mechanically patting the heaving back, Walter Pepper's eyes fell absently on the murky water of the swimming pool. He found himself stifling a sigh.

Gilles, it seemed, was not the only one who had gone in up to his neck.

24

The Laurents' house turned out to be one of the outrageous *fin-de-siècle* edifices on the seafront in Cabourg. Inside, however, it had been decorated with such a stark and minimal elegance Anne was astonished.

Acres of limed oak flooring stretched away across a massive sitting room dotted here and there with pale sofas and low tables. Save for a green pottery Chinese lion squatting snarling on the hearth, the only ornaments were architectural arrangements of twisted willow or glass bowls full of polished crystals. A single print depicting a Japanese ideograph filled the wall above the fireplace.

Anne sighed with envy. It was exactly the type of decor she had always wanted but never even contemplated attempting because it was impossible to maintain alongside the clutter of normal family life. Judging by the piles of books, magazines and personal belongings all over the place, the Laurents also found it something of a strain. Nevertheless, 'Gosh, you're good at interior design,' she breathed to Brigitte, trying to keep the jealousy out of her voice.

'What's that?' Following the direction of her eyes, Brigitte laughed. 'Oh, heavens, you surely don't think this is my doing? I couldn't design the interior of a garden shed. No, it's not even our house. It belongs to a man in André's department at the university. He kindly lent it to us this year because he's gone on a pilgrimage to Tibet. To discover his Inner Being,' she added with a giggle.

André came through from the kitchen carrying a black papier-mâché tray holding two bobbly wine glasses, a saucer of pretzels and a chilled bottle of rosé – 'Chosen especially for you, Anne.'

He pulled the cork before turning to wink at Hayden. 'So, shall we go and discover our inner tee-ing?'

Brigitte groaned. 'Are you off again?'

'I certainly am.' Scooping up a medieval Filofax from a side table, André shoved it in his back trouser pocket. 'This time to play golf. We'll take Hugo and Verity to the station on our way.'

'Wouldn't it be a good idea to take your golf clubs too?' Brigitte cast her husband a mocking little smirk.

'Oh, yes.' Looking abashed, André disappeared back into the kitchen and then re-appeared with them.

Brigitte smiled at Anne. 'Come on.' She picked up the tray. 'Bring the baby and we'll have our wine in the garden.

'As you can see,' she said, a few minutes later when the men had gone and Conrad had mooched off to the beach with Danielle and Carpenter, 'the Orient Express runs out here as well.'

Anne looked round at the black wood decking, the black ceramic pots of grasses and bamboo, the lanterns swaying on sticks and the wind chimes tinkling in the breeze, and then squinted up at the house's gothic arches and Transylvanian turrets. 'It is a funny sort of place to choose that theme,' she conceded. Plonking Martha down on the decking, she settled herself on a garden futon only to heave herself up again to prevent Martha from dismantling a pebble water feature.

'Oh, leave her be,' Brigitte said comfortably. 'She can't drown in it and it is only a heap of wet stones when all is said and done.'

They drank for a while in companionable silence, Anne noticing that the people strolling by on the promenade seemed to be gawping over the hedge at them a good deal more than people usually gawp in that sort of situation. Perhaps she and Brigitte ought to start on a bit of ikebana to entertain them.

'It's a terrible garden for being on show,' grumbled Brigitte, as a red-faced man positively goggled at them. 'We actually had someone stop the other day and ask if we were a Chinese take-away.'

'Offer them peeking duck.'

Brigitte laughed but got up. 'Come on, let's go back inside. I'll make us some lunch and besides – it's clouding over.'

Back in the kitchen, which was all stainless steel cabinets and grooved marble counters, and hence so spookily suggestive of a path lab Anne wondered if they ought to don plastic overalls and rubber bootees, Brigitte seized an exquisite-looking dish of poached salmon from a morgue-size fridge and started putting the finishing touches to it. Whatever her professed limitations in interior design, Brigitte Laurent evidently knew how to cook.

'We'd better save some for Conrad and Dan,' she said, squinting up through the kitchen window at the sky. 'In case they decide to come back. It's gone awfully grey out there.'

Somewhere upstairs a shutter was banging.

'Although knowing my daughter,' Brigitte went on, 'Danielle will doubtless persuade Conrad to grab something on the hoof, as the Americans say. Dan hates sitting down for meals. There.' Fanning a final frill of cucumber slices round the gills of the salmon, she popped the plate on the table.

'That looks absolutely beautiful.' Anne levered Martha back into her buggy.

'Thank you.' Brigitte looked pleased. 'I love cooking. Which reminds me, would you and Hayden like to come to dinner the day after tomorrow? It's Dan's fifteenth birthday and she wants to take Verity and Conrad with her and Hugo to that new American hamburger place in town so we oldies could have a cosy evening together.'

'Sounds lovely,' Anne smiled. 'But you don't want to go to the bother of cooking, surely?'

'As I said, I *love* it. In fact, I love food.'

'Me too, but how do you stay so slim?'

'Thank you again.' The Frenchwoman laughed. 'Except I'd call it scrawny.' Picking up a baguette, she tore it into pieces and chucked them into a basket. 'I know it sounds annoying but I do honestly wish sometimes that I could put on a bit of weight. Yet I never seem to, even though I never diet.

'Not that many French women do diet,' she reflected. 'I think we're too greedy. The single thing I found difficult to understand about English girls when I was at university in London was the way they seemed to spend their entire lives starving themselves.'

Anne gave a wry chuckle. 'And yet never got any thinner.'

The Frenchwoman puffed a little snort. 'Well, I don't know about that.' Opening a plastic bag, she emptied out a pile of blackened red peppers.

'What are you doing with those?'

'One of my specialities.' Brigitte licked her fingers. 'An instant soup of char-grilled peppers and tomato. I really like char-grilling and setting fire to things.' She started deftly stripping the pepper peel.

'Stephanie diets,' remarked Anne, sorting the stuff for Martha's lunch from her bag.

'She would. Stephanie is not a typical Frenchwoman, though.'

'She is in one way,' Anne could not resist saying.

'Oh, right.' Brigitte cast an old-fashioned look over her shoulder. Then, wiping her hands on her kaftan – cheesecloth today, with a monk's hood – she sat down opposite Anne and poured them both more wine. 'I take it you are referring to Gilles's extra-marital excursions.'

Anne nodded.

'Well, that sort of behaviour is not really typically French either, not these days at any rate.'

'Isn't it?' Anne raised her eyebrows. 'I was given to understand by Stephanie that every husband is an automatic adulterer but in France it's all perfectly civilized because the wife puts up with it.'

'Oh, I know that is what *she* would say.' Brigitte waved her glass of wine with a touch of impatience. 'Just as I also know the relish with which Stephanie Dérain relates the gruesome details of her marriage. Stephanie thrives on the gruesome. But she is not typical, any more than her marriage is in modern terms.' She looked sternly at Anne. 'Female emancipation has reached the untutored shores of France, you know.'

'Yes, of course.' Anne felt reproved.

'Oh, I'm not getting at *you*,' Brigitte sighed after a brief but slightly uncomfortable pause. 'It's just women like Stephanie Dérain who irritate the life out of me because they perpetuate these stereotypes purely for their own purpose.' She took a sip of wine. 'As for Gilles, he's no more than a middle-aged saddo who fancies himself as Don Juan. You find men like him in any society.'

'Actually,' Anne put Martha's bowl and spoon on the table, 'Stephanie told me she also has lovers. In fact, I rather got the impression she has one on the go right now.'

'Really?' Brigitte looked intrigued. All agog, she pondered a moment. 'Well, that does surprise me given Stephanie has always struck me as such a cold fish. André said Gilles has some woman in Honfleur but I wonder who Stephanie's bit on the side is.'

'You've no idea?'

Brigitte lifted her cheesecloth shoulders. 'Not the foggiest.' She grimaced suddenly, stood and turned back to her cooking. 'I don't know why those two stay together, when they're so desperately unhappy.'

Anne followed her, her hands full of Martha's food.

'I'll do the baby's lunch for you,' offered Brigitte. 'Just give me a second to finish these.' She was reducing peppers to pulp. 'The fact is Stephanie and Gilles should have divorced years ago. It was bloody difficult for Juno growing up with her parents constantly at each other's throats.'

'She seems to have survived it,' Anne said drily.

'Not really.' Brigitte was chopping away with a knife like a scalpel. 'That is, yes, she is a lovely young woman but in some ways, she's a mess. I expect you know what I mean?' She glanced at Anne.

Anne scratched her ear. 'Um... yes, I suppose so.'

Brigitte turned back to her peppers. 'What it all comes down to, is that it's high time Juno left home.'

'Well, twenty-seven is a little on the mature side to still be living with Mum and Dad.'

'Quite. But you could say that is to Juno's credit. She stays because she feels the need to shield her mother from Gilles – he's *such* a bully, that man. Not that Juno gets anything like thanks from Stephanie in return.'

Brigitte paused, the knife suspended in her hand. 'Anyway, it's all going to change very shortly because Juno is now seriously thinking of leaving and branching out on her own.'

'Good for her.' Anne wished they could talk about something else.

'The latest is she's talking about *really* getting away and going to live in London.'

'London?'

'Yep, London. In fact, she told me Hayden offered to help her find somewhere to live.'

Anne's eyes gravitated to the gleaming mass of peppers. With its feathery flakes of greasy red, it looked like the corpse of some mangled bird. 'When –' Anne heard her voice coming out as a croak and cleared her throat. 'When is she intending to leave?'

Brigitte was now performing a post-mortem on tomatoes.

'Oh, it's nothing definite yet.' She moved to the table to take a quick gulp of wine. 'But very sweet of Hayden, wasn't it? Of course, Juno's old enough to look after herself but it's so nice for her to have someone willing to play the father figure. Given her own is worse than useless.'

The Frenchwoman brandished her scalpel.

'However, I'm sure with Hayden's support it will all work out fine.'

*

Walter Pepper had got himself into a bit of fix. It wasn't his fault, any more than it was Maxine's. The fix began – and looked very much like ending – with Gilles.

He was not proud of pushing the Frenchman into the swimming pool but Walter did think it might have given the silly clot pause for thought. Alas not. No sooner had Maxine stopped having the vapours all over his necktie than Gilles returned for an encore. And what an encore! In any other circumstances Walter would have been tempted to applaud.

Dried off, puffed up and squeezed into a pair of indecently tight trousers, Gilles opened with a five minute rant in French which Walter didn't even bother to listen to. He then switched to English to declare – quite rightly in some ways, Walter had to allow – that pushing him in the pool had been an extremely childish and dangerous thing to do. He was contemplating criminal proceedings for assault or civil ones for damages because he had, he claimed self-righteously, swallowed so much infected water it would oblige him to take in an emergency session of colonic irrigation.

'What the devil's that?' Walter had interrupted to demand of Maxine.

All he could think was that it sounded like some project for watering crops in British India. But once Maxine had explained, Walter decided it was nothing if not typical of Gilles to go in for that sort of disgusting palaver over his innards, when a simple glass of Andrews liver salts would fit the bill – if a bill needed to be fitted. Walter would even lend him a spoonful from his own tin. Saying this, however, had made Gilles foam at the mouth and wave his arms about more than Arthur Scargill.

The situation could not continue.

When at long last it appeared Gilles had flounced off for good – he had waited a bit to make sure – Walter found himself obliged to speak up. The situation could not continue. He could no longer remain at the Manoir.

And no, he had got in before Maxine could suggest it – he was not going back to Paris. Maxine might feel obliged to give him another whistle-stop tour, taking in details of her love life she had omitted to mention on their previous visit. There surely couldn't be too many left but with Maxine, you never knew.

Maxine, however, said she also did not wish to depart to Paris, possibly because their time there did not conjure up what you might call ecstatic memories for her, either. But they had to depart somewhere because one thing was certain: Walter was not staying a minute longer under the same roof as Gilles.

There was Wolverhampton, of course. He could always take Maxine home to Wolverhampton. He had his house there, locked up and dust-sheeted and ready to be sold – if ever he went ahead with that. Yet, try as he might, Walter could not seem to conjure up a vision of Maxine putting her feet up on the Parker Knoll recliner in a semi-detached bungalow in Wolverhampton, quite apart from the fact that there would be nowhere to put Dolores – unless he cleaned out the shed.

Given the way she turned her nose up at everything, but especially Walter, Dolores, Walter suspected, would turn her nose up even more than Maxine at a semi-detached bungalow in Wolverhampton. They could, of course, leave Dolores in France but somehow he could not see Maxine taking kindly to that idea, either. By and large, where Maxine went, Dolores followed. Indeed, it was definitely a case of love me, love my Dolores. Not encouraging, but Walter had had to put up with it.

When it came to Gilles, however, Walter had no intention of putting up with it.

So there was nothing else for it. But no, as he had expected, Maxine didn't fancy Wolverhampton. Actually, he was not convinced she had given it proper consideration since all she was doing was mournfully repeating *'C'est une catastrophe'* over and over. Maxine was given to mournful repetition in times of stress – it could get a trifle wearing. But it meant they were back to square one.

In that case, Walter had concluded, he was off. His bags would be packed and he would be gone within the hour. There was no more to be said. And with that he had risen from the breakfast table.

No wait! Maxine had an idea – an inspiration.

Walter had resumed his seat, but warily. He knew Maxine and her inspirations. There *was* somewhere they could go, she said. If she meant the place in Antibes, Walter said he certainly wasn't going there – it would be far too hot. That again wasn't the real reason. The real reason was that he was not risking meeting any more of the Dérain family who might turn out to be as yampy as Gilles.

But Maxine hadn't meant Antibes. Walter listened while she explained. Well, fair enough. Actually, it sounded all right, very all right, actually. He had always wanted to see that part of the world. He saw himself striding along Alpine paths in a green felt hat with a feather and buying one of those enamel badges to nail on his walking stick – one of his walking sticks.

Fine, he agreed with caution, but how would they get there?

They could drive, Maxine explained breezily. The autoroutes were excellent, if they left now they could be there in nine or ten hours.

Now hang on a minute. Walter wondered how to put this. He had never been one of those gents who made it their business to denigrate women drivers, but the prospect of tearing down a motorway with Maxine at the wheel, let alone careering round mountain passes in the dark, would strike terror into any man's heart.

But that was all right, too. Maxine had no intention of being at the wheel, on the contrary she knew just the person to ask to drive them.

Walter frowned; he couldn't see that working out. Maxine, however, was in no doubt. It was all a question of take and give, she explained. She had given so much over the years and now, *enfin*, came the time for her to take a little favour in return. So – it was settled? Walter had given his dubious assent. In the absence of any other solution, he supposed he might as well go along with it.

Bon. Good.

And with that Maxine had bustled into the house. As soon as Dolores finished packing her *valises*, she would send her along to Walter to do his. Oh, no, Walter had resolved silently as he trotted after Maxine.

Whatever he supposed he might be going along with, he was not letting that bloomin' Spanish maid near his clothes.

*

Down at the beach Conrad was also determined not to let someone near something, and that was his own self and the windsurfer. Sitting glumly on the sand with Carpenter, Conrad watched Danielle guiding it expertly over the choppy water and thought bitterly that she had got the hang of the thing about fifty times better than him. It made him deeply reluctant to have another go. Showing yourself up in front of a girl was not exactly the best way to get friendly with her. Of course, he was already *friends* with Danielle but she wasn't his girlfriend.

There was a difference, a world of difference.

A spate of hysterical yapping obliging him to rush down the sand and detach Carpenter from a Yorkshire terrier with its forelock tied up in a pink bow, Conrad thought how much simpler life was for dogs. If Carpenter fancied someone he just went for it. Conrad couldn't do that. Not in broad daylight on a beach full of people he couldn't. And even if he could, the fear that Danielle might start yapping hysterically made him faint with horror.

It wasn't as if he wanted to *do* very much, he told himself, moodily sifting sand through his fingers. He just, well, sort of wanted to get things on, like, a slightly different footing. The difficulty lay in how to engineer the situation round that way. So far he hadn't a clue.

Aside from the difficulty of having to speak French to her all the time – French might be the language of passion, but personally Conrad found it mega restricting – if Danielle wasn't gliding about on the windsurfer she was talking nineteen to the dozen or swigging Coca-Cola or cracking up empty Coca-Cola cans. Conrad felt he could hardly start slobbering over her when she was cracking up empty Coca-Cola cans.

He looked up as Danielle yelled at him from where she had pulled the windsurfer into the shoreline. Sprinting up the sand, she threw herself into a row of perfect cartwheels, ending with a handstand practically on his ankles. Conrad couldn't help laughing. Dani really was a wild child.

'*Ton tour*,' she panted, grabbing his hand to haul him to his feet. This was the first time she had touched him and, along with the tu-toying, was very encouraging. Except that she immediately released his hand, which wasn't.

And perhaps that was the precisely the problem, Conrad thought hopelessly, as he traipsed down to the windsurfer to make a prat of himself once again.

The wild child was exactly that – a child.

*

'Well?' asked Hugo, as they streamed out into the ciné-club foyer. 'What did you think?'

Turning to him, Verity smiled. 'It was *sick*,' she said sincerely. Nearly all the French might have gone over her head but that didn't mean she couldn't see *A Bout de Souffle* was really groovy. 'A thousand times better than that re-make with Richard Gere,' she added. 'And thanks a million for taking me.'

Hugo looked embarrassed. 'I wanted to see it again myself,' he said awkwardly.

'Let me pay for the tickets.'

'No way.'

'Then can I buy us a coffee or a drink somewhere?'

'That would be good but look.' Hugo nodded towards the exit. 'I think we've got a problem.'

Verity looked. People were hovering around the smoked glass doors, charging out in panicky little flurries with umbrellas raised or macs held over their heads. It was chucking it down outside, the sky pitch black and hailstones as big as golf balls pinging off the pavement.

'Shit!' She pulled a face. 'Do you know anywhere close by?'

'I think there's a bar round the corner.'

'Then let's make a run for it.'

Hugo hesitated, looked dubiously at her dress and then outside again and then back at her dress. After a second he took off his black leather jacket. Underneath, he was wearing a plain white short-sleeved t-shirt. His arms looked nice and brown and sinewy. In fact, Hugo was not too badly dressed at all today. Jeans, a black leather jacket and the white t-shirt, he might not be Jean-Paul Belmondo but he was getting there.

'Put this on,' he ordered.

'No.' Verity took a deep breath and hooked an arm firmly round his waist. 'You hold it over us both.'

*

There were worse things you could do at his age, reflected Walter, as night fell and they wound up the mountain roads, other than scorch across Europe in a motor car that was the equivalent of Betty Grable.

The Porsche, of course, was far too small for the three of them, let alone Maxine's nineteen suitcases and Dolores. But Maxine had led the way round to a row of garages at the back of the manor house, ordered one of them to be opened, and there she stood, gleaming over every inch of her exquisite body – a Rolls-Royce Silver Shadow.

She was so beautiful it had made Walter dizzy to look at her, so dizzy he had been almost on the point of volunteering to drive her himself even though he hadn't been behind the wheel of a car for a decade or more. This was a lady he knew how to handle, an engine he knew piece by piece. It made him feel young again just to look at her.

Then, all at once, looking at the car, he had seen Maggie, as clearly as if she were standing at his side. He had seen Maggie with him at one of the early motor shows; Maggie in a pert little hat over her shining hair and white gloves on her small hands, and wearing a blue dress with big white polka dots and a full skirt, with crisp net petticoats holding the fullness out.

Ladies wore things like that back then. These days you hardly ever seemed to see them in a nice frock and a hat. Even Anne spent most of her time looking as if she was going to work in a munitions factory. But Maggie had always run herself up pretty things to wear. Quite a dab hand at sewing Maggie had been, and that outfit for the motor show had been a smasher.

He could see her now, plain as the day he could see her, unbuttoning the natty little bolero jacket she had made to match the dress. Maggie smiling, Maggie laughing, Maggie saying you're a one, Walter Pepper, when he took her to the firm's stand and ordered her a Pimms Number 7.

It was funny then but, somehow, seeing Maggie like that had made him not want to go on the trip with Maxine, even in the beautiful car. Somehow, all it had made him want to do was go home to Wolverhampton and get out the photograph album and put his feet up on the Parker Knoll and spend the evening with Maggie.

'Wal-tèrre!'

Maxine had suddenly shrieked in his ear making him start so that he nearly slipped and hurt himself.

'You forget your sticks for walking!'

He had gone back into the house and fetched one, only the one – his own – the old hazel twist Maggie had bought him as a surprise that last holiday they had taken together. He had always had a fondness for a nice stick. It was the summer they had gone to Eastbourne, that last summer, the summer before she died.

But Maxine sulked all the way to Switzerland because he refused to bring the walking sticks she had given him. Walter didn't care. All the way to Switzerland he clutched the gnarled and knobbly top of Maggie's, feeling the wood smooth as silk beneath his fingers.

And now, as they climbed up and up, he lent forward in his seat and lowered the side window. Cool air rushed in. Bracing himself on the stick, he strained his eyes up at the sky. Higher and higher they were climbing, climbing until, it seemed, you could reach out and touch the inky blackness riven with stars.

'Wal-tèrre!' Maxine gave an ostentatious shiver. '*Que fais-toi*? I am too cold.'

Walter Pepper did not turn. 'My wife's up there,' he said.

25

'Can Carpenter come in?'

'Of course he can,' said André Laurent, answering the door on the evening of his daughter's birthday. 'Come in, Carpenter, come in, everyone.' Embracing Anne on both cheeks, he stepped back to look her up and down.

'Wow!' He gave a wolf whistle. 'That is *some* outfit.'

Brigitte came swooping out from the kitchen in her kaftan for the day, this time an African tie-dyed one. Gruesome, Anne decided, and then felt mean when Brigitte also told her that her outfit was stunning.

'Makes you look all leg,' she said in awe.

'It certainly cost one.' Hayden plonked down Martha asleep in her car seat. 'Including the arm. Or rather, the lack of it.'

Anne bit her lip.

Her new outfit, acquired with great trepidation at Verity's favourite boutique in Cabourg, consisted of a pair of skin-tight pale pink clam-diggers and a square-cut cropped top in charcoal grey silk jersey, with one sleeve slashed away to leave her right shoulder bare. Given it was the most fashionable outfit she had bought in centuries – even Verity had been struck dumb – Anne was far from convinced it was not too young for her. The last thing she needed was snide comments, especially from Hayden. Come to that, it was most unlike Hayden to *be* snide, let alone to beef about her spending money on clothes.

Anne felt her confidence in smithereens. Since her lunch with Brigitte, little had happened other than Stephanie arriving in the evening of the same day to tell Anne all about Walter Pepper pushing Gilles into the swimming pool. However, despite the Frenchwoman's state of great excitement, this did not strike Anne as particularly *grave*, or even amusing; her father must have lost his temper to do something like that

Anne had found herself being distinctly cool with Stephanie. She had wanted to be more than cool; she had wanted to tell the damn woman exactly what she thought of her and her spiteful little plot to set Anne up for a fall with Alain. But, aside from Hayden's presence making that difficult, she was trying very hard to cling to some remnant of dignity.

Whatever, Anne had found herself noticing an unpleasant gusto about Stephanie Dérain and her enthusiasm for bad news. Or rather, as Brigitte had so succinctly put it – a relish.

Still, Stephanie had also given Anne a letter from Walter, a quick note scrawled on the back of one of Maxine's At Home cards. Walter did not say much in the note, just that he was very sorry that the party had not turned out the way he expected, and that he and Maxine were going away together for a few days. He did not say where they were going. Walter, indeed, also sounded rather cool, or perhaps it was preoccupied. Anne had felt preoccupied herself. How could she be otherwise when it appeared good old Hayden was finding jolly young Juno somewhere to live in London?

Why had he not told Anne about his daddy act, if that was what it was? Unless it was that he was planning to move back with Juno to London to be anything but a daddy? Brooding on this had made Anne so hopping mad that this morning she had rushed out and blown an uncharacteristic fortune on new clothes. Oh, well, at least André appreciated them.

Anne did not know quite what to make of André Laurent. He was very far from being another leering lecher like Gilles, although there was something a touch lascivious about him. However, if he was in complicity with Hayden over Juno then Brigitte certainly knew nothing about it, nor would approve for that matter. No, on the face of it the Laurents appeared to be a perfectly normal, loving couple.

Yet, Anne asked herself, what about the business of André forgetting his golf clubs when he took Hayden to play golf? How many men were going to play golf and forgot to take their clubs? Unlikely as it seemed, Anne could not help wondering if, unbeknownst to his emancipated wife, André Laurent was one more Frenchman with another iron in the fire and anything but a golfing one at that.

Anne watched him prising the cork from a bottle of champagne and griping away at his wife. 'Why can't you wear clothes like that?'

'For the simple reason that I couldn't carry them off.' Brigitte smiled at Anne without a trace of malice. 'With my figure I'd look like a standard lamp.'

Champagne poured, the kids all had a glass and then cleared off into Cabourg for Danielle's birthday treat at the American hamburger bar. Carpenter looked yearningly after them.

'*Courage, mon brave!*' André stooped to stroke Carpenter's head as the dog turned dejectedly to the hearth to wash the Chinese pottery lion's ears. 'You never know with hamburgers and you don't want to end up eating a relative.'

'Is anyone else coming?' Anne peered through the door to the kitchen.

'Malc and his wife,' answered André, straightening up with a dead straight face. 'I know how Hi-den is absolutely pining to see Cindy again.'

Hayden choked on his champagne.

'Oh, shut up, André!' Brigitte thumped Hayden on the back. 'That's not funny. And don't start going on about Cindy and Malc again. They weren't that bad,' she added, but without conviction.

'Are you telling me that a man who hangs fluffy toys from the rear view mirror of his car hasn't got a major design fault?'

'Does he really?' Hayden wiped his streaming eyes. 'Perhaps his wife puts them there.'

'Could you sleep with a woman who hung fluffy toys on your rear view mirror?'

'I once read somewhere,' remarked Brigitte, 'that Claudia Schiffer sleeps with about two hundred fluffy toys on her bed.'

'Ah,' said André. 'Well, in her case I might make an exception.'

'Seriously, Brigitte.' Anne turned to her as the men roared with laughter. 'Who else have you invited?'

'Actually, I asked Juno – '

'Oh, good.' Hayden looked pleased. 'I like Juno.'

'But she later sent me a text to say she was sorry but she couldn't make it after all.'

'Bags I sit next to your wife, then,' André said to Hayden, managing to top up Anne's glass at the same time as feinting a kiss towards her bare shoulder.

'A pity, though,' sighed Brigitte. 'In that Juno would probably have brought along that gorgeous Jean-Pierre.'

André's eyes instantly went beady.

'Because I must say,' Brigitte cast her husband a malicious grin, 'that if one wanted a young lover he'd be the first port of call. He looks just like a young Brad Pitt.'

'And I suppose you fancy yourself as Angelina Jolie?' André said witheringly.

'Goodness, no,' crowed his wife, delighted at the success of her little sally. 'I'm *much* thinner.'

Anne felt her face stiff with trying to smile. 'Brigitte?' she asked in the pause for more mirth. 'Do you mind if I settle the baby upstairs?'

'Of course not. Use our bedroom. It's at the front on the right.'

'Give me a shout if you need help with changing,' called André, as Anne picked up Martha in her car seat and left the room.

The sound of laughter followed her up the stairs.

*

Hugo suggested they all went for a walk on the beach before going to the bar. It was a lovely evening, light and bright if watery, because it had rained most of the afternoon. But Verity wished he had suggested they go for a walk on their own, meeting up with Danielle and Conrad later on.

She didn't want to be mean, and it was Danielle's birthday, but the French girl really got on her nerves with her shrill voice and bossy little ways. And the stupid way she pranced about the beach, demanding they run races or play tag, anyone would think she was five, not fifteen.

Verity found herself feeling almost sorry for her stepbrother. Conrad had a certain hungry look in his eye. But if he was thinking he had a hope in hell of getting anywhere with the likes of Danny boy, he needed his head examining. Then again, Verity realised despondently, she couldn't talk. She wasn't getting anywhere with Hugo. The evening looked far from promising.

Leaving the ciné-club she'd had quite high hopes. They had charged through the streets of Caen, both getting drenched, despite Hugo's leather jacket, because the rain had been virtually horizontal at some points. But this had seemed to make it all the more romantic, especially when at one point a spectacularly vicious gust sent them cowering into a shop doorway.

There they had huddled, breathless – like the film – Verity sneaking little glances up at Hugo from under her eyelashes, and thinking how perfectly irresistible she must look soaked to the skin with her dress all wet and clinging to her body. Yeah, well, Hugo had seemed to find her perfectly resistible.

And possibly because when they eventually got to the bar and Verity escaped to the loo, she saw in horror that the little mascara she'd had on had run in black streaks down her face and her dress wasn't clinging at all. It was hanging stiffly from her body like a wet sack, the lower half of it dark and splotchy in such embarrassing places it looked as if she'd had a very unfortunate accident indeed.

Another deluge on the dash to the station had put the final mockers on progress, Verity by that time feeling so cold and shivery that all she wanted to do was get home and into a hot bath. Since then, she'd only seen Hugo for a couple of minutes on and off at the beach because yet more bloody rain had put paid to anything remotely enterprising. She was anyway fast reaching the conclusion he didn't fancy her after all. Watching Conrad obligingly race Danielle into the distance, she allowed herself a little sigh. She had been flattering herself that he did.

'You're very quiet tonight.' Hugo offered her a piece of chewing gum.

Verity accepted it. Maybe she had bad breath and that's what put him off. 'Am I?' she said distantly.

They walked on a little, chewing.

All at once, however, Hugo halted and grabbed her hand, swinging her round to face him. 'Have you gone off me or something?' he said.

Verity was taken aback. 'No, of course I haven't.'

'That's all right, then.' He pulled her gently towards him.

Shit! Did guys choose their moments! Wondering if she should spit out the gum, which seemed a rather disgusting thing to do, or try to swallow it and risk choking to death, Verity suddenly saw him smile.

'Sorry.' He looked shamefaced. 'I've never had any sense of timing.'

'Oh, I don't know about that.' She was staring at his mouth.

Maybe the evening was not entirely without promise after all.

*

The mention of Juno seemed to have sparked a theme of conversation, because by the time they were into the second bottle of champagne everyone was bitching their heads off about the Dérains, André the bitchiest of all. Anne was beginning to realise André Laurent's mild-looking David Attenborough come-inside-this-anthill appearance was highly misleading. With his crocodile smile and acid wit, there was something Rabelaisian about the way he set about winding everyone up.

'I expect,' he now began with deceptive innocence, 'that poor Juno's cleared off because she's had enough of trying to referee Gilles and Maxine and their constant bust-ups.'

'Don't they get on?' Hayden said in surprise.

'Get on?' André's caustic little eyes gleamed. 'When those two start seismologists faint over the Richter scale.'

'Oh, don't exaggerate, André! And can't you be more discreet?'

Brigitte looked annoyed yet Anne sensed something false, something artificial in her annoyance. It made her wonder if André Laurent's outrageousness and his wife's temperance were not one of those elaborate games some couples go in for.

'Keep mum, you mean.' André chuckled. 'That's certainly what Gilles wants to do – keep Mum. Especially now she's got herself a new boyfriend.'

Anne twitched. André appeared to have forgotten that Walter Pepper was her father.

'Gilles lives in fear and dread that Maxine is one day going to blow the remainder of her fortune on another husband and there will be nothing left for him to inherit.'

'But surely,' said Hayden, with a glance at Anne, 'Gilles inherited a packet from his own father when he died? Your laws on that point are very strict, aren't they?'

'Indeed.' André threw him a silky smile. 'Except with Stephanie patronising every *haute couture* collection Paris has to offer, Gilles's coffers have become seriously depleted. The guy's never had a proper job, idle bugger that he is. And, while Maxine has been extremely generous where her grandchildren are concerned, she draws the line at her own offspring. You might think Maxine slightly bananas with her penchant for making up stories about her life, but believe me, she's all there when it comes to the filthy lucre.

'Hence, if there's a risk of Maxine spending her money on high jinks with another paramour,' he threw a sidelong wink at Anne – he hadn't forgotten, 'Gilles can only ensure life is unbearable for the current favourite.'

'Oh, for God's sake, shut *up*, André.' Brigitte cast a nervously placating look at Anne. 'You're being boring. Anyway, Gilles isn't around much at the moment.'

'Ah, but he is,' contradicted her husband. 'I have it on good authority that his mistress has dumped him and, like a Third World country, Gilles is always at his most volatile following a coup. Honfleur had to put up the barricades.'

'That's strange.'

'What is?' At Anne's remark, Hayden had turned to her.

'Oh, nothing.' Wishing she had not spoken, Anne shook her head. 'Only that I understood from Stephanie that it was the other way round. That Gilles was the one doing the dumping.'

'Never.' André gave a snort of derision. 'That guy's been chucked more times than a discus.'

'Doesn't surprise me,' sniffed Hayden. 'He's such an obnoxious shit. What was his latest like?'

'Oh, a dreadful old crow.' André affected a melodramatic shudder. Drinking more than anyone else, he had acquired the predatory look of a ram in a field of ewes. 'And big with it. When Gilles sailed out with her they used to jam the estuary.'

'Perhaps he used her as ballast.'

'Isn't it funny,' mused Brigitte, 'how men married to really beautiful women so often go for cheesy mistresses?'

André moved to slosh more champagne into everyone's glasses. 'And who says Stephanie Dérain is really beautiful?'

'Now, come *on*,' protested his wife. 'She's hugely glam.'

'She's had more lifts than a hitch-hiker.'

'Well, it hasn't stopped her getting herself a lover,' Brigitte said defiantly.

André paused mid-slosh. 'Who told you that?'

'Anne.'

Anne felt herself go red.

'Is that true?' Hayden again turned to her. 'You never told me.'

'I don't believe it,' scoffed André. "Do we know who he is?'

'No,' Brigitte conceded. 'Except he's a lovely little toy boy.'

'Impossible. She's far too long in the tooth.'

'Oh, honestly.' Brigitte now gave a hoot of derision. 'How sexist can you get? What about all those geriatric film stars and their young wives? Nobody ever said Michael Douglas was too old for Catherine Zeta-Jones.'

'She was so hot to handle I think we felt sorry for him.'

Brigitte ignored her husband. 'Furthermore, think about women. Women like…like Colette, for instance. What about Colette?'

'What about Colette?'

'She was nearly fifty when she had an affair with a sixteen-year-old.'

'Colette was a nympho.'

'Perhaps Stephanie's lover is Malc,' mused Hayden.

'Malc,' André took a long pull of champagne, 'is a wide boy not a toy boy.'

'Hans, then.'

'Too nice a guy and did you see him drooling over Stephanie?'

'Maybe he *is* discreet. Look, no Hans.'

André laughed and then looked smug. 'No, I've got it. Stephanie's squeeze is that oleaginous old prat in the white suit who she was slobbering over at Maxine's party.'

Anne caught her breath but managed to turn it into a cough.

'Really?' Brigitte looked taken aback. 'Who was he? I didn't see anyone like that.'

'He was on the table behind you,' explained her husband. 'But I can assure you Stephanie was doing far more than a Carpenter on his ear. You saw him, didn't you, Anne?'

André turned to her for confirmation and there was a pause.

'Do you know who he was, Anne?' Brigitte had also turned to her.

'You never mentioned any of this to me,' frowned Hayden. '*Did* you know him?'

All three looked at her. Anne felt herself suddenly ringed by peering eyes. 'No,' she said, putting her glass carefully down. 'I've no idea who he was and, if you'll excuse me, I think I'll just pop upstairs and check on the baby. I'm sure that was her crying.'

'I didn't hear anything –' began Hayden.

But Anne had fled.

*

Well, he might have known, thought Conrad, wiping his sweaty face with the back of his hand. Danielle danced the way she did everything – like a headcase. Not that she wasn't a very good dancer, but trying to get your hands on her was like trying to catch a hyperactive kangaroo; the second he got within striking distance she bounced away. He'd have more success with a kangaroo.

And when the jukebox music changed to something slow and moody, all she wanted to do was play the pinball machine. Flip, flip, crash, crash, bounce, bounce, you didn't need an adrenaline surge to keep up with Danielle, it required a permanent drip feed.

I'll defeat this if it's the last thing I do, Conrad resolved grimly, glancing across at his stepsister clinging to Hugo in the corner, if only – and it was a big if – because he had not the slightest intention of letting Verity put one over on him.

*

It was well past one when they got home, the moon risen to its height and the night brilliantly starry. The kids went straight to bed as Hayden carried Martha carefully upstairs and settled her into her cot. He then also cleared off to bed, but Anne lingered in the nursery, pointlessly folding little vests and pairing tiny socks and fiddling about with Martha's toys. She felt utterly shattered and yet at the same time wide awake and twitchy. Somehow – God knows how – she had got through the evening, but the effort had left her jangling more than Martha's cot rattle.

The dinner party had passed in a blur, a cordon blur as far as Brigitte Laurent was concerned, the Frenchwoman having indulged her pyrotechnic addiction not only in char-grilling red peppers, but in igniting entrecôte de boeuf in Calvados and flambée-ing great pans of crêpes suzette. Indeed, by the time they got to them, there was so much smoke in the kitchen Anne felt she had been burnt at the stake. Ducking her head, she sniffed her new top. It stank of cooking fumes.

Oh, what the hell. Hayden didn't like it, anyway. If this evening had been anything to go by, Hayden didn't even seem to like *her*. He had largely ignored her, spending the entire time fooling about with André Laurent.

With a last caress of her daughter's blonde little head, Anne left the nursery and went to the loo. She let herself quietly into the bedroom, expecting Hayden to be asleep.

She blinked. There were no lamps on but moonlight streamed through the open curtains showing Hayden still fully clothed and standing in front of the window looking out. She closed the door behind her.

'Why aren't you in bed?' she said nervously, because there seemed something suddenly oddly menacing in the outline of her husband's broad shoulders. But the next minute he had turned, crossed the room in a single stride, and pulled her roughly into his arms, burying his head in her throat and shoulder.

'God, you look sexy in those trousers.'

At the touch of his mouth on her bare skin, Anne felt herself turn to jelly. 'Hayden?' she began feebly, but before she could get another word out, he had thrown her back on the bed, pulled off her clam-diggers and pants in one, unzipped his flies and entered her.

Whether it was the release of tension, or simply because it felt unbelievably erotic to have him fully clothed pumping away at her naked from the waist down, Anne started to reach orgasm so quickly and so noisily that Hayden had to place a hand over her mouth. Just as well. One of them needed to remember the thin walls.

'*Ooh, là là,*' he breathed a moment later, rolling off and gathering her against his chest. He cuddled her and stroked her hair. 'Must be something in the air. Or those trousers.'

'Clam-diggers,' Anne corrected contentedly, as she lay listening to her husband's heartbeat and breathing in the lovely, familiar smell of his body.

She felt weak with relief. She had been insane, *absolument folle*. Whatever she had imagined Hayden had been doing, it had been simply some bizarre madness on her part. It was all over now.

Now everything would be perfectly all right.

26

Anne woke with a jolt. She had been so deeply asleep that for a moment she couldn't think where she was. Then she felt the sun warm on her cheek, pouring in like the moonlight had through the open curtains last night, and saw her pink clam-diggers lying in a ring on the floor with her pants still inside. Stretching luxuriously, she turned over to reach for Hayden.

She sat up. The bed was empty. She looked at her watch. It was gone nine.

Downstairs round the breakfast table, Hayden was immersed in *Le Monde*, Conrad equally immersed in an old *Hugo* French dictionary, and Verity hovering about six feet above the floor, starry-eyed with what were evidently the transports of first romance. Martha was immersed the remains of boiled egg and toast soldiers, Carpenter just the toast.

Not one of them deigned to acknowledge her.

Anne poured herself a cup of coffee. 'Good morning, Anne,' she muttered, feeling her meagre little store of contentment seeping sourly out of her like a gas leak.

Conrad raised his head. 'Did you know,' he said wonderingly, 'that the French word for to lie down can also mean to get longer?'

Le Monde twitched.

'Sorry, Dad.' Conrad blushed. 'I just meant I wouldn't want to be misunderstood.' He buried himself back in *Hugo*.

Glancing at the dictionary's name, Verity gave a happy little shiver. Anne could almost see her daughter's tail wagging the way Carpenter's did when you mentioned a walk. On the table, Hayden's mobile phone rang.

'Yes?' he said absently, picking it up. 'Indeed,' he then said more crisply, lowering his newspaper and looking at his watch. Flicking a covert glance at Anne, he stood up. 'Sorry, this signal is a little weak. Could you hang on a sec?' And with that Hayden walked quickly out of the front door into the garden.

Jumping to her feet, Anne rushed to the door and peered out after him. Her husband was still talking on the phone but, as he had gone to the farthest point of the orchard, she couldn't make out what he was saying. Five minutes later he was back, his face set in an odd, half apprehensive, half speculative expression.

'Who was that?' Resuming her seat, she picked up her coffee.

'I'm sorry, darling.' Hayden lifted his shoulders in a shrug so exaggerated his neck disappeared. 'But I'm afraid I've got to go away for a day or two.'

'Go away? Go away where?'

'Paris.' Hayden shifted his eyes. 'That was the... um... people from Caen. Something's cropped up in... Paris. They... well... the point is that they want me to go to Paris.'

Even discounting the tell-tale little pauses between phrases that people always leave when they're lying, Hayden looked incredibly shifty. 'What for?' said Anne, fixing him with eyes like a gimlet. 'What precisely has cropped up?'

He looked away. 'Oh, it seems there's a team of American academics there in Paris who may turn out to be good future business, so they want me to go and help schmooze them.'

A team of American academics in Paris in August? Oh, very bloody likely. 'But you don't even officially start work for them until next month.'

'No, but... that is, I mean yes, but...' Hayden broke off and shrugged again. 'Well, you know how it is,' he finished, and bared his teeth at her.

I know that you're lying, Anne thought angrily. But instead of saying this, she decided to call his bluff. 'Very well.' She paused to place her coffee cup very precisely down on its saucer. 'Then we'll all come with you. I wouldn't mind a day or two in Paris.'

'No way!'

'No, please, Mum!'

Two teenage voices had rung in unison. Carpenter gave a muffled bark through his toast.

'There you are.' With what was an unmistakably triumphant nod at the kids, Hayden bustled about, picking up *Le Monde* and pointlessly shuffling its pages. '*Not* a good plan. No, I'll go alone.'

'Good thinking, Dad.' Conrad literally shook himself with relief.

'Yes, you do that, Hayden.' Verity echoed her stepbrother with equal fervour, at which Anne gave up.

'How *are* you going?' she said helplessly.

'Oh, the train.' Poised for flight, Hayden gulped the remainder of his tea. 'I'll just go and pack and then you can drop me at the station on your way to the beach – I take it you are going to the beach. It looks as though it's going to be a nice day for once. I'll phone you later this evening.'

Passing behind Anne, he rested his hands briefly on her shoulders. 'Cheer up, sweetie.' Leaning over, he pecked her on the cheek. 'I won't be gone long.'

Sweetie – *sweetie*? It took Anne a second to realise what he had called her. What a *vile* endearment, if you could call it an endearment. Hayden had never called her that before. She would have slaughtered him if he had. It had a horribly casual ring to it that made you sound like an old slapper.

'Mum?'

Watching her husband bounding up the stairs, Anne turned with an effort to see Verity watching her. 'What?'

'Are you okay?'

'On top of the world.'

'Then do you think I could –?' Verity broke off, disturbed by the expression on her mother's face. Trying to ignore it, she ploughed on. 'That is, would you, like, *mind* if I borrowed your, like, pink clam-diggers? I know they're new and you've only worn them once but –'

'You can have them for good.'

And leaping to her feet, Anne stalked out into the garden before she started smashing the place up. What the hell was Hayden playing at?

*

'Look,' said Hugo, as Verity and he clambered up into the dunes. 'Here's one of the World War II bunkers. They're all along this coast.'

Earlier, after Anne had dropped her and Conrad at the beach, Verity and Hugo had discovered neither of them felt like lolling around or swimming this morning. So Hugo had suggested they instead go for a walk. Verity had offered to take Carpenter with them but Conrad insisted he would look after the dog. He wasn't going in the sea either, he had announced, firmly stretching himself out on the sand, whereupon Danielle went into a strop and flounced off with the windsurfer on her own. Verity got the message. Conrad was playing warfare tactics and he needed Carpenter in his defence line.

Now, as she squinted inside the chipped, graffiti-covered concrete block half buried in sand, she wrinkled her nose at another sort of defence line. Dank and dark, the bunker was full of broken cans and rubbish and smelt grottier than the grottiest public toilet. You couldn't imagine anyone spending five minutes inside there, let alone the weeks and months soldiers presumably had spent.

'It's strange, isn't it?' Withdrawing her head, she turned away, looking over the mouth of the river towards the holiday complex of Port Guillaume on the other side. Pastel pink and blue in the hazy sunshine, the dinky little chalets looked like a row of cupcakes. 'Kinda freaky to think of all that *Saving Private Ryan* stuff going on right here and now it's like,' she lifted her shoulders, 'well, like, just a tourist place.'

'I know.' Hugo nodded. 'The main D-Day landing beaches are actually further along in the other direction, but I could take you to see them if you like.'

'I don't think so.' Verity shook her head. 'I mean, thanks for the offer but I don't think so. I mean, it's not, like, I don't appreciate the sacrifice made by the guys who died there because I do, I really, really do.' She thought a moment and frowned. 'It's just this business of adults constantly saying if we understand and remember, it will stop it ever happening again, when it never seems to, does it? I mean, there are still wars, still atrocities committed in the world. Nothing changes.'

She paused. Hugo was silent.

'But then,' Verity looked down, scuffing her trainers in the sand, 'that's the grown-ups all over, isn't it? They make mistakes, they carry on making them but, boy, do you get it in the neck if *you* dare to step out of line.'

Hugo started to say something and stopped. 'Verity?' he said at last. 'What are we talking about?'

'My mother and stepfather are splitting.' It was funny how she had just come straight out with it like that.

Hugo hesitated. 'What makes you think that?' he said cautiously.

'Oh, I don't know. Things.'

'Hey, come on.' He put an arm comfortingly round her shoulders. 'Are you sure you're not imagining it?' He jiggled her a little. 'I mean, if you took every row *my* parents have seriously, you'd expect them to be in the divorce courts every week.'

'No.' Verity shook her head again but more fiercely this time to prevent herself from crying. 'I know I'm not imagining it. And,' she eyed him, 'I know it's not, like, cool to get stressed over your parents' relationship.'

'I didn't mean that.'

'But it isn't, is it? I mean, like, some of the girls at school laugh about their parents screwing around but, you see, my mother's not like that. Or, at least, she's always said she's not and I believed her.'

'Tell me what's happened.'

Verity breathed in a quick inspiration and then let it out in a long sigh. 'Oh, it was at breakfast this morning – but it's not the first time. There's been something going on for days. Not a row exactly. I don't know exactly what but Mum's no good at hiding her feelings.' She gave a mirthless little laugh. 'Mum doesn't *believe* in hiding her feelings.'

'And?'

Verity trembled suddenly. 'And this morning Hayden kissed her and I saw her. I saw her not just flinch but positively cringe away from him. I thought I was mistaken for a moment but then she watched him go upstairs with this look of absolute *distaste* on her face and then I knew I wasn't.'

Hugo looked as if he didn't know what to say.

'Mum does that with my father, you see.' She had tried not to but she was crying anyway. 'Whenever she sees him that's exactly the way she looks at him. As if he was the biggest shit on earth – a complete waste of space.'

*

The only difference about Danielle and the beach today was that today there was no way Conrad was getting on that poxy windsurfer. That and that today, instead of squashing Yorkshire terriers, Carpenter was trying his luck with an Airedale. However, in view of the fact that even when standing on the tips of his paws with his ears practically vertical with excitement Carpenter's head scarcely came up to the Airedale's shoulder, Conrad thought this a tad ambitious of him.

Nevertheless, Carpenter hung on in there and sure enough the Airedale seemed suddenly to soften up. Carpenter then began to look as though he had got considerably more than he'd bargained for, because the Airedale went so over the top Conrad wondered if he were witnessing the canine equivalent of an erotic fantasy – a big woman turned on by little men. And it must have struck Carpenter that way, too, because quite soon he backed off to take refuge beside Conrad. The Airedale wasn't backing off, however. Perching on powerful haunches next to them, she set about emitting querulous little whines interspersed with flirtatious but hefty bats across Carpenter's ears with one of her gigantic paws.

Carpenter closed his eyes and tried not to wince when his head went sideways.

'I know, mate,' Conrad murmured consolingly to him. 'Women are nothing if not contrary. They either won't leave you alone or you can't get your hands on them.'

'Hey, I'm sorry, is she being a pain?'

Conrad looked up with a start. A plump-ish but really cute-looking English girl was hovering over them. She had braces on her teeth and long fair hair tied up in bunches.

'I'll take her away.'

'No, no worries,' Conrad said quickly. 'Carpenter's just being a wimp.'

'Carpenter? Is that his name?' Kneeling down on the sand, she stroked Carpenter's head, whereupon Carpenter licked the girl's hand so pathetically in his downtrodden I-am-an-abused-dog act Conrad was ashamed of him. Then he realised that the girl was saying Carpenter was lovely. She indicated the Airedale.

'This one's dead flirty.' She flicked Conrad a shy grin. Her teeth under the braces were sparkling white.

Conrad smiled back. It was so great at last to talk to a girl in English. But she got up. 'Well, I'd guess I'd better split.'

'Oh, stay a bit,' he pleaded.

'No,' came an ominous voice and they both jumped as a shadow loomed over them. 'That is not a good plan.'

Bunches and the flirt fled.

'What the bloody hell are you playing at?' spluttered Conrad, when he had recovered from the shock. 'You said you couldn't speak English.'

'No, I did not.' Danielle lay down, coolly stretching out her beautiful lithe body next to his. She suddenly looked about five years older. 'I said I didn't *want* to speak it. And I never do things if I don't want to do them.'

'Well, bully for you.' Conrad looked angrily away. He was really pissed off with her. In fact, she'd made him feel such a total prat he was inclined to bugger off and leave her to it. The next second, however, he nearly left his skin as he felt her mouth on his shoulder. Turning his head, he saw a pair of the clearest green eyes gazing at him from under the thickest black eyelashes. A pink tongue flicked out.

'Sorry, Conrad,' she murmured, and gently bit him.

As if it was the easiest thing in the world, he found himself turning and pushing her back down on the sand.

*

About half an hour after Anne got home Jean-Pierre roared into the drive on one of those obscenely powerful motorbikes. Penis extension, she thought disgustedly. Like father, like son.

Unable to face the prospect of bumping into Stephanie or Brigitte or André or Jean-Pierre – what a lot of people she suddenly had to avoid! – Anne had dropped the kids and Carpenter at the beach, gabbled some excuse about going home to do a bit of decorating, and slunk away with Martha. Decorating? Yeah, sure. The last thing she was going to do was waste her energy prettifying the happy home. However, the trouble was she did not know exactly what she *was* going to do. Once she had got home and transferred the sleeping Martha to her cot, all she had actually done was stand in the middle of the kitchen in a quandary.

How could she check Hayden's story? That was what she wanted to do - but how?

If they had been in some detective drama on television, she would have sneaked after him, stealthily tip-toeing in his wake and dodging behind handy pillars, everyone around this strange woman behaving as if they had suddenly and conveniently lost the power of sight. But even if they hadn't, it was a trifle tricky to stealthily tip-toe after anyone with an eleven month baby in tow, not to mention two complaining teenagers and a dog.

There was always the option of rushing upstairs and turning all the drawers and cupboards out onto the floor in search of – what? Evidence of intrigue, she supposed. There wouldn't be any. If there was any evidence of intrigue to be had, it would be on Hayden's mobile which he had, of course, taken with him. And then she'd only have to put everything back in the drawers and cupboards...

So it was that by the time Jean-Pierre roared up on his motorbike, all she was doing was sitting at the table, sitting there in anything but a happy trance.

*

'What the hell do you want?' she snapped, as he stepped into the kitchen in a biker jacket and boots to grace the Gestapo.

'I came to see you. I look for you at the beach.' His eyes flicked round the room. 'But Conrad tells me you are home alone.'

'Hayden's not here, if that's what you mean.'

'Yes, Conrad tells me Hayden has gone to Paris.'

'Which, of course, you already knew.' Anne threw him an unpleasant little smile. 'Courtesy of dear Juno.'

'Dear Juno?' Jean-Pierre frowned as if bewildered. 'I do not understand. Why do you say 'dear' in this way and why should Juno know where your husband is? Besides, since the party I leave Le Manoir. I go to stay with friends in Trouville so I do not see Juno.'

There was a short pause as he studied her. 'Why do you not go to the beach?'

'What is it to you? But if you must know, I'm busy.' Yanking *Le Monde* towards her, Anne pointedly opened it.

'Doing what?'

'Improving my French.'

Jean-Pierre cocked his head sideways to look at the newspaper. 'It is better if you read him the right way up.'

Not trusting herself to speak, Anne silently righted the paper. In the silence that followed Jean-Pierre then parked himself opposite her, unzipping his jacket with an X-certificate rip. Anne tried not to look at him, wishing she had the nerve to tell him to fuck off. But it was very difficult when your husband had buggered off with a bimbo and you were faced with testosterone on legs.

'Actually, I came to apologise to you,' he said after a moment.

'What for?'

But Jean-Pierre ignored her question, this time looking past her shoulder. 'Do you always put the flowers in the electric kettle?'

Swivelling her head, Anne caught sight of Walter's wilting dahlias and blushed. 'Yes,' she said coldly, resuming her scrutiny of *Le Monde*. 'Now please go away.' There followed yet another pause, this time so quiet Anne could hear him breathing.

All at once Jean-Pierre jumped noisily to his feet. She looked up.

'I know what.' He treated her to a puppyish grin. 'I take you for a ride.'

'I beg your pardon!'

'On my motorbike. We go for what you call the burn-up. You are sad, it will make you happy.' Glancing at her bare arms, he shrugged off his jacket and held it out to her. 'Come, I borrow you this.'

Gaping at him, Anne had split second vision of her zooming round Normandy with a penis extension throbbing between her thighs, naked breasts pumping beneath a biker jacket *à la* Marianne Faithful. How disgraceful. 'And what am I supposed to do with the baby?' she demanded furiously. 'Sling her round my neck?'

Jean-Pierre's face fell. 'I am so sorry. For a moment I forget your baby.'

'Yes, well, you and your father both seem possessed of a highly convenient loss of memory, especially when it comes to such *in*convenient matters as a baby.'

He stiffened visibly. 'I am not my father. Do not paint me with the same brush.'

'Tar,' Anne corrected automatically.

'*Comment*?'

'You *tar* with the same brush – oh, forget it. Just go away.'

'No. I know you are angry with me.'

'Yes, well.' She gave such a huge shrug her neck clicked. 'I wouldn't let it worry you.'

'But it does worry me, Anne. I thought we were friends.'

She looked away.

'Listen to me, Anne, please.' Resting on the palms of his hands, he leaned across the table and looked urgently into her face. 'I now know the true story of your *affaire* with my father but I did not know it before. I swear this. When I make the secret arrangement for you to meet with him, he has told me only that you were friends, the good old *friends* from a time long ago. He tells me it would be a surprise, the *good* surprise for you. Please, I speak the truth – believe me.'

Anne contemplated him for a second and then slumped, suddenly sick and tired of the whole idiotic mess. 'Oh, I believe you, all right,' she said wearily. 'I've since realised you were probably being used, actually. So just forget it.'

'No, I will not forget it. I am *not* the same as my father. I know he is not a good man in many, many ways but –' Jean-Pierre trembled, looking all at once terribly young and vulnerable, 'he is my father.'

Anne felt a shaft of pity. 'I know,' she whispered.

'And listen.' Jean-Pierre shrugged back on his jacket. 'I do not wish to upset you further but I must also tell you that my father is saying he wishes to meet again with you.'

'Why the hell would he want to do that?'

'Oh, you know.' Jean-Pierre now looked wise beyond his years. 'My father is a man who does not like the – how do you say – the unfinished business?'

Unfinished business, reflected Anne, that's a good way of putting it. But she felt a twinge of alarm. 'You're not telling me Alain is going to come here, are you? That your father knows where I live?'

'I cannot say. I have not given him your address but he knew you were here in France because somebody told him that. Maybe that same somebody…?' Jean-Pierre left an eloquent little pause.

Stephanie, Anne thought dully. What's to stop Stephanie and her latest pillow talk? 'Jean-Pierre?' she said carefully. 'Forgive me for asking you this but is your father having an affair with Stephanie?'

'An affair with Stephanie? Stephanie Dérain?'

Anne nodded.

Jean-Pierre frowned. 'No, I do not think so. Oh, I know they like the flirting but an *affaire*? Pah!' He puffed his sensual lips out in a scornful little noise. 'No, I am certain they are not.'

'How can you be so sure?'

'Because,' he said, looking rather grim, 'since I am a man my father always tells to me the exact details of his mistresses.'

Anne pulled a face. 'How vile.'

'Maybe, but it is how I know he has upset you and why I give him the hard time.'

'Thank you.' She managed a wry smile but once more it was followed by silence, both of them aware that, despite the restored goodwill, they had nothing left to say to one another.

'Anne?' Jean-Pierre floundered slightly. 'I think now is the time for me to say *au revoir* or perhaps *adieu* is better because tomorrow I return home to Paris – for my work.'

'Oh.' Anne was surprised by her pang of regret. Ten minutes ago she had wanted the man out of her sight forever and now she felt curiously reluctant to let him go. 'You know, I saw some of your sketches,' she began, adding quickly as Jean-Pierre's eyebrows rushed together, 'By accident, I hasten to add.'

The eyebrows relaxed. 'Please do not tell me what you think of them,' he said nervously.

'But I thought they were beautiful!' Anne gave a vigorous nod. 'In fact, they reminded me of Leonardo's drawings.'

As if disbelieving, the young Frenchman eyed her for a moment. Then he inclined his head in a tiny bow of acknowledgement. 'Thank you,' he said simply. 'You are very kind. Particularly as my father tells me I am wasting my time.'

'Don't listen to him. He's probably jealous.'

Jean-Pierre made as if to reply and then hesitated. 'Anne, if my father should arrive here…?'

'Oh, don't panic. I'm not going to shoot him.'

The young Frenchman's mouth turned down. 'And why not?' he demanded, with mock severity.

Anne smiled. 'I haven't got a gun,' she said.

*

For ages after he had gone, Anne remained sitting at the kitchen table, staring into space. Then, suddenly grabbing her mobile, she sent a text to Hayden telling him not to bother ringing her that evening because she was going out. As soon as she'd collected the kids from the beach she'd switch the thing off. She was not sure of her motives in doing this but one thing was certain. She needed time to think.

27

It was a pity but it seemed to Walter Pepper that St Moritz suited him no better than Paris. Perhaps it was time he faced up to what until now had merely been a sneaking suspicion: he was getting a touch too long in the tooth for all this high life. Every night since they had arrived he had slept badly, waking every morning in a fair bit of a stew, notwithstanding his waking in a very pretty bedroom with pine floorboards, pine match-boarded walls and a pine beamed ceiling. So much pine, indeed, that for a split second every morning Walter thought he was waking up inside a cuckoo clock.

This morning, however, he determined he would get a grip on things. Pulling on his dressing gown, he therefore flung open the French windows and stepped resolutely out onto the pine balcony. Beyond pine window boxes crammed with great swags of the healthiest geraniums Walter had ever seen in his life, the view rivalled the picture on a packet of Alpen.

Drawing in deep lungfuls of the sweet air he debated whether to try a yodel – Maggie had always laughed at his yodel – and then decided against, partly because he didn't feel in the mood for yodelling and partly because at that moment on an adjoining balcony Dolores stepped out.

Walter stepped hastily back in only to hesitate before closing the door. It had occurred to him that if he stepped out again she might automatically swing back in like the lady on a weather house: Mr Pepper for sunshine, Mrs Dolores for rain. He tried it and she didn't. Instead, she treated him to a hostile glare and commenced bashing a fur rug against the wall as if killing a rat.

Downstairs, the daily woman was laying the table for breakfast. With plaits round her head and cheeks like a Cox's Orange Pippin, she might look as harmless as a costume doll but, when it came to Walter, she was no more congenial than Dolores. As for the fair-haired young lad who came in every morning to lay the fire, he was goose-stepping about the place in shorts fit to grace the Hitler Youth Movement.

Walter sighed. It was puzzling how as you got older, the memories from your younger days did not fade but grew more acute – sometimes spitefully acute. He'd only been a boy himself during the war so it was ridiculous to resent this boy, simply because he reminded you of an unpleasant time in history. It was all so long ago.

I'm turning into a funny old man, Walter reflected glumly. But, before he could pursue this somewhat depressing line of thought, in tripped Maxine, wearing – of all things – plus fours and a deerstalker. 'Wal-terre, it is the beautiful day!' she cried, before turning to shriek imprecations at the shorts lad.

I'm too old for this, Walter decided, trying to shut his ears against the piercing voice and wondering why Maxine could not just sit down and eat her breakfast like a sensible woman.

In due course, however, the plaits lady served up a tasty bubble-and-squeak affair, there was a nice rasher or two of bacon and, once she had sat down and stopped squawking, as Maxine reminded him for the umpteenth time, there was no Gilles to bother them.

With this vaguely cheering thought in mind, presently, if a little unwillingly, Walter began almost to perk up.

*

'What's the matter?' asked Anne, as Verity sat at the breakfast table picking at a piece of toast in a slightly listless fashion. 'Have you fallen out with Hugo or something?'

'Oh, no.' Verity looked up. 'Anything but.'

'I'm relieved to hear it.' Anne smiled. 'He's such a nice young man.'

'Blureugh! That puts the kiss of death on the poor guy.'

Anne laughed. For some reason she was feeling a bit better about everything this morning. Crossing by the window, she caught sight of her stepson doing frantic press-ups on the grass. 'Conrad!' she shouted, and tapped on the glass. 'You'll make yourself sick doing that straight after you've eaten!'

Verity yawned. 'He's trying to get himself a six-pack to impress Danny boy.'

'Don't be mean about her, Verity. She's nice, too.'

'Yeah, I guess.'

'By the way, I've been meaning to ask you. Did you know Juno might be going to live in London?'

Verity said she did, actually.

'Do you know why?'

'Not really. That is, I think she told me but I can't, like, remember.' Getting to her feet, Verity flexed her shoulders and stretched her arms above her head. This made her t-shirt ride up so she stroked her flat stomach for good measure. 'I think she just needs to hang out.'

'Like a line of washing?' Anne said witheringly, but Verity wasn't listening.

'Hey, what are you doing today? Hugo's mum has made him and Danielle go shopping with her this morning to get their gear for next term, so I wondered if, like, you fancy it,' Verity assumed a crafty expression, 'if me and you could take a wander down to that boutique in Cabourg. Their end of season sale starts today.'

End of season sales, the new school term, gloom once more descended on Anne. Summer was nearly gone, the carnival was over. That old Seekers song popped into her head. *Say goodbye, my own true lover, as we sing a lover's song. Though it breaks my heart to leave you –*

'Are you okay, Mum? I wasn't suggesting we wander down to the local morgue.'

Anne pulled herself together. 'I'm fine,' she said briskly. 'And yes – let's hit the boutique and squander. I'll buy you a new dress or whatever you fancy.'

'Fantastic! Hey, thanks, Mum! I'll just rush and wash my hair. Hugo said there's a great photo exhibition on in Houlgate – Man Ray and stuff – so we were going to pop along this afternoon.' Verity started for the stairs.

'Verity?'

She turned. 'Yeah?'

'I meant it when I said I'm pleased about you and Hugo, but, well, you are still only fifteen and, anyway, you will remember everything you've been told about sex and so on, won't you?'

Verity looked exasperated. 'You don't need to say that, you know.'

'Okay. Sorry. I know these things are private but, well, Hugo is quite a bit older than you and –'

'That reminds me. I remember now what Juno said about why she might be going to live in London. It was something about her having this English friend. I remember now because she said whoever it was, was, like, really mature and successful and loads older than her which was, like, good because they wouldn't be intimidated and patronised by her parents the way Stephanie and Gilles so often intimidate and patronise her friends.'

Verity swung on the bannister. 'Why did you want to know, anyway?'

Anne stared at her daughter. 'Oh, no reason,' she said brightly. 'Just idle curiosity.'

*

The boutique in Cabourg turned out to be anything but fantastic and not only because Anne and Verity could not find much to fit either of them – sales always went in for size six bargains which were fine if you were a model or a midget. But because raking through the rails faster than a ferret and buckling under the weight of her monster husband's credit cards, they found Stephanie Dérain.

It was quite an eye-opener, even if you were intimately acquainted with a shopaholic. Anne bought herself a black pencil skirt and Verity a pair of white jeans, but by the time they left the boutique, the three of them – and Martha's buggy – were festooned in designer carrier bags, ninety-nine point nine per cent of which pertained to Stephanie.

Stephanie had bought seven silk shirts, five linen jackets, two pairs of cargo pants and, as a reluctant afterthought, three pashminas; reluctant only because she already had six and pashminas were a little *passé* now. Oh, and four bikinis when Anne mentioned she might be going to the beach. Stephanie hadn't brought her bikini with her today, but she would so adore to go to the beach and it was easier than going back home to fetch it.

Fine, rationalised Anne, as, feeling like a designer refugee, she manhandled the creaking buggy down to the seafront. Anyone could be tempted by a convenient bikini when the beach beckons, but why *four*? Was Stephanie going to wear them all at once? Did she intend to emerge dripping eight A-cups like one of those multi-breasted African fertility goddesses?

Anne did not, however, get the chance to find out because, sitting on the top step of the stairs leading down to the beach and clad in what seemed to be 1960's purple loon pants, they found Brigitte Laurent.

'Oh, there you are at last, Anne!' she cried, unfolding her wafery legs like a pair of garden shears. 'I've been waiting ages hoping you were going to come down. I tried to call you yesterday evening but your phone seemed to be switched off.'

She paused to greet Stephanie in a cursory fashion.

Anne started to tell the kids she would meet them at the usual time when Brigitte stopped her. 'Actually, Anne, I was going to ask you all to dinner this evening. I gather that Hayden's been called away on business so I thought you might be feeling a bit blue on your own.'

''Ayden?' As the kids and dog trooped off, Stephanie turned to Anne in surprise. 'Your 'usband 'as gone away?'

'*H*usband, *h*as and *H*ayden,' corrected Brigitte, with the kind of silky malice she must have learnt from her husband and made ten times bitchier. 'Being French doesn't automatically oblige one to drop the H-bomb, you know.'

There followed an unfathomable little pause until 'I think,' Stephanie said suddenly, grabbing her carrier bags, 'I think that maybe the beach is not for me this day. Goodbye, Anne.'

And without another word the Frenchwoman staggered off.

Anne rounded on Brigitte. 'Christ, Brigitte, was that necessary? I realise you don't like Stephanie very much but did you really need to humiliate her like that?'

'Well, what did you drag her along for?'

'I didn't *drag her along*. I bumped into her in town and she came of her own accord. Don't be childish, Brigitte. We're not playing Odd Woman Out.'

'Oh, I'm sorry, Anne.' Brigitte's bony shoulders suddenly slumped and she looked contrite. 'Truly I am. I'm just so angry and worried.'

'Angry? What about? Worried – what about?'

'Angry with Stephanie and her *salaud* of a husband. It's not just your father they've forced out with their nastiness.'

'What do you mean?'

'It's Juno.' Brigitte faced her with a kind of despair.

'Juno?'

'Yes, Juno. I've been trying to ring her since the day before yesterday but she isn't picking up or even responding to texts. So this morning I got so concerned I actually went to the Manoir to find her, but she wasn't there and nobody knew where she was, either. All they knew was that she hasn't been seen for two days.' Brigitte looked on the point of tears. 'Anne, she's simply disappeared.'

The women locked eyes for a second. Then Anne felt a touch of impatience. 'Brigitte, I don't want seem unsympathetic but aren't you going a bit over top about this? Juno is twenty-seven. I don't suppose for one moment that she's *disappeared*. She's doubtless just cleared off somewhere without telling anyone, the way girls of that age do.'

There was another tiny pause as the Frenchwoman again looked straight at Anne. But this time her expression was odd. Then, all at once, she dropped her eyes and turned to go. 'Okay, forget it, forget I spoke. I thought you knew but, obviously, you don't. I'll see you later, okay?'

'No, wait a minute.' Anne grabbed her arm. 'What do you mean – you thought I knew? Know what? What don't I know?'

'Nothing... nothing. Forget I spoke.' Gently shaking off the detaining hand, Brigitte quickly embraced Anne. 'Sorry, but I must get back to my cassoulet. I don't want it to burn. I'll see you later, okay? Come round at about seven.'

And without further ado, the Frenchwoman strode stiff-legged off down the promenade, loon pants flapping round her ankles. From a distance she could have been a clown on stilts.

*

Anne was about to start preparing Martha's lunch when Stephanie Dérain appeared on the doorstep. 'I was expecting you,' she said, surprised to realise she had been. Deciding that the beach was also not for her this day, Anne had gone home with the baby.

'I came to see you because you are on your own without –' Stephanie halted, her face so screwed up that Anne thought she was about to sneeze. 'Huh... huh... *H*ayden,' she enunciated on a rush of breath, and then looked victorious.

Anne smothered a grin. 'If I were you, Stephanie, I wouldn't worry about the English aitch. Hayden likes being called 'Ayden. Besides, I can't pronounce the French word for a frog.'

'*Grenouille*?' The Frenchwoman looked incredulous.

'You said it. Don't ask me to. We're quits.' Gesturing for her to sit down at the table, Anne sloshed a glass of wine for Stephanie without going through all that Badôit crap. 'Now, what did you really come for?'

Stephanie hesitated. 'I think Brigitte poisons you against me.'

'Yes, well, that's nonsense and even if it wasn't I wouldn't let it bother you.'

'I know I am a bad mother –' Stephanie began humbly.

'Oh, for goodness' sake, we're all bad mothers! None of us are perfect and if any woman makes out she is, you can bet your bottom dollar she'd make Joan Crawford look like the Virgin Mary.'

'Juno is so difficult, Anne. It is all very good for Brigitte to sit in the judgement on me but if she knew Juno like I know Juno.'

It sounded like a song. Anne started humming the tune in her head.

'You see, Anne, there are dreadful things Juno does which–'

'Stephanie?' Anne said abruptly. 'Do you mind if we don't talk about Juno?'

Stephanie looked taken aback. 'No. Not if you so desire.'

'And Stephanie?' Something else had clicked in Anne's mind. 'Why did you say you had lovers – *a* lover? You haven't, have you?'

The Frenchwoman hesitated again, this time for longer. '*Non*,' she said at last.

'Then why did you tell me you had?'

'Because,' Stephanie said in a small voice, 'I was jealous of you.'

'Jealous of me? Why on earth should *you* be jealous of *me*?'

'Oh, you would not understand – you with your lovely 'Ayden, your lovely children, your lovely baby, your dog.'

Carpenter didn't seem to qualify for the 'lovely' epithet.

'But it was not... not all the untruths,' Stephanie continued jerkily. 'I did once 'ave an affair.'

'What happened?'

'Oh, Anne, it was 'orrible.' All at once Stephanie's face contorted with distress, making her look like a sick old monkey. 'This man *did* want money, too. That was true. 'E asked me for it. Not the francs on the table but a demand that I put up the expenses for his *appartement*. And this I find very bad because 'e 'ad a job, a good job in the Banque Nationale.'

Stephanie brightened for a second. 'But 'e was very good at sex,' she added, as if this were an afterthought, but a vital one.

Blimey, thought Anne, the *Bonk* Nationale.

'But I wish 'e 'ad not been so good because it made me feel so... so...' Stephanie floundered. 'What is the word? I forget it. Meaning not expensive?'

'Cheap?' Anne suggested helpfully.

'*Exactement* – cheap. You see, I believed I was wanted for myself.'

Anne did not know what to say. 'When was all this?' she asked, in the absence of anything better.

'Oh, many years ago.' Stephanie gave a brave smile. 'When I was *yong*.'

There was another pause, a protracted one. Anne drew a deep breath. Annoying as Stephanie was, she could not help feeling sorry for the wretched woman. 'Well, all I can say is more fool him. He was obviously a total jerk.'

'Oh, Anne, you are the good friend to me.'

Anne glanced at Martha in her high chair. The baby appeared enraptured by their conversation. My daughter is going to go far in life, observed Anne, with a flood of maternal pride, if she's such a good listener. She turned her attention back to the Frenchwoman sniffing pathetically into an uncharacteristically scruffy handkerchief. Reluctant as she was to raise this, there was something that needed to be said.

'Stephanie?'

'*Oui*?'

'You say I am a good friend to you – does that work both ways?'

'*Comment*?'

'What I mean is – are you are a good friend to me?'

'But of course!'

'Then why the hell did you tell Alain Duval that I was here in France?' Anne began speaking very fast, falling over her words in her panic to get them out. 'You knew I had a love affair with him when I was your au pair all those years ago, and later on you knew that affair had ended very painfully. You knew I never wanted to see him again in my life because I told you about what had happened, that I had found out he was married and his wife was pregnant. You knew, because I wrote to you and told you. I *told* you. So you *knew*.

'Why then did you tell him I was here? Why did you put him on to me? You say you're my friend. Well, if that's true then why the hell did you want to make such a fool out of me?'

Stephanie looked as if she were about to faint. 'Oh, Anne, that was not *me*. I would never, *never* do such a thing to you.'

'Look, I'm sorry, but I don't believe you. It *must* have been you. Who else could it have been? I know for a fact that it wasn't Jean-Pierre, he was just being used, and nobody else but you knew about Alain and me – oh, shit!'

There was a hiatus as Anne was suddenly hit by one of those blinding flashes of comprehension. She'd remembered what Alain had said about his dealing in art and who handled things for him the French end.

'I've just got it,' she said, staring coldly at Stephanie. 'It was Gilles, wasn't it? *Gilles* told Alain I was here. It was Gilles all along. Jesus, Stephanie, it was your blasted *husband*.'

The Frenchwoman nodded a forlorn affirmative.

'But why? What has Gilles got against me, for God's sake, to do something like that? What on earth did he think he was doing?'

'I do not know. I think at first … maybe Gilles thinks it is amusing, the little joke.'

'I'm splitting my sides. But have I got this wrong or are you saying that, even if you were not involved in it, you knew what he was going to do?'

Stephanie gulped as tears began to course down her cheeks. 'Yes, I knew but I told 'im it is bad, not amusing but very bad, and I begged 'im not to say anything. I begged Gilles so much, Anne, I did not believe 'e would do it.'

'Then why did he?'

All at once Stephanie sat up straighter, her tear-streaked face seeming to harden. 'Gilles finds you attractive, Anne. Gilles 'as always found you attractive, always since long ago when you were the very yong girl.' She fixed Anne bang in the eye, a kind of irony in her own.

'But you, of course,' she continued, 'did not feel the same way. You did not even see this. But I do. I see it then, I see it now. But Gilles will not see it. No, it... angers 'im.'

Jesus Christ, thought Anne.

'And Gilles is friends for a long time now with Alain because they do the deals together – always they are doing the deals together. So Gilles tells Alain that you are here because it is like – 'ow do you say?' Clutching her head, Stephanie looked agonized as she searched for the right words. 'My God, this is so very bad, but it is like they 'ave the competition together, the competition of who can have the *affaire* and –'

'Okay, okay!' Anne felt she'd vomit if she heard any more. 'I get the general picture.'

'I am so sorry,' said Stephanie, looking mortified.

'It's not your fault. Just tell me this. Have you had an affair with him?'

'With Alain? An *affaire* with Alain Duval?' Stephanie gulped. 'No, never! He does not –' Breaking off, her face crumpled as she again started to weep into her grotty handkerchief.

'Alain never finds me attractive,' she sobbed. 'Like Gilles. Gilles never finds me attractive, either.'

In silence Anne watched her, feeling more than a little repelled, yet, oddly, not repelled by Stephanie. What repelled her was that a man like Gilles, such a complete toad of a man, could reduce a woman to this. 'Come on,' she said, presently and gently. 'Stop crying, dry your eyes and drink your wine. I've got to feed the baby and then I'll make us some lunch.'

'Oh, thank you, but I cannot stay.'

Brushing away her tears, Stephanie explained that she had been invited to the opening of the end of summer sale at a boutique in Deauville. She must go because there were so *many* things she needed.

After she had gone, Anne found herself feeding Martha on autopilot. The baby seemed equally preoccupied. But maybe Martha was thinking the same thing.

Stephanie Dérain wasn't just a sad case, she was terminal.

28

People in history were always claiming mountain air aided clear thinking but so far Walter Pepper was failing to persuade Maxine to indulge in either of them – either the clear thinking or the mountain air. Except for a cable car trip up to the peaks, an exercise that, unfortunately, Walter realised too late was not quite his cup of tea, having discovered he wasn't keen on anything that flew a couple of hundred feet above the ground without wings, Maxine refused to leave the village.

So much for his felt hat with a feather, and striding along rocky passes, and Lord only knows why Maxine had taken to plus fours and a deerstalker.

It might all have been better if Maxine had not complained so much. But complain she did, complain ceaselessly. St Moritz was boring, she moaned, not just once but ten times an hour – or so it seemed. And St Moritz looked ugly in summer. Well, here Walter could see a little of her point. Some of the modern hotels would fit better in Wolverhampton, although even there only if smothered in a couple of feet of snow.

Doggedly, he kept trying to persuade her to go out and see things. Actually, there was plenty to do in the area if you set your mind to it. The walks, a couple of museums – not the type he was generally interested in, admittedly, because they were of the folksy variety. But Walter didn't mind what they looked at providing it gave them something sensible to talk about.

Anyway, he was curious to find out what the Swiss had done in history other than being a bank.

However, Maxine would have none of it. Aside from the cable car trip and once dragging him into a restaurant to dine on something called fondue – a dish which seemed to Walter nothing more than do-it-yourself Welsh rarebit and bloomin' dangerous to boot when burning cheese stuck damned near catastrophically to his plate – Maxine spent most of the time grumbling. Except for going shopping, of course. Maxine never went anywhere without going shopping.

Walter hated shopping but he had roused himself and bought a cuckoo clock for Anne (although somehow it didn't strike him as her type of thing), a beer tankard with a lid for Hayden (again not quite right), fleecy tops for Verity and Conrad (they *might* go down all right), and a lovely little red pinafore frock for Martha embroidered with pansies. Now she would look a treat in that.

He also bought Carpenter a new collar. The man in the shop had tried to sell him a waterproof tartan dog jacket, but Walter knew Carpenter would have no truck with waterproof tartan jackets. He had his doubts about Carpenter having truck with the collar, given that too was red and embroidered with pansies.

Yet, even the shopping caused ructions because Maxine had wanted to buy him a new wrist watch. You cannot come to Switzerland, she declared, without buying a watch. No, he was sorry, it was very kind of her, but Walter did not want a new wrist watch. He did not *need* a new wrist watch. His old Timex that Maggie had given him from the money that she had saved out of the housekeeping and her part-time job in the library was still ticking along nicely, thank you.

It touched him to think of the Timex because Maggie had given it to him the year they had Anne. Indeed, she had given it to him on the day that would have been Jack's fourth birthday – if the poor little blighter had lived. 'I've bought you a present, Walter,' she had said out of the blue over supper that evening, and then 'I'm expecting' – all in the same breath.

Seven months later Anne was born.

Of course, he could have told Maxine all this and then maybe she would have understood about the wrist watch. Except Maxine did not listen to anything you told her, not anything *real*, as Anne would say. Funny. He never had before, but now he could see exactly what his daughter meant by that.

It was three o'clock in the afternoon. They were drinking coffee Walter did not want in the Swiss châlet Walter did not want to be in. Maxine started spinning one of her yarns. The sun shone outside, Wolverhampton beckoned.

It was no good, thought Walter, listening sadly to the nonsense. At his age – at any age – if you truly loved someone you could put up with anything from them.

And if you did not, there was not much point in it, was there?

*

'Three o'clock in the afternoon,' Anne informed Martha, 'is always too early or too late for anything you want to do. Now who said that?'

The baby smiled at her and then stretched her perfect little mouth in a polite yawn.

'Yes, I'm being boring, but for your information I think it was Jean-Paul Sartre.'

Martha did her best to look interested but her eyelids fluttered and drooped.

'Okay, you win. Let's get you down for your siesta.'

Standing to lift the baby into her arms, Anne glanced up at the leaden sky. The sun had disappeared and the day grown so oppressively hot and muggy she contemplated following Martha's example and lying down herself for a bit, except that she felt too wired. She felt oddly as if she ought to be doing something or going somewhere but, if so, she did not know what or where.

They had spent a lovely hour or so together, she and Martha, after Stephanie had gone, Anne getting out the play paints and big pad of cheap paper she had bought from the supermarket and spreading them all out on a rug in the shade of the orchard. It had been the first time Martha had shown an interest in play paints – other than trying to eat them. In fact, she had shown more than an interest; she had produced a couple of action paintings far superior to Jackson Pollock.

Anne stood under the still-leaved apple trees, rocking the sleepy child in her arms. It would be so wonderful if Martha turned out to have inherited her talent for art – if it was talent. Anne wasn't sure any longer, just as she wasn't sure about anything any longer. The world turned upside down, she thought hopelessly, and then immediately remembered her father saying exactly the same thing when her mother died.

Anne looked down at the child in her arms, at the paint-stained little fingers spread across her breast like the tentacles of a starfish.

It had been Walter who had first encouraged her to draw, Walter who had spent patient Sunday afternoons with a box of watercolours encouraging Anne to look closely at things, to look at them so closely you could reproduce their image with your eyes shut. He hadn't been a bad watercolourist himself, Walter, when he had found the time. There and then it occurred to Anne, as it had never occurred before, to wonder if her father had wanted to be an artist. Maybe he had cherished dreams, but dreams never to be fulfilled. Walter was the product of a generation in which a man of his class was not afforded the luxury of dreams. Once out of school, he would have simply been ordered by his own father to buckle down and get a decent job to earn the money that would one day keep a wife and family.

Sighing, Anne trudged back across the spiky grass. It had crossed her mind to let the baby sleep out here – it was stiflingly hot in the house, even with all the windows open – while she tried to sketch the landscape. But the light was foul, managing somehow to be both dim and glaring without a single shadow anywhere. She compromised by leaving the baby uncovered in her cot but with the nursery curtains pulled to, went to the bathroom to rinse her wrists under a cold tap that wasn't cold, and then sat down in front of her dressing table to examine her face in the mirror.

Well, who could blame Hayden for deserting this fright? Her hair was dull and stringy, her eyes puffy and her face deathly pale yet peculiarly blotchy. Far from acquiring a healthy summer glow, she might have spent the last few weeks in Guantanamo Bay.

Anne stiffened her spine. What she needed was a damage limitation policy. Get up and fight for him, ghoul, she told herself savagely. While she waited for Hayden to come back she would get a tan and embark upon a rigid diet. Then – when – *if* he returned, however besotted Hayden might be with his callow mistress, he would be greeted by this honed, toned temptress and realise the error of his ways. Good plan. Except there was no sun and Anne was starving hungry.

The perky little chirrup of her mobile phone sounded from the kitchen. She wasn't taking Hayden's calls, but she must check that it wasn't one of the kids.

Getting heavily to her feet, she clumped downstairs.

Well, whoever had phoned her had not left a message and it was a number she did not recognise. Brigitte? No, but thinking of Brigitte recalled Anne to those rosé wine people André had told her about. If André, as he had promised, had passed on her number to them, it might be them ringing her.

Anne dithered. The last thing she felt like doing at the moment was one of her breezy buy-me-trust-me-I'm-great approaches to a potential client. But... she considered anew. If it turned out that she was, yet again, on the brink of being a single parent, she was going to need every source of income possible. She pressed the call-back. It rang.

'Hello?' she said, tentatively.

'Anne! You called me back!'

Oh, *no*! It was Alain.

*

Well, if nothing else, the one thing you could say about Maxine was when she decided to do something, she did it. Walter Pepper could not help admiring a lady who did that. So it was that the moment he began – with caution – to explain that he was not exactly enjoying himself in Switzerland, Maxine declared that neither was she and they would therefore be packed and *en route* within the hour. She wasn't nasty about it, just determined.

As Walter had anticipated, however, it took Maxine, or rather, Dolores, far longer than an hour to pack Maxine's nineteen suitcases, which meant by the time they were ready to set off the sun had quite disappeared behind the mountains.

Yet, before he could voice his opinion that this was not, therefore, a very auspicious time of the day to embark upon a journey, and such a long journey, the young lad in shorts popped out from nowhere like a jack-in-the-box and presented Walter with a walking stick he had carved himself.

Walter found himself quite overcome. 'Thank you. You're very kind. Indeed –' He trawled his memory. '*Danke*,' he finished, feeling a little foolish.

'No worries,' said the lad. Except for a barely discernible accent he might have been that boy of Hayden's. 'You're welcome any time, Mr Pepper.'

And that was it. They were going home.

*

The day had ground on, getting heavier and stickier, the house so stuffy Anne felt the walls were pressing in on her. Even Martha was behaving in an uncharacteristically grumpy fashion, banging her toys about and intoning 'Da-da, Da-da' like a metronome.

Nobody else had phoned or called round; the afternoon was very quiet.

As evening approached, however, it began to feel odd being on her own in the house with the baby. There was an odd sort of silence, the sort of silence where you find yourself wandering about, aimlessly picking things up, and then equally aimlessly putting them down. Anne found herself feeling strangely self-conscious, as though somebody was watching her. Even Martha had stopped grizzling, sitting motionless on her play mat with one finger pointing mysteriously at the ceiling like someone out of a Leonardo painting.

Eventually six o'clock limped round. Never had an afternoon seemed so long, never had she so longed for company. Yet Anne could not face the thought of dinner with the Laurents. No, she would ring and tell Brigitte she was feeling under the weather, a highly appropriate excuse given the lowering skies. The kids could get a taxi home. She hoped André would not answer the phone because he was bound to find some way of teasing her. A little of André Laurent went a long way.

'Oh, Brigitte, I'm glad I've got you. Listen, I'm awfully sorry, but I don't think I can make dinner this evening. I'm feeling a bit under the weather.'

'Oh, you poor thing!' There was a clucking noise. 'Have you got a cold coming? You sound a bit snuffly.'

Somebody in the background said something.

'It's Anne,' said Brigitte to whoever it was. She sounded much more French on the phone for some reason. 'She's got a cold.' Her voice came back to Anne. 'That was André,' she said with a titter. 'He wants to know if you'd like him to come round and rub Vic on your chest.'

Anne gritted her teeth. 'Brigitte, I haven't got a cold. It's only, um, the Curse,' she lied. 'You know, a bad period. I just need to collapse tonight with a hot water bottle. I'll be all right tomorrow. You know how it is.'

'Ooh, do you still get it badly, then?' Brigitte not only sounded much more French on the phone, she sounded much more prurient. 'Perhaps it's the *Change*,' she intoned ghoulishly. 'At our age we do have to think about that, you know.'

Anne now felt like screaming. 'Listen, can you tell Verity and Conrad to get a cab home? I'll pay for it when they get here.'

Brigitte said they could stay the night. Then Anne could go to bed with her hot water bottle.

Anne hesitated. 'That's extremely kind of you, but what about Carpenter?'

Carpenter could stay, too. 'Does he like cassoulet?'

Anne imagined Brigitte serving cassoulet to shame Elizabeth David. 'Bit rich for him. Tell Verity to make him some scrambled eggs – if that's all right by you.'

'No, I'll tell André. His cooking is about dog standard.'

Anne ended the call and then held the phone in her hand, looking at it thoughtfully. After a minute she turned to her daughter. Martha had had her tea but not, as she usually did, dozed off after it. Instead, the baby was wide awake and watching her.

'Come on.' Anne levered back on the espadrilles she had earlier pushed off because her feet had felt so hot and swollen. 'You and I are going out.'

*

Once they were on the motorway Walter found himself unable to stop dozing off. It wasn't very polite to Maxine but he was done in and, in truth, she was looking pretty pooped herself. Drifting in and out of sleep, he found himself confused as a hundred thoughts crossed and re-crossed across his tired mind. He was looking forward so much to seeing Anne again, looking forward to seeing all his family. Yet, these comforting thoughts were interspersed with strange visions of Anne, a younger Anne, a white-faced, frightened Anne, pleading, 'Dad, you've got to make an effort, please. I know Mum's gone but you've still got a life, your own life.'

As the Rolls-Royce sped along, eating up the miles in its expensive purr, Walter Pepper came to his senses and made a decision. His mind eased, he then settled back in his seat and listened to the rhythmic roar of the wonderful engine, lulling him back into the land of nod. He did not need anyone to tell him what he must do. Walter Pepper knew what he must do and he would do it.

At his age there was no time for procrastination. At his age he'd be a fool not to know he wasn't long for this world.

29

If the atmosphere at the house had been peculiar in daylight, after dark it wasn't merely peculiar, it was downright bloody spooky; creaks and groans everywhere, subdued little pops and plops Anne had never noticed before.

Earlier, she had walked down to the village, pushing Martha in her buggy, for the first time appreciating Penny's reservations about living in the depths of the country. She had been in exactly the sort of mood where at home in Brighton she would have gone out for a coffee at a street café, wandered through The Lanes looking in shop windows, ambled along the seafront, sat on the pier, done anything just to see people, life, a world beyond four walls and a baby.

But there had not been a soul to be seen in the village, the bar and *boulangerie* shuttered up and no lights on anywhere. Save for when she stuck her head round the door of the tiny church, and saw a single candle flame guttering at the altar.

It was only when, as dispiritedly she had started to retrace her steps, that Anne remembered Agnes Fenn. She could go and see Agnes Fenn! Hayden had pointed out where she lived, in a house on the edge of the village nearest to the turning up to them. Agnes Fenn would surely be good for a chat or something? Hayden had said Agnes liked a drink – and a smoke.

She found the place without difficulty.

Built in the uncompromising bourgeois style of nineteenth century Normandy, Agnes Fenn's house was set back from the road behind a high wall in which stood a blistered wrought iron gate opening onto one of the most beautiful gardens Anne had ever seen.

Hesitating a second, because the house had also looked discouragingly dark and deserted, Anne had opened the gate and cautiously pushed the buggy up the path to the front door only to find it standing slightly ajar.

'Hello! Anyone home?' She had rapped a knocker in the shape of a lion's head and then, spotting a rusty bell chain on the outer wall, pulled that as well.

But although a tinny little chime sounded from somewhere deep inside, nobody appeared. Perhaps Agnes was a bit deaf? Hayden had said she was quite old. With this in mind, Anne had left Martha in her buggy on the front porch and stepped inside.

There had been no light on in the sparsely furnished entrance hall. Yet, even in the soupy murk, what there was seemed to glow with a patina of age and use that immediately told Anne of a genuine shabby chic rather than the manufactured modern equivalent. A door to the right was standing open onto a large and faded sitting room. Sticking her head in, she saw someone had left a tea tray sitting, untouched, on the nearest side table. But, on the point of investigating further, Anne had suddenly recoiled.

The room was full of buzzing flies.

In the hall she had called out again, her voice sounding eerie in the silence. Perhaps it was this that had at last made her give up. She had shrugged and left, carefully restoring the front door to its semi-ajar position behind her. Agnes must have popped out. Whatever, she did not feel like hanging about.

Bowling the buggy back through the sombre lanes, however, Anne had found herself almost running. She couldn't think what had so disturbed her, only that she was aware of a strange sense of disquiet.

*

Now it was quite dark, but the storm which had been threatening for hours still hadn't broken which meant the atmosphere was intolerably humid. Nevertheless, Anne closed all the windows downstairs and locked the front door. On second thoughts, she unlocked it again and stepped outside for a last breath of the sodden air.

She looked across at the orchard. In the light shining from the house the apple trees seemed strangely contorted, their twisty branches throwing menacing shadows across the silvered grass.

Shooting back inside, Anne once more barred and bolted everything.

What she really needed was a big glass of wine, not to mention a cigarette – which she hadn't got. But, determined to give the diet a decent go, she instead boiled up a mug of mineral water with a slice of lemon and sat down resolutely on the sofa with an article she had found in Verity's *Heat* about how to cleanse your body of impurities. The article was incredibly badly written, incredibly boring, and the hot lemon water made her tongue stick to the roof of her mouth.

Thunder rumbled, Anne's stomach rumbled. She had eaten nothing more than a low-fat yoghurt since breakfast. Surely, therefore, one *small* glass of wine wouldn't do any harm? And then maybe a slice of cheese on to –

Anne was suddenly still. She had heard something outside. No, she couldn't have – Carpenter would have barked. Then she remembered Carpenter wasn't there to bark.

It must have been the thunder. And Carpenter would have been no good with that. He was a complete wimp about thunder and lightning. But at least Carpenter might have fought off all the footpads, highwaymen and maniacs that Anne now began in vivid detail to imagine were casing the joint.

In fact, so vivid were Anne's imaginings of footpads, highwaymen and maniacs, she was only a little surprised when one actually turned up.

*

'If you don't go away this very minute,' she shouted through the closed window, 'I shall call the police.'

Standing just the other side of the glass and peering owlishly in at her, Gerry Underwood looked either very upset or very drunk – or both.

'Please let me in, Mrs Warwick,' he pleaded for about the fourth time. 'There's something I've got to tell you.'

'I warned you!' Lunging over to the table, Anne seized her phone. 'I'm dialling the police now!' She then started gabbling loud and gobbledegook French into it because, unintelligent as she now realised it was of her, she didn't actually know the emergency number for the police in France.

However, it did the trick. In the gloom beyond the window Underwood wilted, seemed to hesitate a second, and then all at once give up. He disappeared, at any rate. Not bad, thought Anne, extremely shaken but also extremely pleased with herself. Never let it be said that she was not resourceful.

Except her knees had gone a bit wobbly.

Regaining the sofa, she gave them a break, and decided that in a minute she would throw away the stupid lemon water and pour herself a lovely big Calvados. She deserved it. An enormous eruption of thunder chose that moment to explode above her head, followed immediately by such a fantastic flash of lightning it lit up the whole room. Good, thought Anne in shaky satisfaction. She hoped it had struck Gerry Underwood down dead.

PLINK!

The lights went out with startling suddenness. Oh, hell, cursed Anne. The bloody storm had knocked the power out.

Determined not to panic, Anne got cautiously to her feet and, hands outstretched like a blind woman, started to grope her way across the now pitch-black room. The next second there was a fearful crash as she measured her length over Martha's buggy. Fucking giving up smoking, she fumed, sitting up and rubbing her shins. Far from giving her a new lease of life it had almost done for her. If she had been smoking she would have had a box of matches or a lighter with her and not nearly broken her silly neck. On hands and knees she crawled over to the sink, reached up and fumbled in the drawer for the torch. There were the candles she had bought for that ghastly dinner party somewhere, but God knows where.

Another bolt of lightning came coupled with an ear-splitting crack of thunder directly overhead as great torrents of biblical rain started hammering down.

In the wavering beam of the torch Anne made her way to the bottom of the stairs and, ears pricked, listened for a moment or two. But there was not a squeak from above. She almost smiled. How was it that a baby who woke up if you had the temerity to sneeze could sleep through this maelstrom?

She found the dinner party candles and some matches, lit one, sat down at the table and shivered. The temperature seemed to have dropped ten degrees in half as many minutes but at least the storm had alleviated the abominable pressure. In a minute she must go upstairs and get herself a sweater. But first she would pour herself the promised Calvados and listen to Hayden's messages on her mobile.

There had been six, all of which she had ignored, which suddenly struck her as really childish. She was a mature and intelligent woman, for goodness' sake, and she wanted the comfort of hearing her husband's voice. She might even call him back. But first – his messages.

'Hello, Anne? Listen, I wish you'd call me back. I need to talk to you – we need to talk. I know you're angry with me and I know that's my fault but you see, something happened, something I never expected and – well, we have to talk. I'm so desperately sorry if I've upset you. I honestly never meant to hurt you but I –'

Anne clicked the end button, shutting off her husband's voice mid-sentence.

So now she knew. Hayden was going to leave her. What she had just heard was the unmistakeable preface to a man saying he was leaving you. Men always said they had never meant to hurt you when they were about to do exactly that. What did they mean? What did they think they were doing? Rage and insult rose in Anne to the extent that before she knew what she was doing, she had deleted every other of Hayden's messages without listening to them.

Then, desperate for some comfort, she started frantically punching out Penny's number but there was nothing, no signal. The phone was dead. The storm had done for it. Even if she had wanted to call Hayden she could not. Lines of communication had finally been severed. Anne sat motionless, the useless instrument in her hand, watching the candle burn lower.

Never in her life had she felt so alone.

30

Early the next morning Anne got up to find the storm blown away in the night and, after she had worked out how to reset the trip switch, the electricity restored. She had just finished giving Martha her breakfast and was opening the front door to knock the toast crumbs off the bread board, when she saw a note stuck to the outside of it with a grubby strip of masking tape. It was from Gerry Underwood.

He must have come back in the middle of the night to put that there, thought Anne, and suppressed a shudder.

Before she could take in what the note said, however, which was not easy at a glance given it was printed in a random mixture of upper and lower case letters peppered with grocer's apostrophes, an ancient Range Rover catapulted into the drive, came to a swaying halt, and out spilled Brigitte Laurent followed by Verity, Conrad and Carpenter.

'Sorry, can't stop!' Brigitte dived to embrace Anne on both cheeks, at the same time as enveloping her in the crochet folds of a psychedelic patchwork poncho.

'Got to take the children shopping for new shoes. How are you this morning?'

Anne said she was fine. 'But Brigitte, you shouldn't have bothered to come all the way out here. It's very kind of you but the kids could have got a taxi home.'

The Frenchwoman waved away the protest. 'My pleasure. Shall we see you all later at the beach?' She glanced back at the Range Rover in the rear seat of which Anne could see sitting Hugo and Danielle. 'The children are going down.'

Wow, thought Anne, 'children' twice over. Verity and Conrad would never have forgiven her if she'd called them that once. 'Yes, if it stays fine.' Although it was still chilly, the weather looked lighter and brighter.

Brigitte squinted up at the sky. 'Quite a tempest last night, wasn't it? Your little dog got dreadfully upset.'

'Oh dear, was he a nuisance?'

'Not in the least. He had a *protector*. Carpenter, indeed, spent the entire evening – the entire night – cowering in the tender arms of his Uncle André.'

'Really?' Anne was taken aback. She would never have imagined André Laurent a champion of frightened fox terriers. 'How very sweet of him. Do thank him for me, won't you?'

Brigitte gave another dismissive little wave. 'Oh, André's always wanted a dog. In fact, he's lovely with dogs and children. It's just adults that turn him into a pain in the neck.'

Stepping back a pace or two, she nodded at the house. 'Very pretty, by the way, although I'm afraid I'm not one for the rural idyll.'

'Join the club,' muttered Anne, but Brigitte did not seem to hear her.

'Must dash! See you later!' And with another swirl of neon crochet, the Frenchwoman vaulted into the Range Rover and zoomed off.

Anne went back into the house. Conrad had disappeared upstairs, but Carpenter, looking bug-eyed, was climbing leg by laborious leg onto the sofa where he turned wearily round three times before collapsing with a mighty sigh into a deep slumber.

Verity was rummaging in the fridge.

'So – did you have a nice time?' Realising it was still in her hand Anne glanced down at Gerry Underwood's note.

'Yeah, sort of.' Sitting down at the table, Verity tilted her chair back as she ripped open the tab on a can of Coca-Cola.

Anne looked up. 'Why only 'sort of'?'

'Oh, like, you know.' Verity pulled a face. 'It's French parents. I mean, French parents are kinda weird, aren't they?' She made French parents sound like some dubious breed of animal.

'Weird in what way?'

'You know, like, old-fashioned, like – *strict*. I mean, at home when Con and I have our friends round you never mind us taking them up to our rooms, but with Hugo and Danielle it was just, like, taken as read that we would sit with their parents all evening, even after we'd finished eating.' She grimaced again. 'It was kinda boring if you really want to know.'

'French parents sound remarkably sensible to me and I hope you weren't rude.'

'No.' Verity thudded her chair forward. 'Hayden phoned by the way.'

'Phoned the Laurents? Hayden phoned the Laurents last night?'

'Yeah.'

'Why didn't you tell me that straightaway?'

'Dunno.' Verity shrugged. 'Forgot.'

'What did he say?'

'Dunno,' she repeated. 'André spoke to him. I think it was just about Hayden trying to call you and not being able to, like, get through because loads of mobile signals were down everywhere with the storm, so he phoned them because he was worried about you and André told him he thought you were, like, okay, but Brigitte wouldn't let him try to phone later to check because she said you were going to bed early and wouldn't want to be woken up.' Pausing for breath, she shot Anne a look. 'Brigitte told *me* that you'd said you had a bad period. That wasn't true, was it?'

'No.'

'I thought it sounded funny. I mean, you don't get bad periods, do you?'

'No.'

'Why did you duck out of dinner, then?'

Anne hesitated. 'I just felt like a bit of time on my own. You didn't mind, did you?' she added quickly.

Verity shook her head. 'No, 'course not. We all need space occasionally.' Careful to keep her face expressionless, Verity was covertly studying her mother. She wanted to ask her what the hell was going on between her and Hayden but she couldn't. Partly because it just wasn't cool, and partly because she was afraid of what Anne might say. She decided to approach the issue in an oblique way.

'Hey, you are still going to, like, stay living here in France, aren't you?' Anne was frowning down at some scrappy bit of paper she had in her hand. 'Mum?'

'I'm sorry.' Anne looked up again. 'What did you say?'

'I was asking whether you are going to stay here living here in France.'

Anne's frown deepened. 'That's a funny question. Of course I am. Why?'

'I just wanted to make sure.' Verity shifted her eyes. 'Because it's weird but I guess I've, like, suddenly fallen in love with the place.'

Anne concealed a smile. 'Really?'

'Yeah, really.' Verity affected a nonchalant shrug. 'I mean, I could, like, finish my education here in France, you know. Hugo told me there's a fantastic international school in Paris.'

'I'm sure there is.' Still Anne kept her face straight but, as she had suspected, Verity's sudden love affair with France had far more to do with a sudden love affair with Hugo.

'So how about it?'

'Oh, I don't know, darling. We'll see.'

'That's Parent for 'no'.'

Anne laughed. 'No, it isn't. I mean it – we really will see. Anyway, listen a minute.'

Folding and tucking Underwood's note into the pocket of her jeans, she concentrated on her daughter. 'I want to ask you a big favour.'

'What?' Verity looked wary.

'After I've dropped you all at the beach, would you be kind enough to look after Martha for me for an hour or so around midday?'

Verity looked at Martha. 'Why? Are you meeting Stephanie for lunch?'

'No.' Anne cleared her throat. 'Not Stephanie.'

'Who, then?'

There was a pause until Verity's face turned black. 'Jesus, Mum, you're not going out with that creepy old git, are you?'

'Look, yes, I am but –' Anne faltered. 'You won't understand,' she finished feebly.

'Try me.'

Anne drew in a huge breath, held it a second, and then exhaled. 'Very well. It's... unfinished business.' She could think of no better description than Jean-Pierre's phrase. 'Alain – that's his name, by the way – phoned me yesterday to ask whether I would meet him for lunch today and at first I refused. But, having thought about it, I've decided I must see him.

'I need to wind things up, to lay a ghost, if you like.' She flicked her daughter a little smile of appeal. 'Otherwise, who knows? The creepy old git might haunt me for the rest of my days.'

'And what if he jumps on you again?'

'Well, he said he would meet me at Le Grand Hôtel in Cabourg, so it would be a bit difficult for anyone to leap on anyone there. But if he does somehow manage it, I promise you I'll sock him in the kisser.'

Verity gave an unwilling snort of laughter. 'Okay. You win. I'll do the nanny bit.' She brightened. 'Hey, Hugo can help me.'

Anne again suppressed amusement. Let's play at grown-ups, she thought. 'Thank you, darling. I appreciate it. Conrad will be there as well, of course.'

'Hmm.' Verity looked dubious. 'Don't count on it. He'll be away on that stupid windsurfer with the French tornado.'

Anne decided to let this go. 'Then I'm relying on you.'

'That makes a change.'

*

By the time the signs for Caen had started to appear at the side of the road it was going on for lunchtime and Walter was half dead with exhaustion. They had stopped at a motorway service station for forty minutes or so in the early hours of the morning, Maxine insisting they all needed coffee and something to eat. Walter had forced down a rather stale cheese sandwich, but found he could not manage more than a sip or two of what Maxine assured him was a cup of cocoa. He hadn't wanted coffee but what he got hadn't tasted like cocoa, more like that instant hot chocolate stuff, except it wasn't hot or even particularly chocolatey. Once back in car he had tried to get off to sleep again, but being outside in the chilly air had woken him up, leaving him unsettled and restless, unable to keep his hands and feet still.

To distract himself, he had spent the remainder of the night thinking.

Now, as they at last peeled off the motorway onto the ring road round Caen, he stretched out a hand across the seat and gently took Maxine's. It felt boneless, weightless, as if should he let her go she would float out of the window away on the wind.

'Walter?' She turned to him, pronouncing his name correctly for the first time. 'It is the end, is it not? The end of our journey.'

Walter did not pretend to misunderstand her. She was making it easy for him. With a flood of affection for her generosity, he gave the fragile hand a little squeeze, feeling the veins on its back like soft ropes.

'I think so, m' dear. You see, I am going home.'

The long hours of darkness had confirmed his decision. He was going home. He hoped Anne would not try to stop him. He hoped his daughter would see that the old had their place and the young theirs.

And his was not here.

'But please, Walter. Please tell me you have enjoyed yourself.' Maxine drew a kind of sobbing breath. 'Tell me you have had the good time.'

Walter thought of the things he'd seen, of the people he'd met. He thought of the polo, the casino, the restaurants and the oysters. In his mind's eye he saw the Alps of Switzerland, the seafront at Deauville and the boulevards of Paris. He saw Gilles and Dolores – both of whom had during those hours of darkness mysteriously lost any power that they ever had to rile him – and he saw Maxine. More than anything or anyone, he saw Maxine.

He knew now that he had never loved Maxine and never could have loved her, even if they had managed to rid themselves of their funny little world of make-believe, even if – and neither of them could have changed this – even if they had been young. He had only loved one woman in his life and he only ever would love one – Maggie. All the memories of the last weeks faded before her. Maggie. She was beside him now and would be till his dying day.

'I've had a wonderful time.'

Maxine gave a sigh of pure happiness. 'I am so glad.'

Releasing her hand, she indicated the drinks cabinet the Rolls-Royce had fitted into the back of the seat in front of him. 'And so we have a glass of champagne to say farewell, yes? There is a bottle in the cooler compartment.'

Walter gave his own little sigh. He didn't really fancy a glass of champagne at the moment, he didn't really fancy anything other than a spot of Bedfordshire, but it would be the last time Maxine would have her way. She was at heart a good woman and she must this last time have her way.

As the vehicle sped along, he unclicked his seat belt, trying to lean forward and stretch out a hand to unfasten the catch on the drinks cabinet. But sitting in an upright position for so many hours had left his back rigid and unyielding, as though he had overnight somehow turned into a wooden doll. This would never do. Taking a determined grasp of the side door handle, Walter shuffled his backside to the very edge of the seat, pulled himself almost to a standing position and, his knees painfully bent, tried again.

The noise of the crash knocked him senseless. That is, he thought it had. Until Walter realised he was still conscious and someone was screaming. Who was it? Was it Maggie? Oh, God, why would Maggie scream like that? Yet, as he reached out a hand to her there was nothing.

Nothing but silence.

31

Anne took so long to get ready for her encounter with Alain – 'Mum, you're laying a ghost, not the guy himself' – that it was gone noon by the time they got to the promenade. Spying Danielle down on the beach, Conrad promptly shot off with Carpenter, but Hugo came striding up the sand to meet them, his long thin legs like sticks in the now sharp sunshine.

'Right, I'll be off, then.' Anne gave the parasol on Martha's buggy a final tweak. 'She's had an early lunch and she's got loads of cream on, and her hat, but you will keep an eye on her with the sun, won't you, darling? And, of course, ring me if there's a problem.'

'I've left my mobile at home!' Verity looked up from where she was turning the entire contents of her backpack out onto the pavement.

'Oh, Verity! You could have sorted that instead of nagging me to hurry up.'

'No, it's your fault for always telling me off for texting.'

'Well, never mind that now.' Anne ferreted in her bag. 'Look, have mine.'

'But I don't know the number of Le Grand Hôtel!'

Hugo arrived at their side. 'I will find it out for you.'

'Or I could borrow your phone?' suggested Verity. But Hugo spread his hands.

'I haven't my mobile with me. My father confiscated it earlier because I was making too many texts.'

There was a tiny pause as Anne caught her daughter's eye. 'Thank you, Hugo,' she said, handing her phone to him.

'In any case, do not worry,' he said, taking it. 'My mother is coming down very soon.'

'Good.' Anne smiled at the boy before turning back to Verity. 'I'll leave you to it, then, darling. The hotel's only just along the front, so you can easily come and get me if you need to.'

'Don't fuss, Mum. We'll be fine. You just make sure you are.'

'I will.' Anne dithered a second, kissed the baby and Verity and then, after a slight hesitation, Hugo, which made him blush.

'Who is she going to see?' he asked curiously, as Anne hurried away.

'Oh, nobody important.' Verity took hold of the buggy. 'A man about a dog.'

'A man about a dog?' Hugo looked taken aback. 'Are you getting another dog?'

'No.' Verity giggled. 'It's just an English phrase that means...' She frowned. Actually, she didn't know what it meant – only that Grandpa was always saying it. 'Never mind. Hey, give me a hand down the steps with this buggy, will you? Sorry about this but I guess I'm, like, mummy today.'

'No problem.' The French boy threw her a naughty little grin. 'So long as I can be, like, daddy.'

*

If Anne was walking unwontedly fast to Le Grand Hôtel it was only because she had a personal dislike of keeping anyone waiting. Of course, it was far from certain Alain *would* be waiting, given she had refused his invitation. But 'I will wait there for you!' he had cried as she was ringing off. 'I swear I will wait for you forever!'

At the time it had chilled Anne to hear this melodramatic drivel. Only later did it occur to her that it had been Alain's stock-in-trade for so long now that it had probably become the only way he knew to express his feelings. Perhaps it really meant something to him. As to her own feelings, she wasn't sure. She felt composed and in control but, as she had felt for some days, not entirely convinced of the wisdom of her actions. *Why* was she going to meet Alain? What did she hope to achieve? It could not be because she was contemplating picking up with him again, or could it? Was still in love with him – was that what it was? She had told Verity that she wanted to lay a ghost. Was it, more prosaically, that she still wanted to lay Alain? Or finally, was this all merely a game of tit-for-tat that she was playing out with Hayden?

As she reached her destination, Anne gave up on soul-searching. It was doubtless a waste of time, anyway. She might be here but whatever he had so histrionically sworn, given his track record, Alain almost certainly would not be.

But he was.

*

'It's some woman talking in French.'

Verity held out Anne's phone to Hugo. 'I think she must have got the wrong number, but she's talking so fast I can't understand what she's saying and she won't go away. Can you have a word with her?'

'I'm covered in sand!'

Hugo was building yet another sandcastle for Martha to smash to bits. Getting up from his knees and giving his hands a perfunctory scrub on the seat of swimming trunks, he took the instrument delicately between his finger and thumb. '*Oui? Qui parle, s'il vous plait?*'

Verity held Martha upright on her feet and let go for a second. 'Oh, Hugo, look at this! She's standing up on her own!'

Martha sat down with a grunt. 'Oh, Martha,' Verity said sorrowfully. 'You were so nearly there.' She looked up. 'Hey, Hugo, did you see that? She really nearly did it.'

Then she saw his face.

*

'My son has given me a hard time on your account.'

'Good.' Anne opened her menu. The prices were pretty faint-making but sod it. On the assumption Alain was paying, she was going to make damned certain she had an excellent lunch if nothing else.

A waiter arrived to take their order; one of those starchy types of the old school, the sort that probably went down a bundle in the days of Marcel Proust, but in the twenty-first century merely struck Anne as pretentious.

In the same way, although the interior of Le Grand Hôtel was undeniably opulent, exquisite even, for her taste that also struck Anne as a bit pretentious. But then she'd never been a fan of all that *belle époque* gilt and glitz. She'd a million times rather be in a nice common-or-garden brasserie with Hayden. Damn, sighed Anne, looking up at the gleaming chandeliers and ornate ceilings. Now why the hell did she have to think of that? She lowered her eyes to rest on Alain.

'You look so very beautiful –' he began.

'No, I don't think we'll start like that.'

Actually, having washed her grey silk jersey top and matched it with the black skirt she had bought in the boutique sale, Anne did for once feel she looked quite reasonable but the last thing she wanted was a load of fawning compliments. She drank some wine. 'I'm not here in search of flattery.'

'What are you here for?'

Coolly, Anne contemplated the man before her. Funnily enough, Alain didn't look too bad today, either. He wasn't wearing his silly white suit, which was fortuitous given she had earlier made a mental resolution to walk right back out if he had been. Instead, he had on a rather worn but nicely unstructured linen jacket and matching chinos the colour of straw. Okay, open at the neck, his denim shirt revealed a little too much chest hair but… Anne peered closer, suddenly spotting the tell-tale dark stains on his skin. Oh, no, the idiot had dyed his chest hair! She flicked a glance at his head and saw for the first time the ebony black of the carefully coiffed Byronic curls – same treatment. Yet, rather than this appalling her, she felt moved to a kind of tenderness. Secure in his charms as Alain might seem, the poor guy was in reality pitifully lacking in confidence.

'I've been asking myself the same question,' she replied.

Their starters arrived. As she could have predicted, each dish was faffed about to the nth degree and presented with ceremony akin to the President bestowing the Légion d'Honneur. Nevertheless, Anne decided, tucking into *coquilles St Jacques*, it tasted absolutely ambrosial.

'And what did you reply to yourself?'

'I didn't.'

Alain put down his fork. He was eating *escargots*; Anne could smell the garlic across the table. Strange choice if he was planning to leap on her. However, his next sally was unexpected.

'Do you know what Edith Piaf is supposed to have said just before she died?'

'Can't say I do.'

'She said, "Every damn fool thing you do in this life, you pay for."'

'Poor woman. If that's true it certainly gives the lie to "*je ne regrette rien*."'

Alain smiled whereupon Anne saw too late where this was heading.

'And that's exactly how I feel about you,' he said eagerly. 'About *us*. I regret it bitterly. I did a damn fool thing with you – and I'm still paying for it.'

Anne chewed and swallowed. 'Eat your snails.' She nodded at them. 'And don't talk crap.'

But he pushed his plate petulantly away at which point a waiter broke the land speed record by sprinting over to ask if there was a problem. Cutting across Alain's irritable response, Anne assured him everything was perfect, and received a surprisingly warm smile in return.

'Come on, eat up,' she said to the sulky man opposite her. 'It's sacrilege to waste food in a place like this.'

Alain pondered a moment. 'Why won't you accept that I still care for you?'

Placing her knife and fork neatly together, Anne wiped her lips on a thick linen napkin. 'Because you don't. Your undying love died over two decades ago – if it was ever alive,' she added.

'God, you're cruel!' moaned Alain, as the waiter returned to clear their plates.

'Look,' she said reasonably. 'Can't we just have a nice lunch together? Can't we drop the *grand passion* kick and behave like two sensible, middle-aged adults who once, *long* ago, had an affair?'

'I'd never let you down again, you know.'

'What makes you think you're going to get the opportunity?'

'You do.' He looked her straight in the eye. 'You wouldn't be here if you weren't still interested.'

Opening her mouth to deny this, Anne hesitated and then closed it without speaking. He had caught her off guard. What was she doing here if she wasn't still interested? And, of course, he had clocked that fatal hesitation.

'Won't you give me another chance?' He leant urgently towards her. 'I swear I'd never let you down again. I *swear* it. I never meant to let you down before but –'

'Alain, you were married. It might have been different if you had simply told me that. At least then I would have had a choice.'

'But I intended to leave her – for you. I did not know Simone wanted a baby until too late. I did not know –'

'Jesus Christ, Alain!' Anne sat back in amazement. 'You really don't get it, do you? You were sleeping with your wife while you were sleeping with me. It wasn't the Immaculate Conception – *you* got her pregnant. In other words, as far as you were concerned, I was your bit on the side. I was your... your *mistress*.'

He gave a dismissive shrug. 'Yes, but that is not so bad. It doesn't mean I –'

'I can't believe I'm hearing this. Not so bad? Don't you understand that I wasn't some old bag like that woman your chum Gilles keeps for a screw at the sodding seaside? When we started I was a kid, a very young girl, a girl barely out of school uniform.'

He was still for a moment, seeming to hold his breath. Then he let it out. 'Okay, I see your point. You're right. I see that now. It was wrong but maybe times were different then for men in my country. How I would treat you now has changed.'

Great, thought Anne. She was back to the emancipation of women in France. At this rate she could write a bloody thesis on the subject. But before she could say anything their main courses arrived – with attendant fandango.

'Very well,' she said neutrally, once the flourishes had finished. There was nothing to be gained by arguing further with Alain. He was always going to make excuses, never see things her way. Besides, she had ordered lobster Thermidor and, never before having been able to afford this the most classic of all classic French dishes, was longing to try it. She looked at Alain. 'What are you actually suggesting?'

The Frenchman's face broke into a boyish little grin, reminding Anne unexpectedly but nonetheless poignantly of the first time she had met him.

She had gone along to one of his life drawing classes, nervous because she spoke hardly any French, and terrified that she wasn't good enough at life drawing not to make an idiot of herself. And he had been so nice to her, so encouraging, so damned *kind*. He wasn't the devil incarnate in those days, she remembered. She knew she would never have fallen for him if he had been. No, he had *helped* her. In truth, he had probably taught her more about the sheer science of life drawing than she had learnt in the whole of her degree. And yet...

Yet, somewhere along the line, the pupil and pedagogue roles had gone too far. Somewhere along the line she had made the classic mistake – a mistake born of innocence – of assuming that because he was such a good artist he must also be a good person. Not that he was a *bad* person exactly; he was just... weak. You could argue that it wasn't his fault; she had expected too much of him. As he had with her, she had believed him something he was not. In a way they were both guilty of cheating.

Alain had begun talking rapidly, his face illumined with hope. 'What I'm suggesting,' he said, 'is that we start seeing each again. That we start *over*. You can call the shots, I promise. I will do whatever you wish and this time I will not let you down. I promise you that this time you can rely on me. I swear you will never regret it.'

Will I not? Anne said to herself. There were promises but no guarantees. She sighed, not knowing how to respond. Lobster, then. Concentrate on lobster Thermidor. Picking up her fork, she leant forward only immediately to rear back, wrinkling her nose. It smelt incredibly cheesy – overpoweringly cheesy. She dropped the fork. There was no way she could eat this.

Fearful of another Usain Bolt waiter landing in her lap, Anne glanced uncomfortably around – and saw Verity, Verity at the entrance to the restaurant, holding Martha in her arms and scanning the room frantically for her mother.

Anne jumped to her feet so precipitately she knocked her wine glass over.

'My God, what's the matter?' she cried, as her daughter rushed over closely followed by Hugo.

'Mummy, Mummy! I'm so glad I've found you!'

For a split second Anne stared dumbfounded at her daughter. Verity hadn't called her Mummy since she was a child. Yet, in the same moment, she saw how standing there with Hugo and Martha, the three of them looked astonishingly like young parents with a baby of their own.

Then she came to her senses. 'What's happened? What's the matter?'

'It's Grandpa! He's had an accident and he's in hospital!'

Anne gasped as though she'd been punched in the stomach. 'What do you mean? What sort of accident? Where is he?'

Hugo took over as Verity started to cry. 'A car accident. They called your phone from the Centre Hospitalier Universitaire de Caen,' he explained.

But Anne was now in such a state of shock and the French bit so rapid that she didn't get it. She simply stood, immobile, staring at Hugo.

'Please, Madame Warwick, come quickly.' Putting an arm round Verity's shoulders, the boy started to usher her back towards the exit at the same time as trying to draw Anne with him. 'Please. My mother is waiting outside with her car to take you there.'

Coming abruptly to her senses, Anne grabbed her bag, making to hurry after them, when at the last minute she remembered Alain. She turned back to the table.

Alain was nowhere to be seen.

*

Outside the main entrance to the hotel they found Brigitte hopping from one leg to the other, the Laurents' ancient Range Rover ticking over beside her. 'Get in!' she shrieked.

'No... look... thank you.' Anne was trying to think straight. 'But I think I'd better take my own car.' Then she clutched her head. 'Except I left it back in the car park in town!'

André Laurent arrived at that moment, hurrying up with his daughter, a white-faced Conrad and bewildered Carpenter in tow. 'The kids came to get me,' he said to his wife. 'What's happened?'

Brigitte told him. Hearing it again made it sound worse.

'I'm sorry, but I must get my car.' Turning to go, Anne swayed suddenly, reaching out a hand to steady herself on the roof of the Range Rover.

With one look at her face, André took charge. 'You can't drive in this state. Give me your car keys and go with Brigitte. I'll find your car and take the dog and all the children back –'

'No! I'm going with my mother!'

There was a second's pause as André treated Verity's face to a brief but equally acute scrutiny. 'Of course you are.'

Seizing Martha from the girl's arms, André turned to open the car door only for Anne to grab the baby from him, quickly followed by Brigitte performing the same action and, in what in any other circumstances would have been a ludicrous confusion, the baby went from person to person like Pass the Parcel.

The next moment they were all still.

André turned to his wife. '*Donnez-moi la bébé,*' he said quietly.

Brigitte complied.

He turned to Anne. 'Give me your car keys.'

She also obeyed.

'Verity, get in the car.'

Verity got into the back of the Range Rover.

'Anne? You get in, too.'

Before Anne could move, however, the restaurant maître d' shot out of the hotel entrance and started gabbling at her in French she could not understand. Shifting Martha to one arm, André Laurent pulled him summarily aside. There followed a low-toned but distinctly curt exchange, which came to an abrupt halt when André levered a wad of euros out of his back trouser pocket and thrust them at the man.

With a quick count, the maître d' shoved a couple of notes back at him before stalking boot-faced back into the hotel.

'W...what was all that about?' stammered Anne.

André turned to her with a bleak little smile. 'It seems your luncheon companion left without paying.' He cocked his head at the car. 'Now, get in.'

Anne could not believe her ears. Alain had not simply scarpered. He had scarpered without paying the bill. Horrified, she stared at André. 'But I must pay you back –'

'Get in the damn car, Anne.' Looking totally sympathetic but totally immoveable, the Frenchman held the door open wider for her.

Anne got in.

'Phone Hayden, André!' cried Brigitte, as she leapt behind the wheel.

They shot off. The next stop would be the hospital.

32

They had only been going about five minutes, however, when Anne's stomach started to heave. Whether or not it was because she was also in shock, the Frenchwoman was driving atrociously, screaming up to junctions and then stamping on the brakes at the last possible moment.

Anne's mouth suddenly poured with saliva.

'Brigitte,' she said, through clenched teeth. 'You'll have to stop – I'm going to be sick.'

Swerving into the kerb, the car came to a shuddering halt and Anne half flung herself out to throw up undigested *coquilles St Jacques* over the mercifully empty pavement to the accompaniment of blasting horns and screeching tyres overlaid by a man's voice shouting something very imaginative indeed in French.

'God, sorry.'

She flopped, sweating, back into the car, fumbling for a handkerchief to wipe her mouth. A bundle of paper tissues was thrust over her shoulder, quickly followed by another folded wad that Verity must somehow have dampened with water.

Anne held the cool pad over her eyes.

'No, it's my fault.' Looking ashamed, Brigitte prepared to pull away. 'André is always telling me my driving is certifiable.'

They drove on – more circumspectly.

At the hospital, there being, as is typical of such places, nowhere immediately obvious to park, Brigitte dropped them near the entrance signed *Urgences.* 'I'll come and find you,' she said, pulling into the side.

Anne and her daughter climbed out with knees stiff and shoulders hunched as if they had been travelling all night in the back of a cattle truck. Five minutes later and they were being piloted into a tiny side room with a young doctor who, given every word of French Anne had ever known seemed to have deserted her, fortunately spoke very good English. Even so, Anne found she could not quite take in what he was saying. Only one fact impinged: her father was alive. He was undergoing tests but he was alive.

Walter Pepper was alive.

*

Brigitte found them in the casualty waiting room. 'Is he all right?' she panted.

As she came flapping up in her loon pants, Anne noticed for the first time that the Frenchwoman had nothing on her top half except the top half of a one-piece swimsuit striped in horizontal red and white bands like a pre-war lifeguard.

'Have you seen him? Is he going to be all right?'

Verity explained what they had been told. Walter Pepper was still unconscious; he had suffered a head injury. That was all they knew at this stage. 'They've sent him for a brain scan,' she said, and bending down, dragged a pink hooded fleece from her backpack. She proffered it to Brigitte. 'Sorry, but would you like to borrow this?'

'Oh, you're an angel, Verity.' Brigitte pulled the fleece over her head whereupon it came down to just below her rather flat chest. 'I was beginning to feel a bit indecent but, you see, I was just changing to leave for the beach when Hugo phoned, and then I was trying to get hold of André because he'd gone into town to the internet café, and all in all I got myself in such a paddy I forgot to put on my poncho.'

'Mum, I'm dying to go to the loo.' Verity had turned to her mother. 'Can I leave you with Brigitte for a minute?' She bolted off without waiting for a reply.

The two women sat in silence until Brigitte asked Anne if she knew how the accident had happened or who else was in the car.

Anne shook her head dumbly. Right at that moment she didn't much care.

'Okay. Wait here a sec.' Jumping to her feet, Brigitte went over to the reception desk and started talking to the woman there in French too low and fast for Anne to understand. She came back.

'No, she doesn't know the details, either, except that, apart from your father, it seems nobody else was injured.'

Sitting down, she took Anne's hand. 'Try not to worry. I'm sure he'll be all right and Hayden will be here very soon. I took a call from André as I was coming in and he assured me Hayden is on his way.'

Anne slowly turned dull eyes on the Frenchwoman. The first shock had given way to a kind of numb bewilderment.

'Hayden?' she echoed. Her voice sounded unused, rusty, as if she hadn't spoken for ten years rather than ten minutes. She cleared her throat. 'Are you saying Hayden has actually managed to tear himself away from Juno?'

Brigitte gaped at her, her open mouth arrested in a rictus of almost comical surprise. The next moment she had shut it with a snap. 'My God, Anne, what on earth are you talking about? Oh, of course, you're in shock.' She glanced wildly about the room. 'I'd better get someone to take a look at you.'

'No, wait!' As Brigitte made to rise again Anne caught her arm. 'You don't understand – you don't *know*. But, you see, Hayden is having an affair with Juno. That's where Juno has disappeared to. She's gone to Paris with Hayden because they are having an affair.'

For a split second it seemed Brigitte might actually laugh. As it was, she gave a kind of incredulous hoot. 'For heaven's sake, Anne, have you totally lost it? Of course Hayden isn't having an affair with Juno! He isn't having an affair with anyone!'

Anne stared at her. 'Then why has he been behaving so strangely? Because he's been lying to me, that's why. I *know* he's been lying to me. And then he clears off to Paris on some trumped-up excuse –'

'Anne.' The Frenchwoman clutched Anne's arm to stop her. 'Hayden went to Paris for an *interview*.' The Frenchwoman then clutched her own brow. 'Oh, I knew this was a mistake. I *told* André – I told him all along that it was a mistake to keep you in the dark. But would he listen?'

Lowering her voice, Brigitte began rapidly to explain.

'I don't believe this,' Anne said a moment later.

It was unbelievable. Hayden's new job had fallen through just before they left England and he had not told her. He had not told her. And then when André Laurent had set him up with an interview in Paris for an unexpected vacancy in his department at the university he had not told her that, either. That's where Hayden had gone. He had gone to Paris after a job. He had been desperate. And he had not told her...

'I know.' Brigitte was watching her. 'I know how you feel. But there's something else you should know as well.'

'What?'

She drew a deep breath. 'Anne, Juno could not be having an affair with your husband or with any other man for the simple reason that she is...' The Frenchwoman broke off, caught and held her breath an infinitesimal second before letting it out in a rush. *'Elle est une lesbienne,'* she rapped, with the exasperation of someone obliged to explain something extremely simple.

But Anne only looked even more bewildered.

'Do you understand what I'm saying, Anne? Juno is *gay*. God, I thought you knew. I really thought you knew.'

Anne swallowed. 'No, I didn't know,' she said hoarsely. 'How could I have known?'

'You seemed to be so in with Stephanie that I assumed she must have told you. Yesterday, when I told you how worried I was about Juno, you even seemed to be in *sympathy* with the woman.' Shaking back her vinegary hair, Brigitte spread her big, mannish hands in a helpless gesture. 'So much so that I naturally assumed she must have told you. She makes a hell of a production of it with everyone else.'

But not with me, Anne thought, her head reeling. 'But Stephanie is so... so *foul* about Juno,' she stammered.

'Quite.' Brigitte's long, ugly/attractive face turned grim. 'Both Juno's parents are foul about and *to* her. They absolutely refuse to accept what their daughter is. That is, her father does, and Stephanie is so stupidly cowed by Gilles that she follows suit.

'It's incredible in this day and age but André reckons Gilles is a throwback, one of those pathologically homophobic men who regard gays as an attack on their own sexuality.' She glanced sideways at Anne. 'You know the type.'

'Yes.'

'Anyway, it's been terrible for Juno. I realised yesterday that you didn't know what I am going to tell you now, but last year she tried to commit suicide, Juno actually tried to *kill* herself. Which is why I've been so desperately worried about her…'

Breaking off, the Frenchwoman bit her lip and stared into space for a moment until, with a deliberate little shake of her head, she collected herself. 'Oh, look, you don't want to hear all this now. You've got something far more important on your plate.'

Verity came haring back at that moment, breathing as hard as if she'd been running race.

'Mum, Hayden's here! I'd just popped outside the main entrance to call Hugo when Hayden arrived.'

The two women jumped to their feet as one body.

'Where is he?' Whatever her husband had done or not done, Anne was suddenly desperate to see him.

'He's coming, he's just parking the car. He was on the train just pulling into Cabourg train station when André got him, so he picked up our car and came straight here.'

'There you are.' Brigitte hugged Anne's shoulders. 'You'll be all right now, won't you? Hayden's here.'

'Hayden's here,' Anne repeated mechanically. 'I'll be all right now.' She turned her head as, at the far end of the waiting area, her husband burst through the double doors, his face creased with concern.

Throwing off the comforting arm, Anne ran towards him.

33

Walter Pepper looked oddly shrunken in his white hospital gown. Oddly, because in reality he was quite a big man, above average height, broad-shouldered and, despite his age, not at all stooped. As the consultant had said to Anne, 'For his years, Madame, your father is remarkable.'

He was badly bruised all down one side of his head and body, he had dislocated his shoulder and his left wrist was fractured; it would take a small operation to set it properly. On regaining consciousness he had seemed very sleepy, which the consultant had initially thought due to concussion. However, it transpired that, on his own admission, Monsieur Pepper had not slept properly the previous night, something that would cause simple exhaustion in anyone, and certainly a person of this age. The brain scan had shown nothing untoward, at least not at this stage. You could not always be certain with such cases. Monsieur Pepper would possibly suffer some confusion. Monsieur Pepper was also in pain. But this they would alleviate and neither of these factors should, at this stage, give great cause for concern.

When Anne at last got in to see him, however, her father was astonishingly chirpy.

'They're jolly polite to you here, I must say. They call me "M'sieur" which makes a nice change from the doctor's surgery at home where all I get is "Can you wee in this bottle for me, Walter?" from a chit young enough to be my granddaughter.'

'Oh, Dad.'

Walter looked about him. 'Nice room – can I afford it?'

'Hayden's sorted all that out. You're fully insured. Don't you remember? He put you on our policy.'

'I do now you come to mention it, and I can't say I'm surprised. Good chap, that husband of yours, one of the best.'

Anne swallowed and there was a pause as she took her father's uninjured hand in hers. His other had been temporarily strapped up. 'Dad... do you know what happened?'

Walter gave a faint shrug inside his hospital gown. 'I'm afraid not, m'dear. I remember some sort of smash but beyond that I can't help you.' He turned his head slightly to look more closely at Anne, the livid bruising down one side of his face making her flinch.

'Never mind. You're okay and that's all that matters.'

Walter hesitated.

'What's the matter?'

'I gather from the doctor chappie that Maxine is all right, too. He wasn't fibbing, was he?'

Anne assured him he wasn't.

'And Juno, and well – Dolores. Juno was driving, you know.'

'So I've been told, but they're all fine. They've all been checked out and discharged.' Maxine had, in fact, chartered a private helicopter to whisk her back to Paris so that she could be checked out by her own doctor, insisting Juno and Dolores accompany her.

'You were the only one injured, Dad,' Anne told him. 'We've gathered from the police that your car was hit by a van. A van apparently drove into your vehicle from one of the slip lanes on the ring road. But we don't know why you were hurt and yet none of the other passengers were.'

Walter Pepper frowned and shifted slightly in bed, the movement causing him to wince. 'Took my blessed seat belt off,' he said ruefully. 'I remember that. Maxine fancied a farewell glass of champagne, so there was I bumbling around trying to get her one when there was an almighty bang and, before I knew it, I was flying through the air with the greatest of ease.' He tried to smile and winced again.

'Haven't been knocked for six like that since I met your mother.'

Anne wanted to weep. 'You said... sorry.' She coughed. 'You said a 'farewell' glass of champagne?'

Walter turned his wise old eyes on his daughter. 'That's right, m'dear. It's all finished with Maxine.' He pondered a moment. 'Not sure whatever it was ever really began but, you know, Anne, she's a wonderful woman. I'm so relieved she's not hurt.'

'So am I, Dad. So am I.'

'Shame about the other lady, though.' The wise old eyes had started to droop. 'I bet she's in a sorry state.'

Anne felt a prick of alarm. 'Dad?' She gave his hand a gently rousing shake. 'What other lady, Dad?'

'Now, she was a *real* lady.'

As her father drifted off to sleep, Anne watched him, perplexed. 'It's okay, Dad,' she said at last. 'Don't you worry about a thing. You have a nice little sleep and I'll be back in a minute.'

And, detaching her hand, she slipped quietly from the room.

Outside in the corridor Hayden was shaking hands with the traffic policeman who had arrived earlier, intending to take a statement from Walter Pepper.

Verity had left. After a quick peak at her grandfather and being reassured he was going to be fine, she had been persuaded to go back with Brigitte. Not that her daughter had needed persuading, Anne had observed with passing wonder. Rather, 'Yes, you'll need me to help look after Martha,' Verity had informed the Frenchwoman. 'My little sister can sometimes be a bit tricky with people she doesn't know that well.'

Verity seemed to have grown up five years in the space of five minutes.

'Anne, darling.' Releasing the policeman's hand, Hayden now turned to her. 'This officer has kindly agreed not to bother your father with taking a statement at this stage. He doesn't speak English, Walter less French and, in any event, I told him I doubt Walter remembers much about the crash itself.'

'No, that's right. He doesn't.'

With a polite nod of acknowledgement at Anne, the policeman sauntered off. Anne watched him go before turning to her husband. 'Listen, Hayden. I'm not sure we shouldn't get him to wait because Dad's now going on about there being another passenger, another woman in the car.'

'Someone else besides Maxine, Juno and Dolores?'

Anne nodded and pulled her ear.

Hayden stared at his wife for a second and then shook his head. 'No, he's wrong. There was definitely only the four of them. He must be confused. The consultant said he might be. It won't help that they've given him all that dope for pain.'

'I agree, but come and see what you think.'

They went back into the room to find Walter dozing, a tiny slit of light between his eyelids showing he was not quite asleep.

Hayden sat down in the chair Anne had vacated. 'How are you doing, Walter?' he said.

'That you, Hayden, m' boy?'

'Yes, it's me.'

The old man's eyes opened properly. 'Good, because I want to tell you something.'

'Fine, but don't worry if you feel a bit confused about things. It's just the bang on the head.'

'No, it's not about the crash.'

It was about what he had decided and Walter did not feel in the least confused. He had a head like concrete. That's what that Sergeant Major had said to him all those years ago when he was on his National Service in Germany and had fallen out of the back of a truck on his head. 'Pepper,' the Sergeant Major had said. 'You're a bloody useless soldier, but you've got a nut like concrete. Anyone else would have fractured their stupid skull.'

So no, he wasn't confused. 'No,' Walter repeated, speaking directly to Hayden. 'I want to ask you a favour.'

'Ask away.'

Pushing with his uninjured hand, Walter struggled a little more upright in bed.

'I want you to tell this girl of mine that I'm not going to be moving to France. I'm very grateful for the offer but you tell her that as soon as I'm back up on my feet I'm going home, home to Wolverhampton. Of course, I'll always come and see you – I'd love to do that if you'll have me – but I want you to tell your wife that she mustn't try to make me live here.'

'Dad, please…'

At the note of acute distress in her voice, Hayden glanced round at Anne.

'I'd never try to *make* you do anything.'

'Oh, yes, you would.' Walter managed a sweet if lopsided smile for his daughter. 'You don't mean to be like that but just like your mother, you are, always wanting your own way and getting it.'

For a fathomless second, Anne locked eyes with her husband. 'Well, I promise I won't this time.'

'Good.' The old man lay back on his pillows with a sigh of relief. 'I'm glad we've got that sorted out. Now, if you'll excuse me, I think all I need is a little nap.'

'Wait a minute, Walter.' Hayden took his hand. 'Forgive me for bothering you with this, but I must ask you something. You said something a little while ago to Anne about someone else in the car – another passenger there in the car apart from Maxine, Juno and Dolores.'

'Another woman, you said, Dad,' prompted Anne. 'You said she was a real lady and that you bet she'd be in a sorry state. Who was she?'

Raising his head, Walter Pepper stared first at Anne and then Hayden. For a second or two he seemed utterly baffled until all at once light dawned on his lined old face. 'Oh, what a twerp I am!' he said wonderingly.

'What do you mean?'

Walter chuckled. 'I was referring to the *car*. The car was a Rolls-Royce Silver Shadow. I went to Switzerland in a Rolls-Royce Silver Shadow.

'And, believe me, she was a *real* lady.'

*

Verity thought Hugo's dad a really weird guy. He was always taking the piss and yet, when it came down to it, he could be dead kind, dead *nice*. Like when she wasn't quite sure what to do about night clothes for Martha, and nappies and food and stuff, as well as Carpenter's dinner, come to that. Neither Brigitte nor André Laurent told her to back off and that they could manage to look after a baby – and dog – quite well without her interference, thank you very much. Instead, they were, like, respectful, encouraging her to make a list of what she thought was needed, at which point André had immediately bombed off to the nearest supermarket and got the lot, including even a cute little pair of dungarees and a t-shirt with a rabbit on the front for Martha to wear tomorrow.

Tomorrow – they'd be going home tomorrow.

She'd really like to go home now to be with Mum and Hayden and, of course, Grandpa. But Mum had phoned to say she and Hayden were staying overnight in Caen, just until the doctor was completely satisfied that Grandpa was out of danger.

Every time after that when she thought about Grandpa and danger, Verity had to really screw herself up tight so as not to start crying. But then Conrad whispered to her that he felt the same way, which was dead nice of him, especially as you could tell he really meant it. There and then, she resolved never to call Conrad a turdy little minger again. She might even try to like Danielle.

Meanwhile, there was Martha to be bathed and put to bed and Carpenter given his dinner and the evening to be got through somehow.

Hugo was helping her give Martha her bath when his mother came in. Looking up, Verity saw Brigitte was still wearing her pink fleece which, it had to be said, looked pretty funny on her. Oh, God, Brigitte had probably come to call them down to another one of her strange and mammoth meals – just when she wasn't feeling a bit hungry. But instead, the Frenchwoman said something surprising.

Once Martha was settled for the night, she would babysit while André took all the rest of them out for a hamburger and a game of tenpin bowling.

Verity hesitated, not knowing how to refuse politely – she didn't really feel like going out and enjoying herself. But Brigitte was straight on her case.

'Go on,' she urged. 'It'll help take your mind off everything. Your grandfather is going to be fine and besides, he wouldn't want you to worry about him, would he?'

Hugo said he thought his mother was right. Then they both gave her a big hug which was...nice. In fact, Verity decided, if everyone didn't stop being so nice to her, she might just cry like a baby.

Thinking of which, she turned to lift Martha out of the bath.

34

'I feel terrible about everything. I mean, what if he had died?'

'I know.' Hayden poured her some wine.

They were in the restaurant of a chain hotel where Hayden had managed to find them a room, Anne having been surprised to discover that with the extreme relief which always follows hard on the heels of extreme shock, she was actually hungry.

'But you know, darling, and please forgive me for saying this, your father is not a young man. He's got to die sometime.'

'But not *now*! Of course I know he can't last forever, any more than any of us can. But what if he had died now, now after me being so vile to him about Maxine? It's that, more than anything, which is making me feel so…so *awful.*'

'Look, stop it.' Hayden took her hand. 'You've nothing to reproach yourself for and, in any case,' he added, Agnes Fenn's words coming back to him, 'guilt is so unprofitable.'

'Yes, guilty is what I meant.'

Arriving to take their order, a harassed-looking waiter scurried up. The restaurant was very full, probably because it was very cheap. But at least the tables were set far enough apart to prevent you fearing you might drink your neighbour's soup by mistake – and to have a private conversation.

'Besides,' repeated Hayden, when the waiter had bounced away. 'If anyone round here should feel guilty about their behaviour, it's me. I've behaved like a complete idiot.' But Anne just looked oddly at him.

'Not necessarily,' she murmured. However, before he could ascertain what she meant by that, she asked, rather abruptly, 'Hayden, why did you offer to help Juno find somewhere to live in London?'

Hayden jerked back in his seat. '*What?*' He almost laughed. 'What on earth are you talking about, darling?'

Anne explained whereupon his expression changed to one of mild indignation.

'Well, I don't know where Brigitte got that idea from,' he said. 'All I did was point Juno in the direction of a couple of on-line property agencies. It was that day I took Martha to the beach,' he went on. 'The day you were painting the sitting room.' Lifting his glass, he drank a mouthful of wine.

'Juno offered to walk into town with me and show me where the internet café was. I was going to do a bit of surfing in search of a job. Anyway, on the way we got chatting about life in general, at which point she mentioned she might be moving to London.' Putting his glass down, he looked suddenly abashed.

'What's the matter?'

'Well, I made a bit of a twerp of myself with the girl, if the truth be known.'

'How?'

'I assumed she would be moving to London with Jean-Pierre. I had assumed he was her boyfriend. And, of course, he is not.' Hayden shook his head in self-despair. 'As I'm sure you straightaway realised – Juno is gay.'

Anne grimaced; the compliment was hard to swallow. 'I didn't, actually,' she said quietly.

'Didn't you?' Hayden shrugged. 'Well, never mind. I seem to have done a pretty good job of making a twerp of myself all round.'

'Not necessarily,' Anne said again.

Hayden considered his wife. She had an expression on her face that he had never seen before, an expression he couldn't quite make out. Just that in some way she looked...changed. 'What do you mean by that?' he asked curiously, but she did not answer the question.

Instead, she asked him to tell her more about the job he had been offered in Paris. He had told her about it earlier at the hospital, but only briefly, both of them at that stage feeling that any revelations were taking second place to Walter Pepper.

'Do you want to accept it?' Anne now asked.

'That depends entirely on you.' Their starters arriving, Hayden began forking up *saumon fumée*. 'Because it's far from ideal.' Hayden paused for a second, looking faintly amused. 'However, it's certainly *weird*, as Verity would say. Because the job comes courtesy of that man who owns the house in Cabourg, the house that the Laurents are staying in.'

'The man who has gone to Tibet to discover his Inner Being?'

'The same.' He threw her an admiring glance. 'I didn't, but I knew you'd remember that.' He started to explain.

On reaching his destination, it seemed the Tibet man had discovered so much he liked about his Inner Being that he had decided to stay there with it. A few days ago he had emailed André Laurent to say he wasn't coming back, thereby leaving André's department at the university with a dilemma.

'A new term starts in a few weeks,' said Hayden, 'and this man was scheduled to teach three courses.'

'Are they courses in your area of expertise?'

Hayden pulled a face. 'I don't know that I'm an expert in anything but, yes, they are in my field.' He looked embarrassed. 'The point is that the university seems to think I am their saviour.'

Anne said so they should. 'But do you *want* to be their saviour?' she added.

Her husband stroked his chin. 'Well, yes, I do, actually. It's a great job, better than the one I was going to do in Caen, in fact, except...' He hesitated. 'The job is, of course, in Paris and we live in Normandy and that's too far to commute.'

'Very well.' Anne pondered a second. 'We'll have to move to Paris, then – or at least closer to Paris.'

'Anne!' Hayden gaped at her. 'You don't want to do that, surely? You love the house here –'

'I don't, actually. At least, nowhere near as much as I thought I would.' She was silent a moment, thinking how much they'd both got wrong, but especially about each other. 'It was all a bit of dream,' she continued carefully. 'The idea of living in France, the idea of living in the depths of the country.'

She paused to collect her thoughts, 'And I now realise that it's nothing like a dream – any of it. That it's life, real life – and we can make it work.' Anne looked appealingly at her husband. 'Don't you think?'

'I do.'

'But I'd far rather do that living in a town,' she said firmly. 'There must be nice towns nearer to Paris, providing, of course, that we can find somewhere that we can afford.'

'Okay,' Hayden said slowly. He stroked his chin. 'Well, if you're really sure about this, I'll accept the job and we'll start house-hunting. As to what I do for the next few months, there might be a solution there, too, in the short term at least.'

'Go on.'

It turned out that André Laurent had offered to put Hayden up at their place in Paris during the week. He and Brigitte had loads of room and would be delighted to have him.

'How incredibly kind of them.'

'Isn't it?' Then Hayden frowned. 'The problem would be leaving you on your own here in Normandy with Martha. It would only be from Monday to Thursday nights but I don't like the idea of... well, of abandoning you.'

'Hayden, you would never *abandon* me,' Anne started to say, only to break off as she remembered that was precisely what she had thought Hayden was going to do. She felt a tiny shiver of shame. 'Listen, I'll be fine. I'll get out and about a bit and start to make friends – '

'I could introduce you to Agnes Fenn!' Hayden looked as though he'd just won the Lottery.

'Hayden, wait a minute. I forgot, but I've got to tell you something.'

'She's quite a bit older than you, of course,' he went blithely on. 'But I know you'd get on like a house on fire with Agnes.'

'Hayden, please – '

'Mind you, I hope she doesn't get you into bad ways because she drinks and smokes like a trooper.' Eyes bright, he began to chuckle with delight.

Until he saw Anne was crying.

*

'She knew she was going to die.'

'She *knew*?' Anne blew her nose. 'God, that's terrible.'

'No.' He shook his head quite violently. 'I don't mean it like that. I don't mean she actually knew she was going to die now. I meant she didn't feel like that, she didn't look at dying like that. Agnes Fenn wasn't... ' His voice trailed off.

'Gerry Underwood came to tell me,' volunteered Anne, as her husband seemed sunk in reverie. 'That is, he left me a note. It was a heart attack. I should have told you earlier.' Anne bit her lip and paused. 'I'm so sorry. I know you liked her.'

'Yes, I did, I liked her very much.' With another quick shake of his head, Hayden exhaled a jerky little breath. 'She was one those rare people you could talk to, someone you could *tell* things to.' He managed a small smile. 'She tried to persuade me to come clean with you, you know, instead of being so stupidly secretive.'

Anne sighed. 'Oh, you're a man. And all men are born with secretiveness as a minor design fault.'

He smiled, if a little sadly. 'Do you forgive me, then?'

'There's nothing to forgive. I'm the one with the problem.'

'What do you mean?'

'I mean, that nobody – not just you – but nobody seems to have wanted to tell me anything. Take Stephanie and Juno. Why couldn't Stephanie tell me about Juno being gay? Brigitte was the same. Come to that, why couldn't *Juno* tell me about Juno? And then... Dad. Even my own father had to use you as a go-between to tell me he wasn't going to move to France.'

'Anne, Walter didn't mean it like that –'

'I don't blame him. It's me.' She trembled suddenly. 'God, Hayden, am I so intimidating? Am I, God forbid, a *bully*?'

'No, of course you're not,' he began.

'I am, you know, and I've got to change.'

'Well, that's up to you but please don't change too much because, at the risk of sounding slushy, I fell in love with what you are and that's how I want you to stay. I *love* what you are.'

'Do you? Do you really?'

'*Yes*. In fact, right now there's only one thing about you that bothers me.'

'What's that?'

'That you haven't said you love me.'

In the ensuing silence, Anne found herself looking at her husband as if for the first time. Had she ever really seen him, ever really understood what he was?

She had thought he was having an affair. She had made the fatal assumption that because other men cheated, Hayden would be the same. He was not. He wasn't Gilles Dérain; he wasn't Anne's first husband; he wasn't Alain Duval. He was Hayden Warwick and he was different. What was it Verity had said? *Hayden wouldn't do that to you, you know.* Her own daughter, at the age of fifteen, had understood her husband better than she did. Well, if nothing else, it was high time she changed that.

She drew a deep breath. 'Hayden, I do –'

They both started as, lying between them on the table, Anne's phone started to beep noisily, causing neighbouring diners to frown at them in disapproval.

'It's all right!' Hayden cried, seizing it and clicking buttons before she could panic. 'It's not the hospital. It's a text message from Verity – with a photograph.' Scrutinizing the screen for a second or two, he then started to smile all over his face.

'What is it?' Anne demanded.

'See for yourself.' He passed over the phone. 'But I'd say that's a picture of our daughter standing up.'

*

In the hushed opulence of her bedroom, Stephanie Dérain flipped listlessly through the soft pile of her pashminas and wondered why they did not comfort her the way new clothes usually did. She took out one of her new linen jackets, looked at it, and then put it away again, closing the wardrobe door with a firm click. She went over to the window.

Down below on the darkening terrace, her husband was berating one of the gardeners about something. The man had a hosepipe in his hand, a stream of water trickling gently from its nozzle into the flowerpot next to his feet. Stephanie smiled. How lovely it would be if the man suddenly turned his hosepipe on Gilles, soaking him from head to toe the way Anne's father had when he threw Gilles into the swimming pool.

But he did not.

The man continued to stand quite silently and abjectly, his head a little bowed under the onslaught of her husband's bullying. Abruptly, Stephanie turned away from the window. The light had nearly gone so she must hurry.

Quickly, she moved back to the wardrobe and took down a suitcase.

THE END

About the Author

Born in the Heart of England, Jane Jennings went nowhere very much until she met a British diplomat in a pub and then went all over the place.

A lifelong fascination with writing began as a child when she won twelve shillings and sixpence (about 50p) for a poem in *Princess*. She can still recite the poem.

Jane Jennings now lives in Cornwall with her husband, with whom she shares a passion for wire-haired fox terriers and all things French.

Nothing Like a Dream is her first novel.

Visit the author's website at: http://www.janejennings.co.uk.

CPSIA information can be obtained at www.ICGtesting.com
Printed in the USA
LVOW05s1138281014

410706LV00051B/2287/P